A BREAK IN THE FOG

MOLLY SALANS

D1738286

Front cover illustration by Cindy Salans Rosenheim

Printed by The Salans Press in the United States of America

First print edition 2021

ISBN: 9798779165044

The Salans Press
2460 17th Avenue #1024
Santa Cruz, CA 95062

www.abreakinthefog.com

For my daughter, Sarah

PART 1

ONE

CLARA

The window was ajar again. Dad did this to remind him of Mom who had kept every window in the house open, *for fresh air, don't you see?* But it was always freezing like now. The cold seeped in with the blaring foghorns and dampened everything.

I threw the spaghetti noodles into the boiling pot of water. Dinner was almost ready. I whisked together oil, vinegar and mustard and tossed it over the salad.

The juice from the chopped tomatoes was running over the counter, down the cabinet doors and onto the floor. I picked up the sponge to wipe it all down, but the more I wiped, the more the gunk dripped. I was on my knees, still sponging up the stuff, when Dad walked in. I hadn't even heard the door open; the foghorns were so loud.

"Smells good, Clara-Bara." Couldn't he stop calling me that? I wasn't a baby anymore.

"This is Dr. Alan Bernstein..."

I stood up still holding that stupid sponge. I tossed it into the sink and pushed my bushy hair out of my eyes.

"Not Doctor, yet, Doctor, but thank you..." His brown eyes looked like paper, they were that thin, and his eyelashes were so light and scanty I could hardly see them. His hand kept twisting something above his mouth, a mustache as invisible as his eyelashes. He held out his very long hand, and I reluctantly shook it, knowing how wet and shriveled my fingers were.

"I'm sorry my hands..."

He smiled and rubbed his own together as if he were sharpening a knife.

I glared at Dad who wouldn't look at me. Wind blew in, and I shivered.

"We'll eat in the dining room, okay?

The dining room? We hadn't been in there for ages; it must be a

dusty, grimy mess.

"Sure."

"So glad you could come, Alan. Clara is a wonderful cook..." Dad's voice trailed off as they walked out of the kitchen.

The pot was boiling over, and the noodles were overdone. I slipped on my oven gloves and walked the pot over to the sink, spilling some of the water, burning my fingers. The pot clattered and turned over into the sink, the fog horns screamed, and the wind blew in from all directions. I shut the windows and ran my red-hot fingers under cold water. Dinner would have to wait another twenty minutes at least.

Dad hadn't brought anyone home in years; let him wait a few minutes longer. Better yet, he could take Alan Bernstein, the good-Doctor-to-be, out to a good restaurant. That's what Mom would have said.

I picked the pot up and filled it with water again. I remembered watching Mom pacing the kitchen floor and yelling at Dad. *Do you ever call me when you're running late?* she had screamed, her face tomato red. She had thrown the steaming kettle at him, followed by her coffee cup.

An owl was hooting from somewhere nearby. I stared out the window, trying to find it. Its call was insistent and forlorn. Who was he looking for? Would he find her? I put a dishcloth with ice over my burnt hand.

In the dining room, the table needed wiping down, but the floor could wait; and at least in this room the windows weren't open.

Back into the kitchen, the water was boiling again. I turned the heat down and threw in more noodles. Dad walked in, hands on hips, eyes narrowed.

"What's taking so long? Dr. Bernstein has to make rounds in an hour."

"Another ten minutes, that's it. I didn't know we were having company..."

"Let's start with the salad." He walked out, calling to the "doctor."

No wonder Mom had thrown things at him. When I brought the bowl of vegetables to the table, Dad smiled and gestured to our guest to help himself.

"Alan is a Cardiology intern at the hospital and has his hopes on becoming a surgeon. He'll be an excellent one at that."

Alan's mouth was full, salad dressing oiling his lips. He tried to smile with his mouth closed. I laughed. He looked ridiculous.

"Clara is graduating college this June, and she is interested in working in a doctor's office. She is a quick learner and..."

"A dancer." My voice was so suddenly low and heated, I wondered if they could feel it.

I ran out of the room to check the noodles. The water was boiling furiously. I put the gloves over my shaking hands and moved the pot to the sink, concentrating on dance steps I'd taught the kids in my classes. *Pretend you're a snail in a park with running children. Point your toes, take deep breaths in and out, and move slowly, while the ground pounds all around you.* I felt the steam on my cheeks.

They were still talking as I brought dinner in: Alan's face squished from all the concentrating he must have been doing.

"This looks delicious."

I sat across from him, next to Dad.

"As I was saying, Clara will be graduating and is looking for a job in a doctor's office."

Quiet settled in like a net. I had no idea what my face must have looked like.

Alan wound his spaghetti around his fork, but as he lifted it to his mouth, the noodles fell. He tried again. The fork scraped against his plate as sauce fell down his chin.

"I'm a dancer," I said. "I'll be graduating in two weeks with a certificate in Modern Dance and I'm going to open my own studio..."

Dad must have opened the windows. I was freezing.

A fly was buzzing from the bottom of the windowsill up to the top and down again. May's usual fog still brought in flies.

"Clara is tenacious and has a strong will. She quit ballet when she was 13, against my wishes..." He smiled at Alan, and his mouth was so tight I thought his cheeks might break. "Of course, these qualities are absolutely perfect for managing a doctor's office, which she will be able to do with great skill."

Alan's long hand rose to his invisible mustache again. I looked down and saw that my thumbnail was chewed to the skin. I hadn't realized I'd been biting it.

Dad was the only one eating. His face was almost as red as the sauce. His almond eyes were concentrated on his fork as he rolled the noodles perfectly. He put the bunch into his mouth with expertise, not a drop of tomato sauce out of place.

The fly's wings had green tints in the room's light. I wondered if I should open the screen for him?

Instead, I sat straight up in my chair, my feet planted firmly on the ground, staring down at my plate. The lettuce was wilting, the cukes softening and the radishes looked red hot.

The doorbell rang. And rang again. Again, and again.

The fly was hurling itself against the window as I jumped up. I tried to steady my legs, which were wobbling.

I opened the door, and Wendy spilled in, clutching her key.

"Fuck Fuck Fuck. What's so hard about answering a fucking door?" She blew past me, her once beautiful blonde hair, stringy, dyed black and falling in splits down her back. Her face was whiter than white, and her body thinner than a spaghetti noodle.

She sat at *my* place at the table and banged *my* fork against *my* plate.

"I need forty fucking dollars like fucking now, or I'm going to get fucking killed, get it?"

"Everything will be okay," Dad said. "Eat something. Calm down."

"Please help me, Daddy." The sudden change in her tone was sickening, from a screaming hyena to a whimpering dog.

"You can't do this anymore." I was standing behind her, touching her shoulders.

"Get the fuck off me. Daddy... please..."

I rubbed her shoulders. She whipped around, fork shaking in my face, tomato sauce dripping all over her lap and the floor.

"I said don't the fuck touch me... Daddy..."

The plates jumped as his fist came down, his face crunched into deep lines of explosive anger. "This is the last time. I expect you at the clinic tonight. Your sister will bring you."

He stood and reached for his wallet. Wendy's face expanded into a sickening smile, one of her upper teeth missing, as he handed her two twenties, enough money to pay for my groceries for two months.

But of course, *she* was his little girl.

Alan looked down at his watch, then at Dad.

"How could I have been so thoughtless?" Dad put his wallet back into his pocket and hugged Wendy. She let *him* touch her. "We have to get you back to your rounds."

"Daddy you're the best ole man, fuck..."

Alan's chair scraped as he nodded, to me and to Wendy, with his mouth still open. He looked like a robot as he followed Dad out the door.

The second it closed Wendy began screaming. "My fucking heart, oh my fucking god." She dropped the money; it floated right into the spilled sauce on the floor. "I'm going to die. Put your fucking shitty hand on my fucking heart..." She tried to grab my hand but immediately thudded to the floor, her entire body in spasms. I knelt and slapped her hard across the face, but it didn't stop so I shook her shoulders hard. Then, I ran to the kitchen and grabbed a glass of water, came back and threw it in her face. When she stopped breathing I hit her in the chest.

"Fu-uck!' She sat up, clutching the spot, "That fucking hurt. Fuck you."

"Fuck you too." I said.

I helped her into the kitchen and put on the kettle, reaching up for the Yuban that used to stand behind Mom's jars of pills. I stood there for a moment, remembering how they'd spilled all over the table one morning. Mom had screamed at me, *What's wrong with you?* But now I was staring at Wendy. Her lips had been chalk white and cracked. I got down off my toes, wishing I were dancing instead.

Wendy was gulping down her coffee as I brought her a plate of spaghetti.

"You have to leave us alone," I said.

She picked up the food with her hands and pushed it into her mouth, dripping it all over the table.

"I mean it."

She kept on eating, but she was crying now, snot falling from her nose and onto her plate. She put her greasy hands on my shoulders and dropped her head. "Fuck. I'm such a fucking fuck. Shit."

I took a rag and wiped her nose and poured coffee down her throat. She spit and coughed and swore but I forced the rest down her throat. Like Mom had done, only with milk, that morning so long ago. Wendy had screamed, *No, Mommy yucky.*

She was quiet when she tumbled out of the kitchen.

"Hey, where are you going?" I grabbed my purse and ran to block the door. "I have to take you to the clinic."

"Fuck that." She bolted just as I was about to grab her and disappeared into the fog, wisps of damp air engulfing her.

The dark night poured in through the glass doors leading to the garden as I wiped down the kitchen table. The owl was hooting again. What other creatures lurked? Feral cats? I had seen one once on our neighborhood street. It was caught in the headlights, its head still and tail upright, waving. And then he was gone. I picked up Wendy's empty coffee cup and stared into it. I looked out into the garden again. My thumb rubbed the mug, up and down. What feral cats lurked? How many? Did Wendy have enough money? Who was taking care of her tonight?

TWO

JOE

A s usual he couldn't sleep. He sat on his creamy white chair in the living room, listening to Pavarotti, trying to calm himself. Clara would take Wendy to the clinic. She had to get better. Anna hadn't gotten better, no matter how he'd tried to help her. Wendy was **not** Anna. Clara knew what to do. Aaron would also help, once Wendy arrived at the clinic. Had to think of something else, before the memories got him. He wiped his brow, took a breath in, Pavarotti's high tenor voice filled the room, his chest. He understood the precision and discipline such singing required. Unlike Clara, who had refused traditional ballet, a cultural dance that traversed centuries. And she had been an excellent ballerina. Showed her gift at an early age. Watching her in her first *Nutcracker*, how old had she been? Five? Six? In the opening scene at the party, backstage she had twirled in her hoop dress, her smile as wide as the rim. And after, the way she had kissed the bright, yellow daffodils he had given her, how she had leapt into his arms, burying her soft, flushed face against his neck. He wiped his eyes, the depth of the singing always made him cry.

And now he saw Miriam again, so long ago, twirling in the pink taffeta dress his Mama had sewn for her out of one of her dresses she no longer wore. He'd kept unbuttoning the white shirt he was choking in, with his mother chastising him, *Yosev, you are going to see the Ballet, you must look like a gentleman.* He'd run away from her, chasing Miriam, and when he caught her, laughing, she'd turned her red-cheeked face to his and lifted her hands. He'd twirled her around until they both fell, giggling. How she'd loved watching the *Nutcracker*, how she would have loved to have had the opportunity to dance.

The thoughts invaded. The body parts, the toes, the fingers. Joe shook his head as if to shake out the thoughts, and the poem *Once on the Pacific* by Robert Frost went through his mind. No one could have prepared themselves for such a long black time, for the rage and helplessness it created.

He picked up his black leather journal sitting on the table near him and wrote:

> *Unseen fires*
> *Smoked out the Jews*
> *Inflamed Nazis*
> *Burnt this Jew-boy to the bone*

He put his pen down. He hated these poems, these bursts of wanting to vomit before he wrote. The huge undaunted faces. Nazis at his door. His Papa boldly saying, *we will not follow their orders.* Joe's chest had swelled believing in his Papa's strength. Miriam holding onto his hand. A milk mustache on her face. His meticulous Mama standing behind Papa, not having time to wipe Miriam's mouth. The earthquake sound of the gun. His Papa toppling onto Mama, Mama toppling onto Miriam. And all of them falling on top of him. How he had lain there for hours. The stench. The goddamned stench. And yet he had not one broken bone. Not one.

He shuddered. The record had ended. The lamplight shone on his open journal. In the silence, he lifted his pen again and wrote:

Skatole putrescine
feces decay
rancid putrid flesh
Rotting
Mama Papa Miriam

He threw the pen down on the table. So many people worse off than himself. Like Mrs. Lincoln who had two of her four children dead from drugs. She worked day and night to make ends meet. This self-pity is noxious, he thought, getting up from his chair.

THREE
CLARA

The following afternoon, I was on my way to the dance studio, and Cat Stevens was rolling around in my head, especially because of that stupid surprise Dad had played on me last night.

The song *Father and Son* was repeating itself in my mind. Especially the part about how the son never felt listened to by his father.

Dad never ever listened to me, and I was so sick and tired of it all.

The gentle, cool breeze pulled at my hair and beckoned me to walk faster. I remembered this same feeling when I was with Grandma years ago, and we were walking to China Beach.

She'd smelled of jasmine perfume, cigarettes and dark chocolate. I'd just finished my last matinee in the *Nutcracker* for the fourth year in a row. I would soon be old enough to be on toe.

It was hard not to skip; Grandma walked at such a slow pace. The air was cool, the wind thick and strong. I loved it that way, and for once my hair, full of spray, stayed down instead of blowing outward and into my face.

We stood on the sidewalk, holding onto the rail, looking at the winding path leading to the sand and the ocean beyond. The pelicans and seagulls gathered in two separate groups, facing the sea. They stood still as though they were in church.

Do you believe in God? I felt her arm stiffen.

Yes, of course. Who do you think made all of this? And she gestured toward the sky and sea.

Then why don't Mom and Dad say so?

You mean, why don't you go to church?

I guess, or do anything that has to do with God? Some kids at ballet say they light candles in church 'cause they remind them of God's light. I especially would like to have one of those things that holds all of those candles at Chanukah.

A menorah?

I couldn't see her face but her voice cracked, sounding like the seagulls who took off suddenly.

Haven't you ever seen them in a window at night? All of those different colored candles standing inside golden holders and their light against the dark panes?

I'd heard that Jesus could take away bad things and if you believed in God, He'd help you be good. I had no idea what any of that meant, but if I lit a candle for Jesus or God, maybe my life would improve. My stomach might not pop out so much, Wendy might not be so bothersome, and Dad and Mom might stop arguing. And a menorah had eight whole candles! Who knew how much good might pour down because of so much light?

In that moment, all of the gulls, hundreds of them it seemed, took off in a V, their intense caws sliding into the sudden silence between Grandma and me.

Their sounds died off as quickly as they'd arisen, and in the quiet, the sun was painting the sky in magnificent oranges and reds, itself a fiery ball in the center that slowly descended into the sea. I wondered what the rays would sound like if they could sing. I could hear in my mind the music in the *Nutcracker* when the Christmas Tree grew — the horns coming in loud and magnificent, pulling the colors outward. The crescendoing notes splashed through the sky, guiding the sun downward as the magic of night descended. Grandma was talking.

Is it a menorah you need or would something else do?

I don't know. It's just that my heart hurts so much when I see beautiful things and maybe, if I had a menorah, it wouldn't hurt so much.

We walked back to the house slowly. I thought that maybe she moved that way because her skirt was too straight, limiting her step. I wanted to bend down and undo her hem so she could skip with me.

I feel that way when I watch you dance. We had reached the front porch of the house. Before unlocking the front door, she held out her arms, and I sank into them, inhaling the jasmine-smoke-chocolate smells, looking up at her powdery face and the round herringbone hat slightly slanted on her white hair.

The memory was so real and her words, my *heart feels that way when I watch you dance,* made me feel as though I had wings; I was flying up 25th Avenue, passing Lake Street and only stopping when I hit the light at California Street. Sweat dripped down my forehead. This afternoon Patti and I were going to go over the details of the children's dance recital and look at next season's schedule. Patti, like Grandma, understood me. *You take to dance like the leaves take to trees -- you are a born dancer,* she'd said the first time we met. *How would you like to have tea?*

We were going to have tea in *real* tea cups. The card table had already been set up; it was covered with a light blue cotton tablecloth, complete with a small turquoise teapot with matching cups and saucers. Red camellias floated in a clear bowl of water that sat in the middle of a plate surrounded by slices of oranges and sour green apples. Since then, we'd made this a monthly ritual.

The wind blew my hair around my face, and I felt like I could dance the entire *Nutcracker* in just minutes. Ahead, two people standing at the corner stepped to the right, blocking my way. They were quite tall and dressed in red-brown robes with matching turbans wrapped around their heads. The woman handed me a rose.

"Good evening," she smiled. Her clear blue eyes shone in the streetlight.

I stared at her, confused. She was right in front of me. To move forward, I'd have to push her.

"Are you happy?" she asked, following my gaze, forcing me to look at her.

The man laughed. "Listen, we are here to let you know about a joy you can have inside your own heart. Have you heard of Krishna?"

I stepped around them. "No," I said.

They moved with me, the woman holding out the rose. "You look unsettled. Is everything okay at home?" She peered into my eyes with more seriousness. Her skin was smooth like fresh ice on a rink.

"Who are you?" I asked.

"We are the Krishnas. Krishna is a God that guides..."

A god that wasn't Jesus or God God? They were crazy. Besides, what with Mom's death and Wendy's addiction, I wasn't sure if God existed. Dad was certain he didn't. Maybe he was right. "Oh, I'm sorry, I have to go." I stepped aside again, but not before they put the flower in my hand.

"There's an address and a phone number hanging from this stem, make sure you contact us."

I ran from them as fast as I could, risking a red light. When I got to Patti's, I handed her the rose, ignoring the fact that the studio stank of pot.

18

"Perfect!" she laughed, cutting the tag off the stem and placing the blossom in a small vase. "It will accompany the bowl of camellias I've already placed on our table."

Still laughing, she swung her long hair back and tied it with a pink satin ribbon, then placed a plate of sliced apples and cheese in front of the camellias.

Patti sliced the cheese the way she danced, her long graceful fingers picking up the knife, her hands landing it perfectly into the cheese, lifting the slice onto the apple and then repeating the motion until each slice of apple held a luscious piece of cheese. She looked me squarely in the eyes. "You look so worried, and we have so much to do, are you sure you don't want a puff?"

"No thanks." I hated the stuff. The very smell made me gag. After Mom died, Wendy smoked it constantly, always blowing it in my face, daring me to stop her. Patti had never done that, but she would press me to smoke with her. Back when I had run from home because Dad had yelled at Mom again, *You pay more attention to your piano playing than you do your own children,* I came to the studio. Patti understood me like Dad had not. She saw how much I loved modern dance, how much I had loved dancing to *A Hard Day's Night.* Only a couple of months after I started taking her classes, she'd asked me to teach the class for kindergartners and first graders.

But when I got to the studio for tea and to discuss teaching this class, Patti had offered me a joint, saying, *Take a drag, it'll take away all of your worries.* And even though I couldn't stand the stuff and vowed I'd never take it, I was flattered that Patti was offering this to me, as if I were her peer, a dancer as fine as she. I'd inhaled and coughed until I was purple.

The mirrors in front of us glinted from the light coming in from the window, and I saw my mouth turned down. Patti was smiling, and her dimples lit up like candles.

"I wish you'd take just one more drag. But, I should cut back. I've been invited to New York to choreograph. You're quite an example for me!"

New York! What would that mean for me?

"Are you listening?" Patti waved her hand in front of my face. "Since you're graduating, I'm going to give you more classes, especially with the younger kids!" She took another hit. "I'd love to come to your graduation..."

Her pupils were large, and she felt distant to me. I saw my reflection again, and put my head down. I played with my wild, black curls. No one graduated on the college stage these days. "There's nothing to come to."

She put her hand on mine. "Never mind, we'll find a way to celebrate. Maybe you'll have one smoke with me before I cut back?"

I shook my head and forced a smile. "I'm tired, I think I'll go..."

"Wait, wait... do you remember that day when you stomped in here, furious with your father? You put on Dylan's *Positively Fourth Street*, asked me to stand like a statue, pretending to be him — who you described as being that rigid — and then you danced to that song, spitting the words at me?"

I remembered it vividly. I had begged Dad to let me take modern dance. But his eyes had bulged angrily as he had yelled, *That is barbaric. Barbaric do you hear? A ballerina is dignified and cultured...* he had coughed so hard his eyes watered. Like Patti's, now. Only she was giggling so much, tears were pouring down her cheeks. I pushed my chair back and took my coat off the small peg, the last line of the song whirling through my mind... I just wish that Dad *could* walk in my shoes; see himself as I do: as a rigid father that I *want* to love but who has confined me to a strait jacket so tight there is no room to move a baby finger, let alone breathe.

It was freezing. I put my hands inside my sleeves. Chills went up and down my arms. Home was only a few blocks away, but I was in no hurry to get there.

And when I did, Dad was sitting in his creamy white armchair listening to Pavarotti.

I looked at him with his eyes closed, his face at peace as he listened to his favorite opera singer, noticing more wrinkles around his eyes and cheeks. He looked tired. The adolescent ward connected to his hospital was an amazing project, and I was proud of what he was doing, attempting to get kids off the streets and off drugs. But if it meant he couldn't even keep his eyes open, if it meant he only had anger left for me, was it worth it?

The early evening sun had broken through, and light trickled in through the windows, landing in slight slants across the purple and white rug.

He opened his eyes. "Clara-Bara, nice to see you. Tell me about your day..."

"Marc and I..." I began a lie.

"Marc... that barbarian boyfriend with the beard and long hair?"

Pavarotti's mournful tones spread throughout the room and escaped out the windows.

"Listen to me," Dad continued. He had put his paper down and was leaning in his chair, staring at me intensely. "You have a steady and safe life ahead of you. Don't waste it."

I met his gaze and then glimpsed the photo sitting on the table next to him. Aunt Miriam. It seemed as though she was looking right at me. What would she have done? Had she been under Dad's scrutiny like this, too, when she was alive? I sat on the couch, slumped back and closed my eyes.

He'd given me her photo at Christmas when I was thirteen; the same year I had quit ballet for modern dance. She'd looked just like me, her dark frizzy hair pulled back in a ponytail, lots of it escaping down her forehead and face, and curly bits stood on top of her head. *She loved ballet*, he'd said as Wendy had jumped into his lap, after Mom had taught her some piano.

Dad had kissed Wendy's head and said to her, *You play well, Princess. Don't you be a quitter like your sister.*

Pavarotti stopped singing. Dad picked up the paper. I couldn't see his face or Miriam's. The night had come in, whatever natural light had been there was completely gone.

~

IN MARC'S arms a couple of days later, I was standing on the steps to my student apartment, ready to go on a bike ride.

"Do you know that Dad is trying to fix me up with one of his interns? He actually wants me to quit dance and manage an office."

Marc stroked my hair and held me close. "I feel so badly for you." He pulled me away to look at me, his eyes so gorgeous, round and blue. "But soon you'll have your own dance studio; don't ever give up on that." He held my shoulders firmly and said it again. "You are a dancer. Get it, babe?"

I melted in his arms, feeling my head against his strong chest. He danced me around our sidewalk and landed me in front of our bikes parked up on the landing near my front door. He let go of me, picked up his bike and ran down the steps with it. He kicked the stand into place, "Coming?"

Laughing, I got on my bike and dared him to race me. With his hair streaming behind him and his cute butt high up in the air, my feet pedaled faster than ever before. We rode across the Golden Gate, the wind blowing so hard I thought Marc was going to fall off. The fog rolled in and out like a crazy fish looking for a place to settle.

When we reached Marin, his black hair was all curly, his cheeks were all red, his blue eyes were like the ocean, and it was so wonderful to bump my bike into his. He pretended to push me off mine, and as I lifted myself off, he lifted me high into the sky and pulled me down close.

"Let's have a party tomorrow night," he whispered, kissing me on the ear.

I tried to pull back, but he held on tight.

"We bought two chickens yesterday and a whole box of veggies, not to mention the pie."

I pretended to laugh. "But I thought that was *our* dinner? What with my teaching schedule and your work with the cabinet makers, I thought we had made tomorrow night *our* time?"

"Remember that girl from Greece I told you about, the one who is staying with my family for a time? It's about time you met her! My parents won't be home tomorrow night, and I thought we could have a party to welcome her. But we'll do it another time." He whispered, "Most important is that you're happy." He twirled me to my bike. We rode back, the fog seeping in, clouding our way all the ride home.

FOUR

JOE

"There's some trouble with the final sum of federal money, I don't know what the problem is."

"Probably a 't' hasn't been crossed on one of the hundreds of pages."

Joe patted his partner, Aaron, on the back. A slight, thin man, precise as a paper cutter, matter of fact and persistent. Like him.

They walked through the ward, not open yet. There were two locked floors, one for males, the other for females. Double beds in each white pristine room, pink curtains in the female rooms, blue for the males. That was Aaron's idea. Needed some color. After all, the patients were kids.

"I'll take a look at the papers."

"Don't bother." Aaron smiled stiffly. "I'll have my secretary write another letter."

In the cafeteria, Joe sat alone at the large, off-white institutional table, opening an egg salad sandwich wrapped in plastic. The walls were cracked like broken bones, and the table was wobbly. The place was nearly empty, except for an elderly woman sitting at another long table a few feet away. Her back was to him, and he could see the lump there. Osteoporosis. Bones. The memories returned.

They were at home that morning, in 1939. The Nazis had ordered everyone in his small village, Koshel, to gather a few things and to dress in fancy clothes. His Papa had refused to follow any of the orders from the new German occupation. This one was no exception.

Out on the street, all their neighbors, the Wawchels, Studnetzes and Adamiaks, were dressed up in their best. They held small bags of belongings in their hands. Mrs. Studnetz had on a long black gown, the one she had shown his Mama on her wedding anniversary years ago. Mrs. Studnetz' graying hair was pulled into a bun held by a comb studded with diamonds. Another heirloom. It was the shine of the diamonds Yosev couldn't take his eyes off.

They'd all been told that they'd be going somewhere special. He stared out the window and waved to his school friends, Jacob and Joshua. His Mama washed up the breakfast dishes. Papa yelled at him to shut the curtains immediately. His tone made him shiver. They were lucky enough to have two fresh eggs and a pint of milk that Papa had paid dearly for. Miriam got a whole egg and a cup of milk because she was youngest, only six. Yosev was almost a man, already thirteen. His Bar Mitzvah was in two weeks. Papa, Mama and he split the last egg and the rest of the milk.

His Papa's square face was wrinkled around the forehead, eyes narrowed. *We don't follow orders from babies. Do you hear?* He growled at Miriam and Yosev, spitting on his plate.

His Papa was a gregarious man. Out-spoken. Demanding. None of them went against his word, ever. He was different that morning. His voice was lower and meaner, like a lion's growl. Quiet, ready to kill. Yosev had never heard him like this.

.Miriam had just gulped down her milk. The Nazis banged on the door. Their cottage was made of thick pine, and even their hard boots

26

couldn't burst through it. Yosev's chest puffed. He knew his Papa would make them go away.

Papa's chair scraping against the floor made the small hairs on the back of Yosev's neck bristle. They all stood as Papa sauntered toward the door. When he opened it, Mama, Miriam and he stood in a line behind him.

His Papa would make them go away. He was certain. Nazis were just mean, dangerous kids. Kids without a conscience. Kids who could kill. The strength of Papa's words rooted into his belly. *We don't follow orders from babies.*

Pack up they ordered.

His Papa spit in their faces.

Certainty grew, and Yosev's chest puffed even more.

He heard a thunderous noise.

They blew Papa's head off.

Those goddamned Nazis with their high-heeled boots. Raised those guns right into his Papa's face. Blood covered him like a Tallit. He toppled backward, landing on Mama. The two of them toppled onto Miriam. They all fell on top of him. The guns went off again.

And again.

He was at the bottom of the pile. The bullets had missed him. All of them. He'd lain still for hours under his family. Darkness covered the entire house.

How could he have breathed for all that time? How was it that he got out from under without a single broken bone? Not a single broken bone.

"Dr. Greenwood?"

Joe first saw the peeling paint and then felt the table wobble as he leaned back in his chair trying to focus. A hunch-backed woman, the one who had sat at the other table, was leaning into his face. Talking to him.

"I'm Mrs. Sandelstein, Bruce's wife. I hope I'm not bothering you. I just wanted to thank you for saving his life."

FIVE
CLARA

T he day after I had that horrible talk with Dad, I left him and that huge empty house in a hurry. I hated Dad for calling Marc names, for not even bothering to get to know him. Marc always made me laugh, made me feel strong about myself, unlike Dad.

As we'd agreed on our bike ride yesterday, tonight we were going to cook and listen to the news as usual, and I couldn't wait. We were both passionate about Black and Women's Rights, as well as the Watergate scandal -- and for the past four years had gone to every peace rally held in Golden Gate Park. Even though the air had stunk of pot, I loved the live music — except for Janis Joplin. My throat always hurt listening to her; her voice was so scratchy.

I loved the entire political feel. I felt in charge for a change and a part of something huge. *We're making history,* I'd tell Marc, as we passed a crowd chanting, *burn your bras*. But he'd kiss me, take my hand and run us toward a crowd of his friends I'd have to meet. I'd follow reluctantly, although I never said anything. He loved to include everyone, but I just wanted him all to myself, like now.

I leaned my head against the window, as the bus rattled on down 19th Avenue toward my apartment. Yesterday, Marc had held me after we arrived home from our bike ride. *You're the greatest Babe, and I can't wait for us to graduate... for you to open your own dance studio, and for me to build the cabinets for it!* He had led me in a waltz, humming the *Blue Danube*.

Out the window a couple was running across the street. It was so windy her long skirt blew up behind her. Her boyfriend caught the back end of it, and when they reached the sidewalk they kissed. In the reflection of the window, I could see that as they parted the woman was smiling from ear to ear. I looked closely at her face and realized it was *me*. I was looking at my own reflection in the bus window. I was grinning like an idiot.

I was a light breeze as I ran off the bus and hopped up the stairs to my building and into my apartment.

There was an unfamiliar black leather coat thrown over the couch.

"Marc?"

No answer.

A strong smell of perfume and something else weird hit my nose; was that incense? Pot? But Marc told me he didn't smoke anymore...

I walked through the kitchen, throwing my own coat over a chair. It thudded on top of the piles of newspapers sitting on the floor.

I walked into our bedroom.

He was stark naked on top of another naked body.

"Oh my God!" I choked on the incense, I picked up a sneaker lying on the floor, Marc fell off her, I threw the shoe and picked up another...he sat up, hands protecting his head, *whoa whoa*, she was screaming, *stop*, and I threw the incense burner...Marc was on me, grabbing my arms, I twisted free, *goddamn you*, ... She was slinky, everything about her was slinky. She slinked her long slinky legs to the floor, and her long brown curls fell down her slinky back as she reached for her black slinky dress. I picked up a white sandal, and Marc grabbed my arms again...

"Marc, I don't get this. We could have invited her..." Her accent was deep and slinky and sexy.

I whipped around toward her — Sonya from Greece. I bit Marc's hand and he yelled and I bent down and picked up her pink scanty underwear and twirled it around my pinky. Before I could fly it into her eyes and smash all that green color out of them, it flew from my finger and she caught it, laughing. I rammed my fist into her stomach.

"I don't like violence..."

"Oh, you don't do you...?"

Marc grabbed me by the waist and threw me on the bed, but not before I kicked him hard in the groin. I ran into the kitchen, Marc running after me. "Please."

I grabbed a chair, lifted it and watched it rise into the air and crash at his feet. It landed on its side and Mark began hopping on one foot, around the chair, toward me.

"Don't..."

He caught me at the front door and grabbed my arms so I couldn't swing. He looked me hard in the eyes, but I did not return his searching look.

I walked out of the apartment, opened the door to the building and walked robotically down the steps and out onto the street, not caring as a trolley screeched to a halt and the driver leaned his head out the window, screaming, *Jesus Christ kid watch where you're going*.

Slinky, gorgeous Sonya; she was everything I was not. Mom had been right. I was nothing but trouble. Everyone hated me. Marc most of all.

THE NEXT DAY, I cleared out our apartment. I barely looked at the things I had tossed into the garbage: cracked plates, burnt pots and practically everything else in the kitchen cabinets. As the things clattered on top of each other, the sound reached such a pitch I couldn't hear my own thoughts. I wished I could have thrown my splintered heart into the trash as well.

I tore down all the curtains and threw out the sheets and blankets. I left the furniture for the mice. Let them shit all over it, the way Marc had all over me.

I'd borrowed Dad's car so I could throw in all the stuff I was keeping. The boxes and suitcases piled up in the back made quite a contrast to the meticulous care he took of it. But I didn't care. Driving home in it now, the fog was so bad, I could hardly see. Cars honked nonstop. I leaned on my horn, shouting, "Fuck you, I can't move!" I banged the wheel with my fists. The fog crept all around the traffic like gas, choking out all visibility except the pictures in my mind: Marc and I, on our bikes, rolling with the fog across the Golden Gate; him holding me, calling me "the best;" and then him naked, on top of Sonya. I felt so trapped in this car, in my life, the way I had felt when Dad refused to let me take modern dance.

When I'd pleaded with him, his voice had risen like fire, and he had yelled, *A ballerina is dignified and is part of a European tradition that traverses centuries of artistic culture and music. You are to continue with ballet, is that clear?*

I had begged him. *Dad, you don't understand, just meet Ms. Jenkins...*

Angrily, he shook his coffee cup in front of my face, as if to throw it, his cheeks puffed and turning red. *I don't understand what? That you have a rich life with privileges and opportunities at your feet?*

He'd slammed the cup down, and black liquid dripped from the table to the floor. He called Grandma Shirley, screaming into the phone. *You are contributing to Clara's downfall. You are sending her in an uncertain and unstructured direction that she will regret for the rest of her life.*

Cars were still honking at me. I leaned on the horn again. Like Mom when she'd stepped on the gas almost crashing into a trolley. *Watch where you're going,* drivers had screamed at her. But all she did was yell,

Fuck you. Now, the fog was worse. What if Dad had been right? What if I were on a barbaric, destructive path? Mom should've crashed into that trolley.

∼

When I finally arrived home, I lugged my two suitcases up the stairs to Wendy's and my old room and stood in the doorway looking in. Sitting on my desk was the photo of Aunt Miriam, with a "Welcome Home" sign lying in front of it.

I moved toward her and picked it up. *Did you love the ballet?* I asked. I saw her twirl. Laughing, I lunged into an elephant dance. *You would've loved doing this, too. If only you were here.* I gently placed the photo back on my desk.

Our room hadn't changed. The two single beds had the same covers; the same night table still separated them. The way Wendy and I were separated now. I remembered following her to China Beach, where she'd gone every night after Mom had died, her face lit by the bonfire, swaying to the guitars the lanky high school guys were playing. Had she been twelve? One of those times, though, we'd been alone...so unusual for the beach to be empty on a summer evening,

Wendy was already sitting on the sand. I'd crept up behind her. *God is watching you,* I whispered in her ear.

She'd jumped and screamed, and I doubled over laughing.

What the hell are you doing here?

Nothing. Just wanted to know what you did here every night.

Nothing.

She wouldn't look at me.

You just sit here, like this, every night?

Yeah. Why?

I played with the sand. I picked some up and watched it flow through my fingers. I listened to the waves gently touching the shore and going out again.

You know what Grandma told me the last time she was here?

She turned her head toward me. She was crying.

What's wrong?

Nothing.

There was a slight breeze, not enough to make her eyes water.

What did Grandma tell you? She asked, looking away again.

First, she told me that Mom had named me after the princess in the Nutcracker, Clara. And then later she said that Mom named you after the girl in Peter Pan. Mom loved Peter Pan, don't you remember? After we'd watch the show, she'd say, 'Now girls, I hope you never grow up. It's never any fun.'

Wendy leaned into me, and I put my arm around her.

It's true. Growing up is too hard.

I whispered, *It's just us now.* Dad relied on me completely to take care of my sister; he'd always been home for dinner, but that was about it.

The night had flowed in, enormous with stars. The ocean rhythm was like a lullaby.

We'd snuggled closer and sat like that for a while.

Without realizing it, I'd picked up the photo of Aunt Miriam, again. I was clutching it so tightly my fingers cramped. *Where is Wendy?* I asked her. The foghorns were yelling, and I had goose bumps everywhere because couldn't Dad leave just one window closed? *I think Dad must miss you, Miriam. Like Mom, you died so long ago. It's so weird, because you don't feel dead to me.* I kissed her cheeks, and placed her carefully on my bedside table. I went to close the windows, when there was a light tap at the door, and before I could get to it, Grandma walked in with her arms wide open! I had forgotten she was coming today. Caught in my images of Wendy and myself, and Mom and Miriam, I shut the windows harder than I meant to, as if to prevent Grandma from flying out with the breeze, the way memories so often do. Her beauty filled the room.

Her custom-made, teal silk suit was exquisite, bringing out her blue-green eyes. A gorgeous string of blue pearls graced her neck. They glowed like her eyes.

We sat down on my bed, and she said, "It's so good to see you, dear. I heard you were moving home. Your father is very happy about this."

I kept my head down, my fingers curled and cramped.

"For your graduation present," Grandma said. "I'm taking you to see Margot Fonteyn."

Ballet? I gazed at Miriam. My eyebrows were raised like hers.

Didn't Grandma know that ballet was outdated and old-fashioned? After all, she had paid for all my modern dance lessons, supporting me like no one else in my family ever had.

Smiling, she handed me a small white box. "From Tokyo." Her home was in Boston, she had just returned from a trip to Japan. She was a world traveler — Paris, London, Madrid — and now, Asia.

My mouth opened. Sitting in white tissue was a jade necklace, encased in gold. Lying next to it was a matching pair of earrings.

"Congratulations, Sweetheart. I wanted you to have something beautiful to wear."

The sun was suddenly pouring through the windows, landing on the bed and Grandma's lap.

I put it all on.

"You look so elegant! Go look for yourself."

Staring at my lanky figure in the mirror, I noticed my long arms and skinny legs. My feet automatically spread out into first position. Why couldn't I have more curves, like Wendy?

But the gems warmed my neck, and there was something about my black hair lying against the green jade that made me look almost beautiful. I opened my eyes wide and stuck out my tongue and smiled. My brown eyes actually looked happy and shiny, just like Grandma's.

She held out her arms and rose to give me a hug. I inhaled her mint and jasmine smells, and snuggled my head into her soft wrinkly neck.

THAT NIGHT before dinner Dad held me so tight, it was as if his life depended on it. "Such a fine thing to move back home. You are wise to listen to me."

My face was against his belly, and I could hear it gurgling. I saw only his white shirt buttons against his blue shirt, smelling of cigar and chocolate.

I gingerly put my arms around his waist, and he held on more tightly. He kissed the top of my head. My body shook, and I swallowed the lump in my throat.

"I hope you've decided to quit modern dance and that you have seen how thoughtless and unstructured it is. You'll have the summer to think about the history and purpose of ballet."

I tried to pull away, but he took my hands in his and kissed each of my fingers. "Clara-Bara, you have all of your fingers. Be grateful! And Maureen in the office can't wait to start working with you. You begin on Monday."

He held me close again. My entire body was erupting. *Noooooooo....* I wanted to scream.

He led me to the table.

The chicken and rice smelled familiar but the salad was a little too bright with its fresh lettuce, tomatoes and carrots. Why the lacy white place settings and matching napkins, the very ones Mom used to use for all those cocktail parties? The jar of Wish- Bone Salad Dressing was in front of me. What if I dripped it onto the lace?

"Why such a fancy table?" I asked. Grandma was still wearing her blue pearls.

"I thought a festive table would cheer us all up," she said.

Tipping the bottle upside down, all the liquid slowly moved to the top, the bottom oily and empty.

Just then, Grandma handed Dad a stiff looking letter, and written on the top in big bold letters was "Temple Emanuel."

The small black-and-white TV sitting on the counter behind the table was on, as usual. Dad always had to have it on. The news, the world, current events were so important to him. Every now and again when something caught his ear he would make us all be quiet as he listened.

"Are you going?" Grandma's eyes didn't leave Dad's.

"This is NBC Nightly News, and I am John Chancellor, reporting on Wednesday May 14, 1975. Today, President Ford ordered the bombing of the Cambodian port where the American ship Mayaguez was seized just two days ago..."

Great. More war. And if I refused to go to the office, I would be in a bigger fight with Dad.

"I am not. There is no reason to do so."

"The temple has recognized your clinic and is giving you a dinner to honor this. Don't you think you should attend?"

"What have synagogues done for anyone? What has any religion done for anyone?" He coughed hard, his eyes bulging.

His voice hoarse, he said, "Do you know what keeps us safe? Do you? *My* daughter working in *my* office. Marriage to a doctor..."

Grandma didn't take her eyes off him, and I couldn't take mine off a spider web in the upper left-hand corner of the wall. It swung from one side of the corner to the next. Innocent bugs were caught in that sticky, impossible substance. Dying there.

"I don't celebrate anything religious; you should know that by now."

I sure did. When I had asked him for a menorah, years ago, he'd shaken his head and said, *that's a religious symbol, not a toy.*

But the kids at ballet had told me that Christmas and Chanukah candles brought in love. If Dad could see how much light they gave, I had thought, maybe Mom and he would stop fighting.

He got up suddenly, throwing his napkin down. I could feel the heat from his body as he left the room, his knuckles white from clenching his fists. If a menorah held 1000 candles, it wouldn't be enough light to help us all now.

I turned to Grandma. "There are many organizations recognizing Dad's clinic, *they* don't offer him dinners..."

But Grandma shook her head. She took both of my hands in hers, face powder falling from her wrinkled cheeks as she smiled and said, "I can't wait to see *Swan Lake* with you."

ON THE DAY of the ballet, I wore a navy-blue, knee-length dress and black pumps. When I put on the necklace and earrings, Dad was elated. "You look like a dignified young woman, the way my own Mama looked when she dressed."

"Really?"

Dad's rare smile lit up his eyes. "My mama was meticulous. And she loved culture."

We were standing in the hallway next to the staircase. Dad grasped the banister and bent his head toward it, breathing hard. Then he stood tall and said, "A ballerina is rooted in her classical dancing and holds her head up high."

The hallway darkened. The light pouring in from the living room windows had disappeared.

Grandma walked in. Her herringbone hat was tilted on her white head, and her blue pearls glowed. "The cab is here," she said. Grandma hated driving and Dad couldn't take us. She was delighted to take a taxi. "That way we can talk all the way there."

⁓

MARGOT FONTEYN DIDN'T DANCE. She floated. Effortlessly. It was as if air and an invisible wind had transformed her into a swan.

I'd never be able to dance like that. It seemed like the whole audience was crying; the woman next to me kept blowing her nose. Grandma had squeezed my hand, thinking it was *me* crying. And when it was over, she had to tap me on the shoulder several times as I was deep in thought. I kept hearing Dad's voice saying, *My Mama loved ballet; she had loved its precision and tradition.*

There are so many traditions, Patti had said to me, *and modern dance is derived from the African cultures that are as old as Western Europe's, if not older.*

My foot had fallen asleep. It hurt to walk. Grandma must have seen me wobbling. She linked arms with me as we walked out of the Opera House.

I saw Dad's rare smile and lit-up eyes again as we left. *You look like a dignified young woman, the way my own Mama looked when she dressed. She wore the family diamonds around her neck.*

The streets were bustling, the cars honking, and the pigeons were all around our feet.

"Did you know Dad's real Mom?" I asked Grandma.

Her arm stiffened. She turned toward me. "Now why are you thinking of *her* after a performance like this?"

I shrugged and linked arms again. Grandma's tweed coat was itchy. I touched my necklace. The sun suddenly broke through, and a bunch of pigeons squabbled over a trodden cookie.

The gems felt warm against my neck.

Later that night, I didn't want to take my jewelry off. I kept it on even as I got into bed. I looked at Miriam and said, *I bet you would have done the same.*

SIX

JOE

S hirley was in the kitchen cooking, skinning a chicken for soup when he walked in from work. She brushed her gray hair from her eyes, mostly out of habit, as there was little to brush away.

"I've been thinking, " she said turning toward Joe, "has Clara ever been to the opera?"

Joe put down his black leather doctor's bag on the kitchen table and rubbed his hands together. "Of course not, she'd hate it. Always walked out when Anna or I had it on the stereo. 'It's old fashioned,' she says, 'not cool like the Beatles, the Stones.'"

"I'll get us tickets, it might be a good idea..."

"Let her get used to working in the office, first. Thank you. It's a good idea, one that won't work."

But it had with him. He could see Anna at the piano. Her blonde hair cascading down her shoulders, huge green eyes concentrating on the score. She'd had the longest blackest lashes he had ever seen on anyone, and he couldn't take his eyes off her.

He forced himself to see her in his mind's eye, but like a minefield, the horror blew up those thoughts and all he could see was the priest, whose left pinky had turned blue from walking in the cold for hours. Finding shelter hadn't helped much, nor the bowl of soup passed around. Two sips each. A guy with wrinkles around his face so deep you couldn't see his eyes or his mouth had gulped down the whole thing. It had been mostly water, probably gotten from the toilet. But it was called soup. The wrinkled guy was punched in the face until he stopped breathing. Joe had laughed. He couldn't stop. The blood. The bowl had filled with blood. "Blood soup," he'd hiccupped out, holding onto his stomach. The room was as quiet as the cold. No one had had any strength to respond. If he had had any himself, he would have killed the guy who punched the old man to death. But he'd had no feeling left. The laughter. The blood. Those hadn't felt real either. As if he had watched someone else become hysterical, crazy.

He'd had no idea at the time how he had been so lucky as to end up at the Greenwoods. Brother John had somehow arranged the adoption. From Italy? From Poland? He still wasn't sure.

But there Anna had been, hiding behind Shirley's skirt; he'd been barely fourteen and she ten years old.

"Anxious Anna," Shirley had nicknamed her. It was a good name. Anna would jump at her own shadow, then laugh nervously. But when she painted or played the piano she was different. Her nervousness disappeared.

He'd agreed to everything the Greenwoods wanted him to do, even becoming a choirboy. Throwing himself into the church had been a welcome relief from being the Jew-boy he'd been, even though he had disdain for God — where was He when the Nazis took over? He became a choirboy more as an escape from his ordeal than to join a religion. He was ready to be anyone but himself. The best decision he'd ever made. Anna had diligently learned the music to all the hymns he had to sing. They'd practiced for hours. She looked up at him with those sparkling eyes. Smiled at him like a star. His voice had baritoned those notes clear out the window, across the neighbor's yards and cobbled streets. She loved Caruso and called him her "Enrico." And he'd been glad to take on a big Italian identity.

Joe inhaled and smelled the sweet scents of Babki baking, filling up the whole house the way it always had, bringing up more memories of Anna. That cake had been their favorite. He felt something timid, unknown, way down deep in his gut. Anna gazing at him as he bit into the soft sweet; she, doing the same, a sugar mustache spreading across her mouth.

And how she'd hung on to him. Clung to his words. He'd felt like a million dollars. Shirley was pleased with their growing closeness. *Anxious Anna,* she'd tease, *has fallen in love with Joe.* He'd grown red, had asked her to stop saying that. But it was true.

He proposed to her after he'd graduated medical school. She had grown into a human angel, with her tiny waist and her charming smile. She was more beautiful than ever and his to take care of.

One summer night came to him in particular. They were out in her garden. The cicadas and grasshoppers were in concert. Her head rested against his shoulder. He had his arm around her. Inhaled her rose perfume and kissed her check. There was a summer breeze. The moon was a sliver. He thought of Yeats' poem, one Anna had loved. He'd memorized it for her sake and had often recited it.

He whispered,

> *I went out to the hazel wood...*
> *and someone called me by my name:*
> *It had become a glimmering girl*
> *With apple blossom in her hair*
> *It was you, sweet Anna,*
> *Who called me by my name and ran*
> *And faded through the brightening air...*

Oh, you're changing the words and she'd playfully hit him. *And I'm right here, not fading at all.*

He ran his fingers along her lips and continued,

> *Though I am old with wandering*
> *Through hollow lands and hilly lands,*
> *I will find out where she has gone,*
> *And kiss her lips and take her hands*

He softly kissed each finger. Her eyes were wet and shining like the night. He'd held onto her fingers, and she pulled.

You're not old, silly. And you're not wandering...

But he continued

> *And walk among long dappled grass,*
> *And pluck till time and time are done,*
> *The silver apples of the moon,*
> *The golden apples of the sun.*

He played with her curls and whispered the last two lines again. The wind rustled. The sliver moon had gathered stars around her, thousands it seemed.

And two years later, when she gave birth to Clara, he was overjoyed.

But Clara's birth gave Anna no end of grief. She had long bouts of crying; often calling him at the office. Sobbed that Clara was turning blue from screaming. She spent hours under the covers. Her head hidden under a pillow. She hadn't wanted to hear the baby cry like that. Another time she called, hysterical. Yelled over the wires that Clara was in the garbage; she needed help getting her out.

He had raced home. Found his baby wrapped in a blanket from head to toe inside the large can meant for the garbage trucks. He yelled his goddamned head off, which got poor Clara crying, too. He'd spoon-fed her, heat steaming inside of him. Someone was pulling the baby out of his arms, but he wouldn't let her go. Not this time. Miriam had been crying. Especially, when those signs had gone up, *no Jews allowed*, in front of her favorite candy store. He'd snuck in and stolen a chocolate bar. She'd thrown her arms around him when he gave it to her. He'd patted her thick curls. *You'll have everything you want. No one will stop me. Not a stupid sign or a Nazi.* He'd look after her, he'd promised. But she'd toppled on top of him, dead.

Joe, you're hurting her. Give her to me. Anna. Tear-streaked cheeks. Eyes swollen red. Clara, red-faced from crying so hard. *I don't know how Clara got in the garbage. I don't remember...but you...you were...look.* She bent Clara's bruised elbow toward him.

He wanted to hug them both, kiss every inch of them, but Anna was crying too hard. He dismissed the desire. Anna needed help. This wouldn't have happened if she hadn't buried Clara like that.

Shirley had flown out and stayed with them for two months, showing Anna how to take care of Clara. *It's nothing,* Shirley had commented often. *Anna needs to be shown a few things.* That's when he'd discovered Milltown and Benzedrine, and Anna had calmed right down. Shirley may have helped some, but he knew it was the medication that had done the trick. And as a result of his success with Anna, he was asked to head a ward for women with anxiety.

Aaron Weinstein had been at Mt. Sinai a good five years longer than Joe. He'd said he knew of Joe's expertise in neurological disorders and how they affect the heart, and thought he would be an asset to the ward; that success gave him the expertise to run the adolescent clinic.

Now, Shirley was calling him. "Joe, we're at the table. We've been waiting for you."

He'd been a huge asset to that ward. But had failed Anna. Nothing he tried had helped her. Nothing. He picked up his black journal and wrote:

Anna
Your piano playing,
Paintings
Your golden hair with apple blossoms
The way you called my name,
How they wove me
How your death
Still unravels me.

"Anna," he whispered. "I've never stopped wandering."

SEVEN

CLARA

I wore my jewelry everywhere including to Dad's office the following Monday, when I met Maureen. Everything about her was wide: eyes, smile, teeth, chest. She smelled of suffocating perfume that made me cough. "How wonderful to meet the doctor's daughter. I've heard so much about you." Her voice was so sexy, she should have been in the movies.

She stared at my necklace and said to Dad, "She's in good hands, Doctor. I'll give her a tour and then put her to work."

Dad, wearing his white coat and standing tall, left us and walked into the waiting room. I watched him from the opened office window.

"Mary Lincoln?"

A large black girl stood up. Her hand was shaking as she reached to shake Dad's. He met her halfway and took her hand in his. He looked her square in the eyes. "It's good to see you." Her face softened. He meant it. "I know you've been to two groups at the clinic…"

She followed him into another room. She was lucky. Not so much to be a drug addict, but to have this simple relationship with Dad.

"Isn't he wonderful?" Maureen had been watching too. "His patients just love him. And they're getting so much better!"

I turned to look at her. Her grin was bigger than the satin ribbons Patti wore. "You're so lucky to have a dad like him."

She looked at my necklace again and picked up a pile of manila folders. "Follow me."

I touched my neck nervously. She had no business staring like that, especially with a butt like hers. I thought it was going to fall off her body, it wiggled so much.

We entered a small room filled with white filing cabinets that seemed to go from ceiling to floor. There were no windows, and the cracks in the off-white walls looked like bulging veins. The opened door kept creaking back and forth, the sound bouncing off the walls.

She pointed to the cabinet right in front of us, and her fingers slightly brushed my earrings. "This is the active file; all you do is take these records and place them alphabetically." She turned to look at me with that grin. "I've just never seen any office girl look so fancy."

The door slammed closed.

AFTER WORK, I walked up Scott Street toward home. I passed dilapidated buildings, some with broken windows and paint peeling off the doors. A child came running up to me, his filthy diapers down at his ankles. His mother was right behind him, a baby around her neck. She looked down at me, her dark eyes weary and bloodshot. She grabbed the older child and dragged him toward her with one hand. The baby started crying.

"Your rich Daddy buy you that necklace?"

Before I could say anything, she had rolled her eyes and walked on.

I took off my gems and threw them in my purse. They were fine for Grandma and her friends, but I probably looked crazy in them. Jade with a white uniform. What an idiot. I kicked some beer cans out of the way. Their tinny sounds echoed as they rolled down the hills. A sticky Hershey Bar wrapper stuck out from my shoe. I peeled it off and hopped on the next bus home. I pictured Miriam and said, *Tradition is old-fashioned and out of date. You would agree with Maureen, wouldn't you? I'm really stupid for wearing something so ridiculous to work.* I opened my closed fist. The Hershey wrapper was torn to shreds, and my hand was smeared with grimy chocolate.

THE NEXT AFTERNOON, I tossed my jewelry inside my dresser drawer. I never wanted to see it again. And, when I was sure that Dad was in his room watching TV, I snuck quietly down the stairs, grabbed my bag hidden in the stairwell and left, praying he didn't hear the click of the front door on my way out.

I walked as fast as I could up the hill on 25th Avenue. The air was clear, and the wind strong. It pushed my hair in front of my eyes and cheeks. I pushed it back playfully, but it flew right back in front of me. As I reached Clement Street I ran the three blocks to the studio, stretching my arms out like a great bird.

I was just in time for the evening dance class. The teen girls were clambering into the studio. They smelled of bubble gum, Twix and Pringles. I sure hoped they hadn't brought any of that junk in. Just the other day Patti had given me a lecture about all the food in the changing room. *We can't have this mess, it will bring in ants and all kinds of bugs.* She had put a sign up: *No food allowed here or in the dance space.*

Chrissy was in a bad mood. "I hate my fucking pimples, and my parents are making me work in their store all summer. Shit."

Dawn pulled at her curly red hair. "At least you're not being shipped off to Tennessee to take care of your 102-year-old grandparents. Won't even be able to play my favorite songs. Shit"

I put on *I Ain't Gonna Work on Maggie's Farm No More* to help them with their tense moods. The girls stood at the barre, waiting. I stomped into the middle of the room and sang, changing the words, "Who ain't gonna work so hard no more?" I nodded to Chrissy to come join me and told the others to wait. Chrissy marched into the middle of the room and bent toward me. I sang, "You're gonna work hard forever more..."

"No, I'm not workin' for no one no more," stomped Chrissy.

"Dawn and Deb, come on in," I shouted.

Suddenly the center of the room was filled with seven girls creating their own steps and moving in all kinds of directions, eventually not singing at all. I slowly moved in again and directed them to think of something they hated doing, then, "Swing your heads down, feeling that thing you hate doing and lift a leg...Deb, catch Chrissy's leg, swing her, Chrissy resist..."

Soon they were swinging, stomping, frowning their way through a dense and moody dance, Dylan's straining and haunting voice weaving it all together. And just before the very last line, I stopped them cold and directed them to swing their heads up. With me leading with different words, we screamed in unison three times:

"I'm just gonna be me, forever and ever more!

I'm not working for no one who can't hear me no more!"

Sweat pouring from their foreheads, laughing and holding on to each other, they kept singing.

I swung them into a circle and said, "God, you guys, that was so good!"

They practically skipped out of the room, and as I walked into the dressing area, minutes after them, Chrissy handed me a handful of Pringles.

Chips in my sweaty hand, the fog hit my face as I left the studio. It fell off the car lights in clouds of mist. I walked home slowly, eating my Pringles before they became soggy. I took my time chewing, letting the salt rest on my tongue. My feet felt heavy. I was reluctant to move. I just didn't want to go back home. I had wanted to crawl into Chrissy's dance bag and have her carry me to *her* house. Not that I knew her family or wanted to work in a store all summer, but what would it be like to have parents who didn't think twice about sending you to Modern Dance?

When I reached the house, I stopped in front of the steps and looked up at the sky. No moon, not a single star. Nothing to see the keyhole by. I'd probably have to either ring the bell or go back to the studio and sleep there. I walked up the stairs, careful not to make a sound. I flung my dance bag over my shoulder and felt the lock. My fingers wandered down to the keyhole. Keeping one finger there I put the key in and turned the lock. The click was louder than the braying foghorns, and the door squeaked open. Everything was dark inside. Breathless, I shut the door and stood in front of it. Not a sound. I was safe. Dad had no clue I had gone out to teach.

PART 2

ONE

CLARA

Fall

I was walking along the Golden Gate Bridge. The fog was everywhere, and everywhere the horns blew and echoed into each other. The sounds were low; every note they hit was in a minor key. Then one would be so high, I wondered if Joan Baez had tried to imitate its notes. The notes single and together sounded lost, like a call so far out to sea no human could hear, yet so compelling and forlorn that the fog formed around it, misting its way across the water. So the lighthouse man, alone and unseen, sounded the horns again, thinking he was steering the ships away from danger when in truth he was only meeting his own lost cry.

I paused and leaned over the bridge. What would it be like to jump? The wind was like a strong hand on my hair, pulling it so far back I had to lean in that direction instead. I remembered Dad and me at dinner last night. His mouth hardly moved, and his Adam's apple bounced up and down. When our eyes met, I saw a depth and sadness beneath his vacant stare. As if to say, *I need you.*

After, when I had cleared the table, the plates looked small in the large sink, like Dad and I did in that mansion. Nothing fit anymore.

And I was sick to death of Patti and her pot smoking. I hadn't seen any signs of her cutting back. When she was high, it was like she disappeared. She didn't listen to my suggestions, and her comments were weird. The other day Mrs. Patterson, a student's mother, was asking Patti questions about her bill.

Am I all paid up for the summer? She asked. I loved her purple miniskirt and long white boots.

How the heck would I know? Patti fumbled through all the junk on top of her desk. *Where's my book?* She threw books and papers onto her chair and floor.

*Oh, you're so busy. Just send me a bil*l. Mrs. Patterson smiled.

After she left, I asked, *How can you be so disorganized?* But Patti laughed, tossing her long, straggly, dyed-blond hair aside and telling me not to take life so seriously.

Not to take life so seriously. That was easy for *her* to say. She could dance all she wanted. At this rate, I would probably end up quitting dance forever. Would she take that lightly if she were me?

The wind was blowing the fog so densely I couldn't see my own hand on the railing. I stared down at it for a while, trying to make out the form of my thumb. What would it be like to disappear?

The wind brushed against the back of my neck and lifted my hair outward. My eyes were watering, and I leaned forward again.

I was stuck living at home, stuck working in his office. I wasn't pretty enough for Marc and reading the paper now made me sick. I saw Marc and me, arguing on the couch, laughing together. The piles of newspaper were sky-high because he refused to throw any of them out. *You often get the facts wrong,* he'd say, his arm tight around me, *so I have to keep the papers to prove stuff to you.* I didn't need any more facts. Everything was just impossible — like bringing Wendy to Dad's clinic. God knew where she was or how she was earning money for her drugs. I'd have to search day and night for her, and then what? Have her spit in my face and fall down convulsing?

I was bone-tired.

I put my hands around the red poles of the bridge. Through the fog I felt how long and thin my fingers were. I remembered how Mom used to tell me that I had "piano fingers" long enough to stretch to the octaves. The wind raced the tears down my cheeks, and I leaned over the railings just a bit more.

Would Wendy be this way if Mom were still alive?

I put my head way down and looked at the crashing waves, mesmerized by how the wind pulled the ocean, the grey foam meshing into the endless fog.

If I were to jump now. . . I felt my heart beating fast just thinking about it. . . my life would become a sorrowful, interesting topic of conversation. People would shake their heads looking at my gravestone: Clara Greenwood, 1951-1975. They'd say, *She was an aspiring dancer who died too young.* I took in a long breath.

I held my hands right in front of me now and looked at them. My wrist bones were thin, and the skin was red, wind-blown and taut. There were scabs forming along the sides of my nails, especially around my thumbs where I bit them so hard they were sore from broken skin and hangnails.

The wind swept the ocean, smashing its waves against the rocks, screaming mist and spray. I kept wondering about how it would feel to fall, as I continued to look down.

Why was I alive? What the hell was the point? Was this how Mom felt? Did she ever ask herself these questions?

Cars whizzed by behind me. The foghorns blew harder and more frequently. An entire flock of seagulls flew overhead. I couldn't see them, but their scratchy, high and irritating calls were so loud, I knew they were near. I looked up to see if I could find them. They were flying in and out of the mist. One headed for the sea, his huge fog-colored wings spread out as he sailed downward toward the waves. I could barely see his body, while his claws fingered the air.

I shivered and tried not to think anymore. I clung to the red bridge pole and put my head over the railing again. I was dizzy. I hung my head further. I was completely unlovable; Marc had proven that to me. Of course, he wanted Sonya — she was beautiful, friendly, mysterious... Who would want me, with a dead Mom who wanted me dead when I was born, and a gorgeous, drug-addicted sister who got everything she wanted? And who would put up with Dad? The only choice left was to marry a doctor and manage his office. I could feel the ocean so far below, spraying all over my face. I leaned over even further, feeling my waist up against the pole. The fog so dense now, if it weren't for the whitecaps, I wouldn't be able to tell the ocean from the sky.

Suddenly, there was a hand on my shoulder.

"Don't you love watching the waves on a day like this?"

I pulled back, startled. A woman was smiling at me. She withdrew her hand and took out a cigarette and lighter.

"I'm sorry," she laughed. "I never meet people who love to get into the waves like I do. You know, leaning way over."

I stared at her cigarette; at the small red fire.

"My name's June." She held out a short hand, her hot-pink painted nails stood out in the fog. We were standing close, and I could see that she was wearing a long woven skirt with orange and green threads, a white puffed-sleeve peasant blouse with pale orange and red embroidered flowers across the chest. It barely rested on her waist, making it look square. Brown Birkenstocks were on her feet.

"I'm Clara."

"What brings you out in such fog?" June asked.

"Oh, I love days like this."

"Easy to hide, huh?"

I looked more carefully at her face and into her small brown eyes. Brown bangs hung above them, a thick braid slid down her back.

Her eyes met mine and stared. I looked away, took a deep breath and looked up at the fog and down at the water.

"What do you mean?" I said, forcing a smile.

"Oh, I don't know, sometimes I like to hide on days like this. You know, when life is hard, and I ask myself what the purpose of everything is. Ever ask yourself that question?"

I looked away again. When I looked back at June she was laughing.

"Sorry. I ask a lot of stupid questions. Which way were you walking?"

We walked toward San Francisco in the direction I had been moving before I leaned over the rail.

"I have four children," June volunteered suddenly.

"What?" Who would ever want so many kids?

"Can you believe it? I can hardly myself, but that's why I'm in the habit of asking questions. My kids ask all the time, 'why?' and 'what's that?' It's very exciting, you know?"

What could be so exciting about kids asking a million questions? Mom had chastised me for doing that. I was losing interest.

"I don't," I said. The silence made me embarrassed. "I mean, I've just graduated college, and I have a lot of stuff on my mind, so I don't have time to ask a whole lot of questions. I have to figure out my jobs, my relationships, you know, boring stuff. Maybe your life is more exciting?" I couldn't imagine having one child let alone four. If I were her I would certainly jump.

"My life has never been so wonderful."

Good for her. I kept quiet. The walk would soon be over.

"Let me tell you why."

I calculated the distance, another half mile or so.

"I'm studying in a wonderful school, called The Ancient School of Ideas. Our teachers are mystics. They've studied in India and Japan and have connections with both Buddhist temples and Hindu Ashrams. Their knowledge of ancient religions is phenomenal, and they show how all of the teachings give the same message of Divine Love."

She went on to tell me about a special dinner the school was hosting the next night. She said the group was inviting just a few people to listen to the teachers.

Apparently, the food -- the produce, chicken, beef and eggs -- all came from two organic farms, one in Petaluma and the school's very own up in Plainville, Oregon.

Everything in the restaurant was homemade, and all the chefs were students. She really thought I'd enjoy the experience.

"You sound like the Moonies," I told her. My chest was beating up against my collarbone.

She laughed and shrugged. "What can I say to that? That we're not the Moonies? Come to our restaurant for lunch, you'll see for yourself how busy it is."

Her tone had changed from light to disappointed. Even if she were part of the Moonies, what harm could it do to see? "What if I'm tired of 'new', tired of change?" I heard my voice crack as I flashed on Dad telling Wendy and me about Mom dying,

She took my hand. "I understand," she said. "I want to help."

I felt her palm in my hand, soft and warm, as we stood there.

AFTER I LEFT JUNE, I walked up the hills until I reached the lookout point overlooking Baker Beach. I gazed out to the ocean. The fog had cleared, and the water was glimmering with dancing diamonds like it had the day Mom died.

On the way home from school that day, I'd been gazing at the ocean in the distance. I couldn't distinguish the blue in the water from the blue in the sky...

Like every day on the way home from school, I'd pictured Aunt Miriam wearing a similar dress to mine, coming to meet me, waving. We'd talk about our crazy hair and getting Dad to talk to me about modern dance. I'd wished to tell him all the things I'd admired about him, how hard he worked and how he cared so much about his patients. Miriam always agreed, that he was the best and that I needed to tell him these things. I'd imagined his wide grin, and us hugging. He would have finally agreed to leave ballet alone.

As I came to China Beach, I stood looking out, the ocean closer now. Diamonds like the glittering fish, like the silver trout in that Yeats poem Dad always quoted, had been dancing on the waves that day as if to say, *Yes, tell your father how much you admire and love him.* My heart leapt like the waves; I couldn't wait to get home.

But nearing our front steps, I'd been surprised to see Dad's Mustang parked in front. He never did that. He always had it locked securely in the garage. And he had never been home in the middle of the day.

The house was completely quiet. No TV. No piano. I shut the door loudly, just to make noise. Dad called to me from the living room. He was sitting on his creamy white chair, holding Wendy who was sobbing, her wet face against his chest.

His shaggy eyes were also filled with tears, the wrinkles around his mouth turned downwards.

In a rare gesture, he held out his arms, beckoning me toward him. I slid into the chair, nestling my head on his shoulder, Wendy resting on the other one. He put his old, square hand on top of my head and stroked my hair.

His voice cracked, *It's Mom... she died a few hours ago.*

I shivered the memory out of me. The air was damp. The wind sharp. Clamped inside my hand was June's phone number, the meeting date and time, and the restaurant's address.

TWO

CLARA

Patti was in New York; the studio was closed for a few days. I couldn't stand being home. I kept thinking about June's invitation. I needed a walk. I threw on my navy-blue sweatshirt over the light-blue imported Mexican tunic I was wearing. The blue cotton, embroidered shirt fell in a narrow straight line down to my knees. It had a collar, and small blue and red flowers spread daintily across the chest. I had taken it out of Mom's closet after she died. It swam on her, she was so small. It still smelled vaguely of vodka. I grabbed my bag, just in case I decided to go to that dinner.

As I walked toward 25th and California Street, the bus headed downtown was waiting at the stop. Forty-five minutes later I was standing across the street from the restaurant. I could see its dark green façade. "The Ancient Side of Eating" was written in script across a blossoming apple orchard. But Market Street at Golden Gate Street was one of the craziest intersections, and crossing it was a nightmare. Cars honked nonstop, and trolleys came to screeching, braking starts and stops. The light took forever to change, and pigeons pecked around my feet as I stood at the crowded corner, waiting. Dinner would probably be over by the time I made it across.

When the green light finally flashed, I was literally caught in the crowd and pushed across the street. I was among men taller than myself and thick-breasted women stinking of perfume.

When I finally made it inside the restaurant, June came rushing up to me, her brown eyes glowing, mouth all teeth when she smiled, her hands on her belly. She grabbed both of my hands and placed them there.

"I just found out I'm pregnant."

What? With her fifth child? Was she crazy? What was I doing here? June led me to my table.

"I wish I could sit and talk, but I have to go speak with Damien. Wait 'til you meet him...!" Mystifying and excited, her eyes shining, her voice trailed off as she ran toward others.

I sat down at the round wooden table covered by a green-checked table-cloth. The restaurant was artfully decorated in a simple old-fashioned way. Black and white photos lined two of the walls. There were pictures of the farm in Plainville, Oregon, showing a charming timeline of the growth of the farm. Apple trees in all stages of growth stood in the back-ground and with each photo looked fuller and more beautiful. And standing in front of those orchards in each photo were the owner and the farmhands at various ages. The most recent one showed the owner glowing and smiling. She looked about forty. Her muscular arms were holding a huge basket of apples. Her uneven teeth showed clearly through her smile. A farmhand standing next to her held up the paper stating she had saved the farm and now had ownership.

Five or six wooden tables, all covered with the same white tablecloths, stood zigzag style on a beige-green stone floor. Vases full of daffodils and tulips sat on each table. There was a longer table set up front with two wooden chairs.

Mom had loved daffodils; there'd been a bed of them in the garden and always a vase on the table. *Ten thousand I saw at a glance...*a line from a Wordsworth poem. Dad had recited it often to us, often:

> *For oft, when on my couch I lie*
> *In vacant or in pensive mood,*
> *They flash upon that inward eye*
> *Which is the bliss of solitude;*
> *And then my heart with pleasure fills,*
> *And dances with the daffodils.*

And then, hugging Wendy and me, after, would say, *I'm not in a pensive mood when I hear you giggling. You are my heart and my pleasure, and my dancing daffodils.*

My own mood now was far from solitary or pensive as I inhaled the incredible, invisible smells overtaking the restaurant. Chicken, rosemary and thyme; potatoes, carrots and asparagus broiling; but it was especially the garlic that seemed to pass through the walls and steam out of the stone floor cracks.

My very skin glowed, drinking in the scents. And for the first time in years, I looked forward to eating.

Dinner was served at exactly 7 p.m., and what a meal! The meat fell right off of its bone without any effort and melted on my tongue. The small new potatoes tasted more like a dessert — creamy, buttery and soft. With each bite, I fell into ecstasy. It had been so long since I had eaten a real meal, having been on so many diets due to Mom's example.

I remembered one afternoon when she had been dieting. She'd been sitting on the couch, and when I walked in the door, she cried, *Quick, Clara, pour me orange juice from my bottle and bring me a piece of bread.* She hadn't eaten for days, trying to lose that small belly of hers. She must have weighed under a hundred pounds.

The two speakers, Damien and Melissa, began to talk. They were both gorgeous, but especially Damien. His brown eyes glowed, and his black hair cut short, along with his well-trimmed beard, gave him a clean, different, kind-of sexy look. His words, like the food, melted into me. I felt that I was being lured into a new kingdom, where the food was purposely intoxicating so that the king and queen could then have their way with me.

I had never been so on fire and relaxed in the same moment.

Damien spoke first. He had a Leonard Cohen voice, low and deep. As he introduced Melissa, he placed a cigarette between his fingers, hands knobby and wide. His smooth white teeth jumped out of his smile and could be seen clearly against his black beard. His navy-blue shirt was slightly opened at the chest, the sleeves neatly buttoned at the cuffs. It was tucked into black corduroy bell-bottom pants.

"Welcome to the Ancient Side of Eating or ASE, everyone. Thank you for coming and sharing this meal with us. This restaurant is created in Service for God, whom we love so much. We who work here are also part of ASI, the Ancient Study of Ideas, a school where we learn to seek His love."

I put my fork down. A school about finding the love of God I'd finish up my meal and go. This wasn't for me. I slowly took another bite. Damien stopped, looked at me and smiled. Well, maybe, I could learn *something* about God.

"Yes, this school will certainly wake you up," Damien continued, still staring at me. He went on to say that they studied the Bible, the Koran, the Zen Buddhist Sutras, the Kabbalah and the Bhagavad-Gita. And then he said, "This school is for those of you who feel life has no purpose, for those who have an inner pain — an ache so terrible that you want to die. Has it ever occurred to you that that very pain is the energy you need to find your True Self...?"

Damien's low voice was soft and kind, and it seemed that he looked at me most often. When I gazed back, my heart leapt like the Russian Dancers in the *Nutcracker*.

Was finding God really that important? I remembered Grandma and me holding hands walking away from China Beach so long ago. I had had such a desire to *be* the sunset, to actually become the color orange and rest among the fire reds and purples as the day came to a close. Grandma had said so convincingly that it was God that had created all that. *But,* she said, *God is a complicated idea, isn't it?*

Yes it is, Grandma, I thought as I sat there listening to Damien. Many images suddenly ran through my mind, one of Wendy crashing in my dorm, screaming, *Fuck, help me!* Her wrinkled hands grabbing mine, the black circles under her eyes darker than the blackest night. Another, of Dad asking me, *Why haven't you brought your sister to my clinic yet?*

How could there be a God?

Yet, when Damien looked at me, his eyes shone with a deep sparkle I had never seen in anyone before. My heart skipped and my thoughts leapt. Maybe there could be a God. Just maybe. He kept staring into my eyes as he spoke and invited me to join the school.

Then a tall, skinny guy at a table behind me stood up yelling, hands gesturing outward, "This is all a bunch of shit! I've never seen so many fake stares, statements and attitudes in my life!" And he stomped out.

Heads turned, including mine. His violent outburst shook me to the core. I picked up my glass of water, and some of it spilled onto my lap. I didn't know my hands were shaking. Could there be something fake here? But at that moment, small round, chocolate desserts were served, and the smell was intoxicating.

Damien laughed and shook his head. He gazed at me intently, his eyes deepening more into their sockets. My heart dropped to my knees.

He bit into the chocolate, chewed slowly, his tongue sensuously moving over his lips, and rolled his eyes upward. "Some people can't handle the truth. We bless that young man and wish him luck. With an attitude like his, he'll never find love, will he?"

Melissa shook her shiny blonde curls, much like Wendy had.

Damien cut into the crusty dessert again and lifted his fork to Melissa, as if in a toast. She did the same with hers, and they made ecstatic noises as they stared into each other. When Damien looked up, his gaze locked into mine. He smiled and lifted his fork to me. My hands were trembling so much, I couldn't do the same. As I took a bite, the warm chocolate crust gave way to pure chocolate-melt on the inside; chocolate under chocolate, under more chocolate. It entered my bloodstream and led my every thought. I was completely intoxicated. June had pulled over a chair, carrying her plate with just a bite of cake left on it. She sat next to me, laughing into my ear, "You look drunk!"

"Well, look at you, scraping your plate!"

June laughed. "Do you want to join the school?"

"I'm not sure," I mused, although I knew I wanted to. "How much do the classes cost?"

"$250 a month. But as Damien said, just come for one month. Try it out as an experiment."

My neck pulsed at triple speed. "That's an expensive experiment."

She completely ignored my complaint and told me that the first meeting was in two days; she gave me her phone number again, letting me know she was moving in three and didn't have her new number yet. "So, if you want to come, time is of the essence."

I looked up at the photos on the wall and saw the owner's smile again. "Tell me more about this farm."

June's face softened, but her smile vanished. She looked over her shoulder and then looked up at the pictures. She shivered. Her eyes rolled up to the ceiling, and she placed her hands in prayer. She whispered, "Please Almighty God, You who know the Truth, let me tell this history perfectly." Keeping her hands in prayer, she looked past me, the way Mom used to gaze, and whispered, "The farm has been in Helen's family for over 100 years. And single handedly, she rescued it from ruin when she was just twenty years old. She had walked for miles, from farm to farm, pleading for workers to come help, as her parents were ailing, and she had no siblings." Her eyes rolled up to the ceiling again and she raised her arms. "Dear Almighty God, let me tell the rest with perfection." Her hands still folded in prayer, she continued, "Helen had managed to get an article into the town paper and get the attention of the mayor, and then the governor. The farm became Oregon's pet project, and soon volunteers and donations were pouring in like the rain in that state." She bowed her head. "Thank You Almighty God."

Chills covered my back. I'd never heard anyone describe anything like this before. Dad had always said, *God does not exist. Be honest, be good to your mother, your sister, to me. Be grateful, and with all of us here, there is no need of God.* I looked at the photos again. Helen's arms looked bulkier. Her uneven teeth and smile more intense. I was twenty-four. I couldn't imagine accomplishing such a thing. I heard Damien's voice in my mind. *Imagine being in a school where everyone is just like you, waking up to your true purpose, finding your innate joy, no matter what you are doing. Nowhere will you find a place like this, or such genuine support.* He'd paused, puffing on his cigarette, smoke winding its way out of his mouth and through his fingers, a dragon of sorts, inviting magic.

Joining would cost a lot of money, but it would be only for a month. Even though the God thing bothered me, a community like this with someone like Helen as its teacher might be just what I needed. It would only be for a month.

JUNE THREW her arms around me when she saw me walk into my first class. Her large breasts were up against mine, and my head rested against her sturdy, soft shoulder. It surprised me how much I wanted to stay right there. We met in the restaurant itself. The tables had been arranged in a semi-circle, facing the longer one where Damien and Melissa sat. There were six other new students. We were all standing about when Damien approached us. He shook each of our hands and said, "Please sit down. The lovely Melissa is here."

Melissa had walked in silently, and swinging her long blonde hair away from her face, she sat down.

We took our seats.

Melissa's voice was melodic and lyrical; it was as if she were singing to us. "Your teacher is amazing, and we do our best to emulate the teachings that come pouring through her. Helen saved the family farm when she was just twenty years old. Her aging parents wanted to sell it off to builders. And that's when Mother Mary came to her in a dream. She told her that She, Mary, would speak through her from now on."

Damien gently ran a finger down Melissa's cheek, wiping her tears.

Damien's voice was so soft I had to lean forward to listen.

"You see how much Melissa loves our Teacher?"

"Helen followed Mary's word to a T, and still to this day, fifteen years later, Mary speaks through her, guiding us to live from our authentic selves. When Helen gives us an instruction, we all follow it because the word is coming directly from the Blessed Virgin."

At the end of class, June, beaming brighter than the sun, hugged me again. She invited herself to hang out with me at home. "I have so much to help you through," she giggled.

"How can a dead person speak through someone alive?" I asked, feeling uneasy. Yet when Dad had given me the photo of Aunt Miriam at my thirteenth Christmas, she felt alive to me, and I had spoken to her often ever since.

I shivered and looked at June's pregnant belly, imagining it bigger than it was.

She saw my gaze and laughed. "Helen *is* Mother Mary; I have no idea how she can channel the Blessed Virgin, you just have to see for yourself. She comes down twice a year from the farm to work with us older students. She can't handle the negativity of beginning students, but she sends her love to everyone."

"Have you told her about me?"

"Of course. And she knows that you're going to stay."

"What?"

"Helen asks Mary about each one of us constantly and is able to read into our auras."

What's an aura? I wanted to ask. But it didn't matter. I took my thumb out of my mouth. I'd just pulled another hangnail off, and it hurt.

"That's not the half of it, though, because when she thinks one of us is in danger, she'll call and ask such poignant questions you would think she was right there inside your mind."

June saw blood on my nail and handed me a tissue.

I clutched it tight as I headed to the door, feeling how soft it was. Damien was standing at the exit, smiling in a way that looked just as soft. "This place is magical," I said, surprised at my words.

He shook his head, smiling, "When God sends you to the right place and you agree to follow, it feels just like that. But there's no such thing. Stay with us, Clara, and you will see the glorious ways of God-Knowing."

THREE
CLARA

A few days later, I was twirling around the living room. Dad was at work, and I had told Maureen I needed a few days off. I was feeling lighter, more hopeful. June was coming over, and I couldn't wait to see her.

Standing at the door, she held out her big Mama arms, and I fell into them, laughing. She placed my unsuspecting hand on her growing belly.

"Feel here, feel here!' she sang, patting my hand with her large paw-like palm.

"Oh!" I laughed, wondering what it was I was supposed to feel as I rubbed her flabby belly. But an unexpected surge of delight flooded through my bones, just imagining a life there.

She beamed, her eyes widening as we stood there.

I pulled her inside still laughing. As we walked through the hallway to the kitchen, she marveled, "What a gorgeous home. Who lives here?"

"Just Dad and I..."

"You live here, with your Dad, in *his* home?"

I was startled by her tone. "It's the home I grew up in."

June didn't say anything, and I didn't like the silence between us. As we entered the kitchen I said, "How did Helen become a psychic?"

But when I faced June, coffee pot in hand, I noticed her looking me up and down. I raised my brows, but before I could ask, "What's up?" she said, with that smile that opened her entire face, "Helen would want you to start dressing differently, hon. Growing into our true selves means giving up so many habitual patterns. And you have many habits that you need to shed, but first things first!"

Surprised but intrigued, I dropped a plate of Oreos in the middle of the table, sitting down with two cups of coffee.

"Oreos! Oh, my gosh! I have so much to teach you. Where to begin?" She took my hand in hers and sat looking at me.

What had I done wrong? God knows I knew Oreos weren't the best kind of food, but whenever I had friends over, that's all they asked for. The few times that I ate them myself, I had fun breaking the cookie in half, eating them slowly.

"Hon, Oreos are junk for the baby. Helen has taught many of us how to make our own baby food! But all of this in time; I think we need to focus on you and your appearance first."

I stared at her peasant blouse that was way too tight for her large, milk-filled breasts, and I flashed back to the Golden Gate Bridge and being a shield for her cigarette.

"But what about your smoking, that can't be good for the baby?" It was her openness, her ease in responding, that kept me wanting to get to know her more.

"Helen's a living example of her own teaching. She's a survivor of breast cancer, and she teaches, through Mary of course, that as you come closer to your truer self, the vibrational level in your body increases to such a speed that it kills cancer cells before they have a chance to form. Therefore, cigarette smoking is safe, as long as you are working on yourself."

I shook my head in disbelief. What would Dad think of that? A cure for cancer: "Come to ASI and get in touch with your true self." He'd look June right in the eye and tell her she was crazy, ask for the studies, for the scientific proof. I was playing with an Oreo, breaking it open, then deliberately licking the cream off one side of the cookie. I wondered if my cells could ward off the calories, given how quick my chest was pulsating against my bones. I exaggerated my tongue movements along the white sugary substance and made loud groaning sounds, indicating how delicious it was.

June laughed. "Okay, enough lecturing. But, don't you want to look sexy?"

I practically spit out my cookie, the question was so unexpected.

"Come," she said, taking my hand again. "Let's look at your wardrobe."

Leaving the half-eaten sweet and the cooling coffee on the table, I led June to my closet. She searched through my old faded T-shirts, long paisley blue and purple skirts, until she bumped up against the tall, knee-length black leather boots Grandma had brought back from Italy for me a few years before. I seldom wore them. When I put them on, June went wild. She said they were the most gorgeous, sexy pair of shoes she had ever seen on anyone. She pointed out how they accentuated my tall, lean figure and my perfectly shaped legs.

I had never seen myself in this way before, and I saw my long narrow cheeks turn red as we looked at me in the mirror.

When she left, my boots still on, I stood in front of the mirror again and stared at myself for the longest time. June's image of me filtered through my own, arguing that my boney rib cage was actually shapely, that my long skinny arms added to the sexy length of my legs, and that my thin waistline was as graceful as a reed, instead of like a boy's.

The sensations of change were so strange and so delightful that I didn't know how to feel, but I began to wear those boots more often.

ABOUT A WEEK LATER, June and I were on Haight Street shopping for me.

We were literally stepping over hippies, so strung out they didn't look human. In high school, I'd made it a point to stop and talk to one of them. The girl, my age, a high school drop-out, told me she had run from her home in New York City, because her parents were bigots. She couldn't clarify what she meant, but she was out on the streets begging until she had enough money for college. Dad had always lectured about not throwing money away on beggars. But I had felt bad for her. Not having a mom myself, I knew what it was like to be without parents. I gave her and others spare change I found around the house. By my senior year in college, the number of people like her seemed to double in size, and it was overwhelming for me to think about them. It didn't seem like the few dimes I gave could really be helping. I mean, how could anyone afford food and a place to live on so little? In fact, the more I gave, the more I felt I had to give. I felt guilty that I couldn't give more; that so many went hungry and I was helpless to do anything about that. I slowly burned out, thinking it was better not to give at all. Recently, the papers had justified all of this. There were reports of beggars stealing purses and pocket wallets. Apparently, June didn't trust them either because she whispered into my ear, "Hold onto your bag."

We walked into the Second Hand Haight Street Shop, directly across from Psychedelic Plus. Although I wanted to go there first, June steered me away. "No, no, you can't look like a hippie anymore. You must dress as though you already are your True Self."

Chills went up and down my back, and I giggled, feeling my mouth spread wide. There was something exciting about having a "True Self."

The first thing I saw was a tailored blue-jean skirt hanging with a white blouse and a matching jacket. It was identical to what Mom used to wear. I couldn't breathe for a moment. I let June take my hand and lead me through the numerous racks, trying on one after another of the outfits she picked. I had been eight watching Mom get ready for a cocktail party. She'd been sitting in her small dressing room at her table that was covered with all her creams and make-up. She'd handed me her hairbrush, flustered, and said, *My hair appointment was canceled today. Keep brushing while I do my eyes.* I'd brushed hard until the tangles were out and her blonde strands hung down her shoulders in shiny curls. She'd placed a pile of them on top of her head, while allowing the rest to fall. I said, *Oh Mom, you look just like a queen!* She'd smiled at me in the mirror, blowing a kiss.

"Stop day-dreaming." June handed me more skirts to try on. My arm ached from holding so many clothes. She rubbed her large belly and smiled. Had Mom rubbed hers when I had been in there?

The clothing was so remarkably affordable that I purchased all the items June suggested for me. When we got back to the house, I modeled one of the new outfits: a light blue V-neck tight sweater that fell to my hips, and a black leather miniskirt. I pulled on matching stockings and my boots.

June clapped and shouted, "Oh, incredible! An utter transformation! Just a few dabs of make-up, and you're all set."

I tried to draw the line at make-up, but June insisted. I was in shock as I looked at the image staring back at me. Black liner, mascara and deep gray-blue eye shadow enhanced her eyes. The figure had a sexy, long, waistline, and the lipstick, so like the color Mom used to wear, was surprisingly perfect. She had bright smiling lips.

I WORE my outfit to my third class the next night. I'd had trouble keeping my hand steady with the eyeliner, and mascara kept smearing under my eyes. Finally, I'd decided to dab my lips with the lipstick and brush my eyelashes quickly. It came out looking wonderful. But I was having trouble walking gracefully in the high-heeled boots, in spite of the hours I'd spent practicing.

June and Daisy were standing inside the entrance. The hallway was an open area, made with the same large, green stone tile as the restaurant. Daisy had been in ASI as long as June. She also had four children. There was a swarm of toddlers running all over the open area. June and Daisy were in deep conversation, their foreheads wrinkled, mouths in serious frowns. But when they saw me, they stopped talking.

"Wow, look at you! Turn around honey, you look gorgeous! Wait until we tell Helen, she'll be so excited!"

I faced the two of them and did as I was told, trying to picture Helen pleased, even though I'd never met her. And as I turned, about nine of the kids turned with me. Spontaneously, I bent down, took two of them by hand, beckoned to the others and had them spinning in a small circle in no time.

I felt like I was six years old again, twirling in and out of my living room curtain, glowing in Dad's praises. The children doubled over with laughter and continued to swirl after I stopped.

"She has a real knack with kids, doesn't she, June?"

I stood with them, smiling and nodding, feeling as free as the sea. I saw this glance that June gave Daisy: raised eyebrows, mouth pursed closed. What did that look mean? I said I'd meet them down in the basement in class. My heart had dropped. Some of that freeing feeling had disappeared. Did I do something wrong?

I walked down the narrow steps as slowly and gracefully as I could. The heels made a loud thumping sound on the bare wooden stairs. I tried to walk more softly by pointing my toes, but that was impossible in these boots.

I made it down. The damp air and unfinished look of the meeting room were such an ugly contrast to the values of the teaching. I stood still for a moment trying to grasp this contrast. It was the first time I'd been down here. The other two classes had been held upstairs in the restaurant. June had said there would be more students in this one, so we'd be meeting down here.

The wooden floor panels creaked underneath a dirty red rug; folding chairs were arranged in a semicircle facing the altar, which was always covered with a white lace tablecloth, a vase of fresh red roses, red wine, crystal wine glasses, glass ashtrays, cigarettes and homemade brownies and chocolate chip cookies.

Damien and Melissa were there, also steeped in conversation, their hands touching, heads close together. Melissa's blonde curls cascaded over her curvy breasts and down her thin waist. Her blue eyes were accented by matching eyeshadow and mascara. The black, halter-top mini dress exposed her cleavage, and her heels defined her well-shaped calves. Damien's sexy ease spilled out of his pores.

When he saw me, he stopped talking to Melissa and put his hand out to touch mine. My heart was beating crazy fast, my knees wobbled and my head spun.

He turned away from Melissa and gazed at me. His eyes were serious and deep, and he didn't smile. He finally nodded and drew me closer. He whispered, "I can see your beautiful glowing energy. You're ready to wake up. I'm so glad you're here."

Still wobbling, like Mom used to, I found a seat. I shook from head to toe. Thoughts swarmed my mind, like the buzz of people suddenly walking in, maybe fifteen of them all dressed up and looking quite lovely...the way Mom had dressed for her cocktail parties, wobbling from person to person as she greeted each one. Even at those fancy home parties, I had never seen Dad stare at Mom the way Damien had at me. And yet, when Melissa sat down next to him, I felt lanky and skinny in comparison; that I would never be beautiful, in spite of all my recent efforts and June's encouragement. Still, I couldn't take my eyes off him. All the other students, men and women, took their seats. No one could have been older than thirty.

Damien and Melissa gazed at each other and then at us. I longed to be like them. "You all look like royalty; the way the True Self ought to look," Damien said, laughing. "And our lovely Melissa created this beautiful altar." He paused, taking her fingers into his hand, lifting her wrist and kissing it. Melissa's cheeks turned red and her blue eyes shone. "Now we are truly able to begin God's work. So many possibilities await you."

Melissa pulled a white handkerchief out of her small, white patent leather purse and dabbed her eyes. Damien put his hand in hers again. "I hope you all love Melissa the way I do, she cries every time she hears how beautiful this work is..."

Her gaze went around the room, and when it met mine, I looked away. Her eyes were filled with a light that was hard to let in. I tried to look at her again, but she was staring at someone else. Her gaze slowly washed over every single one of us, not stopping until we each were touched by her intimate contact. That tall guy's words floated back to me, "fake stares." I smiled. No way. You couldn't fake a glow like that.

Damien was talking again. "I know that you all have experienced that ache in your heart." His tone was gentle, alluring. "It's really about a longing to know God."

I looked down at my hands. That ache was about God? How so, I wondered? Marc and I used to stay up all night with our friends — well, his friends; I was more of a loner — after the peace rallies in Golden Gate Park, putting down the Born-Again Christians. You want to talk about fake, well, those religious groups were unreal! I shook my head, remembering how Marc would stroke my hair and kiss me hard when the meetings ended. *Hey Goddess Gorgeous, let's go to Sambo's for breakfast. Shit, forget Sambo's!* He'd pull me to the bedroom, pushing me down, the way he'd been pushing on Sonya.

Just then, Melissa caught my eye. She gave me a stunning, dimpled smile.

I'd never be able to be joyous like her, but I forced myself to smile back. Thinking she sensed what I was thinking, intense heat burned inside my chest and rose around my face and head. Beads of sweat gathered around my forehead. I was afraid it would drip over my eyes, splashing mascara down my cheeks.

I focused on Damien's black beard and wide-mouthed smile. He was encouraging us all to go to church and learn from the priests.

"I can't do that," I blurted out. "God feels so unreal to me." The room went completely quiet. I should have kept that in. My face was hot.

"Thanks for speaking for so many in the group, hon. Can you say more?" Melissa's voice was melodious, unbearable.

"No, I mean..." Drenched in embarrassment, my tongue clamped down.

Damien looked into my eyes and said tenderly, "We would not be here, if it were not for God. Helen would say that your thoughts about God are really about the ways you doubt yourself. What has been difficult for you?"

I couldn't keep my eyes off him.

"Maybe something happened between you and your father?"

How could he know?

"Maybe, something was so hurtful to you in your childhood that you had to take control of difficult situations?"

I couldn't keep my head up. No one had ever spoken to me so gently.

"When we have hurtful parents, we gather doubt within us, and we believe the false stories the doubt tells us. You must surrender yourself to God and church, and when you have done this, we can talk further."

I looked up at him again and noticed that Melissa's eyes were tearing. I was relieved that I didn't have to answer his questions about Mom, Dad and Wendy.

"Helen would want you to explore your religion. Are you listening?"

I nodded.

"Start to go to church regularly. It's the only way to surrender that unnecessary control of yours...Follow?"

I nodded again. I had no desire to go to church. But if I could shine in Damien's eyes, like Melissa, I would do anything.

After class, June put her arms around me, and Melissa came around. I asked, "Can I go to church with you guys?"

June shook her head. "Finding God is a very private thing. If either of us went with you, it wouldn't be your journey. Go, find a congregation you like, come and tell us about it when that happens."

They hugged me again. "This is your second act of surrendering, and you have been with us barely one month."

The first act, they told me, was changing the way I dressed.

"We're so proud of you, and Helen is already interested in you. I have mentioned your quick progress to her several times now." Melissa's deep blue eyes sparkled, and I wanted to twirl.

THE NEXT MORNING, that twirling feeling drained right out of me as I walked into the office. The space was closed-in, so when Maureen swung her chair around to face me, our noses practically touched. The ultra-clean walls and shining desks made me want to puke.

"Maureen? I need to ask you something."

"Ask away, I love answering your questions." There was a small coffee stain on the left shoulder of her white uniform.

"I have some pressing issues at my church tomorrow afternoon," I lied. "Can I have it off?" I had made an appointment with Minister Kleep at The Clement Street Protestant Church.

"Yes, of course, but your father often comments when you're not here. I'm wondering why he hasn't known? Wouldn't it be better to ask him?"

FOUR

CLARA

At dinner that night, the enormity of quiet between Dad and me was larger than the house we were living in. Being with him was unbearable. I felt like I was in this vast void, watching him take care of his patients; looking into their eyes while holding their hands, speaking in a soft gentle tone, one he never used with me. Now, at dinner, his brown eyes looked vacant, like Mom's had, and I just wished that there was something, anything that could pull me out, that could help me put my arms around him and hug tightly. Even if I could do that, telling him I wanted to take the day off and why would only throw us into a deeper chasm. I played with my food, pushing broccoli around like a street cleaner.

Chewing on the fried chicken, his mouth shining with grease, he said, "Alan is interested in seeing you again..."

I stopped playing with my food. Our eyes met, and again I saw that depth of sadness that had risen beneath his vacant look. I put my fork down and tried to answer, but my voice was stuck.

He continued to eat; his Adam's apple bounced up and down as he swallowed.

I wanted to tell him that I would choose my own husband, should I ever want to marry. The broccoli was mashed — I continued to mush it up, and the silence balled into a thick wall between us. He scraped his chair against the floor and left. I heard him plodding up the stairs.

I looked at his empty plate and then out to the garden. The sun's short rays landed on the grass, the hydrangeas and the roses. The red-orange dusk sky brushed their blossoms.

I picked up the plates and placed them in the sink. Mom had been wrong when she had said, *Everything has its place, the birds in their nests, the sun in the sky, and my drink in my flask.* She'd laugh wildly and then play Mozart, leaving me completely alone, like I was now.

FIVE

CLARA

On the way to the minister's the next day, I pushed hard up the hills. The sun's rays effortlessly beamed most of the fog away, and the day was gorgeous — a cool 60 degrees, unusual for late November. My breath coming fast, I walked faster, pushing the night before away. The harder my rage burned, the more I forced my calves to work.

On California and 24th Avenue, I passed two hippies sitting under the awning of a boarded store. Their dark beards crawled all over their cheeks and chins, and long tangled brown hair fell down their shoulders. They were unkempt and ugly, sharing a joint, a basket out in front of them filled with coins. As I walked by, they yelled, "That one's tight, too tight for our pants." A coke can filled with cigarette butts rattled toward me. I kicked it hard. *At least I wasn't begging,* I shouted to Dad in my mind.

The smell brought up memories of Wendy again. I doubled up my speed. I hadn't seen her since that fiasco at Dad's in the spring, when he had invited Alan over. I never wanted to watch Dad give her another dime. But was I any different than Wendy? I was a stupid dancer who would never marry or have a decent job.

I took another deep breath. The cool air entered my lungs as if to clean them of old thoughts. Going to see a minister...me? I shuddered, thinking of Dad's red face if he ever found out. I remembered over-hearing Grandma and him arguing. Grandma had said, *It was unnecessary, Joe.* Dad's voice was raised, angry, *Unnecessary?* Grandma had shushed him. *All your views about menorahs and God. Clara needs a religious education. Both the girls do.* I hadn't wanted a religious education, just candles. Dad was quiet. *Not in my house, Shirley. It's over now, but I can't bring the fallacy of God into my life ever again.* I'd wished to be invisible and walk into the room to hear more. In that moment, Mom had swished through the hallway with a tray of vodka and cookies. I'd beat it back up to bed.

I ran up to Clement Street and then down to 20th Avenue, the wind whizzing my crazy hair behind me, and I hit the neighborhood like a hungry gull landing on a wave.

Breathless, I suddenly realized I should have dressed more appropriately for meeting a minister, but I was still learning. Long skirts, tie-dyed shirts and sandals were my attire. I hadn't thought to change until now, as the sweat poured down my face.

The tall stone church looked intimidating. The matching stone door was huge. There was a sign that read, "Office around the back." I felt uneasy all over again. I pictured Aunt Miriam. She smiled, urging me on.

I followed a stone path surrounded by grass and beds of flowers to a wooden building. It looked like a small house. The note on the door said, "Church office. Come in."

The reception area was small and cluttered. A large woman sat at the desk, her graying dark hair piled high in a beehive. Her brown eyes looked tired as she smiled and greeted me, white powder caking right off her rouged cheeks.

"I have an appointment with Minister Kleep."

"He'll be right with you, have a seat."

She pointed to a wooden chair sitting next to a round, wooden coffee table piled high with flyers for the next church event. I picked one up. "Dinner for the homeless. Volunteers needed to serve dinner to those out on the streets. Contact Dottie at the office."

I thought of the two hippies I had just encountered. Could they be homeless? Of course, I didn't know. I had never imagined their lives to be anything but begging on the curb. Did they have a place to sleep at night, a place to go when it rained? Did Wendy?

Minister Kleep came out to greet me. Clean-shaven, red cheeked, short and round, he looked so perfect for the part that I imagined his mother writing on his birth certificate, *We would like to announce the birth of* **Minister** *Edward Kleep.*

His handshake was solid, and he greeted me smiling. I followed him into his office. The wooden desk he sat behind was surprisingly uncluttered, and the room itself simply furnished. In fact, the only furniture in the room was the desk and the two wooden chairs we each sat in. A small oak sculpture of Jesus on the cross hung on the white wall behind his desk.

"What can I do for you, Miss Greenwood?"

"Call me Clara, please. I'm ...I want to own my own dance studio." God, what a stupid, idiotic thing to say. If that's what I wanted, *he* certainly wasn't going to help me. I unclenched my clammy fists and spread my hands out on my lap. My eyes rested on the Jesus. His carved face was turned sideways, and His eyes were closed. Dad often closed his eyes when I spoke to him, too.

"And what is stopping you?"

Heat steamed through my chest, and I wiggled restlessly in my chair. Why would he care even to ask that? "I don't think anyone can help me."

He was staring steadily at me, his eyes so shiny I looked down. He cleared his throat. "And what makes you think that?"

The silence made the uneasiness worse. It was as thick as fog. I briefly looked up. I met his steady gaze for one second. This time he was smiling. His cheeks puffed out like a child's.

Did I look like a child too?

"My dear, who is stopping you from owning your own studio?"

"Dad," I blurted out.

"The bible says to honor your mother and father. Honor His advice ,and you will see that God will grant you everything you want."

I looked at Jesus again, dead on the cross. I pushed my chair back, but he reached out his hand and patted mine briefly.

"Has your father ever honored you dancing?"

Daffodils for my glittering ballerina — Dad had always been the first to hug me after each recital. I nodded.

"That was God acting through your father."

I shook my head. Dad would have said no to that one. My face was hot. This wasn't getting anywhere. "I don't know. I need Dad to listen to me. I don't think anyone, especially a hung Jesus, can make him do that."

Kleep rubbed his eyes and then his forehead. I had probably disappointed him.

"Jesus is not dead, not in the way you think. His spirit is alive in each of us. If you call on Him, He will wake you to so many possibilities..."

I saw Damien pull me close, I heard his incredible voice in my ear. *You are ready to wake up. Your energy is beautiful.* I involuntarily smiled at Minister Kleep. Clearly, both Damien and he knew something I did not.

"Come and worship with us every Sunday morning; you will see the many faces of God," he said, as I got up to go.

As I walked out of his office and into the waiting room, I noticed a large donation basket sitting near the entrance door. I pulled out the change in my pocket and threw it in.

THE FOLLOWING Sunday I couldn't wait to get to church. Damien had glowed when I announced I had found a minister. *Your desire to change is impressive. You had expressed your reluctance to go just last week! And didn't I tell you that once you met the right church that would melt your skepticism?* And after class, he sought me out, and hugged me. Skepticism wasn't the only thing melting.

I chose a pew in the back, and I actually saw people I knew walk in. There was Mrs. Johnson with her two girls that I taught dancing to. They each wore puffy, pastel-colored dresses, one blue, the other purple, with matching-colored plastic headbands. They twirled their way into the church aisle, and I wanted to stand and wave but sat silently, willing myself to act like a church person, sitting with a straight back, hands folded on my lap. I didn't want Damien to find out that I had misbehaved.

Light filtered through the stained-glass window, emboldening the images of Christ and Mary. The pew was hard and uncomfortable.

Soon, Minister Kleep was at the pulpit with the choir behind him. He looked small and powerful; his blue eyes scanned the congregation. Sculptures of Jesus were standing on either side of the pulpit. On the right, He was hanging from a cross, and on the left, He was a baby in Mary's arms.

I had held Wendy often when she had been a baby and taken her from Mom when Mom's eyes had been especially bloodshot.

Minister Kleep was speaking. "Jesus died for our sins — and what does the word 'sin' mean?"

I was on the edge of my seat.

"It means to 'miss the mark.'"

He gazed at us, silently letting his words fall. I looked up at him and then around at the congregation. I looked for my little students, but they were sitting up front, impossible to see. I stared at the balding head of the gentleman right in front of me.

"On my way here this morning," Minister Kleep was speaking again, "I stopped to talk to an old man sitting on the curb. I sat right down next to him and asked him how he was. His eyes were sad, and he stroked his grey beard."

Dad had sad eyes, and he helped like that too. I had watched him sit down with his patients. I remembered him greeting Mary Lincoln in the waiting room.

"'I'm a goner,' the old man said. "'My wife has divorced me, and my one child is lost on drugs. I am a poor man without a family or hope.' I invited him to worship with us. I took down his address."

I gazed down at the floor. There was a small ball of dust wrapped around the foot edge of the pew. Dad didn't have Wendy anymore. Would anyone sit down next to her if she were begging on a curb?

"Was he missing the mark, my friends?" Minister Kleep's voice was much louder, almost booming now. "Was he sinning because he was begging for money? Or was he simply, as he said, 'a poor man without family or hope?' Who is missing the mark, my friends? Him? Or us, for not being active, going out there and helping?"

I pictured Wendy collapsed on my dorm floor. And then Mom, her fallen pills spread all over the piano pedal. I had brought her water...but she brushed it out of my hands and started flinging records, shouting, *Where the fuck is it.?* What was Kleep talking about? Trying to save those who missed the mark? How many attempts had I made with Mom, with Wendy? How much money had I given my sister? Had Dad?

I didn't hear another word. When I walked outside, I wanted to wrap myself inside the fog and disappear. An old lady, balding, toothless, with a huge bag and stinking of rotten eggs, stood right near the door.

"The Lord will save you sinners. Yes, He will." She yelled up at the sky, "Hail to Jesus, save these sinners in front of me." She looked toward me, but past, her face shriveled, like hands when they sit in the bathtub too long. "Jesus told me you cannot be saved. Be gone to Hell, you sinners. Be gone!"

She walked away muttering under her breath, her large bag between her small hands, carried like a cross.

SIX

CLARA

A fter that sermon the next few weeks just flew, and it was harder to get to church. I had only gone once more. But June checked on me every Saturday night.

"Hon, are you going to Church tomorrow?"

There was a piercing scream on the other side of the phone and a huge clatter. "Darlene, stop, no Jacob..."Her kids were shouting and must have been breaking and throwing things. "I gotta go."

I wanted church to help me in the worst way, and I wanted to love God, the way Damien did. I was hoping that this would help me love my life, which I was so sick of. But going to church was boring, and it was hard for me to understand God. "Jesus died for your sins," Kleep had said. Why would anyone die for something like that? It made no sense. There must be something very wrong with me.

The next week, after teaching at Patti's, I picked up my large red dance bag and tossed it over my shoulder. It was Saturday afternoon, when Dad was either doing his rounds or playing golf. He had no idea I was still teaching. Walking out of the studio, I practically bumped into Damien who was standing at the entrance.

Cigarette in hand, smoke falling out of his dark beard, he stood smiling at me, his enticing mouth spreading wide. Eyebrows raised and eyes sparkling, he looked into mine as he took my bag.

What was he doing here? My sweaty thick hair was pushed back by a red-pink headband, and wide, obvious wet circles stained the underarms of my brown cotton T-shirt. I begged the wind to whirl away any body odor.

"Hello, my dear. I've been noticing you lately, and so I'd like to walk with you for a while, if that's okay."

Geary Boulevard was busy as usual. Cars and buses honked and screeched. It was damp and cloudy; you could see the sun filtering through the gray-cream sky. We passed a young woman, perhaps no older than seventeen, carrying a baby on her hip. Her long skirt dragged along the sidewalk. Her brows were wrinkled, mouth drawn tightly closed. She looked so uptight and unhappy. Not that I wanted to be pregnant, but if I could be with someone like Damien, would having a child be so bad? The thought really surprised me, and I tripped over a bump in the sidewalk. Damien reached out his arm to catch me. What if I had fallen, and he had to carry me back to his car? Did he know how much I liked him?

Just then, a group of political activists passed us. A light brown-skinned guy with matted braids down to his waist and a beard as long handed us an "Impeach Nixon" flyer.

Damien stopped walking and looked the guy right in the eye, not taking the flyer. "Damien," he said, and he put his hand out to shake the other.

"Hey, Damien, how you doing, man? Steve here..." His boisterous voice was as strong, it seemed, as his handshake. But Damien held Steve's hand in both of his and wouldn't let go.

Steve's smile broadened as his forehead tensed. "What, man?" He finally blurted. "Let go, okay? Peace to you." Damien finally let go, and Steve ran off, his thick braids banging down his back.

"A waste of life." Damien turned to look at me. "He's worshipping politicians and all their negative responses. You're fortunate that you have the courage to come out of your normal self and join us."

He held my hand as we walked again. Please hand, don't sweat, I begged of it. I hoped he didn't feel how tense it was. I moved my fingers ever so gently to relax each one. I was beginning to see what was wrong with me. I had spent my entire six years in college actively involved in political groups. I'd joined the Coalition for Women's Rights and The People For Peace and spent much of the time yelling at cops. I needed to throw myself into church instead. And that was exactly what Damien was talking about.

"I hear you've spoken to a minister, been to church and paid for your third month already. How wonderful! You have begun to transform yourself quickly. Helen is very excited about you." He stroked my fingers as if they were delicate flower petals.

"Will you spend the afternoon with me?"

Weren't Melissa and he together? The thought was wispy like a thread of fog and melted as soon as it arose. Two red sports cars raced down Geary Street at what looked like 100 miles an hour.

"Crazy drivers," I responded stupidly.

We walked through Golden Gate Park. We ended up near the San Francisco Zoo, all the way down by Ocean Beach.

As we reached the beach, we came face to face with an old woman walking along the sidewalk. The sun and fog had wrinkled her face so harshly you could barely see her eye sockets. She was bent over with the weight of the bags she carried. When she saw us, she put down several of them and held out her shaking hand for money. Her face tilted against her bare right shoulder. She was wearing a yellow sundress that was way too big for her. The shoulder strap was falling down, and her small breasts were unable to fill out the chest area. She looked shrunken, dwarfed.

Damien brushed us right past her. "More negative energy." He shook his head. "All the more grateful that you have decided to stay with us. Any one of us could end up like her. When you can separate out the false self from the true, you are saved from that sort of life."

We reached the beach and walked along the boardwalk. Broiling steak and coffee scents mingled with salt-wind as we approached the Ocean Beach Steak House.

"Hungry?" Damien raised an eyebrow, and before I could answer, his arm was around me as he steered me into the restaurant.

It was early enough to get a table overlooking the ocean. The sun was just beginning to set, and the water was quiet and smooth, reflecting the splashes of orange and red rays. I could see a few seals resting on the rocks closer in, basking in the dusk.

I didn't hear Damien order, and I took his hand in surprise when one of my favorite appetizers appeared. Along with the oysters in their shells, he had ordered a bottle of wine that we finished before our salmon came.

My head spinning, I could hardly eat as I listened to his mesmerizing voice, his eyes barely leaving mine. After ordering a second bottle of wine, we clinked glasses and spent many minutes staring into each other, the quiet expanding my chest, the stillness between us teeming. Mom floated through my mind. Her frail, thin body limp on the sofa in the TV room, an empty bottle of vodka and pills on her lap and the floor. The soap opera on as loud as the foghorns. *I'm not like **her***, I yelled at myself. *I'm **not.***

Damien played with my fingers and said, "Remember, hon, every time you have a negative feeling or thought, you simply apply the false self-idea to yourself. You say, 'Unless I am joyful I am living from my false self.'"

Just amazing how he could see my awful thoughts. I looked at his index finger gently stroking mine. The warmth spread throughout my body. I wasn't being like Mom at all. I was sure she had never felt joy like this.

"This school will give you many ways to exaggerate the falseness within, in order to find your true self."

Really, I had no idea what he was talking about; nothing needed to be exaggerated in my life. But right then my body felt so porous and light, I could hardly feel my heartbeat or my hands around the wine glass.

He ordered two slices of chocolate layer cake with vanilla ice cream, along with glasses of sherry. He picked up his fork dripping with chocolate. "You've hardly eaten." He smiled as he gently put the sweet into my mouth. Cold vanilla, warm chocolate, everything was bursting inside of me. We slowly fed each other, allowing the tastes to linger, before taking another bite. When I didn't touch my liquor, I was spinning too much to do so, he lifted the crystal glass in the air and toasted to my new self. His glowing brown eyes melted into mine. He swallowed the sherry in one gulp.

After dinner, we walked some more. I was wobbling a bit and hung on to his arm. I tried looking up to the stars, but fell against him, laughing. I couldn't see them anyway; the mist was thick and the foghorns louder than I had ever heard them. Damien firmly turned me toward him and kissed me lightly on the forehead. I wasn't sure if my head had doubled its spinning from the liquor or his touch; it didn't matter, it was a dance too delicious to understand.

We walked all the way back to the studio and Damien's car, the wind sobering me some. While driving me back home, Damien drank from a flask that he pulled from his coat pocket. I barely took note of that as my heart was beating loudly. My head, though no longer spinning, was foggy, and I wondered why I had been a prude for so long. I remembered Mom wobbling up from the piano, holding her empty glass, moving unsteadily toward the kitchen. Thin and cloudy memories disappeared as soon as they came, only to reappear again. I had so much more sense than she had ever had.

Damien placed his free hand on my knee, and I put my palm inside his. There were my long, tapered fingers, not even meeting the tips of his. I had never thought of my hands as small before, but there they were, half the size of Damien's.

When we reached home, I didn't know what to do. I couldn't invite him in, not with Dad in the house. "Maybe we could go to your place?" I blurted out.

Instead, he took both of my hands in his and kissed each one. "I don't go with the flow," he whispered, staring into my eyes. "That's what I teach, my dear. Everyone is losing themselves in drugs and love-making without ever getting to know what's within." I wanted to skip with my skipping heartbeats. So much for Marc and Slinky Slimy Sonya...Damien was the kindest man I had ever met!

He kissed my forehead with soft kisses. He mumbled something about all the religious teachings saying the same thing: if human beings could separate their "false" selves from their "true" selves, all suffering would end.

His mouth was over my cheeks, biting them sweetly. "It's our under-standing of God that brings awareness," he mumbled between bite kisses. He said something about staying alive in this moment because it was the only moment that was. But then I matched his kisses, and he finally stopped talking.

I snuggled my head closer to his mouth. It was as though I were floating above myself, watching him hold me. It was like dancing --- that feather-like feeling where I could sculpt the air if I chose.

His lips brushed my mouth, and then he kissed each one of my fingers as he slowly let go of my hands. He took a few steps back and we gazed at each other. I could barely stand.

"I could stay here forever talking with you," I said dumbly.

"Of course, my love, I've awakened you and you see a kindred soul standing near you. But there are many in the school; you will see, many."

FROM THAT MOMENT ON, I carried make-up with me all the time. I put it on after every single dance class and wore it everywhere. I just never knew when Damien would show up again. Like a butterfly, my heart fluttered, and I knew I could transform into something gorgeous. And just because I hadn't seen him in a week didn't mean anything. Everything was a surprise in ASI, and that was the joy of it.

And when I saw him in our next class, he winked and smiled at me just before we began. I understood that he needed to focus on teaching...I loved that about him.

He began class by explaining the word sin, as "missing the mark," exactly the way Minister Kleep had defined it. My chest was so tight, I thought it would break. It was too much. These connections with Kleep and Damien, and the sermon and Damien's message. It was as though I were being surrounded by a bubble; Kleep had called it the Christ Energy. Whatever it was, I could feel it so deep down, as if a kind of beauty was being met, or heard or named.

I bawled. Openly, right there in class. All my breath was caught in the middle of my chest. It was dead quiet, except for my insane hiccupping. Damien was staring at me. Between lumpy gasps for breath, I spoke:

"Everyone in this school is so much more beautiful, greater and smarter than I am. I've never seen anyone work so hard as Melissa and June. They're the two most wonderful people here, and they just work so hard, and they're always so nice to me; and I'm not, and I don't, and all I do is miss the mark, but I don't want to anymore."

June, sitting next to me, gently slid her fingers through my tangled hair. She whispered, "Shhh, don't talk now. Clearly you think you've done something wrong, but the beauty of this work, hon, is that whatever you did before you found ASI doesn't count."

Melissa chimed in. "What have you been beating yourself up over?"

Damien laughed, that coughy, deep guttural laugh of his, adding that self-beatings were missing the mark. Everyone cracked up except me. What was so funny? But he had read my mind.

He reasoned, "Seriously, tell us what's deeply hurting you. You wouldn't see this beauty in Melissa and June if these qualities weren't already within you."

I had heard other students talk about their lives, but words stuck to my intestines and wouldn't come up.

"Come, darling," Damien coaxed, "as I have noticed before, it's apparent you are quite unhappy. Why?"

"I don't know." I squirmed in my seat and noticed a bunch of large black ants scurrying across the rug.

Damien looked into my eyes, "What is going on with your mother?"

I breathed in a huge gulp of tears and choked them out. He, Melissa, none of them knew anything about her. What was I going to say? That I couldn't prevent her drinking and I asked too many questions and she despised me because I couldn't take care of Wendy or her? God, could I please stop crying?

June stroked my hand, hard. I noticed Melissa's soft gaze, intently on me. Damien was leaning forward on his chair; his focus was only on me.

"Whatever it is, it wasn't your fault, not any of it." He said this so quietly, I was sure I was the only one that heard. "The Bible orders us to honor our parents; we don't have to love them, or be with them forever. Follow? We can thank them for giving us life."

I stepped on a few ants. They had doubled in number.

"Let us love you and take care of you in ways you can't imagine. You needn't worry about your family any longer; leave them to their destiny while you change yours."

June stroked my hair, and as class ended, Damien and Melissa surrounded me. They hugged and hugged me. Melissa whispered, "Welcome home, hon."

∼

THE FOLLOWING SATURDAY MORNING, I was teaching one of my favorite dance classes. I had put on Neil Diamond's *Sweet Caroline*. And my little students hopped into class, pulling out ribbons from the bin and hunting for skirts and tutus. Two of them had found the same pink tutu and were fighting over it. I dug through the pile and took out a bright red one. Sue, the blondie, reached out her small hands. I gave her the red costume, and Lucy, with her black braids, began jumping up and down in the pink one she had already put on.

I had the girls dancing in a circle, touching hands and then soaring toward each other to "reach out." Hands were stretching to touch small hands. The girls squealed with delight and sang at the top of their lungs. But I was dragging my feet. I saw Melissa glowing. I was so far away from being like her and wanted to be, so, so badly. Such confidence, her hips swung so easily, and her dimpled smile lit up her incredible blue eyes. No wonder Damien couldn't stop looking at her.

As I changed at the studio after class, I pictured Aunt Miriam, and her face grimaced. *I know*, and I frowned back. *Well, what would you do? Dad said you died when you were six, so how could you understand how ugly and incompetent I feel?* Her mouth turned down and her eyes looked so sad. *I can't imagine dying so young, but maybe you were lucky.* I felt that "Christ Bubble" around me again, and I sat down on the tiny bench underneath the coat pegs, my knees almost in my mouth. I heard her say, *You were meant to dance.* The words, like the desserts Damien and I fed each other, were sweet and lifted me up.

*I've already paid for my third month of classes, and I can now attend two classes a week for just fifty dollars more a month. I'm paying the extra money gladly. At least the office job has some **merit**.* Miriam smiled and nodded.

But Damien and Melissa were often all over each other during class. As I looked in the mirror now, brushing my hair, I saw my entire demeanor change. My mouth literally curved downward, and my eyebrows pulled together. It was almost the painted image of a frown.

My shoulders slumped. I forced myself to stand tall. I put on my black leather boots and stood staring at my reflection. He had only been doing his job as a teacher when he approached me that day, instructing the awakening process. It shouldn't bother me that he taught all the women students in the same way. And Melissa and he were together.

If you are not feeling joy, I told myself in the mirror, you are false. My shoulders slumped again, but I straightened them and smiled. *I'm a dancer, learning how to wake up. Anything less than joy is false,* I kept repeating. I forced myself to skip out of the studio; the extra strain in my calves must be from too much dancing.

SEVEN

CLARA

June greeted me like I was a movie star. She gave me a huge hug, turned me around and told me that my make-up job was "perfect."

"You're just glowing, hon." June said.

Feeling cheered, I practically ran down the old rickety stairs, not caring how much noise I made, reassuring myself that whatever Damien and Melissa did tonight would be fine with me.

And sure enough, there they were near the bottom of the stairs, heads together, Damien once again kissing her fingers.

I bit my thumbnail hard. I took it out of my mouth and repeated to myself, "If you're not feeling joy, you are false."

I sat down in my seat and forced myself to think about the latest things I'd learned. I was not allowed to tell anyone I was part of this school; I'd just gossip away the ancient ideas before they had a chance to take hold and work through my being. Finally — a piece of my life that was all my own. I didn't have to tell Dad, Patti, my students, their parents or *anyone.*

My fingers were bloody again. I looked around for tissues and couldn't find any so I put them in my mouth, tasting that metallic flavor of blood. June was next to me. She whispered, "What are you doing to your lovely hands?" And out of her large bag she pulled a small packet of Kleenex. She gently dabbed my fingers and squeezed each one tight. She wrapped new tissues around each finger and smiled at me.

"Don't do this anymore, okay hon?"

I tried to say something, but she interrupted before I could, "Shhh. Damien's talking already, and he's talking to you!"

And indeed, he was speaking. To me.

"Why is it, Clara?"

Everyone was staring at me. I looked directly at him and immediately looked down.

"Clara," he repeated in a soft, gentle tone. "Why are you still living at home with your father and working in his office? A job you hate, you told us last class?"

My eyes widened.

"You've paid for your third month, sweetheart. That means you love this work, or you would have left by now, follow?"

I nodded.

"The money you've invested in yourself speaks volumes about how you have already changed your attitude. And now you are ready to take the next step, toward having your true self. You will only remain a young girl if you stay at home with Dad. Follow?"

My finger from my other hand had leapt into my mouth. June's hand was on it, urging me to leave it on my lap. He's right. It's time I stopped living at home.

"I'm not sure what to do about Dad..."

"You're not the only one with this resistance. Melissa was also living at home, taking care of everyone, weren't you?"

They turned toward each other and smiled. My hand lifted of its own accord, but June was pressing into it again.

"It will do you so much good to fully move out," she whispered.

Damien continued. "So, your first exercise is to face why you are living there. We are your family here..." He was stroking Melissa's hand, lifting her fingers to his lips. "We want you to confront what's stopping you."

"I'm not sure I can leave Dad."

My forehead was sweating again. To make matters worse, there was a sudden, dense swirling of smoke around me. I was aware for the first time that there were no windows in the room, so the cigarette smoke wound about itself creating layers of thick air.

"I think," Damien continued, leaning over, dropping Melissa's hand and putting his own together as if in prayer, his voice soft, intense, "you're very unhappy, unhappier than we've realized."

I looked up briefly, right into those clear sparkling eyes and looked down again. I loved how Damien listened. Leaving Dad shouldn't be this painful.

He was still talking, "Hon, you're no different from the rest of us. Someone your age would be delighted to leave home; would have already left, in fact. What traumatic thing has happened to prevent you from leaving your father?"

"I really don't know," I finally said. June knew how to take care of her kids. She carried a bottomless dirty orange bag that had everything in it. Graham crackers, baby wipes, first aid kits, chicken sandwiches cut in quarters, wrapped in tin foil, pacifiers, baby bottles...She'd kick her children out when it was their time, and she'd have no qualms doing so, nor would her kids have trouble leaving. In my last year of high school, Dad had said, *Don't think going to college means moving out. You can live here as long as you need to.*

"Can you tell us anything?" Damien tried again.

I couldn't talk. My throat had swelled up, and tears burst over my cheeks as I coughed and choked on the spiraling rings of smoke.

After class that night, Melissa, June and other women surrounded me. They all had a story to tell about their struggles with their families. And then, amazingly, Melissa invited me to live with her. "You need to get out of your father's house, hon, and I know you'll need a place to live in a few days. I have a spare room. The rent is cheap. June and I will talk to you over lunch tomorrow, won't we?"

June hugged me in agreement, and my heart danced.

"MELISSA, it would be so great if you lived on Castro Street! Do you know that in college I spent a lot of time there, helping the gay cause? I love Harvey Milk, don't you?" We were waiting for our food.

Melissa's mouth dropped open and her eyes widened, but she quickly closed it, keeping her eyes as open. She reached out her hand and took mine. "Hon, I don't live on Castro Street. The gays have a lot to learn from ASI, but I don't want to get into that right now, okay?"

I was about to ask her what she meant but was completely distracted by the plates of food the waitress brought us in that moment. The burgers must have been at least eight ounces. They looked six feet tall. In addition, the plate was piled high with the fries Bill's Place was famous for. They were made fresh daily, and each had to be as wide as half a potato. I hadn't been here in years. I automatically recoiled from such large amounts of food.

But Melissa and June laughed at my habits. They'd chosen Bill's Place on purpose, insisting that I come and eat as well as talk.

They took turns dressing my burger. Pulling off the top part of the hot sesame bun, they poured a more than generous amount of ketchup on the already mayonnaised meat, placing sliced tomatoes, red onion and sweet pickles on top, insisting that I have "the works." They promised I could not leave the place until I had eaten the entire thing. I heard Miriam say, *Oh, it all looks so yummy! I loved hamburgers.* And then I heard Damien. *You've eaten so little. Food is meant to be enjoyed.* I remembered tasting the chocolate from his fork and seeing the joy in his eyes.

Melissa dabbed her small mouth with her napkin a hundred times after each bite. Her painted soft pink nails looked like candy against the white cloth, and her high-pitched tone rang through her words. She stopped talking when I picked up the dripping sandwich. My mouth was not wide enough to take an entire bite, top to bottom. I bit into it as best I could, wiping the meat juice and ketchup off my chin and neck. My white cloth napkin was soiled a brown-red, and I balled it up, hoping Melissa wouldn't notice. But soon the flavors tasted so good that I completely forgot how sloppy it all was and immersed myself like a drunk, intoxicated with such wonderful food.

Melissa invited me, again, to live with her. Her burger was half eaten, and there wasn't a crumb on her mouth. Just like Dad.

"I live on Potrero Hill, and I just can't wait to have you. But there are some rules you need to understand, as your studies deepen at ASI. Such as, you can no longer be involved with the media."

I nodded, not paying attention, as the waitress brought our chocolate ice-cream milkshakes. They arrived in tall, wide beer mugs, with whipped cream towering over and spilling down the sides.

"Listen," Melissa was tapping her fork against her mug.

I laughed. But she didn't. There was something more serious to this.

June piped in, "It's only a block away from me. We'll be neighbors."

I was spooning rich chocolate ice cream into my mouth, whipped cream lingering on my lips.

"It's really important that you stop reading the newspapers, listening to the news on TV and the radio. The media just clutters the mind and feeds the false self. Follow?"

Melissa's voice sang on. I could do that. My heart dropped. The shake took my attention away from the heavy feeling. The burger and fries were in hard competition with the ice cream. I saw Damien laughing, wiping ice cream from his lips.

"Clara!" June was intensely loud.

"I'm listening, okay? Don't listen to the news anymore. Done. It's boring anyway. Anything else?" My stomach was purring from the food, but there was a nagging pull in the center of my chest. "I am passionate about gay rights," I said.

Melissa stared me right in the eyes. She was serious. "Look, hon, forget about gay rights for the time being. How often have you or your Dad read the papers?"

The ice cream was stuck in the straw. I picked up the long spoon and dipped. She wasn't asking me to give up on gay rights, just to put it aside for the time being. When I lifted the spoon, the ice cream was swimming in fudge sauce. With my mouth full, I replied, "Every night."

"How often has he discussed politics with you? You know, racism, desegregation, Civil Rights..."

Wendy had cried often that Dad cared more about Martin Luther King and Civil Rights than he did about her being bused into *a...fucking zoo. Oh, God, he doesn't get a fucking thing.*

How often had Dad pushed his ideas onto us?

"We need to develop our own opinions that can only come from finding our True Selves. All our viewpoints until then are fed to us by our parents, friends and the media. And this type of 'food' actually creates holes in our True Spiritual Selves..." Melissa had her hand on top of my wrist.

"You don't really have to give up your passions," June added. "The media and our parents' opinions destroy that in us...actually we die a spiritual death due to this. ASI repairs those spiritual holes, saves our lives."

I gazed at both of my new friends. I had already moved away from my political activities anyway. They'd all reminded me of Marc. However, I did read the papers and watch the news. Besides Gay Rights, I was still passionate about Black Power, Women's Liberation and Watergate. But I had never thought about how my opinions had formed...I had friends who were challenging me to eat delicious food, leave Dad and live with them. Most exciting, they were asking me to give up Dad *and* the media, so I could finally have not only my *own* opinions and thoughts, but a truly alive spirit. And when I moved in with Melissa, I would pick up more dance classes and quit the office. God, if Wendy's viewpoints could have been heard, would she be where she is now?

EIGHT
CLARA

A few days later, I had to tell Dad I was moving out. He sat on his chair in the living room, reading *The San Francisco Examiner*. I sat down on the matching couch, facing him. Poor Dad, he'd never have the chance to have his own thoughts. "I've found a great place to live." My voice echoed against the walls, despite the thick rug covering most of the hardwood floor.

He put his paper down and looked at me, his brown, soft eyes full of wrinkles. "Why do you have to make things difficult for yourself?" he asked. "You'll have to pay for rent and food."

I couldn't look at him. He was so old-fashioned, so stuck in his ways. I was giddy and glad to be letting him go. Thank God I hadn't told him about ASI, he would have never understood. "I'm working and can pay for these things."

He closed his eyes and said, "You have no idea how lucky you are, here at home. Being in a strange place with people you don't know, anything can happen."

One of the lamps went out. The bulb must have died. Shadows fell across his chair. The foghorns brayed through the window. I didn't get up to replace the light bulb, and I knew he wouldn't either. We were both too tired to move.

"You can meet my new housemate, and I leave tomorrow. June and Tim are coming to help."

"When you don't live with your family, you find out how alone you really are."

It was getting darker, the shadows across his chair disappeared. I couldn't see his face anymore. "Then you'll come over. You'll love the home I'm moving into. It's old and…"

"…And falling apart, no doubt. And like your sister, you'll be here, asking for money."

"Oh My God." The wind blew in, and I slammed one of the windows shut. "I've been working for years, I can handle all of my expenses. I'm *not* Wendy."

"Don't you raise your voice at me. You know nothing, do you hear? Nothing."

I tried to move toward him but my body felt too heavy. I didn't want to fight anymore. I wanted to give him a kiss; say goodbye more kindly.

He picked up his paper and walked out of the room. I heard him walk up

the long winding staircase Wendy and I had run up and down so often. When I knew he'd reached the top, I walked slowly up to my bedroom, remembering how Wendy and I had used the banister as a barre to practice the pliés I'd taught her.

THE NEXT MORNING, I woke earlier than Dad and quietly walked down the stairs to the living room. I sat on his chair and picked up the photo of Aunt Miriam. She was still smiling, her eyes curious, her entire face comical and engaged. I looked past her, into the field of wildflowers and the Carpathian Mountains beyond.

This time I told her about how badly I felt leaving Dad, that I had found ASI and Damien. *Dad misses you terribly*, I said. I swore I saw her nod and tears fall down her cheeks. She held out her arms and held me close. I remembered that conversation I had with Dad when I quit ballet. His eyes had filled with water. *Miriam*, I said, *Dad told Grandma Shirley and me that you would have died for a chance to take ballet lessons. He couldn't understand why I had quit. He said, 'Our Mama loved the ballet and brought us to Krakow twice a year to watch the Russians dance.'* Miriam nodded and kissed my cheeks — the way Dad had kissed me good night every night when I was little.

I leaned her photo against my face and continued to talk to her. *It must have been horrible for him to lose your mom, dad and you in such a horrible car accident when he was just thirteen. I know that the Greenwoods had been best friends, and they adopted him.*

In awe, that softness flowed into my chest. I carefully, tenderly held the photo in front of me and looked at it more closely. Her eyes sparkled, and the beauty around her small mouth entered my heart. I felt like a small bird whose broken wing had just been healed. I knew it was right to leave Dad. I would fly when I was on my own. I kissed Miriam on her cheeks and put the photo back, when I heard the doorbell ring.

June and her husband, Tim, were here, with their truck.

My friends worked quickly, and by the time they had moved my stuff, Dad had woken up. He stood at the top of the stairs, wrapped in his brown, terry-cloth robe. As he came down the steps, I blabbed out everyone's names not meaning to have such an awkward introduction.

Dad shook hands. "Nice to meet you."

I didn't say anything. Neither Dad nor I knew what to do. I picked up my suitcase, while June and Tim carried out the last of my things. When everything was in the truck, I walked back up to the house to say goodbye. He was standing at the front door, and we kissed each other. His shaggy brown eyes looked wet. "I'll see you in the office tomorrow...and be careful. You can always come home again."

I stood as tall as I could. I nodded and blew him a kiss. I knew he watched me walk down the porch steps. And I knew he couldn't see my own wet eyes. I don't know how long he remained standing there. As we drove away I noticed a "For Sale" sign in front of a neighbor's home; a flock of gulls flew overhead toward the sea.

NINE

JOE

He felt like a stone, sitting in his office listening to Mary Lincoln. He had no feeling left in him after Clara moved out. It was silly. He was used to being alone, on his own. And Mary's life was horrible.

He looked up at Anna's painting, hanging on the wall facing him. In this one, she'd woven in several of the lines from the Yeats poem. A young man was holding a spinning silver trout on a fishing rod. A beautiful glimmering girl was imposed on the fish, her head reaching both a sliver moon and a setting sun. Their rays were actually composed of golden apples encircling her, becoming her hair, her entire body. The same man was kneeling, kissing her shimmering fingers. But as the painting expanded before him, the beautiful girl was disappearing, a ghost-like figure; the man was wandering on a beach, his empty hands open, his mouth drawn downward, his eyes sad.

Mary's droning voice made him look at her. "And my brother was murdered right in front of me, shit I'd never seen so much blood, that's when I shot up the first time.

I was just twelve...Doc, everything OK?"

"Fine." Everything was just fine. Nothing to be disturbed by, not in his life — now, anyway. Clara was growing up. She'd moved out. She'd get Wendy to the clinic. She was responsible that way. Paying attention to the truth by naming facts usually made him feel better. His chest shouldn't feel this heavy. He looked up at the painting again. Nonsense. He wasn't wandering. He was here, with Mary.

"Maybe my life is too tragic for you? My brother and all that blood...you look sad, Doc."

"Sad for you. But let's take your blood pressure." He pumped her arm, the sound of the device comforting, as it began to lessen pressure. "Well, look at that, Mary. Not so sad." He forced a smile, feeling a tightness in his jaw. "Your blood pressure is down from two weeks ago."

Her eyes were shining like stars.

When she left, Joe picked up his journal and wrote:

Dear Mr. Yeats,

Lines of your poem dance on my dead wife's painting, inspired by your writing.

There is a fire in my head

That won't go out

My wife, my golden apple, is gone

She no longer calls my name

The Nazi's hatred killed the fish, the sea

Wiped out the Sun and Moon

I can't see for the wandering

For the time plucked out

He walked out into the late night. A full moon. Unusually clear sky. Millions and millions of stars. Shining from light years away. Old light. Dancing. As if it were taunting him, pointing out what he'd lost. He shook himself; nonsense he thought, as he walked quickly to his car. Think of Mary. But Anna filled his mind. How she opened the back door, greeting him with her enticing smile, and hugs. And as he entered the parking garage, he heard it again. Miriam and Anna's voices chanting the Kaddish.

Yit'gadal v'yit'kadash sh'mei raba ***...May we and those we touch be united with the ever-growing, ever-increasing holiness that unites us.*** Anna's beautiful green eyes shone in his mind. *b'al'ma di v'ra khir ute...****with those that inhabit this world.*** He tried to stop the prayer but it seemed to well up from somewhere so deep inside it couldn't stop. *v'yam'likh mal'khutei b'chayeikhon uv'yomeikhon...****May we be infused with the Majesty that is God now and for our whole lives.*** *uv chayei d'khol beit yis'ra'eil* **and *...in the lives of all those who are members of the community of seekers.***

He reached out to hold Anna, she seemed so real. And, as his arms reached out into emptiness, he shook himself. The Hebrew prayer for the dead. Enough. He walked briskly to his Mustang. But couldn't get Anna's face out of his mind's eye. Her golden hair and her soft voice, *Oh Joe, we're not separate. Not at all. You're united with me, with Miriam, always.*

He needed a good meal. A sound sleep. He hurriedly turned on the engine. Sat back as he immersed himself in its solid, steady sound. A good American car. Ford. Not a piece of dust anywhere.

TEN
CLARA

I'd moved into a three-story building consisting of three flats on Potrero Hill. Ours was the middle one. The building was at the top of a very steep hill. There weren't many trees or gardens like at home, but the brightly painted houses slanting on the hills, their brick rooftops standing narrow and tall, made up for the lack of vegetation. Besides, you could see the whole city from our living-room window. Everything except the Golden Gate Bridge and the ocean. I couldn't hear the foghorns, but there were so many people out and about that I was sure I wouldn't miss them.

The day after I moved in, Melissa made me an omelet and sat down to talk with me. "You don't need to tell your Dad where you're living, you're starting a whole new life!"

How much cheese had she put into this? I nodded, still winding it around my fork.

"And you can quit your office job tomorrow and pick up more dance classes!"

The fork fell out of my hand, clanging on the plate. I grinned, wider than the cow the cheese had come from.

Melissa's laugh was like bells. "Hon, you are the creator of your own life! No more being a little girl under Daddy's thumb! And besides which, your Dad needs his life back. He can't have his children draining the living daylights out of him, now can he?"

This was definitely *the* best decision I'd ever made! Thank God I had left the photo of Aunt Miriam for him. He would be fine without me. And I, without him.

AFTER LIVING with Melissa for a short time, my head was whirling with just how much June and she worked. Literally, around the clock. Melissa managed a bakery and worked sixteen-hour shifts, four days a week. June did the same, only she was a waitress; she also worked at the ASI daycare a couple of days, so she could spend time with her kids. *It's so great to be part of a community. All of us ASI mothers love helping each other.*

When Melissa and June weren't working, they were in class or doing things for ASI. I had stepped up my work as a dance teacher, and Patti and I were both elated. I was now teaching four classes each on Saturday and Sunday, and two every afternoon. Patti was putting together a program for adults, and soon I would be instructing three of those classes.

Friday, the Sabbath! Although I knew little about this, Melissa said it was the *perfect evening for my first women's-only meeting*. She put me in charge of cleaning our house and preparing the living room. Loving this task, I raced around the apartment all afternoon.

Having sat in so many circles through college, and not feeling comfortable in any of them, I wondered how this meeting would go. The political groups, the Coalition for Women's Rights and The People For Peace, began with passing the bong around, as did the Transcendental Meditation group I joined for a brief time. Tom, the teacher, was told during one of his most powerful meditation experiences to "experiment" with pot as it was a transcendent drug if used within a sacred context. Each of us students was given a secret word, one we were not to tell anyone. But shortly after the pot had been passed a couple of times, one of the students started to break out in panic shouting, *My secret name is Maya. Illusion. Maya, Maya, Maya* she had screamed, clutching her heart. Tom had told us all to keep meditating, and he allowed this girl to roll around on the floor. A guy blew smoke in her face and yelled up to the heavens, *Thank you.* He put his hands on her convulsing chest and chanted, *Asha Asha Asha, Hope, Hope, Hope.* And soon, just about everyone was jumping around shouting out *their* words, like vomit. *Om Shanti* someone had whispered, holding the poor girl's feet. *Om Shanti* the group took up. And Tom had kept meditating until all the excitement had calmed down, and the panicked girl had fallen asleep. Then he ended class, with everyone smiling and hugging one another. This women's meeting would be much different.

I grabbed the Windex and sprayed it all over the bay window, standing on a chair. It dripped faster than I could wipe. It didn't help that my hands were shaking.

Shortly after that TM meeting, Wendy had burst into my small dorm room spilling her skinny body onto my bed. Her ankles were the width of toothpicks, and her wrinkled, dry, taut skin and tangled hair were shocking.

She demanded, *Get me some fuckin' beer or fuckin' wine, anything, or like, I'm going to fuckin' die, I swear.* I dragged her to an all-night coffee shop, forcing coffee, bacon, eggs and toast down her throat.

You can't tell Dad. Her mouth was full, her legs beating up and down. I was used to not telling Dad things. Mom had begged me to do the same. *I need fuckin', like one hundred bucks*, she had pleaded while I shoved eggs into her mouth.

She probably would've been murdered if I hadn't given her the money. She held onto my arm with both hands as I walked her back to my dorm. I pushed her into the shower and stepped in with her, forcing her head under the steaming water. I washed her matted, greasy hair, soaping it up three times before foam finally appeared.

I shivered and noticed that the window still looked smeared. I sprayed the glass with Windex again, watching the liquid drip down before I stroked it clean with a paper towel.

The night settled in as I set up the altar. The fog didn't hit this area of the city as often as it did the Richmond or Sunset districts. It was a clear night, and the stars shone through the clean window. The half-moon hung between them, looking more like a picture than reality.

I stared at it and thanked ASI. Not having to give out my address to Dad *or* Wendy was a great relief.

I placed red roses in one of Melissa's crystal vases on the rickety wooden table I had carried in from the street for free. I almost bought daffodils, but that felt corny, cheesy and way too personal. Daffodils belonged to my other life, to that poem

Dad loved to recite.

> *I wandered lonely as a cloud...*
> *That floats on high o'er vales and hills*
> *When all at once I saw a crowd;*
> *A host of golden daffodils*

I searched like crazy for a particular white table cloth Melissa had used. I found it inside the cabinet, at the very bottom of all the cloth napkins and cloth settings. A huge mound of them piled onto the floor as I dug it out. Wanting to throw the entire mess back inside, as it was... knew better. Everything had to be perfect. And besides, I wouldn't be able to live with myself had I done so. Order was important, and I focused on that as I refolded each napkin and color-coordinated them with the place settings. I then shook the white tablecloth hard, watching it billow in the air, looking for dust particles, grains of dirt, anything I could dab off to make it perfect. I finally spread it under the vase along with a cheap bottle of red wine and plastic wine glasses.

I stepped back and shook my head. It wasn't the fine look of lace and crystal Mom had used for special occasions, but no one was that fancy anymore. Briefly, I saw that crystal vase filled with daffodils on her piano; her, sitting on the bench, her back as straight as a paper's edge, her hair perfectly coiffed...perfume wafting from her chiffon skirt, as her fingers ran up and down the keys, flowing like a waterfall.

But there was no time to think about her. It was almost 11 p.m., and Melissa came swishing through the door, her hair in a ponytail. A black sweater hugged her long torso, resting against a flowy red-and-black cotton skirt. Even after working thirty-two hours straight she looked gorgeous. Bursting with energy, she put a platter of goodies down on the rickety table, asking me to arrange it while she washed up.

She hugged me and cooed, "You are an angel, the place looks great." She floated down the hall, disappearing into her room. I danced around the room; moving in with Melissa was the best thing that had happened to me, and cleaning the apartment was the least I could do. I never wanted to forget what a privilege it was to live with her. She'd even given me a break on the rent.

We were expecting ten women, a combination of newer students — although I was the newest — and older ones who had been in ASI for months, or even years, like Melissa.

Just before midnight, everyone had arrived except one. Melissa headed the group and kept looking at her watch. We all knew that being on time for meetings was one of the most important ways to show respect for the sacred work being done here. Tardiness disturbed the energy and disrupted God, who was always trying to help us.

"Anyone know where Judy is?"

Silence.

"Carol, Judy lives with you...know where she is?"

Carol looked down at her hands, her long fingers clasped together a little too tightly. "I know she waitresses the graveyard shift. There's been a big note on our calendar for weeks, so I know that Judy knew about this meeting. Between my job and hers we just never see each other."

"It's midnight exactly, ladies. Let's start the meeting by welcoming Clara and letting her know why we meet."

Susie jumped in. "Oh my God, I live for these women's meetings! I mean, I tell you when I came here I was a lesbian. But I knew in my heart this was against God's wishes. Know what I mean? And these meetings have taught me how to be a real woman. I married six months after I found this place, and I now have two kids. I am just so happy." She lit a cigarette, her hands shaking like crazy.

Melissa looked at her watch again and smiled at Susie. "Anyone else?"

An older student, Nan, spoke up. She talked with her small, thick hands, waving them about every which way, cigarette smoke weaving in and out of her fingers.

"I've been here over a year, and I am so grateful to be waitressing. I'm making more money than I ever thought I could. And since I've come to this school, I've followed every rule. I haven't read a newspaper, listened to the radio, watched television or spoken to my parents for eighteen months. I am a new person! And this is why.

"All of my life, I wanted to be a journalist like my Dad. But I've been so much calmer since I've stopped paying attention to the news. It had never occurred to me that reading about all that violence only creates more of it. And to think I was going to make a career out of all that! You know what the result is from freeing myself from my family? Steve and I are engaged!"

Everyone clapped and hollered.

A sharp pain went down my right shoulder. It must have been from cleaning the higher windows. I thought about Dad, the assassinations of President Kennedy, Robert Kennedy and Martin Luther King. His eyes had turned to slits, he'd been so mad. *We are just getting over World War II, and then these things happen. At dinner* the night Martin Luther King was assassinated Dad had slammed the rolled-up newspaper so hard against the table that the butter dish fell, smashing into a hundred pieces. And when Viet Nam hit, he was beside himself, calling President Johnson a fascist and then more recently President Nixon a lying dictator. That time we were in the living room, and he'd swung the newspaper at a moth fluttering against the lamp, and the lamp had crashed to the floor.

As I looked out the bay window, there was only darkness, and slivers of fear passed over me like shadows at dusk. It struck me how violent the world had been, how violent Dad's responses were. ASI had something going here, and I was glad I was part of it. There was so much whistling and hugging of Nan that it was hard to hold onto my thoughts for long. Then, Judy walked in, late as hell. That never boded well at ASI.

Silence fell.

Judy stood in the doorway, her brown hair oiled tight into a bun, cheeks pale, and wide black circles under her eyes.

"Sorry I'm late," she said, coming in like a mouse.

Melissa met her halfway. She towered over Judy by about five inches. Her arms, waist, and legs were long and graceful, like reeds; Judy's head reached just below Melissa's shoulder. Her hips and legs were wide, her short feet pointed outward awkwardly, like a duck's.

Melissa gazed down at her, lifted her hand as if in slow motion and slapped her across the face.

The sound stung *my* face. Every head in the room was erect, everyone staring somewhere else. Except for me. I watched every single move.

Judy did nothing.

Heat rose from my lower spine right up through the back of my neck. My thoughts were tangled inside the hot air exploding around my face.

Melissa slapped Judy again, and then again.

ELEVEN
WENDY

Winter

What like fucking time is it, 2 a.m.? But who the fuck cares? I'm freezing, and my hands won't stop shaking, and I'm gonna fuckin' die. God damn this fucking, slimy sweatshirt piece of shit. Who the fuck stole my coat? Who, huh?

"Hey, fuck you!" Some drunk guy. "Stop pulling my fucking hair. What did you do, take a bath in your fucking whiskey?" Like I'd never drink that shit. I'm no fucking drunk like Mom. Like fuck her. The rain was drowning me, my head was pounding, and I was gonna fucking cut off my hair, it was too wet, heavy. Jesus fucking Christ I'm gonna die; I was gonna call Dad. Fuck. Why the fuck not? Nowhere else to go. I ran into a phone booth, and there was like a bunch of guys across the street, a weird-like light coming from their cigarettes, it was fucking foggy. Fuck.

I had to have a fucking dime. I had to have one, but my hands were like shaking so fucking much like I couldn't search my pockets. I could barely even read the neon light that's fucking flashing about a block away: *The Ancient Side of Eating* it said. Fuck that.

I knelt down on the fucking, soaking sidewalk, and I kept combing my pockets. *Come on come on, there had to be a fuckin' dime there's gotta be.* Empty bottles of speed, unwrapped fucking peppermints and used Band-Aids fell out of my pockets. No dimes. Like not even a penny. I sat down on the curb, crossed my legs and put my head down and my hands out. I like heard a bunch of people making loud noises, laughing or yelling. I looked in the direction and saw like about ten people coming out of the restaurant.

Fuck this fucking rain. Shit. I shook my legs up and down; my knees almost hit my fucking chin. Like I'm just a worthless fuck anyway, a goddamned bitch, how the hell...? That crowd ran past me laughing and shouting to someone else.

If I like keep my hands out they're going to fucking freeze off of my wrists.

But what is this? Like a bunch of change dropped into my lap. "Thank you," I yelled and looked up. But the person was walking fast, disappearing. I was like, laughing, I looked down. Fuck. I had more quarters than ever...I could make *five* phone calls if I wanted.

I was jumping up and down and yelling *Thank you* at the top of my lungs and like laughing, and then I lunged into the phone booth, slammed the door and like called Dad.

The phone was ringing, and that neon sign from the restaurant keeps fucking flashing; I wanted to fucking smash it.

Like what the hell was I fucking doing calling my fucking *dad*? Oh my god, I was going to die. Fuck. Answer the fucking phone.

Fuck Dad. Someone's head got too close to the phone booth door, trying to get in to escape the rain, so I like put my foot to it. I've got the phone. Fuck you.

."Hello?"

My heart was coming out of my body, it was pounding so fast. "Dad, it's Wendy. Please, Dad, like I need help. Come get me." I couldn't believe like what I said. There was this voice screaming in my head like to shut the fuck up, and another that was talking, like saying *I need help*. Shit.

How the fuck was *he* going to help me?

"Dad, I'm on Market and Golden Gate. Come down and get me, I don't know what to fucking do anymore. I need help; I need some food. I'm freezing. Like...I have no place to go."

My voice sounded...like as if it's coming out of some kind of cave, my speech was fucking weird, squishy or something.

"Have you called Clara?"

"Fuck you!" I screamed. "Is that all you can fucking do is ask for Clara?"

But I was only screaming into a fucking buzzing phone so I slammed it back down onto its receiver.

I was going to go home, I was going to go home and tell my fucking father to like fuck off for hanging up on me, he was a fucking doctor and had he ever helped me? Who's ever helped me? Like 'call Clara?' He had some fucking nerve. Clara hadn't answered her phone for fucking months. She left her apartment, and her fucking phone was disconnected. Dad would like do any fucking thing for Clara, but what had he ever done for me? What? What?

I was walking up and down in the pouring rain, waiting for the bus. A few of the kids across the way approached me. They surrounded me. I smiled. I like held out my hands to them. "What the fuck do you want, boys? Huh?"

They wanted my spare change. They threw me to the ground; I saw fists and felt slamming pain go through my jaw, and my head like explodes...

TWELVE

JOE

He hadn't been sleeping, but when Wendy called he must have been because the ringtone sounded like it was far away. He hadn't spoken to her in so long, her voice startled him. She hadn't made any sense. She was freezing? Hungry? His Wendy?

He remembered her huge green eyes, so like Anna's, widening even more with her joy. That day so long ago, when he'd brought home daffodil bulbs. A patient had given them to him. An Irish gardener. That weekend, Anna, Wendy and he planted them in the yard. Wendy's small hands were almost the same size as the tiny bulbs. Anna, her blonde curls falling down her breast, her green eyes darting from their daughter to him. *Oh Joe,* she'd clapped, *Remember that daffodil poem we so loved?*

He 'd dug deeply into the ground; the solid earth felt good against his hands. Putting a bulb inside the hole, he'd felt a lump in his throat. Things this small were always so fragile, no matter how rooted. Clearing his throat, he'd looked up and saw Wendy and Anna grinning, both with dirt all over their laps and arms. *"Oh Joe,* her smile as delicate and lovely as a flower, *You always were so good at reciting that. Say it now for us.* Wordsworth's poem came back to him easily, and he said:

I wandered lonely as a cloud
That floats on high o'er vales and hills.
When all at once I saw a crowd,
A host, of golden daffodils;
Beside the lake, beneath the trees,
Fluttering and dancing in the breeze.

Wendy had pushed her hair out of her eyes. *Like this, Daddy?* The dirt falling away, as she swayed and spun, and laughed.

The phone rang again. It was the emergency service. Wendy was at SF General Hospital. Could he come right away?

He hurriedly put on the same suit and tie he'd been wearing for days. He tied his bowtie haphazardly as he ran down the stairs. His hand brushed against his rough chin, another morning without shaving. No time. But Aaron was worried about him, said that he had never seen him look so unkempt. He'd promised he'd shave and have his suits cleaned. He'd get around to it.

His thoughts raced with his speeding car. Clara was supposed to have brought Wendy to the clinic. Clara. He hadn't heard from her since she'd moved out. A few months ago? Had it been that long? He'd wanted to call her but realized he didn't have her phone number. He'd meant to do something about that. About her quitting the office, too. The adolescent ward was more work than ever, and he'd been completely absorbed. Emergencies had occurred often. If she had called him, he wouldn't have known. He was hardly home.

When he entered Wendy's hospital room, he involuntarily took a step back. She was unrecognizable. Pale and skinny, with long, straggly strands of oily, black hair falling unevenly across her thin, bony shoulders; two bruised black eyes; swollen cheeks. Her leg was in a cast from her foot straight up to her thigh.

He moved closer. This couldn't be Wendy. His body froze. She looked like an escapee he'd seen in the mountains long ago, a human skeleton, impossible to know if it was male or female, so bony it looked like there was no skin. The skeleton's shirt had hung down like a dress; the pants could have fit a five-year-old. He was so bent over Joe didn't know what height he had once been. He forced himself to move closer to the hospital bed. For God's sake, he chastised himself, this is my daughter, *Wendy*. His little girl with golden curls, and so completely changed.

"What's happened?" He asked. She slowly turned her head toward him. He held her bony hand.

"Dad..." her voice was quiet, tiny. He put his ear close to her mouth. Tears were dripping down her black and blue eyes. "Dad, please stay. I don't want to go back out there. Help me."

SO MANY SLEEPLESS NIGHTS. Picturing Wendy's swollen and beaten face, her broken leg, the bastards who'd done this to her. He threw himself into making after-care plans for her. He secured a bed for her at the Rehabilitation Drug Clinic in Monterey. Once detoxed, she could come to his ward. It would be a week, at least, before he could get her out of the hospital.

His chest pains and shortness of breath were a nuisance. He had an irregular heartbeat...atrial fibrillation. Downing a beta-blocker, he paced his study, Anna's old art room. He'd converted it about a year after she'd died and kept several of her paintings up. And it was a strange thing to think that...at least...Anna had been spared Wendy's troubles, now.

In spite of the pill he'd taken, his chest pains increased. He'd have an EKG tomorrow. But really, he wasn't as scared of death as he was of going crazy. Even so, the Kaddish rose up in him again.

Yit'gadal v'yit'kadash sh'mei raba **May we and those we touch be united with the ever-growing ever-increasing holiness that unites us.** Again, Anna's beautiful green eyes shone in his mind... *b'al'ma di v'ra khir'utei* **with those that inhabit this world.** That damn prayer he couldn't stop... *v'yam'likh mal'khutei b'chayeikhon uv'yomeikhon.* **May we be infused with the Majesty that is God, now and for our whole lives.** *uv'chayei d'khol beit yis'ra'eil...***and in the lives of all those who are members of the community of seekers.**

He took deep breaths. Swallowed. Shook his head. Where was the union, here, in his life, now? Clara had lied to him, promising she'd find Wendy and send her to the clinic. He needed to get a hold of her.

And all of their past arguments invaded his mind. After Anna had died, their fights escalated to such a point that they'd both agreed not to talk about dance. As long as they didn't, there was peace between them. The foghorns were loud and low. Nonstop. And this time his gut would not relax. What was the feeling there? A sickness? An ache? Anna. The ache beneath his belly increased. He'd loved how she greeted him every night; running toward him, her hair pulled back. Curly strands would fall down over her eyes. She would throw her arms around him, *Oh Joe, I'm happy you're home. You must be very tired.* Her kiss was warm. He'd loved holding her small hands.

The foghorns blew their deep, low cries.

His heart calmed down. He made a pot of coffee. He hadn't grocery shopped for a while. There wasn't any food. He'd buy breakfast at the hospital. He looked down at *The San Francisco Chronicle* sitting on the table. More news about the People's Temple. Jim Jones. He had too much power. He had churches all over California. One was right here — up on Geary Street. He ran homes for the elderly and the disabled. A goddamned Reverend, in charge of the helpless. Goddamned religion. Heat rose inside his head. Hitler had done the same. He'd gotten the youth to worship him. Thousands of kids, younger than Wendy. Younger than Clara. *Worshipped* him. Thank God Wendy had never gotten involved with Jones. He liked to rescue drug addicts too.

The world was being pulled apart, families, children; the violence of others, creating this. If there was to be union, reasoning and education had to be emphasized. That was one of the plans for the clinic -- to have respectable, well-educated doctors and staff who understood old-fashioned common sense.

He sipped his coffee and shuddered. It tasted like shit. Too bitter. Had no idea how to make the damn stuff.

~

His first patient was Mrs. Lincoln, Mary's mother. An obese, church-going woman who'd lost one daughter to drugs and two sons dead. Most likely, drug-related deaths as well. Had finally quit both jobs as she'd secured a small café on Divisadero Street. A huge success for her. The funding coming from the Black Coalition for Small Businesses.

She sat down, sighing. "The People's Temple wants me to give over the deed to the café."

"That's not a goddamned church. Don't ever give that deed to anyone, do you hear me?"

"Are you alright? Your eyes are bulging...what do you have against Reverend Jones. He's a man of God..."

Both fists came down. He saw her jump. He didn't mean to scare her, but he couldn't stop the force that rose inside him. He had his paper-weight in her face. "A murderer, an assassin, a thief of the elderly, the children, the helpless, a man of God? You call him a man of God? Would you call Hitler the same? Would you?" He was shaking the paperweight at her nose. She'd stood up, backed away, but he followed her, pinned her against the wall.

"Our Father who art in Heaven..." she prayed.

Yosev, you are united with us...pounded through his mind.

"...hallowed be Thy Name..."

V;yam:likh mal;klutei b; chayeikhon uv' yomeikhon.

"...Let Thy Kingdom come..."

She wouldn't stop. The Lord's Prayer, the Kaddish, voices mingling and crowding his reasoning. She'd slipped underneath his arms. A huge woman like that. The door was open as she left, and he kept hearing, *v'yam'likh mal'khuteh chayeikhon uv yomeikhon...**May we be infused with the Majesty that is God, now and for our whole lives**. uv'* *chayei d'khol beit yis'ra'eil...* **and in the lives of all those who are members of the community of seekers.**

He was going crazy, hearing voices. He was sure of it. He was not a seeker; he had his head in hands, leaning against the door. What do you want from me, Miriam? Anna? You're dead. You've left me here, alive. I'm not seeking anything. Only a sound mind. Everyone around me is losing their capacity for reason. I can't lose mine. And I won't. He walked slowly to his desk and put the paperweight back in its place. He'd no idea how it had gotten into his hands, or why Mrs. Lincoln and he had been standing so close to the door. He'd only wanted to educate her, to prevent Jones from harming her.

But she wouldn't listen, like Clara. It made him so tired.

THIRTEEN
CLARA

"This is dangerous work," Melissa explained the next day. "You can't be half-assed. You either do it or you don't. And you can't pretend to work on yourself once you've been here a few years, like Judy. For that reason, she was kicked out."

Hitting someone was wrong, but maybe in some cases it was needed, like with Judy.

The bus I was on arrived at Kleep's church, and I was dressed properly, but despite Melissa's warnings -- to take going to church seriously -- I had placed my beach clothes inside my faded red dance bag. I changed in the church bathroom and made a beeline for Baker Beach.

And when I reached it, I swayed and breathed with the sound of the waves. It was so good to be here. I rolled my jeans up, took off my shoes and socks, and left them in the sand.

The ocean rolled over my bare feet; the waves pushed them further into the sand. Wet and caked, I pulled them out of the water, picked up my shoes, and walked to the dunes.

I climbed them steadily, and when I reached the top I sat and gazed at the Golden Gate. It was colder and windier up here, and the fog came in shifts, thickening the sky and hiding the sun every couple of minutes.

I was happily and deeply involved with dance. Not only was I teaching six days a week, but I was also helping Patti manage the studio. In addition, Melissa had helped me land a waitressing job at Joanie's Diner — graveyard shift, four nights a week. Finally, I was working as hard as she did. Damien would be so proud of me.

The fog rolled into my hair, curling it in every way possible. Twisting bits of it with my fingers, I closed my eyes and lay down on my back. The wind whirled around me, and I could have fallen asleep, except for the smile that was spreading across my face. Damien had been amazed at my questions about the Bible in ASI class. Just last week, I had asked him, *Why was it a sin for Eve to eat an apple and make love to Adam?*

Because they were disobeying God.

But, I protested, *if I had listened to Dad, who was controlling my life, I'd never have the life I have now.* Damien smiled and winked at me. *She's a hot one that Clara is,* he said to Melissa. This spurred a lively discussion, during which I completely spaced out. As Damien spoke, I noticed his thick fingers and remembered how kind they felt when I'd kissed them.

The wind blew sand around my eyes, and I sat up. I wasn't supposed to be here. I needed some time to myself, and no harm could come from taking that. But the sky was darkening quickly, and it looked like it would pour. Not wasting any time, I flew down the dune, as if I could go faster than the rain, which caught up with me.

When I got home, sopping wet, June was waiting for me. She was standing on the porch, arms folded. "Lying bitch." She stared at me, hard. "You've been in ASI long enough to know better, but you are as fake as Judy. What the fuck have you been doing this whole day? Going to *church*? Really?"

A toddler came running out. Not one of June's.

The sky was black. The drops of rain were strong and hard.

"Jerry, go back inside, hon."

Jerry? Wasn't that Judy's son?

We faced each other, June's brown, long hair was pulled back in a greasy, sopping-wet ponytail; she probably hadn't washed it in days. Her wide, flat face was breaking out in pimples, and she stank of sour milk.

"Stop staring at me as though you have no idea what I'm talking about."

I looked down and stared at June's Birkenstocks. She wasn't wearing any socks.

"I've been following you for the last month."

"You what?" I looked up again, as water dripped down my nose and hot fury rushed up and down my legs. I turned to walk into the house, but her words whipped me around.

"You're unreal. All you do is pretend and hide."

"Goddammit, just shut up and leave me alone." I turned my back on her again. "I'm not one of your kids... and what is Jerry doing here, anyway?"

She grabbed my hands and forced me to stand close to her. Her strong grip surprised me, and I stopped fighting. We stared at each other, the rain soaking us. Her eyes softened.

She was right, of course. I was a fake. I *had* lied all this time about loving church; I had brought up religious questions without really being interested in them. I was a louse. I didn't deserve anything as glorious as ASI.

The rain let up as suddenly as it had started. She put Jerry in a stroller, and we walked over to the Potrero Hill Café. We were silent while the waitress brought the coffee.

"I'm waiting," she said.

"You had no business following me." I'd let her down, and I couldn't face that. Maybe it was time to leave ASI.

"I'm your mentor, don't you get it? I'm responsible for you. Didn't you learn from Judy? She was always complaining, and then she lied about the work she was doing. Constantly. You can't fake this work, you just can't. Jesus."

Jerry squirmed in his stroller. She pushed him back and forth a bit too quickly.

"And what's he doing here?"

"Judy's too negative to be around him. Helen took him from her and gave him to me."

Despite my being caught, June didn't say anything, and all my God questions must have impressed even Helen, because the next night after class Damien pulled me aside. Lifting my hand and kissing my fingers, he told me that I had earned quite a privilege for my hard work.

"You get to work in the kitchen," he said, fondling my hands while looking into my eyes.

I dropped my purse, and everything spilled out: gum wrappers, make-up, change. I bent down, wondering what color red my face was, and clumsily threw everything back in again. I thought you had to be in school for three or four years before you were evolved enough for kitchen work.

When I stood up again, Damien was laughing. He explained that since Judy had left, Helen had been looking for someone to take her place. " She isn't picking just anyone, she wants you. This is a great privilege. And, you start right now."

It was midnight. Now?

"But I'm all dressed up..."

Melissa waltzed over to us.

"Are you arguing again?" She spun me around. "Silly, there are all kinds of old clothes in the kitchen closet. That way we all can get to the kitchen before and after class without having to worry about what we're wearing. Come on." She pulled me away from Damien, "I'm going there, too."

INSTEAD OF GOING through the restaurant to get to the kitchen that night, I followed Melissa around the back to a separate entrance. We gingerly tiptoed around the potholes in the back alley, careful not to bang into the garbage cans or breathe in the rot.

I wanted to ask why we went that way instead of through the restaurant, but my question was stopped on my tongue as we entered the steaming kitchen. The loud dishwasher was stampeding through its cycle, and there were three or four students doing all kinds of tasks: cooking, chopping, mopping; they were like ants, running everywhere, each on a mission.

Melissa swished me right into the adjacent "changing room," an area large enough to be a single studio apartment. There were two dressing rooms, one for men and one for women, and to the right of us was the biggest walk-in closet I'd ever been in.

There were shelves of jeans and T-shirts, all marked small, medium and large, dozens of shoe racks, some with working shoes, others empty for the good shoes we had on. Above them were shelves with neatly folded socks.

Hanging on hooks were all kinds of scarves and hats designed to keep your hair from falling in your face. In addition, there were hundreds of hangers and empty shelves to neatly stow your good clothes.

There were also two shower stalls, complete with clean towels, soap and bottles of shampoos and conditioners. When you knew your kitchen schedule you could plan accordingly.

"So," Melissa explained to me, "when you work all night here, you bring your day-job clothes with you. You can shower after your shift, dress for your day and be ready to start work, just like always."

I wasted no time picking out an old pair of light blue jeans and a long green T-shirt that said "Go Ask Alice" on the back. Humming the song, I followed Melissa into the kitchen and took my first orders.

FOURTEEN
WENDY

"We have a new member today," the group facilitator announced. He was like talking about me. Shit. Then he looked at me. Shit, I was supposed to fucking talk.

"Well ah you know, like I'm a drug uh...Shit ,I hate this shit...I hate it." My voice sounded like a fucking crow. It was high-pitched and like fucking annoying. I'm not really a fucking drug addict, that's not who I am...God, a joint would be beautiful right now; I don't know how I ended up here. Like my mother's fucking dead and my old man's a doctor. He used to talk about people like you guys. Shit. I'm the only white person here.

My fucking thoughts wouldn't like fucking stop. I looked around and saw white, black and yellow faces staring at me. I stayed silent. My fucking head down.

Fuck. Dad like used to talk about all of you fucking poor black people who didn't have fathers, whose mothers worked three fucking jobs to support you, and you had no opportunities like whatsoever. And here I was, like given all of the fucking opportunities in the world, and I still end up shit-faced and on the streets, and I'm poor as all of you assholes. Are you happy?

"Wendy, please pick your head up and look at us. We won't bite."

There was all this fucking laughter. My fucking head was like almost to the ground, and I was so fucking embarrassed. Fuck.

"I hate this fucking quiet."

My head shot up. Some girl in the group had just jumped out of her chair. She was like fucking pacing and repeated a million times:

"My house was fucking quiet. Mom was always passed out. I never knew my fucking Dad."

I couldn't fucking look at her. My memories like stampeded in my fucking head. When Dad told me all of those fucking stories I used to feel guilty, like it wasn't fair I had so much and they had so little. I used to cry myself to sleep, especially when I was being fucking bused, the only rich kid in that fucking school.

"Jessa, you need to sit down. I understand how painful your life at home has been."

"Fuck you, Freddy." Jessa was fucking screaming.

"Yeah fuck you, Freddy. What the fuck do you know?" That was from Diane, apparently Jessa's best fucking friend.

"Hey! What the fuck? You all stop blaming him. It's not Freddy's fault you're all so fucked up." Louisa. She had her fucking head up her ass.

This group was fucking crazy. I didn't want to fucking talk.

Like when I was in seventh grade, this black girl, Ruthless Ruthie, turns to me and she says, *Wendy girl, is your white-ass Daddy rich?* And you know I had no idea what the fuck she was talking about — *your white-ass Daddy rich?* She asked me that a million times. *Did you whore for your money? Is your white-ass Daddy rich 'cause you whore for him?* At dinner that night, I had to know like what a whore was. Mom was already dead, and Clara was fucking sitting there, playing with her crazy hair, and all of a sudden I like asked Dad, *What's a whore?* He just looked at me, and I said, *Daddy is your white-ass rich?* Clara was biting her fucking thumbnail, and Dad just fucking stared at me. His face got fucking white.

"Wendy. We're still waiting. We'll wait patiently. I know it's hard to talk to a group you don't know."

Freddy's fucking voice was smooth, and cool. Who, like, could trust it? Dad's anger was playing with my fucking mind.

How dare you call me an ass! All I was doing was repeating what Ruthless said to me. I didn't know anything. And Dad was just like, *Don't you ever use those words again, with me or anyone. You are not rich. You are fortunate. You are fortunate to have a home and food every night.*

"Wendy, listen." Freddy was talking. "You've got quite a story, I know you do. I would like to hear it."

When I lifted my head, I saw ten fucking faces wide-eyed, staring at me.

I sucked in a deep, fucking loud, breath. "Dad had just like finished lecturing to me about how fucking lucky I was. I didn't feel fucking fortunate. Mom was fucking dead. I was being fucking bused. Like my life was fucked. Know what I mean? I ran up to my room, sobbing every night. Clara, my fucking older sister, came in and asked what was wrong. And I just like told her how everyone was ganging up on me all because of the stupid busing, and I was now like a white girl in an all black-ass school.

"And that's when I fucking saw that even Clara didn't the fuck get me. I ran down to the fucking beach. I hung out all night long and like met these cool, hip kids who were fucking older than me. I was fucking furious that they wouldn't let me smoke shit with them. So when I was fucking bused, and no one at home fucking got how bad it was, I just started smoking with the fucking kids who were like bothering me. I fucking had to prove myself to them and to those older guys down at the beach."

My head went down again. I was a fucking mess, and I was the one who fucked me up. Fuck. Freddy was like talking again in that cool, Clint Eastwood-like voice.

"The only way to really get better is to face, head-on, all of the resentments you have and to take responsibility for your own actions. The first step to recovery is realizing and admitting that you are a drug addict and that you are powerless over drugs. You've got to start believing in God, babe, or you're not going to get anywhere."

ABOUT A MONTH LATER, Dad was asked to "join us" at the fucking family group meeting. I was so fucking nervous I couldn't like stop my legs from bobbing up and down, twisting and untwisting my hair. I'd been here for thirty-two days and was kind-of like getting used to it. But, still, I had no idea what Dad would say.

We're like sitting next to each other, and I feel him put his hand on my shoulder and I start bawling. Great fucking start. I lifted my head to look at him. His eyes were like red, had he been fucking crying too?

"Like, you have a beard," I teased him.

"I'm trying to be a hippie."

Dad could be funny sometimes. It had been so long. I fucking hugged him.

Freddy had the fucking skinniest, longest legs I've ever like seen on anyone. His arms were just as long.

"Wendy, could you please introduce your guest to us?"

I kept my head up. It was something I'd promised Freddy I'd do. In our last private counseling session, he'd said, *Wendy, you've been here thirty days. Show your Dad how proud you are to be in recovery. Keep your head up at all times, from now on.*

And now, like tears came from nowhere. They were pouring down my face like fucking rain.

"What a fucked-up fuck-up I am." The words just came out. I meant to just introduce Dad.

He turned to look at me. "You're not..."

"Hey, Wendy, is that your Ol' Man?" Christy asked. She'd been here now like for two months. She only had one more to go.

"Yeah, like this is my Ol' Man, Dr. Joe Greenwood." I kept my head up and actually looked around the room. Christy was smiling. She had been like my mentor. I had high respect for her. She had even stopped swearing. Something I was trying to do.

"Dad, ah, this is like my group. Welcome. I've been clean for thirty-two days. And I plan to stay that way. I'm like going to make amends to you and Clara. I've treated you both like the shit I am. Sorry. I didn't mean to swear."

Dad's face crumbled, like his lips started to tremble and his shaggy brown eyes watered. I'd never seen him cry before. And I couldn't fucking get used to his beard.

"I don't know where Clara is..."

What the hell was he talking about? I opened my mouth but like no sounds or words came out. Fucking Clara.

Christy broke the silence. "Jeeze, Doc, you mean you've got two who have gone and done drugs? Wow Old Man. Wow." Leave it to Christy. Jesus, did she have to say that?

Dad looked at Christy and shook his head. He remained quiet.

Freddy took over. "I'm very sorry to hear this, Dr. Greenwood. Christy, we can't make assumptions. Would you like to tell us about Clara?"

Like this wasn't the fucking place for Dad. He's not used to group therapy. But he started speaking.

"Everything will be okay. Wendy is getting better. We'll find her sister."

Fucking Clara.

He turned to me. His face wrinkled, looking like fucking old gum wrappers.

We stared at each other. I still couldn't like fucking talk.

"You look better, Wendy Bendy," he whispered. "Your eyes and your hair look healthier. You look exactly like your mother when she was your age."

I was like stunned. I wanted to look him in the eye, hold his hand, but I couldn't move or do anything.

Finally, words like just fell out of me. "I'll fucking find her. I really will." My chest suddenly felt light. I had a mission, a *purpose,* and Dad needed me. I couldn't remember *ever* feeling like this.

FIFTEEN

CLARA

I spent eight hours scouring the underneath part of the stove burners. Like a whirling top, thoughts just spun around my mind.

I heard June telling me yesterday that *Helen had given Jerry, Judy's son, to me because Judy was too negative for him.* What if Mom had had to give up Wendy for the same reason? I remembered a time when Wendy had been banging on the piano, and Mom had yelled at me, *Stop her! Oh that noise.* Wendy screamed like a screeching monkey as I dragged her off the bench, and at that moment Dad had walked in from work. Writhing in my arms and piercing my ears with her cries, Dad grabbed Wendy out of my grasp. I cringed at her tears and held out my arms again to her. But Mom slapped my hands and shouted, *How dare you play 'Mom' with a real child? She's not one of your dolls.* Dad had held Wendy with one arm and taken my hand with the other. Mom's face crumpled, and she started crying. Dad's voice had been soft when he said, *It's okay Anna. I have Valium for you. A new pill.*

I was on my hands and knees with a hand-scrubber, getting between the cracked floor tiles. Brushing the dirt off as fast and hard as I could, I watched the deep black marks turn white like my knuckles as I held onto the scrubber with all of my might.

Patti had recently told me that Dad had called the studio to talk with me. *He's worried about you. You've quit the office, and he hasn't heard from you.* I had no time to return his calls; besides we both needed to get used to our lives without each other. Sweat was dripping from my forehead as I scrubbed harder.

Damien was suddenly standing above me, blocking the next tile. I kept my head down, not understanding why he was here. My neck was hot and my breath shallow. I sat back on my heels and looked up at him.

I'd never seen him from this angle before. His black shoes, usually shined, were scuffed along the toes. I had half a mind to put my scrubber to them. I smiled involuntarily and heard him laugh. He bent down, still laughing, and pulled me up, holding my hand. I was surprised to find how cramped mine was. Before I could say anything, he folded me into a hug, muttering into my ear that he was so proud of me and how lovely I was, all the while kissing my cheeks.

I whispered that I wanted to wash my hands and take a shower, but he would only let me do the former. I didn't know what to think, my heart was beating so fast. I washed my hands, hardly feeling the hot water and soap go over them. It was as though I was someone else, and I was watching her move toward Damien again.

"You're very sexy, looking like a kitchen maid," he said, bringing me in close to him. His hands were under my T-shirt.

"Here?" I protested, enjoying every moment, although I couldn't feel the weight of my hands on his soft cotton, dark brown shirt.

He walked into the closet and came back with blankets, sheets and pillows. Where did those come from? And what was I doing? The questions were wispy, without gravity, and I continued to float above myself, watching his every move.

His hands looked thick and wide as he unfolded the couch in the small room off the kitchen — a room I'd never paid attention to — and made the bed. As if I were the feathers for the pillows, he lifted me up, and when I landed on the blanket I couldn't feel it. He sat beside me, turning me toward him, opening my mouth with his tongue. His hands were under my bra; they glided over my breasts quietly. Whispering sweet words, he unzipped my jeans, untied my shoes, pulled off my socks and pants.

Eyes closed, lying down, his hand was now under my shoulder, urging me to sit up. I heard fast breathing as I moved and couldn't tell if it was his or mine.

When I opened my eyes, he handed me wine in a sparkling crystal, flute-like glass. We clinked and kissed. He drank his down as I sipped slowly, leaning into his hard, strong biceps. Not having eaten for hours, the wine whizzed to my brain.

The flames between us ignited; the sparks within our kisses sped like fire-crackers, until the sudden explosions so deep inside of me were hot and furious, and was it my body or the bed quaking as if the earth were going to open? And when it had calmed, and the heat kept us close, his chest soft as silk, I wasn't sure who or where I was.

Afterward, Damien rose and poured more wine, handing me my half-full glass. We clinked and drank some more, and he pulled me down again, his animal skin smelling of liquor and tobacco. I would have slept with him like that all day, only he had set the alarm for 5 a.m. so that he could leave and I could go back to the kitchen floor before anyone could find us.

I LOVED my early morning lovemaking sessions with Damien that seemed to go on for weeks. But when he didn't come at the usual time, I decided I'd surprise him. I took off my clothes and just wore my bright red bandana around my head. I drew on red lipstick, enlarging my lips so that they looked much thicker than they were. Smacking my mouth on a tissue, I checked myself in the mirror. I puckered up my lips and undulated my hips. Damien would go crazy. But hours went by and he still hadn't come. Slowly, I wiped my mouth and got dressed. My arms and shoulders were sore, and my body wouldn't move as fast as I wanted it to. It was probably from being on my hands and knees so much.

When I walked outside at 3 a.m., I realized that the buses had stopped running. Taxis were expensive, and I'd heard that late-night taxi drivers were horny as hell. My best choice was to walk the five miles home.

I trudged across Market, making it to the other side in less than two minutes. That was unbelievable, given that this was a street I could hardly get across at any other time of day. Suddenly feeling better, I leapt over the trolley tracks and twirled around in the empty street for a moment, tilting my head back and watching the stars spin. I stopped, dizzy and laughing. I stood there in the middle of Market and Golden Gate, head tilted, completely still, looking at the night sky. I found the Big Dipper and wondered what it would be like to swing through its shape, and better yet to swing through it with Damien!

I twirled to the other side of the street again. That should have been filmed for a movie. No one, I bet, had ever stood in the middle of the busiest street in the world, completely alone, spinning and stargazing. I couldn't wait to tell him about it.

I ran the flat, narrow blocks to 20th and Connecticut streets and practically fell on my face when a feral cat got caught between my feet. But the wind was on my side, pushing me up and pulling my hair back.

Suddenly, the intimidating hills were in front of me. Each one steeper than the last. I kept running up the descending cascade of still stone, past the slanted houses sloping down.

My calves were pounding, sweat pouring down my nose and cheeks. Loud sirens and a loudspeaker came from a car. "Stop running *now*. Police." Completely confused, breathing so hard I couldn't find my breath, I stopped. Two stocky, clean-shaven, shorthaired officers stepped out of the car and walked toward me, each with a gun on one hip, black baton on the other..

"Stay where you are."

The biggest one was standing in front of me. "Open your mouth."

"What?"

"Are you deaf? You heard what he said." The other one's hand clamped down harshly on my shoulder.

I opened my mouth.

"Breath is good. Where're you headed?"

It was hard to get my breath. "Home."

"Walk this block. Where's home?"

I froze.

The bigger officer turned me around. "Walk, I said."

I walked.

"What's your address?"

"534 Kansas St. #2."

"You're good to go. Why are you out so late? Women your age shouldn't be walking this time of night."

They walked away and got into their car before I could answer. The hills looked heavy and cumbersome now, and I just wanted to sit down on the sidewalk and cry. What was I doing, twirling in the middle of a busy street and then running up steep hills at this hour? No one else was around, the lights were out everywhere. I was becoming more like Mom, crazy anxious all the time.

I ran again. That couldn't be true. I was exploring myself, trying to find my soul truth. Mom had never faced herself. But I hadn't been sleeping well, and my hands shook a lot, just like Mom's. That was because of all the coffee I drank. I ran faster and faster until my calves were pulsing harder than my heart.

My apartment was suddenly in front of me, and I stopped dead flat, almost falling.

I was home a good three hours early. If Melissa were up I would need to find an excuse as to why I was here. She was a rule-keeper, and she wouldn't have liked the truth, that Damien hadn't come, and I needed, badly, to sleep.

The lights were off, though, and it didn't seem like anyone was home. I tiptoed into the apartment, across the hallway and into my room. I fell onto my bed, fully clothed, and shut my eyes. I don't know how long I was out when I heard whispers coming out of Melissa's room. Her door opened, and I distinctly heard Damien laughing. There was a noisy smacking, "Just one more..." I threw the covers over me and closed my eyes again, begging God, if He really existed, not to make me anxious like Mom and to calm my nerves so I could sleep.

A FEW NIGHTS LATER, like an idiot, I slept with him again, even though I *knew* he was sleeping with Melissa, knew he wasn't my boyfriend. I couldn't help it; he was a loving Teacher, and I needed his help.

We were snug in the bed in the room off the kitchen, and he had brought candles, along with expensive wine and chocolates. "You're nothing like your mother, hon," he said, as he popped a chocolate into my mouth. "All of this is simply your old self, dying."

His words melted me, like the chocolate in my mouth. The late December rain swept the windows; its continuous beat was rhythmic and hard.

Stroking my thighs, he rolled over and plucked another See's Candies chocolate from its box. Holding one end in his mouth, he opened mine with the other. Biting down on it together, the silky, nutty brown sweetness spread across our tongues, melting us into its soft, endless layers. That's what I loved about Damien, he was always so imaginative in the way he approached me. Once, during August, when we'd first begun to sleep together, he'd brought mangos and squeezed them all over my belly. He had licked me clean, and the feel of the sticky juice and tongue on my skin had made me crazy. I had bitten his fingers like a wild tiger, and after we made love, he poured glass after glass of wine and fell across my breasts, letting me know it was I who made him drunk.

And now, as I was still tasting chocolate while running my fingers through his short, stubby hair, he asked me if I was happy.

"In my life or right now?" I asked.

"Both," he replied.

And I let loose, letting him know how I wanted more control over teaching than I had. "Actually, I'm tired of teaching." I hadn't meant to say that; Damien had a way of bringing out truths I didn't even know I had. "I have no idea what will make me happy, I just want something I can't name." His tongue met mine again. The slanting rain was now a drizzle, its pounding against the sill had stopped.

"You can do anything you want, You just need to trust in God, and in me, your Teacher."

"All I know is dance. I don't know how to do anything else."

"I'll help you. You don't have to teach dance for the rest of your life. You can experiment and even give it up entirely, for just one month." He placed a chocolate on my belly and put another in my mouth. I floated, and the air particles expanded one by one, breathing me into their formations, turning thoughts into drizzle, making it impossible to discern one word from another. The water outside was inside the wind again, pushing itself against the windows.

"I am so proud of you," he whispered into my ear. "You have really taken in the teachings. In time you will discover what you love doing. It will be no problem to quit the habit of dance."

He was inside. I was a breath of rain as I whispered, "Yes."

He lifted his wine glass and poured a bit into my belly button and sipped. He sat up like a satiated lion and wound a bit of my frizzed hair about his thick finger. "I'm not the only one proud of you, honey. Helen is, too."

I reached for his lips, the words not registering. Helen? There was no room in my brain for her.

"Helen wants you to start dating David. He's been working on the Oregon farm..."

I yanked my head away.

He wrapped my hair around his whole palm, pulling my face toward his.

"It's a great honor. She wants to reward you with a man of your own, and she has chosen one of the best students for you."

I wanted to open the door and soak my dizzy head in the wet air. I didn't move.

"But Damien..."

"This is your false self, sweetie, protesting. Think of Noah's Ark. God has said we need to be in pairs..." He poured another glass. "I get so moved when I see my students grow, and I have to let them go."

"That doesn't have to happen...I don't have to date..."

He leaned over and kissed me, long and deep. He picked up the bottle and drank directly from it. He fell asleep.

I got out of bed and paced, pulling my hair harder than he had a few moments ago. I opened the kitchen door and walked outside, garbage and skunk smells rising in the drizzle. There was a huge pothole a few feet in front of me. The ground had just given way one night. It had been sucked downward by some furious dark force. Like the rage storming through me right now. I sat on one of the stones we had placed around it. The wind kicked up, howling, and pulled rain off the few trees standing around. It splashed loudly into the hole, creating a huge filthy black puddle. It looked like my heart felt. A huge weight, darker than the night. I stood up on the stone and pushed out one leg, daring myself to fall. My breath, like the wind, rattled through me. The air stank of sewage. I leaned forward, still on one leg. I never wanted to see Damien again. And I wasn't going to meet David. Ever. Almost losing my footing, I sat again. The rain started up, hitting the hole hard. The way my heart had been slapped, sinking further and breaking wider than the ditch.

I had joined this school so I could have my own thoughts and opinions. I needed to choose my *own* boyfriend, just as I would choose to give up dance or not.

SIXTEEN

JOE

Spring

For six months Wendy had been living in a sober apartment. Unlike Clara, Wendy had been in touch with him all of this time. He was looking forward to having dinner with her, at her place this evening.

But Clara. No address, no phone number. How long had it been? Six, seven months? That ache in his gut. He needed to call that Patti Jenkins. Barbaric teacher, influence the worst over young and vulnerable students. He was in his study, gazing out over the Golden Gate. The lights from the bridge were blinking clearly. No fog tonight. The ocean sparkled like his Mama's diamonds...Miriam. She had loved them... Miriam, so little, sitting next to their Mama, reaching for the jewels around her neck...Mama, always slapping her hands...The root cellar, a *copiek,* where he'd first met John...And the memories flooded him.

They were on top of him. The darkness was everywhere.

The stench, so many bodies, on top of him. He finally wiggled a foot but couldn't feel it move. Something fell off of it, freeing his shin. Couldn't move that either. His right thumb could wiggle. He worked it for a long time and freed his right hand. Breath was difficult, but he forced it out of his chest. Something fell off his right arm. Numb and freer, he moved. Wiggled. Black dark. There were no shadows. He didn't know what he was throwing off. Later, he knew. Body parts. Heads. Fingers. Legs. Standing, he'd felt his way to the door and grabbed a jacket hanging on a hook. Outside, the air was no better; there was stench everywhere.

The silence was worse...He stared about him. He'd...never seen so many empty houses or heard his heart beat so loud. It was the only sound, in the absence of so many. His school friends weren't calling to him. Mr. Leiberman and his Papa weren't standing near the copieks, testing out potatoes, trading stories and predicting the weather. His Papa didn't cuff him on the head, *Eh Yosev, where are you going?* There was extra darkness, because there were no lights on in the homes.

In the silence, he walked to the special copiek his Papa and he had dug out the year before. It kept all the potatoes from freezing.

We will dig one five feet wide and seven feet deep...The Nazis won't know where to find us if we need to hide.

They'd dug out a new one outside the back door. It had taken all summer. Papa shoveled without a cap on his head.

His bald spots turned red from the sun, and his arms bulged as he pitched the shovel in. Leaning on it with one foot, he pushed aside mounds of dirt as tall as the Carpathians. Joe had imitated him...laughing. He'd punched his son in the back...*Before you know it,* he teased, *you'll be as large as a bear.* His chest had swelled.

They worked, even in the rain. The dirt never felt heavy, even as mud. The raindrops clanged onto the shovels. The shovels scraped the earth. The clanging rain and the scraping shovels. It had made great music.

When there was no rain, the shovels' noisy scrapes bounced against the mountains. The noise echoed through the fields. Papa loved those sounds absent of human voices.

When the hole was seven feet deep, Joe had jumped in to test it. He leapt down, but scrambled to get out. His long, skinny legs and big feet pushed at the hole's sides, arms and hands held onto rocks, laughing as the loose dirt and pebbles slid with him. Papa put a stool, two feet high, into the hole.

His Papa placed the small, metal black box with the family diamonds at the bottom. He sawed a wooden cover that opened like a basket lid to fit the hole and placed two metal handles on it. They piled the earth back over the cover and smoothed the earth down. They couldn't see it at all.

Papa nodded. *The job was well done,* he'd said, and his big hands rubbed Joe's head. His chest swelled again. Papa never said things like that.

Joe put his head in his hands and opened the window, feeling the rush of cold wind brushing his bald head. But like a movie, the memories kept playing in his mind and wouldn't leave.

That *awful* night, he'd jumped down into the copiek alone... and a pair of arms had caught him..

The voice was low. *I'm Father John.*

What... He was so numb he couldn't feel the terror shocking him.

John spoke in a tuba-sounding voice. *I'm a priest. I've studied with the Archbishop of Poland. The Archbishop has sent me out to the countryside to help.*

Archbishop? Priest? To *help?* What?

I'm going to get us out of here safely. I promise...Because Jesus will help us, you know.

Joe didn't know. John still had his arms around him. He saw his father's head explode again and jumped, crouching way down onto the pit's dark earth, away from John. He kept jumping and twitching, hearing that gun over and over. John moved closer. He put his arms around Joe again. It was black dark.

You're shivering.

Joe kept still.

What happened?

Nothing.

Nothing?

He was quiet, feeling his own fingers dig like a rabbit into the dirt. They came across the black box holding the diamonds. He heard the tap on the metal. John reached over and pulled the box all the way out, then put it on Joe's lap.

What's that? John's tone was gentle.

Nothing.

May I have a look?

Joe let him.

What is this?

Nothing.

John handed the box back to Joe. *Open it.*

He did.

John whistled and patted Joe's shoulders. The diamonds didn't just sparkle; they lit up the entire hole. They stared at them, their beauty as solid as the sun. A weight lifted and then fell heavier.

John was picking out the contents. He pulled a small flashlight out of his pocket. He turned it on for just a moment. The artificial brightness was hard to adjust to. But he held up an eighteen-inch necklace with his large index finger and thumb. They stared at it and stared some more. At some point he handed Joe his Bubbee's bracelet and pair of earrings. In that moment he turned the flashlight off; it would be very dangerous to keep it on for any longer.

"This is very good," he said. "This is very, very good.

Okay.

These will get you a ticket out of Poland. This is very good."

He was leaving Poland?

In the morning we will leave this place. We will bring the diamonds, but not in this box.

He was leaving Poland? What?

They sat in the hole together. John kept playing with the diamonds.

Before we leave you must swallow all of these.

Joe stared at him.

And then search through your shit, carefully each time you go, and pick them out. We'll use dirt to clean them off, and when we walk by the river, we'll wash them. Once clean, you must swallow them again. Do you understand, son? That way if we are caught escaping, no Nazi will find your diamonds.

Swallow diamonds. Search his shit. Buy a ticket to leave Poland.

John pulled out his flashlight again. He was searching for something on the ground... *Help me find a sharp rock. We need it to break the wire the diamonds are on.*

Relieved to have a job to do, Joe was on his hands and knees digging, the cool grit familiar and good under his nails, and he found several rocks.

Handing the flashlight to Joe, John tested each one against his fingers.

Ouch. Good. He broke the necklace's string and the earrings; then he held the flashlight for Joe, cupping his hands around the light, while Joe did the same with the bracelet. Then he turned the flashlight off.

There were about fifty diamonds in total, all in varying sizes, all laid out in the box. John handed Joe his canteen and a diamond. He gagged at the metallic flavor. But he dutifully drank down one diamond after another.

Joe opened his eyes and stood up. Paced the study. There was no need for these memories. He was here, now, in his home office. He just had to focus.

Clara was a grown woman. Of course, why be so concerned? She was perfectly capable of making her own decisions, wrong as most of them were. He'd given her everything — a good home, education, safety. She had choice, of course, to call him or not. But he'd never treated Shirley like that. Never not talked with her. But kids were different these days. Thoughtless, self-absorbed. Spoiled. Perhaps giving his girls everything had been a mistake. Clara was probably self-absorbed, thinking of her new life, and would call if she wanted to. But Wendy...Wendy had said she wasn't ready to see Clara. *Not ready to see your own sister?* He'd caught his anger and not said anything more.

"It's too confusing, Dad, like know what I mean? I mean I'm just learning who I am, and when I know more of me, then like I can face seeing Clara. I mean we could just go to the studio. But I'm just like not ready."

Maybe he wasn't ready either. He stopped pacing to catch his breath. It was a startling thought. The tension between them, exhausting. Miriam and Anna chanting the Kaddish... *We're united.* Miriam said But Clara and he were not. That ache in his gut.. So heavy. He missed Clara and felt heavier. He sat down. Opened a window. The dark air flew in. They'd grown so far apart.

He shivered and went down the two flights of stairs to the living room and put on Pavarotti. La Boheme. The music sank deep inside of him. More than anything he had to fix this with Clara. She was choosing not to call him. The concept of this choice rattled him, made his breath quiver, the ache way down, unbearable, tender.

Pavarotti's voice had a longing in it he'd never noticed before. He wrote:

Missing
Mama Papa Miriam   Glittering Diamonds
swallowed up
Blacker than black abyss
Anna, my glimmering girl, my Golden Sun
dying too young
Wendy's come home   sparkling spark
We're missing Clara
Missing like breath
In death
I can't breathe for missing

And he heard Miriam again, *Yosev, your family is not apart, you are united with everyone. Your children have grown* up, *not apart. It is the Spirit and the Love that guides us.* He read his poem out loud. "I can't breathe, Miriam. You're not helping; you're dead". But her voice became louder, more insistent. He said, "The spirit and love are wiped out, I can't breathe."

O Mimì, tu più non torni...

The phone rang, startling him.

There was too much noise. He was covering his ears. He stopped the record and was about to unplug the phone, but answered it instead.

"Dad, are you coming over or what?" Wendy sounded anxious.

He'd completely forgotten dinner at her house.

While driving down 19th Avenue to Ocean Avenue, he couldn't get Miriam out of his head. She spoke to him again. *Yosev, your family is not apart, you are united with everyone. Your children have grown up, not apart. It is the Spirit and the Love that guides us.*

He pulled over angry, his chest tight. "Just leave me alone," he said out loud. But why angry? He couldn't control this voice, and at the same time he knew she was right. Clara had grown up. She didn't have to contact him. Unlike Miriam and him, who had never had that chance... A lump in his throat and his head on the steering wheel...He'd never had the choice to leave his parents at age eighteen. It was this lack of choice that was making him feel so out of control; the very freedom of choice was the thing causing so much conflict. He couldn't control Clara, couldn't make her call him. And he felt so apart from her. How was he *united*? How?

He lifted his head. Opened the window. The cool air helped clear his mind. He drove more slowly to Wendy's. Thought about her, instead.

She was living in a sober apartment building on the corner of Ocean, near 19th. For six months now, Wendy had been in a government-funded college preparatory program. The sober hospital ward that Aaron and he started three years ago partnered with this program. It helped kids in recovery receive their GEDs and college education. It was in its second successful year. He smiled.

Wendy had said, *And Dad, don't have like a cow when you see the mess. My roommates don't study at home, but, like, I do. My books and papers and junk like are all over the living space. There's no place in my room to put them.*

He rang her bell. It was just two of them for dinner; her roommates were out for the evening.

"Welcome Dad. Come in to my abode."

Wendy held out her arms. Her hair was shiny blonde; green eyes clear and healthy. She was Anna's look-alike. So much so he had to remind himself who was in front of him.

The table, in the middle of the living space, was covered with a familiar-looking, white lace cloth. Anna's. There was an interesting set of blue ceramic plates with matching cups sitting on top of it. A vase of daffodils sat in the middle.

The place was neat enough.

But her desk. She had warned him. Papers and magazines were scattered there and on the floor. There were several books on Behavioral Psychology. Two were open around her typewriter. But... there were books about Hitler and World War II. He knew she was filling her head with psychology, but Hitler? Easy. Easy. He breathed deeply. He didn't want to be angry. Wendy was speaking but it was hard to understand her.

"I made the quiche and even like baked the bread! And all the veggies are farm fresh! We're having a feast! Sit down."

He watched her slice the quiche. How did she learn to cook something so exotic? This belonged to the French. It was perfectly solid in the middle, appropriately filled with cheese and spinach. *Did she use real cream?* He asked.

She nodded, smiling.

"You should use milk; cream will hurt the arteries. Why so many books on Hitler?"

"The dressing like is already on the salad, and look at how fresh this bread is. Here Dad, doesn't the food look great?" She spoke rapidly, her voice deeper, less high-pitched. She sounded like she was going to cry. He'd been too harsh.

"I've taken like several courses on World War II; it fascinates me. I've wanted to ask you some questions about Poland. I mean like were you or your parents living there when Hitler invaded?"

Shortness of breath. "No." Wendy's green eyes were wide, staring at him. "You know I wasn't...that I came here when I was very little, and that my parents..."

"...died like in a car accident when you were like twelve, and that's like when you went to live with Mom. But you're from Poland, and so like I just wondered."

"Why so fascinated with World War II? Why with something so tragic as the camps, as the victims? Why study something that is long gone?" Rapid heart palpitations. Not good. He needed to calm down. Perhaps leave before... before he became too angry. He stood up. Threw his balled-up napkin down, too hard.

"There are so many other things to study. Hitler does not deserve to be called human." He wanted to hear about her sobriety. About the good things in her life. He breathed in and out. The palpitations were not going away.

"I...I ...I often wonder if like Hitler was a cult leader, Dad. I mean on a much larger scale. You know, like Reverend Moon or Jones? Stuff is being reported about like their cult activities all the time."

"Hitler cannot be compared to anything or anyone." She would not drop this topic. "Wendy..." He tried to soften his voice. "Do you know the circumstances of the Nazi victims? Do you know what it is like to be starving, freezing, to be treated as less than an animal?" He was coughing. Wheezing. She was just like Anna had been. Insensitive to what had gone on before them.

"Dad, Dad, please like sit down." Her tone was heated. "Forget it. Let's talk about like something else. Let me make you some tea. Don't go home this way."

She was as angry as he was. He couldn't say another word. He picked up his coat. She was still asking him to stay. He spewed, "You don't get how this country has turned, how promising it used to be. You kids have turned it all to shit." He choked again, eyes watering. "And Hitler? An inhuman beast who does not deserve to live, not even in history books."

In the car, he swallowed hard. Jesus, it wasn't Wendy's fault. She had no idea what he had gone through. None of them did. Hitler. She should be content with her new sobriety and study something practical like nursing. Was she, also, growing up and apart?

SEVENTEEN
WENDY

I wanted to fucking die. I picked up the quiche and like threw it upside down into the sink. I ran hot water and a half a bottle of soap into it. I left it sitting in a fucking pool of suds and curled up on the floor, sobbing. I banged my fist against the kitchen tile floor like until it was like raw red, and kept fucking pounding. It wasn't my fucking fault that Clara wouldn't contact Dad, that Mom had fucking died. Fuck. My stomach was like screaming, it hurt so much. And then the heaves came, dry, and tears, screaming yelling sobs. Like I just fucking wanted to die.

I was such a fuck-up. Maybe it was because of me that Clara was like disowning us. Maybe she couldn't take me anymore and it was my fucking fault. My dealer's fucking phone number ran around my head like a flashing fucking neon light. Call him call him call him. I curled up tighter and screamed to God for help. I was sobbing harder than I ever had in my life. And like fucking deep within me, I heard my own voice like really small, saying, *if you really want to die you know how. It's living you're not used to.*

EIGHTEEN
CLARA

Spring

After talking with David sporadically for four months over the phone, he was finally back from the farm and at my door, arms full of roses and apologies. "I'm so sorry it's taken so long to meet you, there was so much to do on the farm. But, here I am!"

The flowers were over the top. No one brought a dozen roses on a first date. Already, I couldn't stand him. He was clean-shaven, blonde and muscular. He probably had been a jock in high school. Not my type *at all*. He was twenty-nine years old, four years older than me. At least, he had agreed to go to Ocean Beach instead of an expensive restaurant for lunch.

The air was thick and unusually warm for April , the beach completely filled. Joggers, fishermen, frisbee players and children blasted from all directions. The gulls were equally abundant and obnoxious that after-noon. They cluttered the beach, pecking at small bits of garbage.

We ducked fishing lines and Chinese fishermen, yelling and kicking at the gulls. I could hardly see the surfers crashing into and riding atop the swells. For such a stocky guy, David's stride was strong and fast.

"Damien tells me you're a dancer." He turned to look at me, his small eyes blending in with the fog.

"Well yeah, I've danced all my life, but I'm teaching less now and waitressing more. I hear you're cooking in the restaurant now?"

"Yeah, it was pretty cool working on my cooking with Helen at the farm. She makes you prepare the same thing over and over until it's perfect. At the all-night men's meetings Damien encourages the older students to point out my every mistake and then hit me if they don't think my dishes or attitude are perfect."

We stopped walking. I looked out at the surfers; Mom had loved to watch them. She'd said, *Imagine, Clara, I saw one gliding so gracefully with the waves. And that same surfer practically landed at my feet. I started to say something to him, but was amazed to find that "he" was a "she." Imagine, a girl surfing like that.* I could see her green eyes so large, so shiny. We were near the area where she had died.

He moved closer and waved his arms in front of me. I pushed his hands away. Just give me my space, I wanted to yell. Besides, it was more than I could handle, this punching out and slapping business. I told him so.

He put his arm around my shoulders. I resisted and started walking again, looking down at my feet and then at his wide palms swinging by his sides. His stubby fingers were calloused, and his hands chubby. I couldn't see him gracefully chopping anything.

"Yeah, they punched me out, but only once, you know, to knock some sense into me. It did me good. Helen raves about my cooking."

Good for him. Nobody, but nobody would *ever* punch me...Mom, tugging me, pinching my arm so hard there were marks, and yelling, *We have to go **now**.*

"I'm going back up to the farm in a couple of months to help build the steeple Helen has planned."

The fog became denser, its white transparency continuously touching the waves, the sand, the birds and us.

"I hope to get to law school in a couple of years; that's my dream, you know. I was accepted into Berkeley School of Law when I met ASI. This place had a whole lot more to offer, and of course I gave most of my school money to the farm."

I stopped walking and turned to look at him. His eyes were hard to find, the fog was so thick.

"You gave up law school to find your true self?" That was new, different, out-of-the box. Giving up dance might really help. I was so sick of my own irritations, of thinking about all the bad that had happened, how critical I was. God, could I just be nice for once? I grabbed David's hand and challenged him to a run. He laughed and pulled me close. Fog seeped between us as we kissed, my eyes slightly open, looking at the water. The ocean rumbled and pulled itself out, exposing seaweed, rocks, bits of shells and all of the small sea life that otherwise lay hidden when the tide was in.

When I came home, I was alone, and it was good to be in the kitchen listening to the coffee pot hum. I pulled my sneakers off and rubbed my aching feet. I had only a couple of hours before I had to go to the dance studio. Only three classes today, instead of seven. The machine dripped to a stop. I couldn't move. It was too hard to get up. If I quit dance for just a month, I'd have more time to devote to ASI and myself. Maybe I could become an ASI teacher. The thought was so shocking that I shot up out of my chair. I poured myself a cup and pictured announcing my decision at tomorrow's meeting. I closed my eyes and saw Damien glowing. Suddenly, hot liquid ran down my chest. I'd spilled coffee all over my clothes.

It felt as though that ASI meeting would never come. The next day moved slower than a snail. Things were sluggish at the restaurant where I waitressed, I had trouble concentrating on the orders and customers didn't stop whining. *Where are my extra pickles?...I didn't order a burger...I said **chocolate** shake not vanilla.* My manager had to pull me aside. Are *you feeling okay? Customers aren't happy.* But I kept imagining

Damien's joy, feeling his kisses on my cheeks and his eyes moving over my chest. I just didn't care. Work couldn't end soon enough.

Finally, when I walked into ASI David greeted me at the bottom of the stairs, stretching out his arms wide. I gave him a huge hug and kiss, feeling out-of-my-body powerful. My torso and hips swung easily; I slinked past other male students, sensing their eyes eating me up.

David led me to the seat next to his. I purposely played with his fingers and ignored Damien, stuffing down my real thoughts of David. I didn't want to know.

My eyes looked upward, away from everyone, and rested on a bunch of cobwebs climbing up the right-hand part of the ceiling. Their dusty trails exposed dead black and brown bugs entwined within them.

Smoke filled the room in swirls, leaving yellow film along the walls. David pressed his hand into mine when I coughed.

Melissa was speaking, tossing her blonde curls away from her face. She was speaking to Damien in a voice loud enough for us all to hear. To my surprise, she was talking about me!

"I must recognize one student in particular tonight. She's done a million things I am proud of her for. She's going to church, has changed her way of dressing, stopped taking care of her Dad, moved in with me and has been waitressing a graveyard shift four nights a week. She's even been given the special privilege of cleaning ASI's kitchen three nights a week." She wiped her eyes with her white handkerchief.

Spasms started in my toes and cramped up my ankles and calves. I pressed my palm hard into David's.

"And I have a surprise for you all," I spilled out. All eyes were on me. "Since this school is about breaking habits and finding your True Self, I've decided to stop dancing for one month."

Melissa wiped her eyes again, and Damien leaned in toward me.

David kissed me; I didn't feel it.

"Are you sure? This is an enormous choice of yours. We all know that dance is your life, even you've said as much. Take your time, because if you say yes, we'll hold you to it."

My body was floating. My head hot and sweaty. The love in the room was beyond anything I'd ever experienced. I nodded and said, "Yes," even though I didn't have to. That was the joy of it; this was *my* decision.

"Oh hon," Melissa cooed, "You've probably understood now, that you've been dancing around your own issues!"

Well, I really hadn't thought that far, but Damien was speaking.

"Clara," he leaned even further forward. His eyes locked into mine.

"As you know, the whole point of this school is to teach you to wake up. And by choosing to break this one habit of dance...it's a guarantee, sweetheart." He put his hands in prayer position and bowed. Melissa did the same.

I bowed my head too. I had no idea why we were all bowing. The red rug had tiny white dust particles tucked into it.

"Now you must work very hard. You must surrender your habit to God, and because we are His servants, you must ask all of us, June, Melissa, David and me for help. Follow?"

"You can always go back to dancing, hon." Melissa's eyes were shining like the noon sun.

I nodded.

When the meeting ended, Damien hugged me so sensuously I wanted to rip off my clothes.

But David was hugging me, too. I couldn't tell whose arms were around me when, or whose lips I was touching. Cigarette smoke weaved in and around our mingled bodies, making my eyes water. I coughed hard.

Damien grabbed me firmly and held me close, whispering. "I'm so proud of you. Go with Melissa and talk with her about any resistance that may come in, so you can nip it in the bud... You must surrender now." He took my hand, and kissed each finger. I glimpsed David, nodding and smiling. I held onto Damien's hand but he let me go, pushing me into David's arms.

Melissa glided over to us. She pulled at my hand and said softly, "Hon, let's go get a cup of coffee. I'll treat."

I watched myself float behind Melissa. Drifting away from David was a relief. He was so good. Really. I had to do something about my playing around with him. After all, he was a gift for me, from Helen. He deserved my honesty.

"I get how huge this is for you." Melissa's voice was melodious. We walked side by side, toward the Market Street Coffee House across the street. A cool breeze wiped my forehead. Caffeine would be really good right now.

"...even more than you do, right now."

Linking arms with me, she didn't let go until we were seated. The brown-red plastic seats at the booth were too far back from the table, and the table wobbled with an uneven leg or two as Melissa tried to move it closer. Giving up, she leaned forward on her elbows, palms on her forehead.

"We have to predict all the doubts that will arise from this decision. Our soul knows things our egos can't possibly get. I've known for a while, through things you've mentioned, that there's something going on between you and your Dad. Whatever traumas you've experienced with him will come up to haunt you if you don't talk of them now."

I thought about the time when Dad had found out that Grandma was paying for my modern dance lessons. He'd said to her, *You didn't see what I saw, Shirley. Mama and Miriam loved the ballet. The tradition keeps our family together.*

But he was the one that had been separating us. Melissa and Damien were my best friends and great teachers. Unlike Dad, they wanted the best for me.

"What is it? If you don't talk, it'll eat you alive."

I looked into Melissa's kind eyes. The waitress brought coffee, eggs and wheat toast. Melissa must have ordered.

She prepared my coffee for me, pouring in just a drop of cream.

"There," she said, placing the cup and saucer gently in front of me. "In order to take the next step, you must tell me what is bugging you."

I could hardly hear her. It was as though suddenly wads of wool wove in and out of my thoughts. What I had done was just beginning to hit me. I was crazy to give up dance. But it was only for a month. I could inquire about becoming an ASI teacher... Damien would be interested in me again.

"I mean, honestly, why are you paying us so much money? To be stuck in your past?" She smiled. "You haven't even begun to experiment. This action will change your life...not to mention David, who just adores you."

I poured another cup of coffee. Finally, I spoke up, the events jumbled and tumbling out of me.

"Dad worked a lot, but he came to all of my dance recitals. But when Mom died, he stopped coming and worked harder. Mom loved the beach. Once, when we went together, she stopped to look at the ocean and pleaded, *Please help Joe and me stop fighting.* I'd taken her hand, and we stood there watching the waves. I said, *Please let Mom and Dad stop fighting.* She died there. A few years later. She died on the beach, the police found her body."

"After that Dad was like a ghost. He didn't shave for weeks, and his bow tie was never tied. He went to work and came home. I cooked and cleaned and tried to help Wendy. But she had been bused to a new school and was terrified all the time. She ran to the beach every night. Maybe to find Mom."

Melissa put her warm hand in mine. "The more you tell me, the more these awful experiences will disappear. They always do." And she smiled that glorious smile of hers, already spreading light through my ugly life. No wonder Damien loved her. I looked down at my plate, not only were my eggs smashed, but I had crushed the cold toast with my knife.

It was the first day I didn't dance. I walked along Baker Beach, just a few blocks away from home. It seemed like a lifetime ago, living with Dad. Already a year.

The beach was empty, except for the birds: a few gulls flying overhead, the sandpipers running in and out of the waves, their little feet going so fast, leaving miniature webbed imprints in the sand that washed away as quickly as their feet ran. Like dancing. It was 2:30 p.m. Wednesday. I should be teaching right now. I kicked off my shoes, rolled up my jeans and let the water bathe my naked feet.

Patti was horrified. *You're quitting? You?*

Not quitting, just taking a break. I'm really tired these days.

She looked at me intently. I wanted to tell her everything. But my talk with Melissa was enough. *It's a long story. I'll be back in a month; it's just for a short time.*

The wind pulled at my hair as I pulled my freezing feet out of the water and headed toward the dunes. Two seagulls landed a few feet in front of me. They were both standing on the same small, sandy and waterlogged piece of waxed paper that, probably, at one time had a sandwich or a donut stuck to it. They flapped viciously, pushing each other aside, their squeals irritating. But they took off, leaving the useless paper on the sand.

The warmer, dry sand stuck to my wet feet until my soles were thickly caked. I stopped for a moment and lifted one up to look. Some sand drizzled off, the rest stayed on, looking like a huge mound of wet clay forming to the contours of my sole. What if I found some "sand glue" and clumped this permanently to my foot? Would I be able to dance? I began spinning along the uneven curves of the beach. Falling, I laughed.

I lay flat on my back; the sky was spinning as fast as I was breathing. My instant "dancing sand shoe," gone in a flash.

Standing up, staying still, I forced my arms to stretch way out and did an exercise I often taught the younger kids. I pretended I had eagle wings. As I flew toward the ocean, I was aware of the dunes behind me; winging my arms, I could feel their sloping weight, comforting and inviting. This is where weight belonged, not in my chest or legs or anywhere in my body. I spread my "wings" out again and ran to the dunes. As I climbed, swinging my arms now like a monkey, the sand beneath my feet fell downward. I dug my toes deeper, imagining they were claws, and pulled myself up. Dad would find his way far more easily without me. I was convinced of that, just like I knew I'd dance again in a month. And once I did, I'd start my own studio like David who was going to go back to law school. I dug my feet in deeper, swung my hips and arms faster.

My heart dances when I watch you dance, Grandma had said, her face glowing. I turned around and looked out over the water, my heart fluttering. The Golden Gate Bridge stood majestic, with light wisps of fog spinning about its legs and its highest tips. The middle, cleared of mist, stood strong, its thin, red cables, like tightropes taut and inviting across its mile length.

I saw a black cargo ship way out to sea, and at the shore, the sandpipers looked like small shadows racing in and out with the tide.

I wanted to shout to the ship "I quit dance!" so loud that everyone on it could hear, so that the sandpipers and the ocean itself would stop.

I put my arms out wide to fly up the rest of the dune, but it didn't work this time. Instead, I was a small boat, tugging a cargo ship to land. I continued to climb, more slowly now, sweat pouring over my brow as I finally reached the top, breathless.

I sat down and looked out again at the view, at the deep, varying green-blue colors of the sea, the sunbaked mist basting the waves. I longed to touch that beauty, and it felt so out of reach. Like Dad. For years, I hadn't been able to talk to him about anything important to me.

He was like a rock, impenetrable. His voice had been sometimes sad, sometimes angry, but Wendy and I had never known why. Like the times he'd told us bedtime stories about his family. *I used to help Miriam with math. She'd smile at me and say, 'Someday I'll be smarter than you.'* His voice had cracked, and his lips had lingered on my forehead and on Wendy's, kissing us goodnight.

I saw him sitting at the long kitchen table by himself eating meal after meal, night after night, sitting on his creamy white chair in the living room, reading the paper, and I wasn't on the opposite couch talking with him. At least Aunt Miriam was beside him there.

There was a massive fog bank way out at sea. The turquoise and dark blue water was already fading into the fog, and the bridge was now completely engulfed. I sat watching the fog slowly encompass everything, as if to wipe out existence itself.

NINETEEN
CLARA

The next day I picked up extra hours at the restaurant, focusing like crazy, working a double shift. *You're the best waitress we've had in a long time,* my manager had said. *Next time when you don't feel well, tell me. You'll take the day off.* Never, I thought, not if I want to be an equal with Melissa and June...in terms of hours of work.

But it wasn't just the hours put in, I was realizing; it was also the quality of attention. Like the way Melissa taught, always making me feel as though I were the only one in the room. I studied her, watched her closely. At night, I wrote down what she'd said, word for word. And in my spare time, standing in front of the mirror, I made faces like hers. I practiced raising one eyebrow and making my eyes water by thinking of something sad. When they did, I pursed my lips the way she did and created looks of compassion. In this way, I'd become an ASI teacher and somehow bring dance to the teachings.

Thinking about that all day, I'd come home from the double shift and collapsed on my bed. Melissa imitations repeatedly danced through my mind, the images becoming darker and darker. I was chained to a prison cell, found guilty of being fraudulent and an imposter. Long, sharp fingers dug into my shoulders, imprinting my crime, and a high piercing voice was in my ear.

"Hurry, wake-up! It's June! She wants to talk to you!' Melissa was shaking me. Her normally melodious voice was high and squeaky, blistering my ears. "Take the phone." Her long hands tugged at my shoulders, her attentiveness like a rope around my neck.

Still curled up, the dream not quite gone, I attempted to speak into the phone, but Melissa was ordering me to sit up. Eying her from my tattered wool blanket, I saw her blonde hair wild about her face like a mane, and her pace that of a lion. She kept interrupting the call with her questions and comments.

"Hi honey. Melissa tells me you've done the impossible."

"Get out of bed."

"Hold on June. Melissa! Stop!"

"I'm so proud of you and I am thinking of you every minute; I pray for you every day!"

"No really, you don't have to do that." God, it was good to hear her voice. "All I did was quit modern dance, you know, for just another twenty-nine days, then I'm back." Melissa was treating me like a five-year-old. She put her finger to her mouth and whispered, "Be quiet so that June can go on with her message."

"You must start going to church more regularly. No more beachcombing. Okay, hon? Easter is in just a few weeks. You gotta find a way to take God into your heart more seriously. I gotta go, the baby's stirring."

She hung up before I could say anything else. Melissa pulled me out of bed, her arm linked into mine, her hand clawing my wrist, all the while speaking in her high cheerful tone. "I'll make coffee."

I reluctantly followed her to the living room. I stood near the bay window across from the couch. I didn't want to be by her side. I didn't need to celebrate my quitting dance, and becoming an ASI teacher would probably never happen. Besides, yesterday had been hard enough. The starred night glittered through the window, and my dried-out eyes hurt as I rested my head against the cool windowpane.

"Sit on the couch, so we can discuss plans."

I closed my eyes again and pressed my head harder into the glass. After all, no one told me to quit dance. I shouldn't take my anger out on Melissa; it wasn't her fault.

"Did June let you in on our plans for you? You know you have three steps that must be taken next."

"What?" I banged my head lightly against the glass again.

Melissa's shrieky tone was endless. "Because of this huge step you've taken, you've gained the privileges of older students, and you'll need to work harder. You can do it! You are extraordinary in your ability to make these changes."

I am?

"So, listen up, okay? The first step is to double or triple your hours as a waitress."

"I thought I'd have more time..."

"You'll need to pay monthly dues, as well as your tuition."

Monthly dues? Jesus, tuition was already $250 a month. I banged my forehead against the window, this time a little harder.

"Yes, we older students pay for the rent of our meeting space, food, wine, cigarettes, ashtrays. It all adds up to an extra $20 a week.

"The second step is to create a closer relationship to the priest or minister at the church you've been going to. What are you doing? Stop banging your head like

that!"

My forehead was buzzing and probably bruising. Melissa was by my side, pulling me away from the window. I pushed her slightly, and the blue chipped coffee mug she held flew out of her hands. It crashed hard, blue splinters and brown liquid splaying across the floor.

I leaned back against the window and pushed my head against the pane again. The stars were fading; short rays of light specked the dark, blue-grey sky. Melissa was on her hands and knees in front of me, cleaning up the clattered clay pieces. She asked me if I was all right. No! I wanted to scream. There is something deeply wrong with me. I couldn't feel the relief and joy of quitting dance; instead, I was seething. Teaching at ASI was absolutely impossible. My dream was a premonition. Damien would see through my Melissa imitations, condemn me and throw me out, as he should.

It was almost dawn. The orange-red rays spread like fire across the sky, falling into the room and across the wooden floor. Melissa was still on her hands and knees cleaning up the spilled coffee.

I knelt, too.

"Are you listening? I know it's a lot all at once, I know this, hon." There were some broken mug pieces in her right hand, and her left one held the dirty rag. She put her arms around me and held me to her with closed fists.

"The third step," she whispered, "is that you have to let David in. You can no longer ignore him."

I ended the hug. Sitting on the floor facing her, I picked up a piece of the chipped mug and rolled it around in my palm. It was short and wide, with sharp points. I rubbed my baby finger along the sharper edge, feeling its rough surface dig into the small area around my nail.

Melissa sat cross-legged as she continued to carefully place one broken piece after another into her hand.

I looked up into her wide blue eyes, that sparkle stretching into the way back of her pupils.

"Helen's very intuitive and psychic and has never been wrong in her decisions about others. You're quite lucky, you know. David is the best."

The piece of shattered clay was resting along my fingers. I stroked the softer side of it.

Clearly, Helen, Melissa, Damien and June all were doing their best for me. There was something stopping me from embracing David; everyone could see this except me. There *was* something wrong with me. When I looked up to say something, Melissa had gone to throw out the mug shards, and the floor was clean. Still in my fist was the last piece of broken clay.

"WE WANT to talk with you all about Easter and Passover..."

In class a couple of days later, I wanted to close my eyes, thinking I could fall asleep. But David pressed his hand into mine and fondled my fingers one by one. I forced myself to stay still, opening my eyes wide. They met Damien's, and my heart pulsed in my neck. Could he see it? He was gazing over me, his eyes scanning my palm inside David's. My blood froze, my hand went limp; I felt only the cold sweat on David's fingernails.

"Do you all follow? This is the time of deep contemplation and resurrection. Resurrect your spirits, my dears..."

I couldn't stop looking at him, yet David kept squeezing my hand. "Remember your True Selves..."

At the end of the meeting, David pulled me up, his eyes two brown shiny stars. "Wow, wasn't that inspiring? Let me take you home tonight." He drew me close and I forced myself to relax into him.

Damien and Melissa approached us, holding hands.

"Permit me." And before I knew it, Damien was kissing me on the forehead, on the cheeks, and ever so lightly on the mouth. "To get you going with David," he whispered. Grabbing Melissa's hands, he kissed and pressed them to his heart. "How you resurrect my spirit." Melissa moved closer to him, and gave him her forehead to kiss.

As they turned to kiss other students, my hand weaseled out of David's. "I don't know," I feigned a yawn, "I need to be waitressing in three hours."

But he pushed me up the stairs and pulled me out into the night, laughing. "I love this time of year, don't you? It's all about new beginnings, especially resurrecting love."

I was quiet. I didn't know what to say. The air chilled my cheeks, and the stillness of the hour cleared my thoughts. I loved downtown San Francisco at 2 a.m. There were no cars; the buildings were dark and quiet. The last trolley was waiting in its track on the corner of Market and Golden Gate. The fog rolled in and out of its great green belly, hiding its trolley poles.

I wanted to be a statue and stop time; then David could go home, and I would remain staring at the dark stillness, forever.

David's hand tightened in mine. I let him hold on. Statues didn't have to worry about not feeling attracted to such a good guy.

"I'm sorry, I really need sleep."

He stopped suddenly and swung me around. His smile wide, eyes crinkled. "Well, sweetheart, welcome to ASI! What better way to observe your 'false' self! Breaking the habit of sleep is wonderful!" He twirled me about, but my legs were lead. He tried to dance me down Market, but I slowed my pace. He quit trying and right in the middle of Market Street, practically on the trolley track itself, he kissed me, his tongue tight and wide inside my mouth. He pulled my wild hair and pressed into me harder.

I wished to be a web, the thing the spider and the bug were both trapped by. I wouldn't have to decide whether I was the spider weaving a lie with David, or the bug caught within.

No MATTER how much I repeated, *If you're not feeling joy, you're not your True Self,* I couldn't shake off the lead-like feeling weighing down my chest. In class all l did was gawk at Damien, sure he knew how much I couldn't live up to his teachings. And the more I understood this, the worse I felt. I probably didn't even have a True Self; that part of me smashed to smithereens.

For the past few days, I'd waitressed 12-hour shifts, running from kitchen to table with a smile plastered to my face, the same smile I gave to David, pretending to have that joy meant for everyone else.

When I walked in my front door, Melissa was sitting in the living room, two small empty bottles of vodka beside her coffee cup. This was unusual. I hadn't noticed her drinking up until now. I collapsed on the couch next to her, hundreds of coins and dollar bills falling out of my pockets, clanging to the floor.

I leaned back, closed my eyes and thought I wouldn't move ever again.

"Helen is profoundly disappointed in you." Melissa's stinky breath hit me as hard as her words.

"What?" My eyes stayed closed, her voice stung my ears. Helen didn't even know me, and Melissa's stale alcohol breath made me want to leave, only I couldn't get my body to do so.

"You stink."

"What's up with you that you didn't go to church yesterday, *on Easter?*"

I couldn't answer. My tongue more exhausted than my eyes. I just should've lied. The restaurant had needed me, the tips were magnificent, and the owners loved me; they said I was their best and most dedicated worker.

She stomped to her feet, the noise jerking my head up. "Goddammit, I got you out of your father's home, I got you your waitressing job, I've done nothing but give you encouragement, poured everything I've got into you..."

I opened my dry eyes. Her blond curls were uncombed and matted. Her long, thin arms hung about her waist.

She was right of course. I was a louse, letting her down like this. Proof I didn't have a True Self and wasn't even capable of developing that or I would've gone to church. It wouldn't have occurred to me *not* to go.

"You are stubborn and only think of yourself..."

Each word pricked my insides. Dad's very words to me.

"Damien can't believe you..."

Was the entire school gossiping about me? "Just because I didn't go to church?" I shouted. She was pacing, her voice an icy fire whisper. Gone were the high cheerful notes.

No. Not because I didn't go to church. But because every time I was given direction, I disrespected it. Every time I was asked to do something, I tantrumed. Did I have any idea what it was like to work with me? Did I? Did I have any idea how close I was to being kicked out because everyone was sick to death of my belligerence and whining? Since I was always like this, how could I possibly "turn it off" in the kitchen, huh? It was Helen who insisted on keeping me, because Helen could see beyond the tantrum. I had Helen to thank and had better start doing so. And fast.

I sank to the floor, curled up. The hard wood pressed into my cheek, and chills went up and down my spine. Melissa towered over me; a wad of spit landed near my face and her pounding feet reverberated against the floor as she walked away.

I stood, neck aching, feet asleep. Slowly, I moved into the kitchen, feeling my feet prickling back. I pulled out the sharpest knife I could find. Without looking in the mirror, I put the knife as close to my scalp as possible. I sliced off a huge chunk of hair at the root. Who cared? I didn't need my wild hair anymore. Desperate to find my True Self, maybe I'd find her under this ugly, god-awful mop of hair.

Maybe it was time to leave ASI. I paused and considered this. And create a big spiritual hole inside of me? Melissa was right, she did get me that job, and she did pull me out of Dad's house. I watched the first few hairs drop from the knife down to my feet. I'd probably lose my job if I left ASI. And I had no money saved. My hair was falling faster now. I kept slicing. I didn't want to go home and live with Dad, work in an office. Nor did I want to die a spiritual death or have spiritual holes. Nor did I want to leave Damien. I saw his huge brown eyes winking at me, his warm sweet smile. I was nothing to him. We hadn't slept together in weeks. But I didn't need him. I had David, a gift. I cut more hair. The hidden costs, the cleaning bills for all the clothing in the kitchen's spare room, and the hundreds of boxes of cigarettes stacked up in the cabinet. I held a strand up to the light and noticed how long the waves were in that one black strand. The rent had gone up both at the restaurant and here at Melissa's. I caught a few more strands as they fell, feeling how strong and wiry they were. That's why I had taken on so many extra shifts, just to keep up with the expenses. I examined the knife. It had blood on it. I found that curious but kept chopping. I'd have to move in with Dad and work with Maureen again. And leave Damien for good.

My scalp was beating against my brain. I put my hand to it and felt wet, sticky areas. I looked at the tips of my fingers; they were bright red. I glanced downward and saw my hair lying in a black, stagnant pool around my ankles. I remembered sand falling out of Mom's pockets and landing in similar piles so many years ago. *We are not the same.* I stomped my foot and cut another strand.

TWENTY

WENDY

Spring

I fell in love with this kid Jake who like I met in rehab. And even though we're not supposed to date each other from there, there was only so much Freddy could do to control my life and Jake was like one of the coolest guys I'd ever met.

I was fucking proud of myself for staying sober for 7 months, and it was Jake who like helped me. And Freddy mostly had his head up his ass, when he'd lecture like how we'd substitute our partner for our drugs. It wasn't fucking like that with Jake and me. He was *super* serious about staying sober..

No more of that shit for me he'd claim, looking like right into my eyes. His were the color of strong coffee — that black — although he said they were brown. His hair was the color of the sun, golden and wavy, but he kept it short, not wanting to look like a fucking hippie anymore.

We'd walk all over the city, and we especially loved the Mission District and this Mexican restaurant, La Ciudad De México, Mexico City. We ate there first 'cause we couldn't believe the fucking corny name, like who would ever name a place after a city? But shit, the food was fucking great. We could like watch them make tortillas, and their burritos were out of this world. They had some secret spice that like made us go crazy.

So there we were, sitting at one of the rickety tables, like eating home-baked tortillas filled with chicken, cheese, tomatoes and hot chilies. That special spice made our eyes and noses like run. I choked between bites and like drank tons of water, but oh God I could have eaten there every fucking day.

And Jake was also like going to City College. He was saying that he was majoring in history 'cause he was fascinated with Hitler, 'cause he's Jewish.

"Really?" I mouthed. I was so busy chewing.

"Yeah, but you know I'm not like religious."

"I thought Jewish *was* a religion. I mean how can you like not be religious?"

"Well, Jewish is like Jewish, you know? I love eating lox and bagels, lighting menorahs and eating matzah with a ton of butter on it, but like I don't go to synagogue or pray. I mean does God really exist? I mean, like I know that we're supposed to find God, and Freddy keeps saying, 'Jake, you've got to start believing.' But I'm fucking uncomfortable with this God thing. Know what I mean? I mean look what happens when you follow creeps who say they're like close to God? Look at Reverend stupid Moon, and that other fucking creep, Jones? I mean I can fucking admit I'm like powerless over drugs and shit, but my *experiences* are my fucking God."

My heart was pounding really fast. He sounded so much like Dad. Shit.

"I don't know." I finally answered. "Maybe there are creeps out there, you know? Lots of liars. Fuck. I've known like so many."

I shuddered, remembering one room I used to go to. I had to walk up dozens of stairs, they all fucking creaked, and one I had to hop over, 'cause there wasn't any fucking stair on it. When I reached the room, it stank of beer and fucking vomit. There was always someone different offering me the fucking needle. *Hey bitch, I got what you want. It'll put you in fucking heaven.*

"Hey, come back, are you here?"

Jake was waving his hand in front of my face. I shook my head and said, "Look, we both know how fucking bad it can get out there. And, I mean Freddy always says, like find God in your heart. Who's ever told me anything like that kind of shit? God in your heart. Fucking crazy amazing, know what I mean? And remember like that night when I almost used? You know, I told you, how I heard a voice telling me to live instead? Well, shit. That could have been God, right? That could have been God right inside my fucking heart."

Jake shook his head. "That was just you saying 'what the fuck? I don't want to go out there anymore; I mean, there are fucking millions of crazies out there claiming they have God in their fucking hearts. How could fucking Hitler have done what he did if God existed?"

I shrugged. "I mean all kinds of shit happens, right? Look at my sister, she won't call Dad. He says she hasn't called him for over a year. You could say that if God existed that like wouldn't be happening, either."

"My point exactly."

"But Freddy is insisting that if we turn to God, He'll help us stay sober. And it's not like God can make us give up our habits. We have to try, and then He helps."

"Shit, do you really want to go back to that shit? To that life?"

"Well, no. But like I'm so tempted so often, aren't you?"

He shook his head and stood up. "You just need to remember your experiences. You don't need fucking God to do that."

He sounded just like Dad. I couldn't wait for them to meet. I didn't know when that was going to fucking happen. But I would make sure it like did.

≈

A WEEK LATER, just after my one-year sobriety date, Dad called.

"I want you to stop by the dance studio. I'm sure Clara would be happy to see you sober. Probably happier to see you than me."

I was finally ready to see her and told him so.

I called Jake and like begged him to come with me. "I'm like a wreck just thinking about it. I was such a shit to her. Fuck. She was always following me to the beach, standing up to those Fucks at the bonfire, and I just laughed in her fucking face."

Jake was the best. "Fuck that fucking shame shit. You've been fucking sober for a year. Be proud of yourself."

At the dance studio, *Lucy in the Sky with Diamonds* was floating out the window. "Fucking great." I looked at Jake and rolled my eyes. "A fucking song about drugs. Shit."

He laughed. "I'll wait here." he said and opened the door for me. A real gentleman.

There was no office. I don't know what I was expecting, but it was like I walked into a fucking nursery or something. There were little jackets hanging on hooks, and like fucking socks and shoes spread on the floor underneath them.

A tall, like graceful woman came down the hallway. "May I help you?"

"I'm like looking for Patti Jenkins."

"I'm her."

My legs were fucking shaking; knees were buckling under. Shit. She was gorgeous. Her grey-blue eyes were deep inside her sockets, and they were fucking shining. Her cheeks were like fucking Katherine Hepburn's. How did Mom used to call them? High cheekbones. They made her face look fucking stunning.

I put my hand out and saw it shake. "I'm like Wendy Greenwood. I'm like here to see my sister Clara."

"Well, it's just wonderful to meet you." She looked me up and down. I'm sure she was comparing my short, round body to Clara's fucking tall, lean one. She'd probably heard all about me, what a fucked up piece of shit I was.

"Clara isn't here."

I was ready to run. I forced my head to stay up, my eyes to look into hers. "Oh, ah, can you tell me when she will be?"

Patti kept looking at me. What the fuck? I licked my lips. I brushed my tongue along my front teeth. Did I have like a piece of fucking spinach stuck to them? That was like crazy. I hadn't eaten fucking spinach in I don't how long. Why was she so fucking quiet? Then she finally said, "I haven't seen Clara for a couple of months. She's quit dancing. I've tried calling her, but the phone number's been disconnected."

My mouth dropped open. I stood there like a fucking idiot. I had no idea what to fucking say.

"I'm sorry, Wendy. If I hear from her, I'll let you know. I'll go get some paper and a pen and write down your information."

I stood there like a fucking statue, speaking like a robot. After giving Patty my phone number, I ran to Jake and hit his fucking chest, going crazy. "How could she fucking do this? Just like fucking disappear? Fuck her. Fuck her. Fuck her."

"Whoa, babe, whoa. Coffee?"

He took me by the arm and led me to Bill's Place. He didn't order fucking coffee. Before I knew it the waitress was bringing like two huge chocolate shakes in mugs overflowing with whipped cream.

"What the fuck am I going to tell fucking Dad?"

Jake looked serious. I had never seen him with such a face. His mouth was like turned down, and his eyes had lost their fucking glow.

"It does sound fucking strange. It's possible that she got swept up into one of those fucking cults, Moonies or the People's Temple..."

I was drinking the fucking shake so fast my stomach hurt. "What the hell are you fucking talking about? Cults? Where the hell did that come from? She like disappeared from *me* 'cause like she hates me and who knows maybe Dad, too, and is making sure like we never see her again. What am I going to tell fucking Dad?"

TWENTY-ONE

CLARA

Spring

Two nights after I cut my hair off, I saw her as I made it down the stairs to the meeting room, standing close to the landing, talking quietly with Melissa and Damien. Tall and slim, a lilac velvet gown hugging her small hips as it fell to her ankles, polished, black patent leather boots covering her feet. Her dark black hair was swept into a beehive, wisps of it falling down over small brown eyes covered with lashes as long as my fingers. Liner, mascara, and eye shadow deepened and accented them.. Her brown-red, lipsticked mouth elongated and stretched when she spoke, dimples appearing often, denting any serious gesture with a light, laugh-like touch.

Helen.

I could not stop staring at her, and tears unexpectedly welled up. Still hurting from my Easter fight with Melissa, I vowed to myself that I would listen and follow every direction without an argument from now on.

I wished I had known she was coming. I'd have made more effort with my dress. I was rapidly losing weight, ten pounds in the past two weeks.

My plum, boat-neck sweater hung down like a bag, my skirt needed closer ironing, and I had wrapped a black wool scarf around my cropped head. It fell down my back, scratching my neck.

When we all finally sat down, Helen first stared into Damien's eyes. She gazed at him for some time, and the silence between them was flammable.

"What would we do without God?" she finally said.

If velvet could speak, its voice would sound just like hers, soft, deep and calming.

He laughed. "We'd be screwed."

She nodded, her eyes widening, face aglow against the vase of red roses. She gazed at us, cigarette in one hand, a glass of wine in the other. "It's all up to you to find the truth. You all must speak to your rabbis and priests, ask them questions about God."

Damien cleared his throat. "Helen, may I tell you what we've been experimenting with?"

She stared at him.

"We've been exploring what the 'false self' really is, how it manifests in our lives, how we have no control over it."

My leather boots. They were scuffed at the toes.

"Go on." Helen's voice was water over pebbles, clear and bubbly.

"We have a prodigy student here who is already working in the kitchen, a privilege you so generously gave her without even meeting her..."

My face was heated. It was hard to breathe.

"Instead of working on herself in a prime moment when she was tired, she flew off the handle, ending up in a verbal argument with Melissa of all people. And instead of owning her own misbehavior..."

Everyone was looking at me. Helen coughed. I looked up, only to see her take a long drag on her cigarette, eyebrows raised. Our eyes met, and I felt I was boiling over.

"But she was confusing her false self with what she thought was her True Self. Follow?" Damien was leaning in, telling all of us how stupid I was.

Helen and Damien gazed deeply into each other; making me squirm.

"Go on." Helen responded.

"She didn't care what she looked like on the outside, twisted our words and decided that the only way to find her True Self was to defy her outer beauty, a very gift from God. She dangerously chopped off all of her fine, silky, feminine hair and is now as bald as a Vietnam vet."

I couldn't even lift my hand to wipe the sweat off my face. Helen was probably going to ask me to leave. She couldn't have anyone shaming God — shaming ASI — like this.

"Clara, dear," her voice was soft, sweet. "I have heard so much about you. Your hair will grow back, and when it does, I hope you will remember your lesson. What do you think it is?"

How must I have looked to her? My mouth wide-open, this black, holey rag twisted around my head...

"Clara, hon, I am talking to you." Her tone was a bit less bubbly.

"I'm sorry about everything. I'm confused. And I can't do anything authentically." I couldn't stand my whiny voice.

The room fell quiet. I kept my head bent, staring at my left ring finger. So many women in class wore circles of gold there.

"Damien," Helen's tender voice waved across the silence, "We have a real gem here in Clara..."

My head jerked up.

Damien grinned and nodded until it looked as if his head was going to fall off his neck.

"Hon, until you find God, your false self will continue to badger you, as it does all of us. You must heed the following instructions: Speak to your minister about allowing God to come into your heart. I know he will help you..."

I pictured Minister Kleep's clear blue eyes.

"Buy yourself brightly colored silk scarves that flow and symbolize your true inner beauty. I'm sure Melissa will help you."

"Of course." Melissa's sunshine tones floated into the room.

"Take photos of yourself so you will remember what your false self does to you." She lifted her gaze to the whole room. "This is why it's so important for you all to take in our instruction. We will always lead you to deeper truths about yourselves."

Helen's eyes scanned my face. I tried to look into them, but they had too much light for me to take in. I would do anything and everything she asked.

As I WALKED OUTSIDE, the dark wind hit my cheeks, smells of tar and concrete entered my skin. My feet were feathers, and I twirled my way into the alley, past the garbage cans, their stench rising, invisible and shadow-like. I opened the kitchen door quickly and spun in.

I changed my clothes, exchanged the scratchy, black wool scarf for a cherry red bandana and grabbed a pair of orange rubber gloves, the brightest I could find. I decided to scrub all the pots and pans, including their copper bottoms, until I could see my face in them. My hands whirled through the steaming water and disappeared into the soap as it foamed to the top. I took the scratchy green pad, dumped out the soapy water and began to work. I was mesmerized as each burnt spot disappeared.

"As the stained black spots disappear, so does all my falseness," I chanted. My body was on fire as I worked. I had never felt so alive, so seen, so completely accepted. I even felt attracted to David. Maybe I could forget about Damien, as I had hardly looked at him. The tension in my forehead left, and I was surging with energy. It was time I embraced him, to really show my gratitude to Helen. It was such a relief to understand this. The water and the dishwasher were running. They were so noisy and I was so focused that I didn't hear anyone come in.

I jumped. I was suddenly grabbed from behind by the waist and thinking it was David, I screamed playfully and turned around, laughing.

I felt light-headed while Damien pulled me toward him. "Oh, I'm a mess, I look awful, let me clean..." I stuttered, stupidly. I ran to the bathroom and looked in the mirror. I re-tied my red bandana, remembering how the hairdresser had shaved my scalp completely, treating the scabs with great care. Never mind that, the sweat and all the hot water had steamed my face beet red and I looked stark, like a rat; my eyes bugged out, and the contours of my angular face sharpened my already deflated cheeks. My entire body craved Damien, while my head argued for David. And if he walked in right now, Jesus, anything could happen, including a threesome, and that thought just made me want to vomit.

As I entered the kitchen, I muttered, "Let's get together tomorrow night." That way I could be ready for him. Make sure it would be only us.

But he stroked my face with his finger and kissed the top of my forehead, making his way down to my cheeks. I tried turning my back, but he spun me around. I pushed him away, but he thought it was a game. He stank of whiskey.

I remembered seeing a bottle of unopened wine standing in the corner on the counter, way down past the dishwasher.

"Wine," I said, pointing where I thought it was. "Don't you want a glass first?"

I was unnerved when he nodded. I re-tied my bandana even more securely and ran out of the kitchen, down through the restaurant and out the door, tripping over the mat. Let him chase me if he really wants me right now. The wind was swirling, and I felt dizzy again.

I knew David would be looking for me, but I had no idea where he was. It was unusually warm outside, and I could see every star. When Damien drank too much, his neck grew red, his eyes blurred and he lashed out senselessly; hopefully he wouldn't come after me, drunk. The way Mom had. *Where are you going?* She had yelled at me. *You must come with me.* Drunk, her nails had dug into my wrists as she pulled me into the car. Flask in one hand, the other on the steering wheel, speeding down those hills.

Exhausted from all these thoughts, I walked back into the restaurant and sat down on a folding chair by the front door. I bent over, putting my head way down between my legs.

I heard voices drifting up through the floor and assumed Helen was talking to David. I closed my eyes. My hair would grow back. So would my confidence. I would talk to Minister Kleep. Maybe he really could help me find God, or my True Self. Or some semblance of happiness. I breathed in deeply, grabbed my ankles and pulled my head down further. I slowly lifted myself up, vertebrae by vertebrae, noticing how light my head felt without hair, and saw David smiling and standing in front of me.

"Let's go, Pretzel Girl," he said, pulling me up.

LATER, I couldn't stop thinking about either of them as I walked to the Clement Street Church. Damien, David, Damien, David.

I'd wrapped my new cobalt-blue silk scarf around my head like a turban and felt like I belonged to a new religious sect.

David had hated the scarf. *Cobalt blue makes your eyes look smaller. You need lime green, hon."*

Lime green made my skin look yellow. He was constantly telling me what to do, how to do it and when. He even told me *how* to believe in God. *You just need to get on your knees and say the Lord's Prayer. Then ask Him to come into your heart. You'll feel happy immediately.*

Church bells echoed across the sky, announcing the hour. I was walking so fast that I reached the park in less than an hour.

There's something about the word God that is hard to swallow, I'd barked. *I don't know how to take Him in. What does everyone mean by saying, 'Believe in God, and you'll always be your true happy self'?*

David's mouth had a way of dropping all the way down to his chin when he was unhappy. His eyes drooped down along with it, all shiny with water although he never cried.

I felt like a worm when that happened. I let him kiss me and spent the night, vowing for the millionth time that I wouldn't argue with him or anyone else anymore.

The breeze blew about me, and I wished I could rest in its arms. I swayed with its rhythm, but my feet were hot, and inside my black pumps a blister was screaming up my left ankle. They were not made for walking. I kicked them off and ripped the nylons. I hated wearing them. I slid my thumbnail up and down the delicate material, tearing runs that flew down my thighs and knees. I rubbed my feet against stones, feeling the rough surfaces meet my soles as the holes grew wider. I stood behind a nearby tree, and, hoping no one would notice, I held the ripped hanging stocking of each leg, lifted my dress, and tucked them into my underwear.

I stepped out from the tree gingerly and stole over the rocks until I hit the sidewalk again. My feet were freed. I thought of a dance exercise. I pretended I was a turtle, moving toward water. *Feel the heaviness of his shell on his back,* I'd instructed, *and remember, turtles move very, very slowly.*

TWENTY-TWO

WENDY

I had to wait a whole week to get up the fucking nerve to tell Dad about fucking Clara. Jake and I had wanted to like look for her, but we had no idea where to begin. Patti hadn't called us either. Shit.

It was Saturday afternoon. I walked up the stone stairs slowly, as if I was going to a fucking funeral. My heart was giving me a fucking cow it was beating so fast. I rang the bell and put my head to the door. What was I fucking doing? What was that door made of, fucking steel? You couldn't hear..."

It opened. There was Dad. He looked fucking awful. His hair around his ears was like shocking white. I hadn't noticed that before. And his eyes, I had to like look down they were so sad. Come to think of it, I hadn't seen him for like a month, although we'd talked.

"Come in, it's good to see you." He said, like always.

I wanted to like make a pot of coffee. But there was like something definitive about the way he sat down in his chair. I sat on the couch across from him. The Oriental rug was fucking filthy. There were like black lines around the edges. I didn't like say anything. Dad got mad so easily.

205

"You look good."

But he said it in like a dull tone. Was he happy to like see me?

"You know how you like asked me to go to the fuc...I mean the dance studio?"

He nodded. Was that all he could fucking do? Couldn't he like sit up, or like lean further toward me or like smile?

"Well, I met fuc...I mean like I met Patti Jenkens. You should like see her..."

"How's Clara?"

I gulped. He finally sounded excited. I looked down and mumbled, "Patti said like she quit fucking dance. Sorry. I didn't mean to swear..."

"Did I hear you correctly? Clara has quit dance?"

He almost looked fucking happy. Did he think she quit like modern dance and went back to the fucking San Francisco Ballet?

I lifted my head and forced myself to look at him. He was leaning further toward me.

"She like quit dancing and quit without notice and changed her fucking phone number and Patti can't reach her and I have no way of like looking for her."

Dad paced the room like a trapped, wild animal. His eyes stared, unmoving, straight ahead, and like he didn't deviate from his path; just walked from one end of the rug to the other. He was like too thin, had lost his belly and his cheeks looked hollow.

"We will just have to find her."

Yeah, I thought. Like fine. Just fucking find her. How big was San Francisco, how big the fucking Bay Area, how big the fucking world?

TWENTY-THREE
CLARA

Minister Kleep didn't remember me. We sat in the same stark office, across from each other, with the same small statue of Jesus hanging from a wooden cross on the white wall staring at me. Or rather I stared at it; Jesus had his eyes closed.

Kleep's clear blue eyes met mine, and then he looked past my shoulder.

"I want to know how to bring God into my heart."

"He's already there. You just have to know that."

His tone was dull.

"I don't understand."

"Neither do I." He continued to look past me.

"What?"

"Even though my daughter is missing, He's still here. Do you see, my child?" His eyes were so clear they looked dead, glassy.

Did he mean have I seen his daughter, or did I understand?

"She may have flown off to Sweden to join a commune with her hippie friends, or she may have run off to sea with her sailor boyfriend. I have not heard from her for two months. Do you see?"

He leaned over the wooden desk as if to capture me and this time wouldn't let my gaze leave his. "The Lord is still with me. Like Job, all is taken from me, my child. And still, I serve the Lord. Do you see?"

Nothing moved. Not my eyebrows, not his gaze, nothing.

"I...I'm sorry about your daughter. I'm sure she'll turn up."

"Ah, how can you be convinced of *that*, and not of God?"

"I'm confused about God."

"No, my child, no. Be confused about life, be confused about how children disappear. But God never goes away. Don't you see?"

Would he stop saying that? I stood up.

"Where are you going?"

"I...I'm going to think about what you are saying." I sat down again. "So, even if you are confused about people who love you, God is still there?" I remembered asking Dad, after my one and only Sunday school class -- Grandma had insisted that Wendy and I attend, but Dad pulled us out after one class -- and I'd asked, *How can God be Jesus's father, if He doesn't exist?* Dad had answered, his smile as big as our room, *Your **family** exists. We are alive and well, and all you'll ever need.* He'd kissed both of my cheeks and gently rubbed my head. *Good night my Golden Apple.*

"Never give up on people who love you. God sends loving people to us," Kleep said. "And He'll also send us enemies, so we must learn to love our enemies, those on the outside and those within us."

He was dead quiet, so quiet he didn't look real. I slowly moved my chair back, and he didn't even blink. I wanted to wave my hand in front of his face but thought better of it. I tiptoed out, looking over my shoulder one more time. He was sitting in the same position. His secretary didn't look up as I tiptoed past her. I opened the big wide door; the sun was shining more brightly than it had in days.

I tightened the turban around my head, and the sidewalk was warm against my bare feet. My soles were soaking in the sun, as though quenching a long-held thirst. I walked to the Five and Dime Store to buy a pair of socks and sandals. *We're all you'll ever need.* Dad may have needed me, but I didn't him. It was a matter of trust. Obviously, Minister Kleep didn't trust his daughter, or he wouldn't have been so worried. And I didn't hate Dad. I found the sock/underwear section and laughed out loud, as I suddenly felt my stockings again, tucked into my underwear! No, I didn't hate Dad, I just didn't need to contact him. I saw Aunt Miriam, looking puzzled. *He needed to have his life fully, to trust like I did,* I explained. *Kleep thinks his daughter is missing, but what if she's doing the same thing I am? Giving her father the chance to find his True Self, without her leaning on him all the time?* And as I pictured Miriam's eyes, they softened; I heard Kleep say, *Never give up on people who love you,* and tears were running down her face.

Miriam spun me around and brought me back to a time when I had called Dad because Mom had fainted. He came home late that night without her. And I had comforted Wendy as usual.

Well Clara-Bara, Wendy-Bendy, what keeps you up?

He looked into my face, and I searched his eyes, noticing a small red

pimple on the left side of his nose. I touched my own, relieved there was no pimple there.

You did a great job calling me! He was beaming at me. *Your mother is fine. She'll be home tomorrow. She just needs to rest.*

My chest swelled. And I couldn't help but smile, even though I felt bad for Mom.

Why can't she rest here? Wendy yawned, her mouth as big as the question.

Your mother needed to be more quiet. Now up to your room, both of you.

There's something wrong with Mom, I said as we climbed into bed.

No. Dad said she was fine.

She isn't.

How do you know?

I saw her. She isn't fine, there's something's wrong.

Like what?

I can't figure it out. She smells funny all the time now.

Dad said she's okay, She'd turned her body away from me, crying.

I snuggled into her bed, and curled my long legs around hers. At nine, she was still so cuddleable, adorable.

When Mom and Dad are out of the house, I'm in charge of you. Wendy's hair was soft against my hands.

Dad walked in and kissed both of us. *Everything is fine.*

We sat up. Wendy reached out her arms. He picked up her hand and kissed it all over. *Such warm, soft fingers, Wendy-Bendy.* And he smiled watching her giggle. *You'll see Mom at the piano when you come home from school tomorrow.* He kissed her again and patted her thick blonde head.

Then he held my hands. *You're so helpful, Clara-Bara. You did all of the right things. He kissed* me solidly, twice on both cheeks, while keeping his hand in mine. My chest warmed like a flower in the sun.

As he left, I said, *Sorry. You're right. Mom's fine. And you know what?*

Wendy rolled over to look at me. *I **do** do a good job of taking care of you, and I always will.*

Promise?

The question startled my heart. *Promise*, I'd whispered.

I stood outside the Five and Dime and shielded my face from the blinding sun. I'd no idea how Wendy was doing without me. Or Dad, for that matter. In any case, I didn't need either of them. I started to walk to the bus stop, but my new sandals felt floppy. When I looked down, one of the toe straps had broken. Miriam was shaking her head. Such a small, insignificant thing affecting the entire shoe, the way one action can destroy all the words in one promise. I took off both sandals and threw them hard against a tree. They fell in pieces, the breeze covering them with dead leaves.

TWENTY-FOUR

JOE

The doorbell was ringing nonstop, and Joe barely heard it. He'd thrown himself into his work. This was what he knew how to do. Work. The Adolescent Ward for Drug Addiction at Mt. Sinai was booming and brought new worries, worries that piled on top of the ones he had for Clara. Those were deeply buried. And when they rose in the middle of the night, when they woke him with his chest pounding, he read piles of articles about addiction and heart disease, rewrote the talks he was scheduled to give and scribbled lists of things he'd have to do the next day. He was immersed in one such article when he heard: "Dad...Shit...what the fuck..." along with pounding on the door and the leaning on the bell. The noises startled him, interrupted his concentration, but these days she was his spark. He was glad to see Wendy. There were bags under her eyes, and her hair looked as if she hadn't combed it for days. Was she using again? "You look pale," he said, "But come in. It's nice to see you."

"I have to talk with you about Clara. Can I like make us some tea?"

If she had been using, she wouldn't have wanted tea. He watched her pull out mugs and tea bags and fill the kettle with water. The kitchen noises were comforting. He'd been in the absence of them for so long.

"What if she's like missing? What if she's in fucking Korea in a fucking mass wedding…? What if she's like…"

"Wendy! Everything is okay. Let's not jump to conclusions."

She came over with the tea, sat down next to him and put her head in her hands. Her hair was a tangled mane. "It's surprising that she's quit dancing and she hasn't left a phone number," he said. He wanted to pat her head as of old. But kept his hands wrapped around the steaming mug.

"She like hates us, why else wouldn't she fucking call?"

"Of course she doesn't hate us. Everything is okay." He stood up and paced. Hearing his very thoughts from her mouth was uncomfortable. He sat down again, rubbing his hands together. Clara joining a cult. He had thought of that as well, vaguely. But, Clara had common sense; it couldn't be. Clara was stable. Strong-willed. A perfectionist like him. She was probably involved in some kind of project. She wouldn't contact him until it was done, making him proud.

"She will call soon," he reassured. "I'll phone the San Francisco Ballet. She might have decided to be a ballerina after all. She might be too proud to admit that I was right." Wendy shook her head, hair falling about her face. He doubted she had returned to ballet. Nonetheless, it wouldn't hurt to call.

"No. It's not okay. It's my like fault. If I hadn't used…"

He couldn't hear her. She had no idea what it was like to be at fault, what it was to hear guns so loud you couldn't move, even as you watch your Papa's head bleed, even as you knew you should have thrown yourself on top of your own sister. She had no idea what it was to "not have been as others were/to have not seen as others saw."

But her face was in his, her huge eyes full of concern.

"What are you mumbling? Poe, the most like depressing poet on the planet? I must've said something to send you spiraling down to think of him… Fuck. Everything I say makes you sad…I'm so sorry."

He sipped his tea, and patted her head. Had he been mumbling? Sad...No. Not sad. And really he had no time for this nonsense. "I'm busy, preoccupied. You are getting help now. That's what counts."

TWENTY-FIVE

CLARA

May

Everything around me was dancing. Small blossoms swayed in the small gardens on the sides of the buildings and cafes we passed. Daffodils and tulips waltzed along the pathways to the front entrances, and the sky was a deep May blue.

I bet if Dad knew I had quit dancing, he'd try everything in his power to keep me from starting again. It was a good thing, after all, that I was leaving him alone. He always ruined so many dancing moments anyway. Like the time when I was little and had been skipping to Mom's music. He'd been sitting on his creamy chair with his eyes closed and smiling. But then a bottle dropped, and his face reddened as quickly as a match to gasoline. I slid under his chair to hide. *Goddammit, Anna,* he'd yelled at Mom. *Can't you do without for once?*

I shook the memory out of my head as David swung me by the hand. We were walking to the restaurant, and I had this incredible idea about returning to dance that I couldn't wait to tell him about. Patti was going to be choreographing in New York and Boston this coming summer. I'd seen the announcement hanging on her door. It had been one hundred and seven days since I'd quit. It was time to start dancing again. But David was harping on my conversation with Kleep, especially the part about God.

"Would you stand still for a moment?"

Instead, I ducked under his arm, laughing.

"That thing Kleep said about loving what we hate...For God's sake, stop."

I stood still, putting my arm on his shoulder and positioning myself to twirl.

"I mean look at what happened to the poor guy...and still he loves the Lord."

I couldn't listen. I twirled again, in and out of his arms, pushing on his shoulder to make him dance with me.

"Guess what?" I finally interrupted him. "While Patti's gone, she might need a substitute teacher here for the summer. I'm going to drop by and ask!"

David finally spun me about so I landed in his arms. He almost tore my rotator cuff, his grasp was so stiff. He pushed me into a turn again, but despite his clumsiness, I didn't have to pretend, my whole body lifted without effort.

"There's something even more exciting," he said, as he held me now, in a tango pose. He pulled me up, holding me tight and close. Kissing my ears, he whispered, "I know it's time that you dance again, but a tremendous thing has happened. Helen's invited you to the farm this summer. We leave in one week."

I stepped away from him. "What?" My eyes searched his. Maybe he was joking.

This was beyond a huge privilege. From the moment I joined ASI, I'd heard so much about the farm. The only way you got to be there was by invitation. My excitement about dancing deflated. David sensed this. He held me tight, kissing the top of my scarf. "I know, hon, another dilemma standing in your way. You will dance again, just like I know I'll be in law school soon. Helen can't wait to have you up there, she's building a steeple and needs help..."

I ran.

"Hey, where are you going? Goddammit, all you do is tantrum when..."

But I wasn't tantruming. I had to run from David to get my mind clear. Getting back to dance felt like a stepping-stone to becoming an ASI teacher. But maybe it was the other way around. And Damien would probably be up at the farm. Still, I so wanted to be at the studio this summer. Dance felt like a part of me...but maybe it was just a part of my false self. My boots hit the pavement hard, and I ripped off my silk scarf. Fog curled around the exposed, tiny black baby hairs on top of my bare head as I turned back now and beat it toward class.

DAVID WAS in the meeting room before me, already talking with Melissa, when I arrived breathless and a complete mess. I had hit some puddles on the way, and my well-worn leather boots couldn't handle being splashed. On top of that, sweat stained my armpits, and my blue silk scarf had caught on a tree branch and was ripped down the center.

Melissa pulled me aside. "Why are you looking like this, hon? The best news in the world has just come your way, and you show up like a tramp?"

"Too much excitement," I said, noticing her skinny neck. It would be easy to rattle her.

"I know, hon, everyone gets scared at first. But you'll see, you'll *love* the farm. Come on, I'll walk you to the bathroom and fix you up myself. You can't be in the meeting as an older student looking like this."

She handed me her flask. "Take a sip."

I drank while Melissa put me back together.

She pinned up my hem; washed my face with hardly any pressure at all, patting the area between my eyes ever so gently. Her touch was surprisingly soft. She rolled her fingers over my bald head. "They're lovely," she whispered, "the small dark, baby hairs covering your scalp." She folded the ruined scarf and wrapped it around my head.

"And there's such a surprise waiting for us, hon, I can hardly wait to show you."

She shared her flask with me throughout the process. I saw Mom at the piano years ago, one hand shaking over the keys, as she lifted her bottle with the other, gesturing toward me. *Fill it, that's a sweet girl.*

Melissa's warm hand was in mine as she led me outside. The sidewalk was spinning and standing in front of us was a huge Greyhound bus, the smell of diesel making me gag. Sweat poured down my face as I saw the bus spin on the spinning ground. I held onto Melissa.

More students gathered, running after their wired-up toddlers and carrying babies too small to walk. They were screaming and swearing and pulling the caught kids by the arms, hauling them onto the bus.

Melissa whispered, "We're leaving for the farm right now! And I've packed a bag for you!"

What in the hell was she talking about? Got me all dolled up to go on a stinky bus to a muddy farm? I whipped around to look at her, but she was pulling me onto the bus, my head was about to split open.

I heaved all over the bus steps and Melissa's shoes.

"Oh hon," Melissa's voice was syrupy liqueur, "You're not feeling okay? Why didn't you tell me?"

David was beside us. A bucket and mop already in hand.

"Come on," Melissa linked arms with me and pulled us, once again, onto the bus. Still wobbly, I moved slowly, watching my feet shuffle across the floor. Dry heaves rose up and down. I let go of Melissa, but she continued to push me.

I whirled around. "Goddamnit, stop!" Was that my voice screaming?

"Hush. The bus is full, so we have to walk to the back."

"Get your fucking hands off me…"

I saw my shaking body turn, and my hand pushing Melissa away from me. She held onto me more firmly. We were walking single file down the narrow bus aisle.

"You better stop, now." Her whispering heated me up. "You're just drunk. As soon as you're seated, I'll get you some water."

My hand balled into a fist, and I had to hold onto it so I wouldn't punch her. I wasn't drunk. I was *not*.

"Here's your seat. I'll help you into it."

"No, I can do it." Bitch. My head was spinning again.

A mother looked at me across the aisle, with a finger to her mouth.

"I don't remember saying anything." I was annoyed. A sleeping baby was buckled in tightly beside her, and I realized that there was a toddler sleeping in the seat next to me. She gestured that he was hers as well.

I bit my tongue and slumped into my seat, my back aching and my new baby hair follicles hurting from all the tension. I looked at the toddler next to me. He was sleeping soundly, small blonde head slumped against the window, his little body practically falling off the seat. I took the blanket at my feet and covered him, looking around to his mother. She smiled and nodded her approval.

Funny to think that this little guy was the "older" sibling. I couldn't have been much older than him when Wendy was born. I lifted the blanket and looked at him more carefully. His hands resting on his lap looked no bigger than my thumbs, and it seemed that my middle and index fingers would barely fit into his shoes. And yet he was the older one. Just like me. Ever since I could remember, maybe even at Wendy's birth, I felt I knew more than she could have ever known. And yet, if I had been as little as this guy sitting next to me, how was that possible?

The bus whined and shimmied and shut its doors; Melissa stood at the front, asking for our attention. She said something about beginning a tremendous

journey. I didn't bother to listen. It occurred to me that I had eight hours to myself, away from her. As the bus took off, the heat came on. I leaned back. The pulsations between my shoulder blades calmed down, and I massaged the top of my head, my hands working slowly toward my temples. The toddler's even breathing and the darkness spilling in made me relax further. I would see June in the morning. Damien would be arriving the next day.

TWENTY-SIX

JOE

Summer

Clara had disappeared. But she was busy, Joe reasoned again. She would call soon.

He walked faster and thought about Wendy. Stubborn as ever. Insisting on that B.A. in psychology with a minor in history. Suddenly short of breath,

He called Patti Jenkins, but she told him the same thing she'd told Wendy. She hadn't seen Clara for three months. The San Francisco Ballet had had no word from her either.

His chest pains. Aaron suggested heart surgery. That wasn't necessary. But Aaron was excited about this new treatment: Ablation Surgery. Joe, too, was curious and had done some reading, what little there was. He took walks after work for a few hours and didn't get home until midnight. The exercise was good for the heart. It tired him. Helped him sleep through the night.

Fillmore Street. No fancy houses, restaurants or people. He relaxed in the clear night, under the full moon.

A few kids were loitering outside the Round Table Coffee Shop. Its doors were open. James Brown was playing on the jukebox. The kids were pushing each other, laughing. He couldn't tell if they were Black... some Chinese? Not Caucasian.

He walked faster and thought about Wendy. Stubborn as ever. Insisting on that B.A. in psychology with a minor in history. Suddenly short of breath, he slowed down.. . Her boyfriend, Jake, loved to build things, she told him — just like he had. She was excited. When she was like that, it was impossible to have a conversation.

Jacob sounded unstable. A woodworker. Another hippie who thought he could live on the things he built. He ought to discipline himself. Sit down and study. Prepare for a real job.

Appearing unexpectedly, an old man was sitting on steps to a boarded-up building. Fallen nails were everywhere. The old man held out his hand. It was shaking. Joe pocketed a few nails that were sitting too close to the old man and handed him a couple of dimes. His eyes were yellow — jaundice probably. He looked thin. When was the last time he had eaten?

Hands in his pockets, playing with the nails, Joe continued to walk. Jake was Jewish. And he was headed for an unnecessarily unstable life. Hadn't there been enough of that in this country? The riots, Watergate, the assassinations of the Kennedys and Martin Luther King? A nail's dull head pressed up against his hand. He pressed it harder to still his tachycardia. Jake, Wendy had no idea how fortunate they were, their opportunities, why *choose* to be unstable?

He looked up at the dark sky. The moon as round as that gun hole, the bullets hidden inside those bodies, the blood on the white snow, brightly lit by the moon. The memory as vivid.

There he was once more in the mountains, the two Nazis dead in the snow, the weapon smoking in his grasp. John, the priest, waving his hands. He was praying to Jesus for all of them. The blood was pouring out of their mouths and chests. They weren't even gasping for breath. It was him, Joe Greenwood, the kid who had pulled his sister's hair all of the time. *That* kid had just murdered two people.

The wind had picked up. Its bite against his cheeks brought him back. He bent over. The nausea was painful. Sweat poured out of his armpits. The oxygen was leaving his head.

He heard Miriam again. *Yosev, don't you see you are no longer that boy? You are a successful doctor.*

Miriam? He said quietly as he leaned his head against a lamppost, *is that really you?*

You were just a boy. There was no way you could have stopped those Nazis

He rubbed his forehead. A slight bruise had formed from resting it on the pole. *Shooting those Nazis was self-defense. It couldn't have been helped.* He leaned again against the lamppost and pulled the rusty nails from his pocket.

Someone tapped him on the shoulder. A tall black teenager towered over him. "You okay, ole' man? My Mama runs the café down the street. She saw you over here and wondered if you were okay. She says there are too many broken people in this world, and would you like some fried chicken?"

The nails slid out of his palm and rolled toward the gutter.

TWENTY-SEVEN
CLARA

Summer

I t was hot and clear, unusual for the Oregon Coast. I stepped off the bus, and the first thing that caught my eyes was the Pacific Ocean banging against the cliffs. The untamed grass was sprinkled with blue and gold wildflowers. In front of me stood a stone lodge with windows from ground to roof and a wide wooden front deck.

The wind smelled of salt and mountain, and I heard Dad's soft voice at bedtime when he'd told Wendy and me stories about his life in his Polish village at the base of the Carpathian Mountains.

When Papa and I had walked on the trails, he shushed me if I spoke. 'When we are quiet we can hear the mountain,' Papa would say.

I stood as still as the trees, trying to listen.

"Come on, what are you standing around for? It's past eight, we're already late for breakfast." Melissa's voice was as obnoxious as the crows.

The children clamored off the bus. Hungry and excited, they were as wild as the ocean waves. They ran this way and that, calling and screaming to one another.

Parents with babies attached to their chests called to their children, and June, with her clan of four and her baby at her chest, came lumbering out of the house, wrinkles around her eyes, and rolls of fat over her belly and torso. Her children — all under ten — ran in every direction, and she walked faster toward us, sweat dripping from her nose. Judy's oldest son had been given to his father to care for, as he'd ended up being way too much for June to handle.

I ran toward her, arms out, intending to smack into her with a hug.

She pushed my palms away and held my hands. The skin under her eyes was caked with old make-up. Mud-black lines encircled the area. There were folds in her cheeks and neck.

She smiled, clearly a labor, and her eyes wandered toward the children. "Have to get 'em all together." The words fell out of her mouth, thick as rocks.

Before June could stop me, I ran after the youngsters, feeling like one myself, the wind gathering my scarf and pulling its long blue ends behind me. Dancing and leaping, and like a choreographer, I directed and spun the children back to the lodge.

AS WE ENTERED, cheeks hot, I halted. Wide pinewood covered the walls and floor. A long, shining oval wooden table stood on top of a woven rug of muted orange, red and brown. The table was set with matching, hand-quilted mats and red napkins. Beige-orange pottery plates and cups lay on top of the mats. Someone was serving eggs and bacon to the other seated fifteen students who had been on the farm for as long as June, and a basket of homemade toast with freshly whipped butter was passed around. The strong scent of coffee mingled with that of the toast, bacon and eggs.

Helen was at the head of the table, black wisps of curls falling down her cheeks, her vast amounts of thick hair tied back.

"Hello, Clara," Helen greeted me, her eyes boring into mine. "How nice of you to bring in the children." Her smile disappeared, and she grimaced at June.

I followed her look, feeling some of the joy drain out of me. But my plate was being filled. There was so much activity. Mothers from the bus were greeting their husbands, children were jumping on their fathers' laps, and the food smelled so good. It seemed like a long time since I'd eaten.

"Oh," June said, gulping down her eggs, "it was so nice of Clara to do that." We smiled at each other. It was good to see her.

"The children were excited to be here; you know how much they love this farm, Helen, and when they saw their little friends running off the bus, why they ran helter-skelter, and Clara, being Clara, decided to help."

"June?" Melissa jumped in, pointedly.

Silence fell around the table. My fork scraped against my empty plate. What happened? Even though June was way across the table from me, I saw how quickly her fork went from her mouth to her plate. Melissa's eyes didn't blink, and Helen's were also boring into June's. She ate faster.

Melissa cleared her throat. Her eyes never left June, but she spoke to all of us. "As you know, this is a place of hard work, on every level of our being. And I strongly suggest that you observe your falseness like crazy right now. What is the real reason that Clara took over the children for you?"

I never took over anyone's children. I was ready to protest but Melissa jumped in again.

"June?"

June kept eating. Finally, she answered. "I'm exhausted. And the falseness tells me that I can't handle so many kids on my own. I'm grateful, because I can see where I'm stuck."

Helen's voice was low, like thunder. "Your most recent reading with me showed shadows, and Mother Mary warned you of this. I've told you since that reading that not a sliver of falseness could come from you." Helen picked up her napkin and dabbed her eyes. Melissa was quick to pull out one of her silky white handkerchiefs. She gave it to Helen, who smiled at the gesture.

Melissa cooed, "I didn't know that your reading even predicted such a fall for June. I feel responsible..."

"You are angelic. Your aura is pure, and you have done wonders with Clara here. You are not to take responsibility for June."

"I'm afraid, dear..." and Helen's eyes filled with more tears, "that you have not heeded your spiritual reading from Mary and have become a terrible example to those who are new here. I'd hate to have you leave and never have you see your kids again. They cannot be around such negativity, as you well know."

Reading? Melissa's aura, pure? June not seeing her children again? Because I helped round them all in? *It's not like that*, I wanted to shout. *It's not June's fault; it's mine. I did it!*

...I did it, I did it. The words echoed throughout my head. Dad and Mom had been screaming while Wendy squirmed in Mom's arms, and I was between them, shouting, *I did i!* Someone was pouring coffee into my empty cup, and Helen was still talking.

"You've lost the privilege of taking care of the children. You'll spend the day cleaning all of the cabins. Mary will instruct us going forward. In the meantime, Clara, your aura is pure and your mind quite clear."

Helen sighed, and the sparkles in her eyes fell over me. My heart was skipping, and my neck stretched to the ceiling. It felt like I could float right through it.

"You'll be in charge of the children. Vicki, who is at the brink of falling out of herself, like June already has, will be with you. You're to help her, yes?"

"I want to help June..."

Everyone stared at me. A knife clanged to the floor.

Helen's smile was mesmerizing. "Of course you do. She brought you here. Filling your quota, right hon?"

My head fell into my shoulders, and my neck snapped downward. June wouldn't look at me. *Is it true? Talk to me,* I begged silently.

"By helping Vicki, you'll be helping everyone, including June. And you can turn people around, just like this," Helen snapped her fingers. I saw Melissa tipping her flask into her coffee.

My thumb was bleeding. I had torn a long hangnail off. I expected June to take my hand in hers and wrap soft tissue around it. Instead, it throbbed, resting on my lap. June had to change, just like Wendy had had to. Pictures of her floated in. She had skipped school and hadn't come home for a couple of days. When she'd finally snuck in, her swollen eye was ink black, and she had told the teachers I'd hit her.

"It's seldom that such a clear aura as yours sits at this table."

My head swayed to the ceiling again. I gazed down at June. She was looking at her hands instead of taking care of mine. No, June was nothing like Wendy. I imagined June laughing, her incredible smile spreading a mile across her face as she watched me put on those Italian leather boots; emptying out her huge, crazy bag to find make-up for me; and most of all not telling anyone how I had gone to the beach instead of church. A quota? It couldn't be so. I'd been pressing down hard on my hand, but it hurt. Like my breath, which was hard to catch. I gazed into Helen's dazzling eyes, and I couldn't feel the insult in my gut anymore. I was finding a new self within me that could do anything. June could do the same. Hanging out with her wouldn't be good for me right now, this new self was instructing me.

TWENTY-EIGHT
JOE

Joe walked with the tall young man, still trying to grasp what he'd just heard from Miriam, but the boy wouldn't stop talking.

"My Mama saved my sister's and my own souls, seeing how much we all needed the Lord, and we had gone and listened to her, otherwise I'd be on the streets, missing, disappeared, just like my younger brother...or dead, like my other one."

He was alert. His mother had a missing child?

"She knows how to fix what's broken in a human being, she does. She'll be right glad you're coming over."

Broken. His head was in a whirl, and the chest pains were gone. He must be going crazy, hearing those voices, like a schizophrenic. There must be a rational reason. Of course, he didn't blame himself; it was a horrific event. It happened so long ago. He wasn't broken. He stood taller. He was the doctor. He examined those with high blood pressure, irregular heart-beats. He was in charge...his patients, Maureen and his office, the adolescent ward. It was terrible that this young man's siblings had died.

As they entered the café, the smells of fried chicken and apple pie made his stomach growl. So embarrassing. There were a handful of black women sitting around a couple of square wooden tables, pushed together. They each had an open Bible in front of them. That was the problem with the Blacks he knew; they depended too much on religion. Believed too much in God's Creation. A nice story, but not based on facts. Nothing to do with Darwin or Newton.

The place was spotless. White porcelain salt-and-pepper shakers stood neatly in front of ketchup bottles and silver-colored napkin holders. There was an old jukebox standing beside the door. Aretha Franklin was singing something about a bridge over troubled waters. The song was haunting.

"Well, if that isn't Dr. Greenwood!"

Mrs. Lincoln?

"Georgie, pull up a chair for the doctor, and then get him some fried chicken and potatoes; why are you standin' there?"

Her son Kevin was missing. Her daughter, Mary, was doing well at the clinic.

There was a commotion of chairs scraping across the well-worn floor. He squeezed between the women and sat. Georgie gave him a huge plate of golden-crisp chicken and mashed potatoes.

"The Lord does work in mysterious ways, don't he?" Mrs. Lincoln's smile crinkled her eyes. She laughed, and the other ladies nodded.

"Let's all pray for Annie, 'cause her youngest girl just run off with that Billy man, ten years her senior," Mrs. Lincoln said.

"Always had a hard head, that girl." The women bowed their heads.

Although the meal was delicious, the prayer was hard for Joe to stomach. He asked, "Has Kevin been found?"

"Lord have Mercy, not yet."

Perhaps she didn't remember that visit with him, was it last year? He'd tried to have a conversation with her about Jim Jones. So far, this evening, he hadn't been mentioned. Maybe she'd listened after all. His thoughts were drowned out as the women joined their voices, reciting Scripture. "Even though I may walk through the valley of the shadow of death, I will fear no evil, for Thou art with me." Then one of the women bowed her head and said quietly, "May You find Kevin, Dear Jesus, and help him find his way home to us." The others joined her in prayer, nodding.

"Did you hear about the minister's daughter, that one way up on Clement?" Mrs. Lincoln asked as she lifted her head.

"You must mean Minister Kleep's little girl, that one who ran off to sea with her sailor boyfriend?"

"No, no I hear she got caught up with some hippie commune all the way over in Sweden."

The momentum of their voices and sound of prayer were giving him tinnitus in both ears. He stood up, ready to go, but he paused and sat down again, needing to hear more.

TWENTY-NINE
CLARA

On the first day of the second week, I lined all the children up single file, had them hold hands and led them down the narrow path between the ocean and the orchids. The wind whipped up leaves and made the birds fly slanted. The waves rushed to the shore, spraying their salty wet breath on the tips of our hair, including my own new, soft, longer strands. I flung off my scarf. Our hands, inside one another's, were also dewy and damp.

We headed toward the natural pool, an area where the fresh water dripping down from the mountains fell into a waterfall wading pool whose stream trickled to the ocean. It was one of June's favorite spots on the farm.

We'd dip our feet and do some "bird" dancing before lunch. I wanted to teach them all how to dance and give Helen a show at the end of the two weeks I had been assigned to the children.

I was zigzagging the line, trying to make it look like a flying ribbon or a slithering snake. I couldn't decide which. Vicki was holding up the rear.

The kids screamed, "Snake! Snake!" and a few of them fell on their bellies wiggling about, laughing their heads off.

I fell down too. "Wiggle just your torsos and keep your heads up. Hiss!" They copied me as I writhed up nose-to-nose with a couple of them, stuck my tongue out and "sssssssssssssed." Vicki was standing near me.

"They're fucking filthy, the mothers will kill us. Helen will have another fucking vision..."

"You need to work on yourself, you can't be reacting like this," I said.

"Yeah? You tell me how to get these kids up and out of the mud. It's your fucking fault, getting down and getting fucking filthy with them."

"It's just your false self speaking." I was surprised at how easily I could teach her. "Have you prayed to God, or brought Jesus in?"

I looked up into her eyes, the way Melissa often looked at me. I did this with such ease, practicing to be an ASI teacher.

"Look, hon," I said, standing and forcing her white clean fingers into my muddy ones. "It's just like Helen has said, these kids are reminding us of a freedom we've forgotten we have. Don't hate them for being so free. It's just the false self that hates this process."

She pulled back as I grabbed her firmly, making her twirl and run about with me the way I had done with Wendy when Dad had found out I'd quit ballet. We sang *A Hard Day's Night* at the top of our lungs. I swung her around and felt Dad glaring at me.

I hear, Clara, that you want to quit ballet. Mrs. Bronson says that you haven't been to class for two weeks. I kept swinging Wendy around, but she sat down, and I was the only one dancing and singing.

*You were chosen, **chosen** by Mrs. Bronson to be one of her prime students. And you want to quit?*

His hands had flown out in front of his chest, and he looked intently at me, as though he were looking right into the heart of my future, predicting the kind of bum I'd become if I quit ballet.

"Stop. *Stop.*"

Vicki was screaming at me. "You're fucking dirty," she was crying and laughing as I pulled and spun her faster, spinning Dad out of my mind. The kids sped up their slithering and followed us on their bellies, hissing louder than ever. I hissed back at them and then at her. "You should play, it can really get the negativity out..."

But she spat out, "Jesus fucking Christ. Look at these kids, will you?"

They were completely covered in mud, spitting dirt off their pink tongues.

"Goddammit, we have no towels, tissues, clean clothing, nothing."

This was true. "We can always wash them off in the wading pool."

"And dry and clothe them after, with what? Goddammit..."

There were a couple of shrill high screams from the kids. Vicki burst out crying, her straight brown hair falling into her face.

The sun was breaking the clouds apart, and the sea breeze picked up, whooshing around us, freezing my uncovered head. Suddenly the shrill sounds coming from the kids curled into frightening screams. We flew the few hundred yards toward the noise, only to see Rosa, June's oldest, and Lisa, Damien's niece, scratching and punching each other. They were the same age, almost eight, but Rosa was a much bigger child.

They were rolling away from the rocks over the path and edging close to the wild, raw ocean. The waves tumbled furiously on top of each other, curling under as they got close to shore, crashing in opposite directions, and rising and curling together again, creating a deep and dangerous undertow.

I ran to them as fast as I could but not before Lisa had fallen in such a way that her arm was flung out oddly. They were both crying, as Rosa rolled off of her onto the sand. They were just a few yards away from the ocean.

"Oh my God, Vicki, quick! Run. Get Melissa or June, or call 911. Lisa, hon, can you move your arm?"

Another child came toward me holding my abandoned scarf. With a filthy thumb in his mouth, he handed it to me, looking down at us, snot falling out of his nose.

I wrapped my scarf around Lisa's small elbow and forearms. Her face contorted in pain. "It really hurts, huh?"

I looked up for a moment, and realized that I was alone with nineteen muddy, filthy, crying children. I got them away from the sea.

As I raced to get ready for class that night, I kept hearing Lisa's scream. She'd broken her arm and would be in a cast the entire summer.

Classes started every night at 8 sharp, right after dinner, and I wasn't going to be late. Everyone had to be there on time to show respect for God and Mother Mary. To be exactly on time meant that our highest selves were in gear and our negativity gone. There was an excitement in the room as we all arrived, honoring this rule; there was no telling what could happen, and every class was different, completely unpredictable.

And it was advised to skip dinner rather than be late. We weren't allowed to eat after class, because it would mess up the established sacred energy that was created there. Going to bed hungry was a great way to work on your false self. Breaking the habit of eating made you so clear inside. And sometimes, Helen suggested *all* of us skip dinner, just so we could experience ourselves differently as a group.

We sat on cushions in a semi-circle on the floor. Helen and Damien ran the meetings, with Melissa sitting next to Helen.

Silence fell over us, and my eyes focused on the night falling in through the windows. The ocean rustled faintly; if there was a wind, I couldn't hear it. There were no foghorns, and the evening felt extra quiet. Except for my loud heart beats. Helen's wrath was awful.

"It's not the situation, but rather our negativity, that makes our lives so miserable. You are all very privileged to be here, to learn, to study how to rid yourselves of this negative way of life." Helen looked around at all of us. "Tim, for example."

Tim was June's husband.

"I am so proud of you. Every plank you carried for the steeple's foundation, you carried with love and without a single negative sliver touching you."

How could she know?

"But the others..." Helen's voice moved to a slow rumble, her eyes deliberately falling on about five other men. "You were all resentful, thinking, perhaps, that guys back at home get paid for doing labor like this, yes? Thinking that you were being used by me, isn't this so? Forgetting completely how you are free to walk out at any moment?"

She sat up straight, her long neck curved forward slightly. Dark curls swept over her forehead and fell to her chin.

Lisa's scream, her body with her arm stretched and curled in that awful way on the beach and the ambulance screech kept showing up in my mind. I stared out the window; moths, hundreds of them, were fluttering against it, near the one outside lamp.

She would lay into me, next.

"... forgetting completely about your true selves, and how you must pay with your negativity first, correct? If you give up your negativity, you will be richer than rich!! You are serving God here, yes?"

Her eyes were flashing. The men were slumping, including David who was working like the rest of the guys, 24/7. I couldn't imagine what he was going through. We hadn't talked for a week.

"Everyone on that crew, except for Tim, must undo every single plank laid down this morning as the entire project must be redone."

I'd been told often enough that waking up took extra effort. And it seemed to me that people *were* being taught something. But me, I had hurt Lisa with my negligence. That was completely unacceptable — in a category all of its own. Mom's rage scorched my mind. *What's wrong with you?* Her coffee cup had lain broken on the kitchen floor, coffee spilling off the table onto her lap. Wendy had been tantruming in the mess, shards surrounding her. *You made me do this, scaring Wendy and me, coming in so quietly.* Squirming now in my seat, I glanced at Damien who was looking at Helen. He probably hated me for hurting his niece, thinking I was the most irresponsible person he'd ever met. I wished I had been hurt instead. Anything would be better than this stabbing feeling in my chest. I could feel David's eyes on me so I stared at him. He looked exhausted.

"By dinnertime tomorrow night, triple the amount of work you did today, and this time without a single thought of resentment. Tim, you will oversee the project."

I saw Tim nodding out of the corner of my eye. I don't think anyone was breathing.

A few tears fell down Helen's cheeks. She turned her back to us, and Damien started in.

"Helen loves you all so much. You can't know why she does the things she does. Follow?" He paused and looked at each of us in turn, but his eyes hardly lingered on me the way they used to.

I wiggled in my seat. Helen probably was psychic. And sensitive. I longed to let her know that I knew what this was like, to be so misunderstood. But then, I was nothing like her, how could I even pretend to understand her, this, the goings on here?

"June, you are responsible for a large part of the resentment going on around here," Helen said. "You have been with us for seven years, and you still have a pout on your face. I must say that I am afraid for Tim."

Helen turned around, her shining eyes still moist. She dazzled her smile on Damien. "I think, June, I will give you time to turn this around. You can go to the solitary cabin for three days. Clara and Vicki will look after your children during the day, and Melissa and Tim will take care of them at night.

"Use this time to reflect and change. If you can't..." She shuddered, a tear or two slowly falling out from under her lids. "I'm afraid you'll have to leave..."

My legs, arms, head felt like cement. The moths didn't stop. I wanted to take a hammer to the window. Smash them.

"And if you do go, I'm afraid for your mental state. To leave with as much knowledge as you have, without waking up, is to die a spiritual death, and that is the worst death of all. You could become psychotic, and the children can't be around that."

Damien cleared his throat, and the abrupt noise made me jump. My knuckles had turned white, I was clenching them so hard, just like Dad's. "Before we end tonight's meeting, I want to acknowledge Clara who's done a phenomenal job with the children. Even Vicki looks better tonight."

What?

Helen beamed, "Seldom has a pure energy like Clara's come into my vision. June, filling your quota with Clara was a remarkable gesture. As you go into silence contemplate on that."

She was *really* going into silent confinement for three days? *I* was the one who deserved that kind of treatment. *I* was the one who brought in the children that day I arrived, interfering with June's sacred work on herself. I should've told Helen, I should've told Dad so many things and didn't. Like when I had caught Wendy taking drugs at the beach; when I had filled Mom's flask as she had demanded, *Don't tell your father, do you hear me? It's our special secret.* She'd kissed me on the cheek, opened her hand, her wrinkled fingers shaking as I took the quarter quivering there... And that day in the car with her, *What are you doin' lady?...fuck you lady...*making me promise I wouldn't tell Dad.

"Clara dear...you are invited to come to my rooms tomorrow morning for a reading." Her velvety voice brought me back. "In three nights we'll have a women's meeting after our regular one."

As I walked toward the door, Damien stretched out his hand. Our fingers lingered as he spoke with Melissa who was standing with Tim. I thought I saw Miriam nodding and smiling, and unexpectedly the possibility of becoming a teacher here occurred to me again. I'd work so closely with Damien that our relationship would be even more intimate than his was with Melissa. And when June came out of confinement she'd be a great mentor for me. Outside, the cloudy night was getting lighter. There were only a few moths fluttering. I was too excited to sleep, and anyway the kids would be up the minute the sun rose.

THE FRONT of Helen's cabin faced the ocean. With wall-to-wall windows, the morning light fell across the wooden floor. Wicker chairs faced the wood-burning stove, and the spotless kitchen was toward the back. Instead of a loft, wide pinewood stairs led to the second floor, where I imagined an enormous bedroom, spotless, with the sun and the stars pouring through curtainless windows.

I sat in a straight-backed wicker chair, facing her rocking one. A round, brown-orange cushion softened the seat, and a woven rug, much like the one in the lodge, covered the floor around us. The wood sparking inside the stove gave off a smoky, pleasant smell.

"Welcome. Thank you for being so prompt."

Helen wore a long, silky turquoise skirt that fell in pleats to the ground. A golden top flowed over her chest and down toward the floor, turquoise lace lined the neck and sleeve cuffs.

I felt awkward in my torn jeans and muddy green T-shirt.

Helen closed her eyes and asked me to do the same. To my great surprise she said nothing about the way I looked.

"Mary has many messages for you, hon. You must listen without interruption. If there is time for questions at the end, you may ask. I will do all the talking, but it is Mary speaking through me, yes?" She widened her eyes.

"Mary is saying that you were born to dance."

My eyes opened in shock.

"You needed this gift to escape your family. Your mother drank too much, and your sister took drugs. Your father wanted you to be something you couldn't, so you danced for hours and entered an entirely different world."

I stopped breathing. Helen kept her eyes on me, and didn't stop.

"You recently gave up dancing because your soul knew that you did not need it any longer. You will dance again, in time. Right now, it will only hurt you...you are in the middle of building a beautiful spirit... repairing so many holes."

Helen's face changed. Her cheeks puffed out, and she was leaning over, her body frail, like an ancient old lady. Her voice deepened.

"God has sent you to ASI to find your True Self. You have found the family you were always meant to have. Helen, Damien, Melissa will not lead you astray, and you are ASI teacher material."

I froze.

"Oh!" Helen clapped her hands and her perfectly straight white teeth glistened as she smiled. "I had *thought* this was true, but now I have real confirmation! It's more important than ever that you open your heart to us." She paused.

The wood was popping in the stove.

"And that brings me to your longing... to be with Damien."

Good God. This had to be real. I had never spoken about my feelings for Damien to anyone.

"He's tapped into your longing, but that's his gift and his work at ASI. Every time you feel longing for Damien, or anyone, in fact — your sister, father, mother, dance -- know this is a longing for God. He exists right here," she pointed to the center of her chest, "inside of each of us, and it's here, you'll find real love."

245

I couldn't close my mouth. Kleep had told me something similar.

Helen blinked, yawned and smiled "You are a gem. I'll do everything in my humble power to help you."

She closed her eyes. I tiptoed out of the cabin. Sunlight poured through the tall trees. The sea wind caught my scarf, blowing its ends behind me. I walked slowly down the path to the beach, forgetting where I was, what I was supposed to be doing.

THIRTY

WENDY

I walked into Minister Kleep's office, and there was this like grey-haired older lady who looked like she was still living in the fifties. Dad was already there.

This round, bald-headed man came out and greeted us. His eyes were like fucking bluer than fucking blue. He led us into a completely empty office except for some chairs and his desk that he sat behind, and motioned Dad and me to sit across.

"Yes, my children?"

He had to be kidding. Who was he fucking talking to?

Dad shook the minister's hand and like introduced us. The minister nodded again, waiting.

Dad cleared his throat. I like jumped in.

"We know that your daughter is missing like my sister, Clara, and we're here because we like want to know if you know her."

Dad's face was fucking red hot red. And his eyes fucking shot bullets at me. Well, shit, someone had to say something.

Kleep raised his eyebrows. "The name sounds familiar. A girl who enjoys dancing, I recall."

Dad sat up. "You know her?"

"She comes to worship from time to time and has been in here asking me questions about God."

"When?" Dad was up almost like at Kleep's throat.

"I don't know." He pulled his head away and like cleared his throat. "Please sit back down, Doctor. I know what it feels like to have a missing child..."

Dad like ignored him. His tone was low, his nose close to Kleep's. "She's been missing for months, and you sit here and tell me you don't remember when you last saw her? You don't have an address, you don't have any idea?"

"Mine too. My daughter has been missing for months, but the Lord..."

"Yes, that's why we're here." Dad said quietly.

Kleep looked closer at him and spoke more slowly. "Yes, Doctor, my daughter has also been gone for months. I have no idea where she is. No one has heard anything from her."

We were all like quiet. Dad finally withdrew his face but not his eyes. The two men stared at each other. I couldn't like see Dad, but Kleep's eyes were teary, and he put his hands on top of Dad's.

"It's a horrible thing." Dad's voice was softer.

"It is, Doctor."

"How are you making your way?"

"Jesus, Job, Jonah..."

Dad like shook his head. I could barely hear him. I had to put my head like really close to his. He didn't notice. "I can't... I can't... You don't see..."

"You've suffered greatly. We've daughters missing. We've that suffering in common. God brings us who suffer together, so we don't have to be alone."

This fucking minister was like fucking amazing.

"Never has God felt so palpable to me. He beats with every one of my heartbeats. I can help you find Him."

Dad lowered his eyes. He whispered so that now both Kleep and I had to lean closer to him to hear. "I don't think that will be possible for me."

Dad always looked like he was going to murder someone when God or religion was even mentioned. But this time there was like a weird awkward silence, like I didn't know if Dad was suddenly going to leap from his chair and throw it at Kleep or what, and my heart was fucking racing. No matter what happened, I knew Kleep was the minister for me.

"Here," Kleep responded. He gave Dad some paper and a pen. "Write down your phone number. If your daughter comes again, I'll call you. Right away."

We all like shook hands. I couldn't believe Dad's calm demeanor, or my fucking good luck. A fucking minister who not only knows Clara but who could also actually help me find God in my heart. This was fucking great! I couldn't wait to tell Jake. We'd like come to church every Sunday, we'd find Clara, and I'd have my answers about God, finally.

Dad looked sadder than I'd ever seen him. Fucking Clara. I was more determined than ever to fucking find her.

THIRTY-ONE

JOE

Joe was deep in thought as he walked with Wendy to Tom Yein's Chinese Restaurant, just a few blocks down Clement Street. Minister Kleep, Father John. So similar. John's belief in Christ had been as solid as the minister's. John's mission was to save their lives... and Kleep's? Possibly, the same. Both spoke gently, both genuine. At least Clara was still in San Francisco. She wasn't in Korea and probably wasn't a Moonie. That was a relief. Wendy was distracting, what with her leaping ahead and then stopping to wait. That girl could never stay still. He pictured her at six, leapfrogging around the park; he couldn't help but smile as she bounced back toward him, gesturing wildly. She was much better.

"Watch it Dad!" And she yanked him by the arm. "Like, you're walking against a fucking red light."

Jesus, she was right.

"You fucking gotta pay attention. I can't lose you too. Shit."

"You swear too much." She said often that she was trying to work on it, but he hadn't seen much progress.

Jake was waiting for them at the restaurant. Joe had had no idea what to expect, but certainly not what he saw: a tall, lanky young man with short blonde hair and black eyes

After they ordered, Joe said, "Wendy tells me you're Jewish."

"What the fuck?"

"Wendy!" He admonished his daughter again.

Jake swallowed and nodded.

"You look German." A stupid comment. There were thousands of German Jews with blonde hair. Wendy's mouth was wide open.

"That's right..."

"What are you doing with yourself?"

The waiter placed their dishes on the table. Shrimp in Lobster Sauce, Beef and Broccoli, Chinese Eggplant, General Tso's Chicken.

Wendy piled almost the entire platter of chicken onto her plate and topped it with more than half the rice.

"Working on a commune in Berkeley, mostly..."

"You should see the apartment he just fucking put together, fucking out of this world..."

"You're spitting your food..."

"Hey babe, it's okay. Here." Jake took his napkin and wiped her mouth. She burst out laughing, spewing bits of rice and chicken everywhere.

They were children. Kids. Having fun. But no sense of responsibility. Jake couldn't make a living working on a commune. German Jewish. Polish Jewish. True responsibility had been wiped out. Excerpts of Poe's poem, *Alone*, went round and round in his mind.

From childhood's hour I have not been
As others were — I have not seen
As others saw...
And all I lov'd — I lov'd alone...
From the thunder, and the storm —
And the cloud that took the form
(When the rest of Heaven was blue)
Of a demon in my view –

He'd loved being at the Greenwoods, doing every chore they asked, from planting bulbs in the garden to getting straight "A's," all through school. Every Mother's Day, every Father's Day outdoing himself for Neil and Shirley and making sure Anna was a part of whatever surprise he'd planned. Creating that "play" of how he'd been adopted and how happy they both were to have each other, how grateful they were to Shirley and Neil. And Neil had treated Joe like his own and had never discussed Poland with him. But Neil loved poetry, and they often read at night — Yeats, Wordsworth and Poe. Perhaps it was Neil's way of letting Joe know he understood suffering without directly talking about Joe's loss, which Joe had purposely buried. And when Neil died of a sudden heart attack in Joe's junior year, he'd delved into Poe in his English class at Boston Latin. Sorrow had filled the Greenwood home. Sorrow had unraveled from his writing. His long paper on Poe. On tragedy. On death.The bill was in front of him. Money grew on trees for these kids. He was annoyed. Jake didn't even offer to contribute. But Wendy was standing behind him, her arms around his neck, her hair tickling his checks.

"Thanks," she said, "We'll find Clara, I just know it."

THIRTY-TWO
CLARA

"Well, June, what do you have to say for yourself? You've been given the opportunity to be solitary for three days and nights."

All the women were gathered for the women's meeting.

"Poor Lisa, arm in a cast because Rosa was out-of-control. And why was she, June, hmm?"

June's face was puffy and pale, and her eyes were red and swollen.

We were sitting around the large eating table in the kitchen. The lights were low, candles burning, and the full moon had risen over the ocean, its faint blue light seeping into the windows.

I twined and untwined the ends of my scarf.

"I've been doing so much thinking these last few days." June answered. "I've been plain exhausted from parenting and have fully forgotten about the Light I truly am..."

Helen banged her hand down on the table.

Melissa jumped, I let out an "oh," and covered my mouth.

"June!" Melissa's voice was sharp, pointy, scratchy. "You had three full days to turn this around, your own daughter was picking up your negativity. Don't you get it? That's why she broke Lisa's arm..."

Helen smiled at Melissa.

I wished I had my hair back so I'd have something real to pull and feel. The scarf was too gentle. I put my thumbnail in my mouth and bit hard.

"Your first sentence *began* with a negative. 'I have been plain exhausted...' You could have said, 'I have renewed energy to shine the light I truly am'."

It was a loud, tense silence as Melissa paused. Her eyes remained on June, whose head was down.

"It's time to go." Melissa relayed, pointedly. "You've been here for seven years, and your negativity is shameful. There should not have been a false thought within your being as you greeted the kids coming off the bus."

It's my fault! I did it. I did it. I did it. I couldn't lift my tongue, or even a finger. Was she really going to leave and give up her children? And what about Tim? I didn't know about him, but what would I do without her?

But then, we hadn't seen each other for months. I swallowed and found my breath. Mary, of all beings, had spoken to me. If Helen deemed June too negative to be around, mightn't there be some truth to this? I bit my thumb harder. Mary should have been around for Mom and Dad, especially when Dad accused Mom, which was often. *Those are dangerous,* Dad had yelled at her, *Why can't you keep an eye on her?* Mom had thrown a book of music at him. *Fuck you,* she'd screamed. Wendy crying so hard. The book smashing against a window sounded like June's chair as she scraped it back. I was frozen, on my own, covering my ears, even as I wanted to run after her.

Helen was speaking to me. "I want to commend you, Clara. You handled that emergency with the children beautifully. You will make a wonderful mother after you marry David."

What. Married? No. But her word, like Dad's, was difficult to disobey. With Helen, *everything* came from Mary. I'd better knock all negative thoughts right out of my system and be grateful. I took my thumb out of my mouth. The nail was deep red around the edges. I pushed my chair back to run after June, but Helen smiled at me again. Her teeth struck me. They looked different than the photos back home. They were no longer crooked. But June was at the door before I could even say good-bye.

Every woman in the room was hugging and congratulating me. Things were happening so fast, I had no time to think.

Someone must've left the door open, because as I was embraced, I heard Lisa crying. "Don't go Mommy!" I looked down at the floor. There was a small crack running from beneath a chair leg up to the edge of the woven rug.

THIRTY-THREE
WENDY

Fall

"Mind-control exists in a two-person cult, such as in a marriage, in small groups — even in families — and in massive, mastermind cults, such as the one Reverend Moon runs. Those who have left The People's Temple have called Reverend Jim Jones a cult leader.

"Here's what we've been doing about this..."

I was like mesmerized. I couldn't keep my eyes off of Dr. Beatrice Goldman. She was short and round, with this like red hair that curled all around her face. And her face was sprinkled with freckles; I mean, I'd never seen so many spots on anyone in all my fucking life. She wore like those gold Granny glasses, and a black suit with a tie. She was the guest speaker for our Family Systems psychology course.

After class, Jake and I were in the student lounge, and I like couldn't stop talking about her.

"I think she can help us find Clara. She's a fucking 'debriefer,' Jake. I mean she's been to fucking *Korea,* and she like brings whole *families* over to have like family therapy sessions with the cult victims once she frees them. She's fucking amazing."

"Well that's like great, if you can fucking afford to go to Korea to have a fucking family therapy session."

"She's has like fucking government *grants* 'cause she's brilliant."

"I hope she's not too busy to help you."

I loved it when Jake was like agreeing with me. "I'm going to tell Dad about her."

"I wouldn't."

We'd bought coffees, and I poured fucking twenty small creamers into mine. "You're so fucking pessimistic."

He leaned on his elbows and moved closer in. I melted. His black-brown eyes were like fucking deer eyes. So gorgeous.

"Your Dad would never go for someone like her. She's too weird. Who's ever heard of like a fucking 'debriefer'?"

I leaned over and kissed him. That like ended that conversation.

FUCK. I should have like listened to Jake. He was so fucking right.

Dad and I were sitting in his studio on the third floor. I missed Mom's fucking art room. All those like turpentine smells. I think *that* was like the first thing that ever got me high. Just inhaling all of that fucking turpentine when I was young.

He was at his desk, and I was on the window seat. The windows were open. It was freezing, but Dad didn't notice. The foghorns sounded so fucking forlorn.

"A 'debriefer'?"

"Well, you should just fu... I mean you should like call her. You never know. She may have something really smart to suggest. I mean you won't go to the police..."

"How many times have I told you? Both the adolescent drug recovery wards are in full swing."

He put his hands to his chest and closed his eyes.

"Dad, like are you okay?"

"Everything is fine. I'm tired. Working long hours. The wards. I can't let this leak. This Beatrice person. We don't know her. Perhaps she has heard of the wards. Perhaps she will tell a news reporter. Then the story is out. My name is ruined. Do you understand?"

Then he pulled out a photograph from underneath one of his piles. He sat down next to me, and we both gazed at Mom, Clara and me sitting around the huge art table Mom used to have. Mom's hair was falling out of her loose braid, and both Clara and I were sitting close, but she was looking at me with a huge, glorious fucking smile.

Dad was talking.

"I'm happy you're well. I'm happy you have Jake. Be grateful."

Looking at Mom, I felt an ache in my chest and a lump in my throat. I wanted her back. Her smile was so contagious, I couldn't handle looking at her and put the photo down, only to pick it up again. I pulled it in close, and my heart stopped. I saw God in her fucking smile. That's what'd made her so gorgeous. I said to Dad, "I miss her so much. It's so hard to feel ok. Like there's a piece of me missing. Nothing will feel right until I find Clara."

"We'll find her. Everything is ok." But he kept staring at the photo. And his voice had no feeling in it.

And suddenly all of this fucking frustration exploded out of me. "God, fucking damn Clara. All she does is cause fucking trouble, all the fucking fights you guys had, no wonder Mom fucking drank."

And his face, red as the Devil's, was in mine. "Get out. Your attitude is repulsive. Repulsive, do you hear me?" A thick, medical journal went whizzing, slamming against the door. Another was in his hands. "Get out." He was sputtering, spitting. As I left, the journal crashed to the floor.

THIRTY-FOUR

CLARA

E arly the next morning, David woke me with strong hugs and kisses all over my face and neck.

"Wake-up! We've until 1 today to be together. We're going down to the beach."

It was still dark, not even 5 a.m., as I reluctantly rose to help him pack fruit, veggies and sandwiches.

The ocean shone cold and silver in the early dawn, its waves sparkling like stars. The wind banged against my back, pushing me faster down the steep slope than I wanted to go. David ran like a wild man, loping down the rocks, yelling at me to hurry.

I wanted to go back to bed. My nails were bitten down to the skin, and layers of dirt lay beneath them. My arms looked like sticks, and my body like a boy's.

David was yelling to me from the beach. He held out his arms, wide. "They're so cold without you, hon. Hurry up!"

I resisted the wind as best I could and slowly made my way down, studying the dew on the wildflowers, the small night insects still plopped on the petals. I imagined the nectar and scent luring them. They looked drunk, and if they weren't careful the morning sun would kill them.

"Come on, what're you doing? Time is going!" He came bounding up and folded me into a hug, smelling of strawberries. I pushed him away but felt sorry. I grabbed his hand, as if I had been only playing. When we reached the beach, he led me to a sandy spot between the rocks, up and away from the water. The sun was rising, its deep red rays blushing the ocean below, and the whitecaps held fast on the swelling waves.

David pulled all sorts of groundcover out of his backpack: a blue tarp, two black, down sleeping bags, unzipped, that he lay close together, two real pillows, a couple of blankets, large canteens filled with water, jars of berries, and fresh bread and cheese.

The rocks dug into my shoulder blades as he got on top of me, and his sweat dripped down onto my chest. My body would not respond. Dry and hurting, I lied to him throughout the process, bearing the pain of him inside of me as best I could. When it was over, I rolled to my side, my back to him.

"Helen is the best, don't you think?" David said, rolling over, too, stroking my baby hair.

"Yup." I said softly, hoping to express sleepy contentment, her perfect teeth flashing through my mind. I was about to ask him about them, but he wanted to talk.

"You know what I want to do? Apply to law school when I get back. I spoke with Damien and told him I'd like to represent this school: be the lawyer for it. Damien thought it was an incredible idea."

"It is!" I was suddenly interested, turned around to look at him.

He laughed, patting my head. "I like you bald..."

I tried to picture myself in his eyes. Bald. A gull suddenly landed on the ocean's edge, he flapped rapidly toward us, his ugly head wobbling. One of the most disgusting birds on the planet.

David threw a rock near him, and his curdling scream seemed to roughen the waves.

I stood up, gathering my clothes.

"Baby, hon, what happened? Come here, sweetie." Sitting up, small grey-blue eyes wide, he spread out his arms again. "Sit down. You can't just walk away like this."

But I did.

He was in front of me in no time, picked me up and carried me in his arms like a baby back to our sitting area.

I kicked and cried, but he kept kissing me, making loud smacking sounds that eventually got me laughing.

Placing me back down on the sleeping bags, he massaged my shoulders and spoke so softly and kindly that I nestled into his arms.

Pulling me back underneath him, he made love to me again. It was not much better this time. The howling wind moved in between the rocks, making the waves crash like crazy. I imagined each grain of sand, every flower petal, wings of birds and all of the unseen crawling and flying critters, soaking wet and crushed from the wild and raw ocean spray.

The sky darkened suddenly, and rain came down faster than the waves were crashing.

We dressed fast and rapidly walked single file up the path in silence. David had said, "I know a lawyer who can write up a contract for ASI and me. The contract will say that I can take time off from ASI, but the minute I graduate and begin work, I give ASI half of my income for five years!"

Maybe there was a reason, after all, to be with him. If he could get back to law school with a contract like that, I could get back to dancing and finally open my own dance studio. In spite of the instructions from my reading with Mary, the desire to dance was still enormous. But, first things first. Once I was an ASI teacher, dance would fall into place.

~

I WAS WALKING toward the main house in the rain after leaving David. Melissa came bounding up to me, like Tigger. "I've got great news for you!" She was startling, with her crazy high-pitched voice and excitement. I was walking toward the main house in the rain.

"You get to work in the kitchen with me. You'll take June's place and help me create recipes. It's a lot of fun...!"

"Am I really the right person...?"

"Don't be silly, hon -- Helen has commented often on your purity..." We walked toward the kitchen, linking arms.

"Tim and I will look after her children. I don't know why June became so negative. There's a part in us that just can't rise above that place, you know... but if her kids couldn't have reminded her, why couldn't Tim?" She giggled and flipped her hair about. We were almost flying.

Damien had told me a long while back, *never take anything at face value, hon, you'll see weird things going on, but remember whatever you think is happening... it's just the opposite. All of us teachers are here to help you wake up.*

Soaked to the bone, we peeled off our socks and shoes. Water dripped from our heads to our shoulders as we walked barefoot into the kitchen. Melissa, giggling too much, opened a cupboard and pulled out two pairs of sandals. She pulled me toward a counter. "Create anything you like," she sang. "Here are some recipes, make one up if you like!"

Garlic bulbs hung in small baskets over the windows, and fresh bunches of basil, oregano, mint and thyme were sitting on plates, all just picked. In addition, cucumbers, broccoli, kale and spinach were near the sink, washed, chopped and ready for cooking.

Three crystal vases filled with orange and red wildflowers were placed evenly on the counters, adding color and joy to the kitchen.

While Melissa sizzled onions, I made cookie dough, realizing we'd have to have milk with them, and the very thought made me see Wendy's face turning blue from choking and milk all over the table. *Do it,* Mom had said, *Do it, now.* The dough was like Wendy's baby fat and as thick, as I rolled it into a thick ball, my fists clenched. And I was trying to pick Wendy up, and Mom was saying, *You're going to drop her, for Christ's sake, she's not a doll.* And someone was breathing down my neck, telling me to chop the butter more, and I turned, clenching my jaw and threw the entire ball of dough. I heard Melissa cry out. She was over my shoulder, only trying to help, and suddenly there was cookie dough stuck on her face and falling in chunks down her hair.

"Bitch!" she yelled, and took some from her hair and rubbed it on my cheeks and forehead.

"Asshole," I said taking up the left-over butter and smearing it across her chest.

She grabbed a plateful of chopped spinach and threw the entire thing at me. I ducked; it smashed against the wall, and I picked up the whole bowl of dough and tossed it at Melissa's head. Chocolate chips, bags of flour and sugar, and all sorts of herbs and veggies went flying.

We fell on the floor, I yanked her hair, she screamed and bit my hand. We hugged tightly, rolling around like dough in the fallen flour and sugar, pulling each other's hair, crying and then finally laughing so hard we cried again, clenched together like a pair of fists.

EVER SINCE THAT FOOD FIGHT, I'd felt more like a peer to Melissa. And that October, after I'd come home from the farm, I threw myself into my waitressing job and all the extra chores at ASI. I'd always loved October. The early darkness always felt cozy and made it easier to clean the ASI kitchen, do the towel-and-sheet laundry there, or rearrange and purge junk from the shelves. David had remained on the farm, as he continued to work on the steeple.

Melissa had asked me to be home at a particular time. And when I walked into the kitchen, she couldn't contain herself. "Helen wants you to be a mentor for new students. Congratulations!" She grinned, beckoning me to sit across from her at the table. "She says that Mary has finally given her the OK, and that this is your Thanksgiving gift."

I smiled, unable to speak. This was the first step in becoming an ASI teacher and then back to dance. Helen really did care about what was best for me, unlike Dad. I imagined him reading his paper, watching the news and sports on television. It wouldn't occur to him to do otherwise. He held desperately onto things, unlike me, who was truly learning to let go.

There was a coffee pot, a stack of business papers and two brand new, blue-inked Bic pens between us on top of the table.

As Melissa leaned in to hand me one, I detected small dark lines underneath her eyes. The "pink cotton" nail polish was too thick on some of her nails, unusual for meticulous Melissa. Tim was still on the farm, and due to the daycare up there, the kids were with him. Once he returned, Melissa would be moving in with him.

She took out her flask and poured whiskey into her coffee, offering me the same, but I refused. She was careful not to spill a single drop onto any of the papers. The stack was at least two inches thick; "Bank of America" was written in bold black letters across the top.

"Hon, what this means is that you will need to step up even more as an older student, but more importantly this signifies that Helen is actually inviting you into our family."

"Aren't I already a part of that?"

"Not officially." She shook her head, blonde curls looking oiler, dirtier than usual. "Helen brilliantly created a Family Total Bank Account for us teachers and mentors. We all pool our money into the account, and Helen, along with her accountant, has complete charge. When you give me money, I give that to the accountant, and he places it all into the Total account."

I lifted my eyebrows.

"The account will pay for your rent, utility bills and all expenses for ASI. You'll receive an allowance of ten dollars a week but given that all expenses are paid, you won't even need it! If you decide to leave ASI, you receive back all that you pooled-in, minus whatever expenses you may owe."

This was absolute heaven. No more money worries. I bit down on my nail and quickly took my index finger out of my mouth. I'd still have to keep working hard to pay for the expenses, but as Melissa pointed out, when all that money was pooled together, it made a ton of interest.

"If I understand this correctly, I give you all my money. As long as I keep up my earning with my expenses, I am earning interest for the account. The ten dollars a week is drawn from that interest. But, if for some reason, I can't keep up with my expenses... then I can draw on money from the account. But by doing this, I am running up a debt, and more money will be tacked to my monthly expenses."

Melissa nodded. "And the moment you sign the agreement and put in your cash, that is the moment you begin training for mentoring. If you decide not to do this, we need to consider how serious you are about being here. Helen will understand by your negation..."

I dug into my pockets and pulled out piles of coins and dollar bills and laid them on the table in front of us. I poured the last cups of coffee, and Melissa emptied her flask into hers. She picked up the stack of papers, pounded them on the table so all the corners met and pushed the first pages in front of me to sign.

"These explain what the account will do for you..."

I signed each and every paper. I hadn't slept for at least four days and had had little else to eat other than pots of black coffee.

I was elated at my good fortune.

I T W A S our usual meeting time, around 1 a.m. a few days later, and we were sitting in the restaurant, at three tables pulled together. Helen had flown in from Oregon and was at the head, dressed in black velvet.

"You have all shown such significant dedication to ASI, which is why I have exclusively invited just the handful of you to help me out with my new idea, which must be launched in two weeks' time."

I knew that tonight I was glowing like her. She had told Melissa that she was so happy to have a 'daughter' like Clara pool into the Total Account, and that I would be "one of the best mentors ASI would ever have."

I couldn't sit still; I'd be meeting my first new student in just a short time, although I didn't know when.

"We need more students, and I have many exciting future plans for expansion, but first things first."

The restaurant was dimly lit; the photos of Helen and staff had their own lights, like paintings in a museum. The light gave a soft, impressionistic grain to the still faces.

"Starting next Friday, I'll be giving weekly luncheon talks. We'll call them, *Conversing with Helen*. The topics of discussion will be the importance of organic farming and the necessity of families staying together. You all know how opposed I am to divorce and this crazy idea of 'free love.'"

Free love? I shuddered, remembering how I'd pulled Wendy by the hair, dragging her off the beach. She'd fought me off and said, *I'm my own woman now*, and had kissed that much larger, greasy, long-haired guy with the guitar... I sat up as straight as I could. I was here, with Helen. My new family.

She raised her hands up to heaven, the bell sleeves falling up to her elbows. "Dear Mother of Jesus, Sweet, Wonderful Mary," she cried, looking upward and then back down at us, "Your Sacred Design for us humans is family, community, health, education and love of the earth.

The purpose of marriage is to push one another to our deepest and highest selves, and divorce is an escape, a farce!"

She brought her hands down and looked around. "We are servants of the Creator, yes? If you bring children into this world, you must take care of them.

"But what if you can't? What if you go crazy trying to do this work, as so many have? Here at ASI, we have community, we have dedicated and educated people studying together, so that when one member must leave, we are all here to protect the children. Yes?"

Her eyes were unblinking as she made contact with every one of us. I could have sworn that those photos on the wall became five- or six-dimensional. I was still, like a four-year-old, engrossed in a story.

"We'll be selling tickets to these luncheons, and here's how." Helen clapped her hands excitedly and her tone became light, like a child going to her own birthday party. The difference in her voice was stunning and difficult to adjust to. Like Wendy's had been, black circles under her eyes, skinnier than a toothpick, one minute had screamed, *Give me 100 fucking dollars, now*, and the next she was sobbing on my dorm-room floor, looking like a small tick in the blankets I'd given her. She'd said, *Tell me a story, the way you used to, remember?*

My feet beat up and down, making an unwanted tapping sound. I slammed my hands down on my thighs, willing them to stop. She's not my family. She's *not*. Still, the memory fell in. I'd sat on the floor, tucking her further into the blanket bed I'd made. Stroking her wet hair, I'd said, *Remember how Mom played Mozart, and we sat with Dad in his chair? And while she played, he told us about the daffodils? 'I wandered lonely as a cloud/that floats on high o'er vales and hills/When all at once I saw a crowd/A host of golden daffodils.'* Wendy recited the last line, *'Beside the lake, beneath the trees/ fluttering and dancing in the breeze.'* And then, she whispered, *Remember how Dad would say, 'You are my little dancing daffodils?'* And she stroked my cheeks so gently, as if she saw me as that.

Helen's voice was excitable again, like a strong wind tossing me back into the room. "You'll stop people spontaneously on the streets and convince them to buy tickets for a lunch they'll never forget! I am expecting no less than thirty people every single Friday for the next two months! It's a wonderful way to observe your negativity and turn it around!"

There was a sudden buzz all around the table, as if a hive of bees had just been let loose. The idea was brilliant. I felt inspired. A small fire was spreading through my belly, smoking out all memories. This was the way I used to feel just before I went on stage. I was sure I could sell all the tickets in ten minutes. I saw myself riding the buses, inviting the regulars I saw every day. I pictured Karen, the nurse who rode the same route as me at 6 a.m. She always wore blue uniforms and squeaky white sneakers. Her dirty-blonde hair was usually pulled back with a black clip. We were both up all night, she with her patients and me with my customers.

"You must sell them in pairs; this is a community, remember? If you sell by yourself, you do not have as much of an opportunity to observe yourselves. No one pushes you like your sister or brother beside you, yes?"

Jesus. That would be impossible. So much easier to do this on my own. Between work and class, there weren't even three minutes, let alone a few hours, to schedule this with anyone.

Melissa caught my eye. She nodded, as if to say, we'll sell together. She looked awful. Her normal bouncy curls looked flattened, oily and almost matted. Something was up with her. And I didn't really care. And yet, as her peer, that probably wasn't ok. I smiled back at her and nodded.

The problem was that she had never seen me as an equal; yet, everywhere I went, there she was. She took a hostess position at one of the evening shifts I worked. She was there on the same nights as me. And when at times I had to change my shift, she also changed hers. She'd shrug. "Remember, we need to be at the same meetings at the same time?"

She gave me a huge hug, clinging to me, as Helen said, "You understand, Melissa? No less than thirty people every Friday noon." Helen's tone was sharp, her

brows raised and mouth pursed together.

A FEW DAYS LATER, I was already fifteen minutes late to our first ticket adventure. My hair, finally growing out, was matted with sweat as I galloped down Castro Street to the Castro Street BookStore. The dusk sky was darkish blue, and it was cool — a breezy fifty degrees. Crowds of people moved as one, impossible to shove past.

Campaign signs touting Harvey Milk for City Supervisor were on every storefront. Transvestites and gays were handing out pamphlets that read "Gay Rights Now," "Down with Anita Bryant," "Jesus was Black," "Jesus was Gay," "Jesus was a Transvestite." I couldn't help but laugh, feeling an odd camaraderie with all of this. Everyone was "coming out" and "being themselves," just like me. And yet ASI's entire philosophy went against the notion of homosexuality. Gayness was a defense against the True Self. No matter how hard I tried to understand this it didn't make any sense to me. You were born with sexual tendencies, and that was that. How could it be wrong to follow your heart? Melissa, on the other hand, cared deeply about setting the gay population straight. I giggled at my unintentional pun.

But none of this was funny to Melissa who was on fire to fix "these broken people" by bringing more into the school. "We'll go to Castro Street and sell tickets," she'd suggested, her eyes shining. "We'll even try to get Harvey Milk to join... huh? Can you imagine? That way we can truly apply the beauty of ASI's teachings. Gayness is an egoic defense, and now we have a chance to help."

Occasionally gay people had wandered into ASI. Some stayed and married, like Sue, but the others had left, stormed out. Emily had been kicked out for being too negative in her thinking and behaviors. She had refused to drop her "gayness."

Dad's stories had, after all, instilled a sense of justice inside of me. He had always said that there wasn't time for prejudice when you were saving lives, whether you were White, Black, Chinese, Japanese, straight, gay, poor or rich.

How long had it been since I'd seen him? What if Wendy had died? I ran faster. These thoughts are from the past, pay attention to what I have *now*. I lifted my knees higher, and my feet landed harder. After all, Helen had called me 'daughter'. I smiled, and my body felt lighter. For sure, I'd dance again, all the while bringing in new students. And Damien, so proud of me, would want to be with me, always.

I saw the bookstore awning finally. A huge navy blue sign with white letters: The Castro Street BookStore, and there was Melissa standing under it, her cheeks red flame, and her eyes not happy.

I was a rag of sweat, unable even to say hello, I was breathing so hard.

We stood silently until I could catch my breath. "Sorry. If I'd paid attention more closely and worked faster to clean my station at the café, I wouldn't be late now. You know how that inner falseness works, right?"

"You can't be late anymore. Not as a mentor." Melissa's mouth stayed nearly closed as she spoke. Her eyes were not sympathetic. "That's how Judy was kicked out, remember?"

I opened my mouth.

"Don't say a word. We just have to get to work. We need to stop those who really can pay for ASI; I am sick of these useless hippies who can't afford anything."

The sky was darkening, the first star coming through. The wind was sharper, and the sweat around my neck was cooling.

I frowned. Another huge judgment from Melissa. Had she ever stopped to talk to a panhandler? She was more than just unsympathetic. There was nervousness in her tone and tightness in her closed mouth that I'd only noticed recently. The corner of her upper right lip twitched uncontrollably several times while she spoke, and her threats about me being late didn't scare me, as they normally would have.

Melissa elbowed me hard on the side. "Pay attention."

I followed her gaze and saw two men coming toward us. Melissa stopped them and completely changed her mood. Slowly dancing around them, she asked, "Don't you love healthy food?" She moved more wildly, singing the question. Who was this person changing from tight-lipped to loose and creative, just like that? The two men stood staring at her, one taller than the other, with tattoos down his arm and his mouth open.

Her blonde hair, perfect tonight, fell across her shoulders, and her high black heels made a clicking sound against the pavement as she swirled.

I joined her. I moved in opposite directions, playing off of her food idea.

"Can you smell home-made bread?" She sang.

"Mmmmmmm," I responded and twirled.

"Can you taste the freshly whipped butter, straight from the cow?"

"Ooooooooooooh," I purred and then asked, "Where?"

"The Ancient Side of Eating, the best health food restaurant in the city..."

She swung me playfully and then turned her back, standing between the two men, making sure they couldn't make eye contact.

At that point, the taller of the two said, "Well you are entertaining enough, thank you. Dan?" He made a motion for his partner to start walking.

Melissa stood in front of Dan, and I faced the tall one. I motioned him to step aside so I could explain.

"Let Melissa be her crazy self, while we talk." I said, staring into his weary blue eyes and smiling. What the hell was I going to say to him? How could you explain ASI to anyone?

He continued to stare at me. "What is it? Because I'm tired, and I need to prepare..."

"Have you ever eaten at the Ancient Side of Eating?" It was the best I could do.

He shook his head.

"Do you enjoy fresh farm food, but I mean, the real deal?"

"Of course, dear, but I need to..."

"Would you like to buy two tickets to the most extraordinary meal you'll ever have?"

"Not really..."

A sharp pain hit the inside of my upper right rib cage, right below my breast. I opened my mouth to breathe more easily.

"Okay, well, I do hope you enjoyed our dance and song..."

"Look, ah... what's this all about? What tickets to a luncheon?" His eyes had softened. He was probably feeling sorry for me.

"Oh nothing." I put my head down on purpose. "I mean I'm really sorry we bothered you."

"Not at all, dear. What is it you're selling?"

I looked up at him, that sharp pain rolling into rapid heart flutters. "Tickets to an extraordinary luncheon and conversation with the owner."

"Do you have a flyer? I'll read it over..."

"We're a very creative group." That brilliant statement just fell out of me. "We don't like to take the easy road." Wow how true. "We take the road less traveled, just like Robert Frost says (thanks, Dad, for your constant reciting of poetry), and so, when we have events at our restaurant we like to hand-pick our customers and sell tickets spontaneously, you know, on the spot. That way the event will be more alive and clear..." I was on a roll. I never knew I could speak about ASI like this. It must have been my passion shining through, because he took two twenty-dollar bills out of his wallet and handed them to me.

I waved to Melissa, trying to stifle my excitement. But as she joined me I noticed that there were deep red blotches on her cheeks, and her eyes were screaming.

"What a jerk," she breathed into my ear. "Don't tell me they're coming? Helen will kill me, he was an arrogant S.O.B."

Melissa's jaw was clenched tight, and her fingers balled into fists. Here I had sold my first tickets, recruited my first two guests, and she was having a hissy fit. She should at least congratulate me. Where was her enthusiasm, support; in fact, where was her positive attitude? She grabbed my arm and we walked.

"What happened?"

"We got talking about gay-versus-straight..."

"What?"

"And before I knew it he was telling me that I didn't know shit about the True Self and that I should go join that orange juice Anita Bryant Bitch from Florida."

"Melissa." Chills were creeping down my back and along my arms. How could she have had the nerve to even talk about gayness? That conversation was meant for class, a teaching of ASI meant only for those of us who joined. *Just be yourselves,* Helen had said when she gave us this project, *no mention of any ideas that ASI teaches, because no one will understand.*

"You didn't accuse him of being gay, did you?"

"Why would I do that? And how many years have I taught this work? We just started talking about gay-versus-straight. And suddenly he was saying the most horrible things to me, as if I had threatened him..."

My arms swung by my side, my hands remarkably calm. Images of Melissa filling her coffee cup with whisky, of her unkempt appearance, floated into my mind. I heard Helen say to her, *No less than thirty a luncheon, yes?*

Something was up for her. Or she wouldn't have spoken like this. What if she were kicked out, like June? I was the apple of Helen's eyes now, not her. My heart was fluttering, and in spite of the cool evening there was sweat on my forehead. God, what would it be like to be free of her? No more Melissa... *I* was the one that got that guy to pay for those two tickets.

We stopped at a light. She turned toward me.

"That was good work. I know I said I didn't want them to come, but they will be perfect, you'll see."

Her voice was shaky, but she spoke without hesitation. It was a long light, more people gathered, and shmushed us closer.

I kept a steady gaze on her, much like I did with Wendy years ago, when I had wanted her to do something for me. I felt a familiar warmth tingle through my bones and knew for the first time that Melissa was scared, and that I now had something over her.

THIRTY-FIVE

JOE

Late Fall

It was Saturday, a grey, miserable foggy day. Another sleepless night. Anna had come running to him, her hair pulled back. Curly strands falling down her eyes. She'd thrown her arms around him and said, *I'm happy you're home. You must be very tired.* Her kiss was warm. He'd loved holding her small hands. Waking from these dreams was difficult. He grabbed his black journal and wrote:

> *The Nazis' hard steel-like boots*
> *Stomped on translucent skin, broken bones*
> *They ripped children from families*
> *like wings from birds*
>
> *Decades later*
> *Anna, in her high heels, wobbled like a small bird*
> *And died in the spring.*
>
> *I look down at my tired feet*
> *aching, worn out*

from their shoes.

He closed his eyes, hoping to sleep again, but he still heard Wendy yelling, *No wonder Mom drank...* He hated throwing things, hated it. But despised most of all Wendy's insensitivity and inability to think before she spoke. She could at times be just the opposite — kind and understanding — but he couldn't tolerate her impulsivity, cruelty and utter disrespect. Nor could he with Clara, for that matter. He never ever spoke to Neil and Shirley the way his girls spoke to him, the way Wendy had spoken two weeks ago. He understood that her frustration at Clara's silence was getting to her, as it had to him, but there was a way to discuss this. He was reasonable, after all.

And Wendy could not know the difficulties he'd had with Anna. He recalled that difficult conversation he'd had with Aaron so long ago. They'd grabbed turkey sandwiches wrapped in cellophane and found an empty table in the hospital cafeteria. The place stank of bad soups, and the walls needed a paint job. Slowly and carefully he'd unwrapped the cellophane, knowing the sandwich would taste like cardboard. *What's on your mind?* He'd asked Aaron.

Have you seen the latest article in the AMJ?

I haven't read the American Medical Journal for weeks.

There's new information about the effects of Valium.

He watched his fingers push the plastic off the sandwich.

Apparently, it's severely addicting.

Joe shot out of bed.

He didn't notice that it was just past dawn as he reached Ocean Beach. The wind was blowing hard, and he zipped up his thin jacket. The fog moved like a monster, fluid and fused together both at once.

Miriam continued to speak to him during the day, while Anna appeared in his dreams at night. He walked faster, and the fog moved even more rapidly over the ocean, covering it completely. The foghorns were loud, nonstop. Anna had loved them. *It would be so fun to bring a piano to the beach and make the fog dance, oh how wonderful that would be!* She'd loved this area, so much so that she lost track of time, sometimes staying out all night.

And on that dark morning when she'd walked in at 3 a.m., he'd confronted her, so worried. She'd said, *I took a long walk up and down the beach and found this cliff with marvelous rocks, and they had faces, Joe, some were wise and old, and some laughing, so I walked on them, talked with them, they were so inviting, don't you see? And I sat listening to the ocean.*

I don't understand, he'd tried staying calm. *It's 3 a.m. You're telling me the rocks had faces and told you to climb them?*

The ocean is so mesmerizing. You've said so yourself so many times. And I lost track of time.

She was nervous, raising her voice and pacing the floor.

You know how that is, more than anyone. All of those late house calls when you didn't call me to tell me you wouldn't be home for dinner.

Her face had reddened and she looked around frantically. *Where's my Valium?*

He'd put her suede coat over a kitchen chair. She'd walked unevenly to it and searched her pockets for pills; handfuls of sand spilled out of them and piled onto the floor. She'd sat right down on the pile, put her hands to her face and cried.

And a year later the cops had found her body on those same rocks. The Kaddish rose up from him again, and again he tried to stop it, but could not.

Yit'gadal v'yit'kadash sh'mei raba... **May we and those we touch be united with the ever-growing ever-increasing holiness that unites us.** *b'al'ma di v'ra khir'utei...***with those that inhabit this world,** *v'yam'likh mal'khutei b'chayeikhon uv'yomeikhon...* **May we be infused with the Majesty that is God, now and for our whole lives.**

uv'chayei d'khol beit yis'ra'eil... **and in the lives of all those who are members of the community of seekers.**

And Wendy had said, in one of her more thoughtful moments, *If you're going to help addicts, then you have to help them believe in God too. Like God is Love, and Love shows up in some fucking weird ways.*

God was a made-up notion by those who wanted full control of your mind, heart and soul. Addicts, controlled fully by drugs, cleaved to another drug-like belief system, in order to keep the status quo. Facing what he had had to was not anything these kids had endured. Wendy included.

Chills were building on chills up and down his arms and back. The sun was shrouded in grey mist, and the tide was up. His feet were freezing and made squishing noises inside his wet shoes as he strode quickly back to the car.

THIRTY-SIX
CLARA

Winter

I was on an incredible roll. I had brought over forty people to this first month of luncheons. That was an average of ten a week, or eight hundred dollars for the school. Quite a feat!

David, still on the farm, kept calling and telling me how proud he was of me, and didn't I think less and less of dance as I focused more and more on this task of giving back to Helen?

"I mean, that's how I'm looking at things. She's also given me a great privilege: she's put me in charge of the entire temple project! And the more I work on every single detail, the less I pay attention to law school."

I was in high gear as I boarded the city bus. Caking make-up on just before it arrived, to hide the deep black wrinkles under my eyes.

"And where are you headed this morning?" I asked the young woman sitting next to me.

She tossed her great black, Cher-like hair, permed and falling down her shoulders. "Dance class."

My eyes, already bloodshot and dry from lack of sleep, widened. That pain inside my upper right rib began to pong. "Oh?"

"I'm auditioning to join the classical troupe at the San Francisco Ballet."

This was completely unexpected. I scrambled to keep up my high energy. "Really?" I had even stopped listening to music lately, as every song I had ever loved reminded me of a dance I had been a part of.

"Yeah! I'm going to a callback. I'm so excited!"

"Of course." I swallowed, wondering when was the last time I'd had a glass of water. My hands were wrinkled, and my fingers scaly, not to mention the deep cuts along my nails. I was turning into Wendy, with her shriveled and shrunken fingers. Mine were not like that. I'd lotion them as soon as I could.

Looking into this woman's moist, deep brown eyes, I said, "I'm doing something exciting too. How would you like to come to the most extraordinary luncheon at the healthiest restaurant ever, listening to the owner herself..." I barely recognized my own voice. It sounded like a seagull's.

"I just love healthy, I'd love to come..."

Just before she reached her stop, she rummaged through her bulky green bag and fished out two crumpled ten-dollar bills. "Here you go, I'll see you Friday. Oh, my name is Becky."

"Clara," I said in response. Holding her money, I watched her tall graceful body sway to the bus's jolts as she made her way up to the front. Helen had told me at the last luncheon that the next new guest who joined ASI would be the first student I'd mentor.

BECKY'S EYES lit up when she saw me at the restaurant. She came bursting in, her massive hair roping down her shoulders and back. She flung her green bag on a chair and came galloping toward me.

"I was so afraid I would be late, you made such a point..."

I laughed and tugged at her hair playfully. "Just didn't want you to miss a second."

"Where are you sitting?"

Damien and Melissa always sat on either side of Helen, but Helen had asked me to sit near her as well. Becky's vibes probably weren't high enough to join me, although I wouldn't know.

Melissa glided over. "Don't tell me, Clara found you on the streets!"

They both laughed, and I moved a bit closer to Becky. "I think it's fine if you sit next to me."

"Becky, you have such long legs... like a dancer."

"Oh! I am a dancer..."

"How wonderful! Just like Clara..."

Becky turned toward me, but Helen had arrived, and we all sat down. All heads turned as she undulated across the floor, sparkling from the inside out.

"Welcome," she smiled, her eyes crinkling, her face alive. "I am the founder of ..."

As she spoke, the minestrone soup was served. The pinto beans had soaked all night and cooked for hours. Organic tomatoes, carrots, zucchini, summer squash and onions thickened the broth. The croutons were crusted from leftover homemade bread, and the noodles, too, were made right there in the kitchen.

"Oh my gosh." Becky was groaning, her eyes rolled up, head thrown back, hair almost touching the floor.

"Good, huh?" I laughed, seeing myself in her, two and a half years ago.

"We have a school here," Helen was saying. "We study the ancient aspects..."

Becky looked at me and mouthed, "School?"

"The best part is that every student here gets to learn how to cook like this. This soup, the entire meal..."

Becky scraped her bowl clean.

Helen's golden voice filled the room as I took in the smells for the first time in a long while. They seeped into my nostrils, so used to smelling cigarette smoke, whiskey, wine and coffee. Even the diner I worked in smelled more of these things than bacon and eggs.

My chest was tight, and I was surprised to feel tears thicken inside my throat. Maybe Becky wasn't such a great idea. Her enthusiasm was irritating, and her bright, panting breath made me want to shake her. I wanted to chop her hair off. My fingers were rubbing the table knife. I imagined how ridiculous she'd look if I took the knife near my plate and lopped off some of her hair. She wouldn't even hear me doing it, Helen's voice hiding the sound as I chopped away. Becky would cry, much like Wendy had, when I'd cut the bubble-gum that I had given her out of her tangled hair. The salmon steaks were served. Slices of pickled ginger lined the green plates, along with little matching saucers filled with the soy-ginger sauce. I picked up the knife smiling.

All thoughts disappeared as the salmon melted on my tongue. I forgot about Becky, how tired I was, how much pressure I was feeling to complete all of my ASI tasks. The flavors washed over my tongue, soothed all the batches of tears ever to have been caught in my throat and glided down my intestines, coating their caffeinated walls. Everyone was groaning, putting their forks down, their hands to their hearts and hastily picking up their forks again.

"We are a loving, honest community." Helen paused. She looked around, allowing her eyes to drop onto each one of us.

"How much?" Becky, intoxicated, was waving her checkbook.

Helen entranced me with her gaze, she loved me like no other.

"Welcome my dear. Clara is your mentor."

Melissa was squirming, moving one leg over the other, then switching again. Cigarette smoke was intruding on the meal we'd just finished.

Helen stared at me again. Our eyes locked for a long while, much longer than usual. This time, I noticed a seriousness behind those eyes. There was something unrelenting, iron-like there. Unexpected chills crept up and down my arms, and I suddenly jumped in my chair as Melissa banged her flask down on the table. Helen didn't blink, and I returned her gaze. I willed myself to stay still, searching that iron depth I had never seen before. The smoke inside my throat made me gag. How much had it cost to get those teeth fixed? I coughed hard, like Dad had when I'd asked him about the milk mustache on Miriam's face... *Where did you hear such a thing?* he'd whispered, his eyes narrowing, coughing so hard it'd scared me.

Helen turned to Becky. "Well, dear, indeed you are very lucky. Clara will bring you to the first meeting, and she will be your go-to girl. Yes?"

THIRTY-SEVEN
CLARA

S ince Melissa had moved in with Tim, Becky moved in with me, at Helen's suggestion.

Swan Lake was playing in the living room again. Becky was doing back bends and splits; she loved ASI and was still free to do as she pleased.

My toes burned from waitressing. I'd taken the night off to clean our meeting room, and I was deep in the red with what I owed ASI. They covered all my expenses, but what they covered exceeded what I had paid in. Being in debt was a sign of negative energy, but it seemed my expenses kept increasing. I was now responsible for paying for one eighth of the restaurant rent, half the cigarette cost — even though I didn't smoke — all the wine, and cleaning products. Not to mention Helen's teeth. And then there were my own personal expenses, including the cost of monthly tuition. It all added up to $750 per month. I was earning half that. A fortune, if I could think about it that way, but it was striking poverty in the eyes of ASI.

I marched in and turned off the music.

Becky looked up, shocked.

"Sorry, hon," I faked a soft tone of voice, "the music is grating, and I need to sleep."

"Join me, come on. You are longing to stretch, you've said so yourself."

She turned the music back on. *Pas de Quatre*, Act Two. The pain rose up my calves. I took off my shoes and rubbed my soles, watching Becky fly into splits, back bends and pliés. She pirouetted across the floor, reminding me of Wendy before the drug days. When Wendy entered a room, heads used to turn. She was immediately the center of attention. But then she'd have a way of drawing me in or would immediately copy what I did. If she told a story, she would include me in the storytelling, or if I ate some of the nuts sitting on the coffee table, she would, too. Becky did the same, made heads turn when she entered a room, and she could also draw me in like she was now.

The music tingled my fingernails, tickled up my arms. I found them winging me up, and I began to move — creak, really. I dared the splits and could only go halfway down, my inner thighs screaming with pain. Nineteen months. I stood and swung my arms into first position, my feet arching as I pointed. Second position, they turned all the way out. Becky clapped, her low voice full of encouragement. "That's right, plié all the way down, back straight, head up..."

The movements came back to me readily, and soon I was swooshing my head and stomping my feet to the *Pas de Quatre*. How ironic. There we were, a mismatched couple of dancers, one pirouetting and splitting, the other stomping and swaying, and, like animals in a jungle, we moved in our own way across the floor.

Becky hugged me when I stopped. "Why did you quit?"

Falling onto the couch elated, I said, "There are just some things you're not going to understand." I stretched, and tousled her hair. In my room afterwards, I was on fire, tears burning my cheeks. I sucked in a deep breath and did the splits.

I pushed myself to the floor, and with my thighs yelling, I dropped my head to my knees. Wendy and I were lost to each other, and it just couldn't be any other way. I lifted my torso slowly and threw my head all the way back, hearing Wendy's voice in my mind. She'd been bused in the 7th grade. *Fuck it*, she'd said, *I'm dumped into a fucking huge crowd of huge black kids. Donny feels me up every day, his fucking black hand running up the inside of my shirt, and he's Ruthless Ruthie's boyfriend... and I can't get him off of me... I'm going to get fucking killed...* I'd tried to get Dad's attention from behind his paper. *Dad, Dad,* but he wouldn't look up. *Dad,* I'd said again, *Wendy's really unhappy at school.* He'd remained behind his paper, *She's helping our city make history and should be proud.* I ripped the paper out from his hands, and his face got so red I thought he was going to choke to death. *Don't ever do that again. You kids are barbaric. You need to be grateful for all you have. Now, give me the paper.* I threw it at him and ran upstairs, with him coming up after me. Wendy was nowhere to be seen and had probably snuck out. That's what she was — sneaky; while I fought her goddamned battles. I wanted to scream at Dad that *she* was ungrateful, not me.

There was nothing to miss about her. I'd pushed myself all the way to the floor. And my head was touching my knees again. I still had flexibility and strength.

291

THIRTY-EIGHT

WENDY

Winter

"I don't want to see Dad ever again." Jake was pulling me toward the restaurant. "I'm so fucking ashamed. He should've thrown the entire stack of journals at me, knocked me unconscious. I'm such a fucking fuck up."

"Stop the shit." Jake was still pulling. "Self-pity only leads to more drugs. You fucked up and are learning, and even you said that that minister told you to do what's fucking right, so do it. We're not breaking your date with your Dad."

And there he was, already seated. I ran to him, "I'm so fucking sorry about that fuck, I mean dinner, you know like two weeks ago ..."

He smiled. "Thank you. Sit down. No more talk of what happened. I know you had something you wanted to discuss."

Like, really, he was OK? I raised my eyebrows, and Jake nodded. And besides, we were at TomYein's again. I fucking loved this place. "I'm going to church, and I've spoken to Minister Kleep privately. And he's told me I need to follow like what's right to do. And I'm like really interested in World Religions and Family Therapy. And there's this institute..."

"Family *what* and World Religion?"

"It's called Family Therapy, and I'm so excited about it. The treatment looks at patterns in families, like alcohol and drug abuse..." Terrified, I couldn't look at him.

"Patterns in families?" His tone was so calm, I looked up.

"Doctor, it's very like interesting. The science behind it says that the addictive gene is like passed down from generations."

That's what I fucking loved about Jake. He could make anything sound smart.

"Yeah, Mom was addicted to alcohol, so like she had the addictive gene, and I fucking received it from her." Dad kept looking at me. He wasn't eating, like at all.

"I'm surprised to hear this. Heart disease is genetic. Are you saying that addictions are similar? I'd like to see the studies."

"That's it, exactly. There've been many studies coming out of Stanford University." I put my fork down and was like practically hopping in my seat.

"Wendy, stop fu... like kicking me, okay babe?"

I nodded, laughing. "Dad, 1 can't wait to share my articles with you. They'll like blow your fu... ah... mind." My smile was so wide I could feel my ears like stretching.

"Bring me the articles. Now, what is this talk about you going to church?"

Dad's smile got frowny really fucking fast. He looked like he was going to have a fucking cow.

"What's up with you and like religion? I think it's like really great. You take God right into your heart..."

Jake elbowed me fucking hard.

"Ow! Fuck you! Are you trying to fucking... Oh, I'm really sorry, but you don't have to elbow me like that. Shit."

"Doctor, I share your views about religion. It's just another drug. I know that it is important in recovery. Many kids get well because of it. They substitute their addiction for Jesus. It works. But there is still a rigidity in their thinking.

I was like diving my chopsticks into my crispy noodles. "But you guys, here's like what you don't get."

"Stop talking with your mouth full."

"Fuck..." but my chopsticks slipped, and fucking Mu Shu Pork slid all over the fucking table. Fuck. "What you don't get is that there's something called spirituality, which is like different than dogma..." Jake took his napkin and pushed all that junk into his hands. There was fucking grease everywhere. I tried wiping up the grease, only it kept spreading. Shit.

"You're too excitable Wendy, just like your mother. You need to..."

"From what I know of Wendy's mother," Jake fucking jumped in, "she's nothing like her."

Dad's eyes became fucking slits.

"Whoa... deep breaths. Shit. I'm just like Mom. Fuck. An addict, only she didn't have fucking spirituality, fucking *love*..."

But Dad pushed his chair back, and the noise made Jake fucking jump, and the mess in his hands fell on the floor. He pushed his chair back, fucking facing Dad.

I wanted to fall through the floor. But I slid between them. "Please you guys,, please... I'm fucking like Mom, and I'm different like spiritually. Mom didn't know about it, and it's about fucking love, and I can feel Mom when I'm like spiritual..."

Jake suddenly started laughing, like a fucking duck, clucking and heehawing and like so hard he was bent over, wheezing — like he couldn't catch his breath. And Dad fucking took his hand and felt his pulse and led him over to the table.

The fucking waiter was sweeping up the mess, and I pushed chairs away so we could all sit. I held Jake's other hand, and Dad said, "Take slow deep breaths."

Jake was wheezing, gasping for breath, following the instructions. And I was like fucking dumbfounded at how gentle Dad could be.

THIRTY-NINE
CLARA

The pressure was so intense, I thought my head would split open. I was the apple of Helen's eye, but Melissa was in big trouble. In the women's meeting a few nights ago, Helen had surprised us with a visit, flying down from Oregon. And she wasted no time.

"There are only two reasons why you are still here, Melissa hon, and one of those is because Clara continues to go beyond herself." Helen fondly looked at me. "The second reason is because Tim and his children need you."

They were June's children, too.

"The more you are in the mother and wife roles the more your spirits will lift, and you'll be able to shake this downward frown you've put on all of us, yes? But if you continue to spiral in the direction you're going, we'll have to dismiss you."

A couple of women grabbed tissues and were sniffling like horses. I pretended to do the same but used the tissue to hide the grin that wouldn't stop spreading across my face.

"I expect you, Clara, to continue to excel, and because you're in such a vibrant space, I now put you in sole charge of making sure the meeting room is set up perfectly for our gatherings, yes?

Melissa was glaring at me. That had been her job ever since *forever*.

"Melissa already has five children on her hands; she doesn't have time to clean."

But we both knew she was being stripped of a major privilege. She washed and dried and shined Helen's special wine glass, ashtray and pottery plate for her desserts. Helen wouldn't let just anyone touch those things.

She yawned, lit another cigarette and smiled into my eyes again. "You are serving Becky quite well, and now that she has paid for her seventh month you may even ask her to help you set up. I think that would be great for the both of you, yes?"

A huge honor! Unbelievable! I took my bitten-down thumb out of my mouth and imagined cleaning Helen's wine glass and arranging yellow roses in the crystal vase, their perfume filling the room.

IT WAS our first night setting up the classroom together. Becky brought a portable tape player and put on Joni Mitchell while we set up. I stopped the tape immediately and told her we had to concentrate.

"That's how I focus, with music."

"Becky..."

"Please?" She turned it on again. She was stubborn, like Wendy had been.

I turned Joni off and handed Becky a dust rag. "Wipe down the legs of every chair until they shine."

"I can work better with music."

"Look, hon…" I wanted to put my hands on her neck really badly. "The room has to be gorgeous…"

"But this is a really ugly place…"

"All the more reason to shine it up. Work on yourself. Experiment. Do the best you can while you shine the legs of those chairs."

We worked in silence. I rubbed the wine glasses and ashtrays.

I'd send Becky out to buy the roses and desserts as soon as she was finished with the twenty-five metal chairs.

I vacuumed and dusted everything but the chairs, and Becky was daydreaming away. It was getting dark. I'd given us three hours for this task; by myself it would have been completed by now. Becky was hopeless.

"I'll do the chairs, hon, you run out and get desserts and roses. Here's the list, the place to buy everything and the money. It should take you about twenty minutes. Go, I'll time you." Wendy used to run as fast as she could when I sent her on errands. She loved being timed.

Becky took the list, the directions and the money, and promised she'd be back quickly. I worked the chair legs like crazy and was completely done before she returned. And return she did, forty minutes later, with the most dilapidated roses I'd ever seen.

I collapsed onto a chair, my head in my hands.

The roses looked almost dead, and if Helen didn't like them it would be the death of me. I ran in my heels as fast as I could to the florist, whose shop was now closed. There was nowhere to go, and those flowers couldn't be used.

I ran back to the restaurant, cut the roses off their stems and floated them in a glass bowl. I clomped down the stairs, placed the flowers on the table, told Becky to find her seat and clomped back up the stairs. From the changing room, I grabbed a pair of jeans, a holey sweatshirt with SF GIANTS written in gold letters across the back, sneakers and socks. I banged out of the restaurant and ran as fast as I could. Class was starting. I ran up Golden Gate all the way to Van Ness Avenue, having no clear idea where I was heading. A fleeting thought flew into my mind that I would get hell for running like this, but my feet banged the pavement so hard, it was driven out. I didn't care. My calves were flying, and there wasn't any pain anywhere in my body. I made a right and continued up Van Ness past Post Street. When I hit California, I turned again, heading out to 25th Avenue, my old neighborhood. I ran down El Camino Del Mar toward Baker Beach.

I ripped down the dirt path; tree branches hit my forehead and scratched my cheeks. Vines caught my ankles, tripping me more than once. There were monstrous, looming shadows everywhere, and besides my own breathing the only sound I heard was the crashing surf. When I fell onto the sand, I couldn't see the waves; the whitecaps were absent in the windless night. I sat cross-legged on the sand. My heart beat like the surf, and I dug my fists into the hard sand and pounded. It was useless, I thought. I was useless. I looked out at the waves, the water always so inviting.

Dad's home was so close. Our bedroom window had always been open, the sea air and the faint lapping of the waves so soothing as I had snuggled with Wendy, holding her close. I had held Wendy so often, singing and telling her stories, trying to comfort her, the sound of the sea from the opened window, comforting me.

Unlike now. The ocean was roaring, and the wind had picked up. I uncurled my stiff fist, red from pounding the sand. I heard voices approaching and running feet. A woman came screaming onto the beach and ran a few feet ahead of me, toward the water. She didn't get far, because a much larger guy had caught up with her. My fist froze on the sand.

The waves pushed into each other, the sounds never stopping.

He pulled her by the hair; they were standing right in front of me.

I tried to push myself backward more toward the path, but my legs were heavy, unmoving.

He was in front of her, facing me. But he didn't see me.

There was an enormous thump. Something silver gleamed and disappeared. The ocean was streaming out of her chest and mouth. The ocean? How could that be possible? No. It was blood. The gleaming silver was a knife beside her.

I found my breath, but lost it again, my heart was beating so hard. I slowly pushed my butt away, moving backward like a crab.

Once I was on El Camino, my shaking calves made me gallop. Dad's house was just a few blocks away, but my body took me back to the restaurant, my heart hammering so hard I thought it would fall right at my feet, the way that woman seemed to. The way Mom had died, the tide climbing to the foot of the rocks she'd been sitting on, swallowing her up. Accident? Suicide?

Back in the kitchen, the sudsy dishwater was soothing as I washed, the ammoniac smell sharp in my nose.

TWO WEEKS PASSED without anyone mentioning my absence that night. I was beginning to think I'd gotten away with it. Still, I kept my head down, working harder than ever, scrubbing the dishes until it seemed I might break them, the kitchen tiles until they glistened like the knife that guy had used. No matter how hard I worked, I couldn't get that scene out of my mind. It was past midnight, I had just finished scrubbing the tiles when Damien walked in.

He pulled me toward him, and I collapsed in his arms. We snuggled in bed, and as he stroked my hair, my thoughts unraveled like a torn garment, and I told him everything that had happened two weeks ago.

He was quiet for a long time. All I could hear was his heartbeat.

"My poor Clara..."

My chest loosened like a noose, and his kind tone massaged the brokenness I felt there.

"Something is up with you. When horrible things happen like this, it means that God's intervening."

I felt as though I was at an entrance way of an unreachable, whole new place that glittered with possibilities. Here, I could become an ASI teacher; I could dance again. They sparkled like distinct crystals. I was truly leaving Dad, who angered at the smallest thing — like modern dance. If this was God intervening, I wanted more of it.

Damien was touching my hair, playing with my curls.

"When I understood this, years ago, my entire life pulsed with new meaning."

I lifted myself up to look at him, our eyes met, and I was lost within their blue continuum. I floated on his soft tone.

"I lived in eleven different foster homes starting at age five. I'd no idea who my father was, and my mother often entertained different men; that's how she supported us. When her visitors came to our door, she'd ask me to be the 'gentleman' and show them to the living room to wait for her."

I stroked his short hair and listened as his voice deepened, as there were tears caught in his throat. I wanted to cup his whole face in my hands, prove to him that I was the one who could make his pain go away. Instead, my chest was tight, and the words caught.

"I remember one guy," Damien continued, "whose arms were as muscular as a boxer's, and I shook like a stupid coward as he pulled Mom by the hair, yelling, *teach your son to be a man*. He grabbed me by the neck and threw me to the wall. They were both arrested, and I never saw my mother again."

I could only look at him, wishing I could do more. I knew what it was like to grow up without a mother, and, unlike Dad, who also lost his, Damien's experience was like nothing I had ever heard before. I couldn't imagine living in so many different homes. Dad had hardly talked about his mother, no matter how much I had asked about her. *If you want to know about your Grandmother, go back to ballet.* His voice had hardened, and his eyes watered, making it impossible to ask more about her. Damien finally looked at me.

"Hey, don't look so concerned." He ran his fingers around my mouth. "I was a different kind of kid-smart. I outwitted every foster parent."

I breathed deeply and snuggled closer to him, feeling his warmth spread through me.

"When I was seventeen I was finally released from state care. I'd heard about Helen's farm and went to work for her. There, I realized that everything that had ever happened to me was for the divine purpose of helping others wake up."

I saw strength in his eyes. He was just remarkable, and I was so lucky to be this close to him. If only I'd known him years ago, when I was struggling with Mom. Things would've been so different. That car ride wouldn't have ever happened. *Stop. Stop,* I'd screamed, the trolley just missing us. Perhaps if I had had a "Damien" to teach me about God back then... and then I saw the gleaming knife, the blood pouring out of that woman. I put my head down on his chest, to stop the shaking, the thoughts, hoping that his confidence in God would rub off on me.

"You're waking up, and everything that happens to you while you're in this school is an Angelic Intervention. You've something big to learn from what you witnessed."

He took me into his arms, and I melted with each kiss. There was such a thing as Heaven on Earth, and it was Damien.

AND THE NEXT AFTERNOON, I felt like I had wings as I flew through the kitchen, making coffee and pulling out scrub brushes. Watching the water splash into the bucket, warmth splashed over me again, thinking about how beautiful last night was.

The noises were wonderful. The coffee dripping, the fridge humming and the swish of the brushes as I scrubbed the wall tiles. The phone rang, interrupting my rhythm.

"Clara, dear, it's Helen. It's time for another reading."

My hand trembled.

"Leaving that night was a sign that you're in deep trouble. Mary has been requesting a visit with you. We can do this over the phone, now, yes?"

The pot of coffee was ready. Holding the phone to my ear, I poured another cup and jumped up on the counter to sit. My head banged on one of the cabinets; I had to lean forward, straining my neck.

"I guess so. I'm in the middle of..." Even though Damien had been kind, you just never knew with Helen. Her moods changed like the weather.

"Close your eyes, now. Take three deep breaths and quiet your mind. Allow yourself to open..."

We were quiet for a few moments, and then a voice that was different from Helen's said, "Hello, it is I. Mother Mary."

And then it was Helen's voice. "Thank you, Mother, for coming. What is your message for Clara? She is flailing."

Mary returned. "The whole reason you witnessed that accident is because you needed to witness the stabbing of your own soul, as negativity is like that. Few people have such a privilege; it ought to wake you, make you take heart. We know that though you were near your father, you chose to come back to your true home."

I reached for the pot of coffee, but its handle was unexpectedly hot, and it fell out of my hands, crashing hard. Black liquid swirled all over the ammonia-clean tiles, and big chunks of glass splayed across the floor while small shards dispersed into the spilled coffee and the cracks. *Everything you experience in this school is Angelic Intervention.* Damien's words, his soft voice, echoed in my mind.

"I just dropped…"

"Are you listening?" It was Helen, again.

"Go on…" I was shaking from head to toe. I was trying so hard to believe her, Damien. Still holding the phone, I jumped down from the counter and kneeled on the floor. I put my tongue to some of the sharded coffee. The glass was sharp on the tip, and I wanted to crunch down on it. Experience what that poor woman had.

"I understand your longing to dance, dear one, and how fed up you are with Becky. But you see, she is very valuable to you because she is a real dancer in a troupe, earning money, meaning she was good enough to be accepted into the prestigious San Francisco School of Ballet. Whereas you were a mere teacher at…"

I'd stopped listening. She sounded like Dad. I picked up a larger piece of glass. I wanted to run it along the tip of my right index finger. *A mere teacher*. That's all I was. I didn't deserve this school, Damien, all the good that I'd seen last night. It was me that should have been stabbed.

I put the glass down, staring into its blunt light. Through it, I saw Mom, slumped on the couch in the T.V. room, years ago. Dad had said, *What are you doing with this?* He was so sad. I'd wanted to fill her flask, like she'd often asked me to. *Fill it up, there's my girl*. But Dad had said, *Go, you're in the way*. His fists were white, clenched.

"But this experience has earned you another privilege, I'm happy to say." Helen's voice sounded like a chirping bird.

"I want you up at the farm this June. ASI will pay for your flight. You've earned it."

What? This was so unpredictable, crazy. The generosity was overwhelm-ing. I threw away the piece of glass and felt sorry for the stabbed woman. I pushed her out of my thoughts. I had to make myself worthy. No more complaining about *anything*. I flew through the muddy mess, whisking it up in no time, my thoughts whisking faster. I must already have a True Self that had guided me to witness that stabbing, a True Self that would change me from a "mere" teacher into a fantastic dancer, that would guide me to be worthy enough to become an ASI teacher.

I'd earn my way into being Damien's equal. I pictured him in my mind and felt his kisses all over again.

FORTY

WENDY

Spring

I needed a new outfit for church, and like I needed it now. I walked into the Second Hand Shop on Haight and laughed. Jake couldn't like believe it either. Displayed in the window was a "Jax" outfit from like the early 1960s. It wasn't like exactly Mom's clothes, but it sure looked like them. I like *had* to like try the outfit on. If Clara was around she'd probably freak. It was a fitted blue-jean skirt that reached my knees, a tailored pink shirt and a blue jean jacket. The whole thing looked fucking great on me, and I was like Mom's image. But that was beautiful 'cause Mom was fucking gorgeous. I know she was a fucking drunk, but before all that happened, well, she was like fucking great. I wanted to remember her that way.

Jake, at first, wouldn't go to church with me. We got into a huge fight about that. I told him he needed to help me find Clara, and could he please like come anyway?

"Jesus, Wendy, I'm fucking Jewish. Why would I want to go hear about Jesus?"

"You're only Jewish when you want to be, like fuck you, just come." He hated it when I cried, and I like couldn't help it. It just fucking happened when I thought about spirit shit. I was sure that if I kept going to Kleep's church, Clara would show up. Finding her and finding God had like become one and the same.

Jake was feeling more and more like family, and that made me feel like whole, like I fucking belonged to someone. We found a pew and sat down on the hard bench. Couldn't someone like put a cushion down? I was like sick and tired of my fucking butt hurting all the time.

I whispered to him, "This seat is so harsh, I feel like I'm being punished for something." He laughed.

"Welcome to the religious communities... for like, centuries." Jake had this like dark sense of humor. I had to stifle my fucking laughter.

Minister Kleep was talking about Job. The sermon like fascinated me. It was all about the questions I had. Job had worked for everything, and yet God took it all away. The point was, Kleep was saying, that God wasn't about the material things. He was about perseverance, patience and family – even through the darkest of times.

And then he like beamed at us, at everybody there... a bright, huge, heartfelt smile. "I know this to be true, because during this time that my daughter has been missing, I have never once doubted the love of God. And now, my daughter has just returned from the sea. She and her boyfriend have traveled far and wide."

The organ music started up, and then we all stood, singing a Hallelujah hymn. I like hummed along. Who the fuck knew, maybe I'd like even join the fucking chorus. The music was fucking beautiful.

Afterward, everyone was hugging each other, there was so much joy in the church with Kleep's news. God had to be fucking great. That's what I kept hearing. And he was. That little voice inside me that had told me to live was fucking God's voice. And I listened. No matter what Jake might say, God helps when you listen. When Dad and I met Kleep that first time, all Kleep like kept saying was, "Take Jesus into your heart." I have, and He's kept me sober, every moment. I hugged Jake, "You see? God has to exist. This wouldn't have fucking happened, otherwise. Take Jesus into your heart; that's all I had to do. I know we'll find Clara, Jake, I just know it 'cause that like *spirit* inside of me *knows.*"

FORTY-ONE

JOE

"Hey Dad, are you fu... home?"

Wendy was running up the stairs to his study. She burst through the door, carrying a bucket of Kentucky Fried Chicken.

"Come down and have like dinner with me, I have great news!"

She was too energetic, exaggerated too often. "Slow down," he demanded, as they headed for the kitchen. He sat at the table watching her set up everything; the plates, the chicken, potatoes and the cole slaw.

"Guess what? You'll never like believe it, Kleep's daughter is back." She was waving her chicken leg in the air. Like a banner or a flag.

He looked up at her, dropping the thigh he was about to eat. "Is that so?"

"Yes, and like, he says that it was the hand of God..."

"Wendy!" Trying to convert him, pretending to have some kind of "spirit." He couldn't stop the fire, rushing up from his belly. She shrank back. Cleared her throat and looked down at her plate. He kept swallowing, as if gulping down the flames leaping from within. He didn't want to yell again. When she spoke, her voice was quieter.

311

"What I'm trying to say is that like what I'm learning is that the whole reason why I took drugs was to stop that fucking pain I had when like Mom died. And now that I don't have the drugs anymore, like I have to live with that hurt, and sometimes, I swear Mom is with me, and then like I feel all this love pour into my heart..."

She looked up at him, her huge eyes full of tears.

"... and Kleep says that God brings that love to me through her 'cause like she's gone back to being spirit, and spirit is like God's love..."

Family was everything, he could agree to that. Relieved that the anger was contained, he patted her head. "God doesn't exist, but our family does. Of course... we both miss your mother, and now Clara..."

"There's like such a hole, right Dad? God, you feel that, too, right here?"

She pointed to her chest. His opened unexpectedly. The sharp pains increased. Wendy was annoying, overly emotional, but she had a way with her. She had a rare understanding... a compassion not easily found in others. It was difficult to speak.

Wendy reached out her hand and placed it in his. They sat like that. Silent. The chicken grew cold. She spoke first.

"Not only like am I going to church, but I'm like learning to meditate. There's like this Buddhist center I go to sometimes... it's like amazing, Dad. I hope you'll come with me sometime... it's like so beautiful. It says everyone has a spirit, just like Jesus says, only like there's no Jesus... but if you want to bring Him in quietly to yourself, like you can..."

He couldn't stand it. The continual mention of God.

"Ow. You're fucking hurting me."

He'd put full pressure on her hand without realizing it, crushing her fingers with the force of it. "You must stop this nonsense..."

"But it isn't fucking nonsense... You're full of nonsense. Always quoting Poe — what do you always say from him? *'And all I lov'd, I loved alone…'* You believe you loved alone… That's shit. You think you're the only one that's loved Mom and Clara because of that stupid Poe. "

She kept going, quoting:

From the thunder, and the storm/And the cloud that took the form/when the rest of heaven was blue/of a demon in my view — Fuck Dad all you see are fucking demons. You should read Jane Roberts and fucking Walt Whitman, ever heard of them? Jane Roberts says, *Suffering isn't good for the soul, unless it teaches you how to stop suffering, that's its purpose,* and Whitman, God he's so fucking great, *I celebrate myself, and sing myself/and what I shall assume you shall assume/for every atom belonging to me as good belongs to you.*"

Fire was rising up from his belly, and flames licked his tongue. He wouldn't be spoken to like this. He said, "You've no idea what it is to suffer, to be hungry…! You don't know what it is to feel, toes…" he sputtered, stopped himself, but had to continue… "Your mother and I gave you *everything*, and you *chose* to be miserable, to put a few drugs in your system…"

"A few fucking drugs in my system? Is that what you think my fucking life's been like when I was out on the streets, freezing, starving… just wanting relief, just wanting someone to fucking take care of me… and fucking Mom dead, and Clara gone, I couldn't call or reach her…"

His hands were shaking; a lump, dry and big, caught in his throat. She slammed down an apple pie she'd bought. She picked up her huge black bag and swung it over her shoulder.

Let her leave. It was best that way. He heard her stomp toward the door… But he followed her. Grabbed her by the shoulders and turned her toward him. Tears dripped down her cheeks, and he wrapped his arms around her. She was clean. Had been for over a year. That's what mattered most. He wanted to say this to her, to apologize for hurting her.

Instead, he led her back to the table. He sliced the pie precisely and gave them each a huge piece. They ate in silence, the dessert tasting unusually sweet.

~

JUST A FEW DAYS LATER, while Joe was interviewing psychologist Dr. Ed Friedman for the clinic, both Roberts and Whitman were mentioned again. What in hell was going on in these recovery programs?

"One year into my recovery, I knew I had to understand the deeper meanings of the psyche. Hence my doctorate in psychology from UC Berkeley..."

"Interesting, 'the deeper meanings of the psyche.' Did you study more Freud or Jung? "

"Neither really. I've studied Carl Rogers and John Bowlby the most. I like Rogers' approach about having kind regard for every patient, and Attachment Theory is fascinating..."

Aaron had given Joe Bowlby's book a few years ago. "Bowlby says that if we don't attach in a healthy way to our parents, we won't have healthy adult relationships either."

"Exactly," Ed jumped in.

He was overly enthusiastic, like Wendy.

"And to find the why of addiction! It's beautiful to see how an unhealthy attachment can lead to such a suffering..."

Joe's fingers curled into two fists on his lap. Poe ripped through his mind, *And my soul from out that shadow that lies floating on the floor/shall be lifted — nevermore.* He swallowed hard. "And do you think religion has a place in these deeper so-called sufferings?" Joe saw Ed Friedman grimace, probably at the tone of his voice. He looked past the young man's forehead, hearing Wendy's voice: *Meditation helps you calm down. You should come...*

"I know that the new Reborn movement has spread like wildfire, but unless the addict keeps working on the 'why' it happened, that becomes another drug. I'm not into the God thing myself, preferring Zen Buddhism, where there's no God... but there is suffering..."

"The Beatles." Joe smirked, remembering that they'd been to India and were introducing here some foreign Eastern ways of thinking. Or was that Hinduism? Zen Buddhism, he remembered, was Japanese. At any rate, he'd suggested to Aaron that they play Bach and Mozart on the ward instead of all the God-awful rock-and-roll stuff. Give the poor kids real music, real culture. Aaron had thought that would drive the adolescents right out.

"If you were to be employed here as one of our psychologists, how would you handle this new Jesus movement?"

"Practice 'kind regard' for the patient. I'd have to let it be, Doctor. I can't tell someone else what to believe in. I can teach them how to believe in themselves..."

"It's the belief in oneself that's most important, isn't it?" Joe responded. "And when one suffers, how does one gain that belief in oneself back again? Do you think it's possible without this so-called 'faith' that is so important in recovery?"

"Not only is it possible, but it's essential. I think that suffering is beneath the need for religion... I mean Jane Roberts says..."

Joe tried his best to smile. "My daughter has also mentioned her."

"She's phenomenal, Doctor, there's so much hope in her books... *Seth Speaks*. She channels..."

"Ever read Poe?" Joe had to change the subject. He was the expert, the interviewer. He would choose the subjects they spoke of. And a well-read team member would be an asset.

Ed's eyes had widened. "I love poetry, all kinds. Poe was a favorite in high school."

Joe's mouth dropped, and his fingers relaxed on his lap.

"*The Raven*... Poe was some dark figure. If I'd had time, I would've studied English Literature along with Psychology. And Poe would have been the first I'd study."

Joe put one leg over the other and banged his ankle against the desk. The pain pulsed, as if it were swollen. "What other poets do you know? Do you read Walt Whitman?"

Ed leaned forward in his chair, a huge smile lighting up his face. Dimples emerged, and he looked like a young boy. "I could talk about Whitman forever. His detail of the human condition...*Song of Myself*...you know, so many have looked at Whitman as conceited, but I see him, the *Song of Myself* as a reclamation of the human spirit... it's just beautiful."

The blood was rushing around Joe's ankle, repairing it. He said, "Poe and Whitman, two opposite men, one exploring the darker aspects of the human condition, the other the more positive ones. Both sides exist in each of our psyches. The addict has to choose which to throw his weight behind."

~

JOE'S own words followed him home that night, and he read Whitman for a time:

> *I harbor for good or bad, I permit myself to speak at every*
> *   hazard*
> *Nature without check with original energy*

And he wrote in his journal:

> *No one human is the same*
> *Though we all have two arms, two legs,*
> *ten fingers and toes, one heart*
> *As children   innocent*
> *With the Rabbi*
> *we tried to name   that same core*

Severed

Nothing is the same
very few managed
too many like me
damaged

FORTY-TWO

CLARA

Summer

W hile I couldn't wait to go up to the farm, time passed slowly. Damien had left shortly after Helen invited me, and David had called me non-stop, saying the same boring things.

"I can't wait to see you! And wait till you see..."

The clouds had just parted, and I had to shield my eyes from the sun pouring in through the windows. David's voice was too loud, and I hated myself for feeling so irritated with him. This was the hundredth time he'd called me. If I wanted to be a teacher, I'd *have to* marry David.

"I can't wait to come up." I said, feeling my heart drop to my knees. But that wasn't a lie. I'd see Damien every day,

"I'm in charge of building the steeple."

"That's great." I wasn't being false, I told myself. I was acting the person I wanted to be. The sun was getting brighter, and the living room hotter. There weren't any shades or curtains, *so we can always be translucent,* Melissa had sung shortly before she had moved out. *We are the Light, and the more we can feel the sun, the more we are reminded.* I'd

319

been too busy to cover the windows, but she'd been right. I just had to pretend until I could feel the joy, always.

THE FRESH OCEAN breeze hit my face as I got off the airport transport bus. To my great surprise June was running from the main house to meet me. I fell into her big Mama arms, a million questions falling out of my mouth.

"How, what, when? I mean how did you get back here?"

Her mouth dropped downward, and her eyes filled up. There was something serious behind those tears. She lit up again, smiling. "How are *you*? We must find a time to talk. I have some important things to tell you..."

She laughed, not quite sincerely, not really her deep laugh. I stared at her. And still, I couldn't believe my good luck! Being here on the farm *this* time would be spectacular.

"We'll find time, I'm sure!" We hugged again.

ON MY SECOND MORNING, I rolled out of bed at 4:30 a.m. and put on yesterday's filthy jeans, red T-shirt, socks and work boots. I piled my unbrushed hair into my faded dark-blue baseball cap.

Tim was already starting up the truck loaded with new trees to be planted in the orchard that morning. He must be happy, too, to be back with June.

I stretched out my arms, sore from all of that shoveling yesterday digging holes for the new trees. Tim and so many other guys had cleared an entire forest to create the new orchard. Today we were going to plant almond trees. Helen had instructed those of us appointed to the orchard during two late-night meetings.

The reason we're planting almond trees is precisely because they are hard to grow in this region. We cross-pollinate and spray them with our organic protectant. Yes? We will have crews around the clock, and the way you take care of these trees is the way you take care of yourselves — you neglect a single detail, you kill the whole tree.

I knew how to pay attention to detail, and already I loved the labor of this effort. The sheer physical stamina it took to dig out those holes yesterday made my biceps stronger and broadened my shoulders. The hot sun had felt like balm over my tired hands, and the welcoming sea breeze embraced my cheeks. I felt like I was digging myself out of a hole as I dug deeper and deeper. Helen and I both knew I was glowing, Damien knew also, although I had hardly seen him, we were all so busy. I was proud to be planting almond trees.

The rickety truck kicked into gear and slowly made its way down the rocky road to the orchard.

I walked down the path that led to the beach, gazing at the sunrise as it brushed across the different blues and greens in the sea. One last star gave off its fading sparkles as it disappeared into the light. The ocean sang deeply and crashed the waves, its song searing through the red-orange sky. The wind was absent this morning, and the orchard stretched on like the sky, endlessly quiet.

The truck rumbled up where I was. Tim and Damien were shouting to one another. I took in a long deep breath, trying to swallow the beauty as I moved upward toward them. I stayed at the point of the path where the truck couldn't go anymore. The guys would have to bring the trees down the short path to the orchard. I could see them, but they couldn't see me.

"Careful," Damien warned, "treat them like babies, follow? They're living beings and need your firm but gentle touch." Damien, David and Tim were standing at the back of the truck, and four other male students watched from the roadside. They were all looking at the trees. Their backs were to me. I was standing close enough to tell that David had lost weight. His body had a gaunt look to it. Gazing at him, I realized that he was more like a brother to me than a lover. He'd already yanked out a tree, pulling it apart from another its branches had entwined with.

Tim saw him do this.

"Bastard. Can't you follow directions?"

David glared at him, standing a few inches taller.

"Can't respect the trees like you can't respect yourself?"

David suddenly punched Tim in the face.

"Fuck you, bastard." Tim hit him right back, knocked him down. He stood over David. "You Goddamned fucking asshole. No wonder you don't have a fucking wife. Is this how you'd fucking treat her?" Tim was holding him down with his legs, fists looming over him. David screamed, "Fucking asshole. You didn't even know what the fuck I was doing..."

Damien laughed and nodded to the other four men. "Come on guys, leave them alone, let them fight this one out. You understand that Tim was right, follow? Treat these trees like you would your women, with care and firmness."

I beat it down to the orchard. Fighting things through was something Dad had never allowed. He was always right no matter what. *You are helping Clara become a barbarian,* he'd told Grandma when she paid for my modern dance lessons. *She will live to regret this for the rest of her life.* He'd slammed the phone down and refused to have a discussion with me. At least David and Tim had the chance to figure this out; it was a relief that I didn't have to.

But David lumbered down toward me and placed a sapling in my arms, a little too harshly. He pinched my butt, forcefully. "That hurt." I hit him back lightly, trying to make fun of my pain. He rubbed his arms and bent to rub his knees. His small grey eyes were dull, without glow. Something wasn't right with him, but I couldn't figure out what. I shrugged it off. He'd just been hit pretty badly, and he must be hurting. After all, he'd lost the fight. He'd never let on, though. Just like Dad, he probably wouldn't work it through. Still, I had this weird feeling in the pit of my stomach.

"Everything okay?" I asked.

"Of course, babe, of course." He pinched my butt again and walked back toward the truck.

The night before, another busload of students had arrived. Becky had been invited to come this time. She must have arrived while I was observing the fight. I was surprised to see her standing in a ditch beside mine, crying.

"This is way too hard, I can't do this. I'll callous my dancing hands; no guy will want to touch them in a show."

"You must observe yourself, you know? Of course, you can't do this, but the True 'I' in you can. That's why we're here together, to help each other out. This is the perfect opportunity to observe your false self." I sounded just like a teacher. Proudly, I began to dig.

"But I've been up all night, I've had two hours of sleep..."

"Come on, Becky, you really need to see where all of this whining is coming from. This is your opportunity to bust through all of that. You must try harder."

"I am, but my body hurts, and I'm hungry."

"You're not listening!"

"I'm feeling faint. My heart feels funny."

I fixed my eyes on hers, weariness creeping up my backbone. Out of my peripheral vision I could detect the rows and rows of ditches, and the hundreds of trees that needed to be planted before sundown. The entire orchard had to be finished by the end of the day.

The sun, though just risen, was already beginning to beat down on my shoulders, adding to the soreness I was feeling. But no one said teaching was easy. I stood up tall.

"Look, where's your resolve? Think of the hours you put in rehearsing for ballet. You have the discipline..."

She keeled over. Fainted, right at my feet; a tremendous thud that swept the gulls into sudden clusters, their raucous cries resounding throughout the orchard. I dropped to the ground, the shovel clanging on top of my back, and poured a pitcher of water on her head. "Becky, you can't do this now... Huh?" Becky was Wendy, writhing on the kitchen floor, screaming and swearing. I was slapping Becky across the face, not realizing how loud I was yelling. A large, rough hand grabbed my own and pulled me up. Struggling to get free, I was caught. David whipped me around, forcing me to face him.

Becky came to. Tim had her in his arms.

"What the hell?" David's face was in mine.

"It's nothing. We're fine." I tried to loosen his grip. My cap had fallen off, and my hair, now grown fully back, was a tangled rat's nest, the knots matted and blowing across my eyes.

He pulled my hair harder, our faces close. An image of Mom ran through my mind. Her face in mine, pulling me by the hair. *We have to go. Now.* And then, in the car, her wild driving, and the trolley so close, *Stop, Mom, stop.*

"What the hell? I asked you." David was still yelling at me.

"And I said 'nothing'."

Tim helped Becky up.

"She's alright."

"Yeah." Becky said.

It was barely audible. Was she going to make it?

"We have to get these all planted by the end of the day, you ladies get that?" David's eyes were hard, and he'd grasped my biceps.

"Let me go, okay?" My voice was unsteady. Like Mom's in the car. *No one understands me, no one...*

David pinched me again, harshly. Something had changed him in the seven months we'd been apart. He let me go and walked up the path with Tim.

I picked up the two shovels that had fallen and handed one to Becky. "Come on, hon, let's get to work. I'll be beside you all day."

The clangy iron sounds pounded with the pounding waves, and the forceful wind whirled the unplanted, unsteady trees all over the ground.

We lifted them up and placed each inside its own hole. When Becky stopped to rest, I did as well. Squinting, I could see a line of us planting one tree after another. Cormorants in the near distance rested on trees, their tired, wet wings spread out on the limbs to dry.

We put down our shovels as the night came in softly and full of stars. The phosphorus danced on the white foam, welling and falling on invisible black waves. I put my arm around Becky and drew her close. We were quiet, our breath mixing with the air, dried sweat cooling our necks and cheeks.

And then she whispered, "This place is crazy. Not fun, wild crazy, but crazy crazy."

Before I could reply she started the walk back to the lodge. The waves were crashing furiously; the tide was coming in. Most of the sand would be swallowed up in no time. We walked in silence up the steep path. Like animals, we found our way back and made it to the meeting on time.

It was 11 p.m. I left class to go back to the trees. It was my turn to spray their leaves. I tiptoed out, holding my breath, making sure the door opened and shut without a sound. Helen hated to be disturbed once she began running a meeting. Walking out soundlessly meant we

325

were not bringing attention to ourselves and were intent on the job at hand.

The chilly air bit into my chest and froze my thoughts. I put on work boots and gloves as the air dried my lips and chapped my cheeks. I looked up at the stars. The wind whirled the wisps of clouds, and it looked as though the stars were moving, revealing deeper and deeper layers of light.

I walked quickly down the black path, trusting my feet to find their way. I was doing my best with Becky. I'd put myself in the role of being a beacon for her, trying to reflect the light that was already inside of her. I looked up at the sparkling sky again. The amount of stars was overwhelming; it was hard to separate just one out. Maybe my efforts were like that, insignificant and lost in some deep continuum.

I moved even more quickly, daring my feet to stay steady, the wind loud behind me. The ocean was slapping against the rocks, the sea spray hitting my face. I intently paid attention to my mission. In the orchard, the lithe saplings stood like dutiful children, all in their rows. They bowed in the wind, their small branches leaning as if to greet me.

A two-sided stepladder was lying beside the tree nearest me. Even though the trees were small, a ladder was needed to rise above the leaves to see more clearly any fungus that might be growing on them. I removed the flashlight attached to the ladder and belted it to me. As I sturdied the ladder I was aware of the amount of work ahead of me.

I climbed two of the steps saying to myself, "one leaf at a time, don't think about what lies ahead." *This place is crazy crazy.* Becky's words haunted me. Could she be right? Who sprayed trees like this in the middle of the night? Balancing on the ladder was easy and a relief. My long years of dancing were helping me. I balanced myself on one step, swung out my arms and the other leg. What was it like to be a branch in the wind? I focused on the tree trunk in front of me, and while the wind wobbled my outstretched leg, I stayed still. Sweat poured out of my armpits, and my heart beat quickly. I almost forgot where I was. I felt that I could jump, turn, leap and land perfectly. Perhaps it *was* crazy taking care of the trees at night, but it was different and even fun. I'd talk with Becky about all of this in the morning.

I brought my foot back in and picked up the spray bottle. I flashed the light on the leaves. As I checked the first ones, both my feet now firmly planted, the wind played tricks on me. It whistled and whispered, and I became aware of all the night creatures skulking about. It was a moonless night, everything was in shadow, and the flashlight brightened the leaves in a surreal, shadowing way. I stuck to my mission and scanned for evidence of bugs, for any holes, no matter how small. I spoke out loud to the trees, needing to hear my own voice. "I'm here to take good care of you." I felt the leaves listening, almost speaking back. It seemed like they lifted themselves of their own accord to be nearer to me. I was feeling more and more at home as I sprayed.

Victorious at completing my first tree, I climbed halfway down the ladder, excited and intent on working on the next. But I was yanked by the waist the rest of the way down. Too frightened to scream, I fell forward onto David, who was laughing his head off.

"What the fuck are you doing?"

"Nothing." His body looked bigger in the shadows.

He held me so tightly I couldn't wiggle out.

"You know you want me."

"I don't really." I was confused. I'd been so intent on those trees. What was he doing here? What did he mean, 'I wanted him?' I didn't. Not in the least. But he still held me from behind, and started to tickle me. I giggled, turned around, and he put his hands on his jean zipper. Holding mine, he led my fingers down until his jeans slipped down to his ankles. I picked up the flashlight and said, "Your legs aren't very sexy you need..." But he pushed me to the ground, and I fought him, saying, "Wait a sec... you're hurting me." But he held me firmly.

"You know you want this, bitch..." And then he changed his tone, "I'm sorry, hon, it's been so long for us..." I gave in, feeling sorry I'd been bitchy to him.

He ripped off my shirt, tearing it in places, while he held me down. "Just let go a little." And reluctantly, I let him inside, pretending to enjoy every moment.

He pushed hard. Ignoring the pain, I caressed his arms, his face, trying to calm him. And I must have softened him, because with his sweat dripping onto my nose and mouth he said, "Oversee the steeple... fucking assholes screwed up... My goddamned fault. Helen... I have to pay. No more law school." His hands tightened around my throat as if to choke out his pain.

Skunk stench was everywhere, and fishers screamed like babies being tortured. I couldn't breathe and struggled to pull his hands down to my breasts.

"I'm ruined. The fucking steeple... thousands..."

His sweat was dripping onto my nose, my mouth. Breath shuddered through me, my throat pounding.

"I'm fucking trapped... poured my heart into that steeple.." He fell to my side. Cold and shaken, I rolled over to hold him, to comfort him, to offer him money, but he stood up, shouting. "Where the fuck are my clothes?"

I got onto my knees, feeling my throat throb, searching for his jeans. I found them against the ladder. We dressed in silence, the wind still stinking of skunk and the ocean pounding the rocks relentlessly, its white foam rising with fury.

The sky was black and clouded, frozen. The night swallowed David as he trudged away back up the path. I pushed the ladder to the second tree. Trembling, I climbed it and willed my hand to be steady as I once again sprayed, holding each leaf as carefully as I now held David's pain. I sprayed a few leaves. Something wet was dropping on my hair and bare hands. I lifted my face to the sky; gentle rain was falling everywhere.

FORTY-THREE
WENDY

Summer

I'd gotten to our AA meeting early to be alone, because the room had this old piano, and like I hadn't played since I was fucking fifteen years old. I was fucking twenty-three. Fuck.

It was like an upright old thing. When I pulled back the brown lid, dust blew everywhere. I guessed that no one had played it in like years. I sat on the bench and put my hands on the keys, and the tones were fucking shit. I didn't care. I had to fucking play.

I kept running my hands up and down the keys. I felt Mom sitting next to me and I heard her voice in my like ear again. *That's right. Put your thumb on Middle C and stretch your whole hand down to the next C. Put your pinky on that C and... Oh, that's perfect...*

I kept at it, like finding myself playing Mozart's Concerto in C Major. It just so happened to be the theme to Clara's and my most favorite fucking movie, *Elvira Madigan.* When Mom like taught me how to play it, I'd no idea a fucking movie would use it! It was a story about a tightrope dancer and a fucking soldier who'd gone AWOL from the army. A love story. Just like Dad had said, *Family is everything.* If family isn't like a story about love, like I didn't know what was. I played with all of my heart. It felt fucking amazing. It was Clara's fucking life — being a fucking dancer *and* AWOL. Fuck. She'd disappeared without leave. Maybe she'd hear me play. Just like it said in like those books *Seth Speaks* and *The Nature of Personal Reality*. Like energy can fucking travel...

Maybe Clara would hear me playing from my heart, and somehow it'd reach hers. Maybe she'd come home then. Clara, can you hear? There is nothing like family, Clara. Would you just like show the fuck up?

Jake was like shaking me, and there were all these people hanging around. I lifted my head from the keys.

I fell into his big fucking arms and like sobbed on his fucking shoulder until some guy yelled that the meeting was starting.

FORTY-FOUR
CLARA

There was a police car in front of the main house as I walked up from the orchard. As I drew nearer, I saw an officer talking with Helen. She waved urgently to me. I ran the rest of the way up the path. A flock of yellow finches took off, twittering and streaking the early morning sky.

The cop turned to me; his eyes were wide, brown and intently looking in mine.

"Did you know David...?"

"He's dead, suicide." Helen's voice was low, firm.

"I'm sorry, Miss...?"

The breeze picked up. Gulls were cawing loudly, squirrels, hundreds of them appeared out of nowhere. The one I saw was really fat, and he'd an equally fat black walnut between his paws. He looked right at me, eyes unflinching, and then at his nut. He turned his back on me and ate.

"Miss...?"

The cop was talking to me still or again. He was asking my name. "Clara. Call me Clara." My voice was muffled, hidden.

"Can you describe your relationship...?"

I looked at him unable to think. Relationship? *Mom is gone, she died early this morning.* Dad had said. Wendy was sobbing. Dad had looked so unkempt the next morning I'd hardly recognized him. David? Suicide?

The fat squirrel had disappeared.

"We can't rule out suicide, Clara." The cop was talking to me again.

"What?" The cops had come to Dad's office with Mom's things in their hands, her shoes, purse... *We found her out on the rocks early this morning. We think she drowned...* the cops had told Dad. On the ground near the rocks to my left, black ants were bustling everywhere. Their purpose was to serve their queen. Or was that bees?

"We believe he was quite drunk early this morning when his truck smashed..."

There were thousands of ants. And each one was so tiny. I could crush their entire colony easily.

"...against the mountain just a few miles down the road."

Helen called an emergency meeting.

"THE POLICE REPORTED that David had high levels of alcohol in his system when he smashed the pick-up into a cliff about ten miles down the road. They weren't sure if it was a thought-out plan or an accident. However, Mary says that this is suicide."

June and Tim were sitting next to each other on the other side of the room. We hadn't had a chance to talk yet. Damien was next to Helen, and Becky was near me. I was sitting near the door.

"Suicide is the angriest, most rageful act any human being can possibly commit." Helen's tone was sharp. "David has just released an entire hurricane of rage that we all now must breathe in. It is of utmost importance that you all take the incense being handed out and cleanse each other and yourselves. It means that every single plant and every single thing we have built here must also be cleansed with sage, and immediately."

My heart dipped down into my belly. I felt David's hands around my waist. *Of course you want me...* I could still taste the salty sweat that had dripped from his forehead and onto my mouth. My legs were crossed so tightly, they cramped. He couldn't be dead.

"...and Clara..." Helen's voice was very quiet.

I looked at her.

"You were the last to see him, yes?"

My lip was sore from clamping down on it.

"Yes?" Helen's tone was sharper.

I nodded.

"I am quite worried about you, your energy has dropped dangerously, or David wouldn't have done this. He must have been drinking in your negativity, and that's what killed him."

The room was dead silent. My lap was filled with sage and matches someone had placed there. I felt Damien's eyes boring into mine, as if to say, *Really, is this what you've become, after all I've poured into you?* I could hardly lift my eyes, they felt so heavy. I was pure scum.

"I have messages from Mary for you. You are riddled with spiritual holes."

My head shot up. Helen looked so tired there were black lines under her eyes. I must have done that to her. I'd devastated a saint, and yet... Mary still came through her, talking to me..

"Three days in the solitary cabin will restore you. During this time, you must reflect on your True Self. Follow everything Helen asks you to do, and you will see, these spiritual holes will close over time. Once this is done, you'll be able to dance again, and Helen will consider you, once again, for a Teacher's position.'"

I'd never have that privilege.

"'You cannot have a single negative thought, do a single negative thing, or you will die a spiritual death, the worst death of all. Schizophrenics, drug addicts and murderers, to name a few, have all died spiritually."

FORTY-FIVE
JOE

Summer

He was doing his rounds on the ward, wondering about Clara. Missing? With Jones? He knew his suit was wrinkled, his tie not tied right. He'd shaved hastily, his cheeks still rough. His shoes squeaked on the clean floor. But, good light was coming in from the windows. At least the ward was in good order.

Sandy ran past him. One of the youngest on the ward, just thirteen. Her mother had died from heroin, and her father had disappeared. She'd never known him.

"Slow down. Good morning." She stopped dead in her tracks, her thick brown hair falling down her face. Some of it was in her mouth. Sucking furiously, she said, 'Hey Doc. Morning. Late for Dr. Friedman. Gotta go..."

She was hopping from foot to foot, now putting more hair in her mouth, now taking it out. She was as hyper as Wendy, who never stopped running when she was a child. Except for that one evening, when she was so limp.

"Doc, everything alright? Hate to keep..."

He kept looking at her young, soft face. Acne spread across her forehead. Lively brown eyes. Wendy said she'd taken her first acid at Sandy's age. Anna had died around that time.

"Fine. Go. No running..."

But she had taken off like a deer, loping down the hall.

Nurse Linda stopped him, asking him questions about meds for a couple of the patients, and a few more kids greeted him.

Andy shot passed him, and he yelled to him. The broad, short, 16-year-old waited for Joe to catch up with him.

"What are you doing here on the female ward?"

"Visiting a friend."

"Do you have permission? A note?" Andy looked through his pants pockets, obviously pretending to look for one.

"Fuck, doctor, I must've left it on my bed..."

"Then you must go back and get it."

"I'm sixteen, and I'm my own man, and I'm so fucking tired of being told what to do!" He was waving his arms, stomping his feet.

Something about the stomping. Andy's youth, that arrogance. Joe felt it in his bones. A hot trembling, a rumbling, heat, coming up from his ankles. His Papa's voice strong, *We don't take orders from babies.* That certainty Joe had always felt with his Papa collapsing like a lung.

"Doc, that..."

Goddamn Nazis... Andy was yelling, "Doc, it hurts let go."

Joe let go of Andy's hand and looked at his red fingers, horrified. He'd had no idea he'd grabbed the young man. "You need to follow orders, from *me*." Then, he softened his tone. "Some rules are created to harm. The ones here on the ward are not those."

Joe saw the surprise in Andy 's eyes.

"Thanks Doc. Fuck. I'll get permission."

At the nurses' station, Joe filled out the slip and handed it to him. He watched Andy lumber down the hall, his gait uneven. When he was a young boy, he'd been shot in the leg on a hunting trip. His father had been drunk.

Having these kids here, helping them through their brokenness made him feel like he was doing his small part. He walked by Ed Friedman's office, the ward's

psychotherapist; the door was ajar, and he heard him say to Sandy, "Suffering is unnecessary…"

Joe walked in and saw Ed shift in his seat, his mouth open.

"Doctor Greenwood…"

"Hey Doc," Sandy jumped up. "Am I late for something? I haven't done anything… I told you I was gonna be fucking late for Doc. Friedman…"

"You're in the right place, Sandy. Slow down. No need to get your heart rate up again. No more blood clots, OK? No more Cocaine. Ever. You're doing a good job, and I'm giving you a pass for psychotherapy today."

She jumped up and down, clapping, yelling, "Really? No kidding, Doc?

Don't kid me." She ran out, yelling for her friend.

Joe pulled up a chair and sat across from Ed. It was uncomfortable, not a proper office setting: him behind his desk, seated in his own leather chair.

"Why do you think I interrupted your session?"

Ed shook his head.

"You've no idea? None?" Joe couldn't believe the stupidity in this highly educated, in-recovery young psychologist.

"Inform me."

His tone was insolent, arrogant. That heat rising up. Joe tried to push it down. *Pack your stuff*, the Nazis had said. No one had had any choice. "You've no right to tell anyone they can't suffer." Joe said, twisting his hands.

"You interrupted me before I could say more..."

Joe's face was puffing out, his chest was tighter than it had been in a while. He lowered his head and observed Ed's platform shoes... those heavy Nazi boots.

He stood up suddenly, picking up the wooden chair he was sitting on. He stopped himself from throwing it. Putting it down, he stood and turned toward the door, his back to Ed, breathing hard.

Now Ed was at the door, concerned.

But Joe thrust out his arms, thinking Ed was trying to bolt. "Sit down." Ed did so. And he sat too, still trying to breathe rhythmically. At least the young psychotherapist listened. Enthusiasm was gone from his eyes. That was good. So full of his own

God damned ideas. "You've no understanding of hardships... they don't go away. Everyone knows they don't 'have to suffer' as you glibly say. It's that they can't help it, suffering never stops."

"With all due respect, there's more information."

"Where? With that Seth person you people love? Always escaping into some fantasy about how suffering has no purpose... as if to say their pain..." He stood up and began pacing furiously. He opened a window, not noticing Ed shivering, glued to his seat, leaning in to hear him better. Joe was almost whispering, now. "I need decency in this ward. Sandy only knows suffering... no parents..." His hands were shaking. He understood. He'd not even been thirteen, lying under his murdered Mama and Papa...

His heart was beating out of his chest; he saw Ed rush to him. "I'm OK. Everything is OK." He sat. Breathed hard. Ed sat across from him, confused. All Joe had wanted was an old-fashioned, Freudian psychiatrist, someone stable, and educated in this well-established work.

He slowly walked out. Aaron had been looking for him. Greeted him with a big smile.

"CBS evening news wants to interview us. They've heard great things about this ward."

FORTY-SIX

CLARA

Becky walked with me to my cabin. Her ropey braid slapped against her butt like angry waves.

She stopped and turned toward me, her brown eyes weary. "This kind of thing isn't for me. I'm leaving."

We stared at each other in silence, the ocean slamming against the shore. The last support I had was shattering. "You can't mean that?"

"I'm exhausted. I'm going to sleep on the bus all the way home. And then we'll talk."

The wind howled through the trees. The sea crashed forward and receded, furiously returning with greater force. Becky couldn't leave. I would never become a teacher. "I'll be strong in three days, you'll see. Let's talk then. You're just tired."

But maybe she should go before I killed her, too. The solitary cabin was pitch black, and I decided not to turn on my flashlight. I paced the cabin like a defeated tiger, my head between my hands. I sat down on the bed and stood up again.

I walked outside; the cold black air was welcoming. The sky was a massive, multiple-layered sparkle of every star that ever existed.

The ocean had quieted, and the hooting of the owls echoed against the mountains. My throat began to throb. I closed my eyes and took in the sounds. I opened them and looked up at the sky, breathing deeply. I asked David if he was here with me. Of course I received no response; the dead were dead. But was he really? I could feel a softening around my throat. And a great heaviness thudded into my gut. I sat on the earth, doubled over, my back against a tree. I cried, howled, called out for him. My insides were cracking open, expanding past my body's ability to hold them.

"I should have helped him... I did it. I did it. I did it," I cried to the waning moon. I was sweating profusely. I threw off my top and tore off my bra and curled up like a baby beneath the tree, pounded the ground with my fist and bit small rocks. My teeth ached. Spitting out bits of earth, I sat up and leaned against the tree. Its rough bark cut into my bare back. I tried to see Miriam, but she didn't appear. The fishers' wild, guttural cries and the coyotes forlorn howling screamed into the black, then blacker night.

Shivering, I grabbed my clothes and walked naked and barefoot back to my cabin. I never could help anyone. I'd failed miserably at helping Mom. That time when there were a bunch of guys sitting on the front steps, as I'd approached home. They were inhaling pot and sharing acid, their long, unkempt hair tied back in ponytails, wearing long tie-dyed shirts and blue jeans. One had said, *Wow, a free concert, man, all to ourselves. Hey, who has guitars? Let's jam, man.*

The living room window was ajar, and Mom's piano playing was floating out. They were calling *that* a free concert? I'd taken decisive steps up the stairs, using my pointing toes like a walking cane for the blind to mark a safe and open space in which to step.

A long arm smelling of patchouli oil had grabbed at the bottom of my bell sleeve. It had been a feeble attempt, and I hardly had to move my arm to brush him off.

Come on honey, have a smoke, one of them had said, his eyes squinted, lungs filled. Their collective laugh made me run into the house.

Mom was slumped as was the usual case, and her eyes were red and blotchy. A bottle of Valium was on the piano bench next to her, overturned, a few fallen pills underneath her feet. An empty bottle of vodka was standing on the piano itself, without a coaster. She was in her pale blue bathrobe. It was half-opened, exposing her breasts. Her hair was uncombed, wild-looking.

I gently put my hand on her shoulder. She shuddered and looked at me.

Mom, I'd whispered close to her ear, *Mom! You have an audience. You must be presentable. I'm going to go get you a glass of water, and I'll bring you some clothes. Just stay here and keep playing.*

Mom had looked at me as I pointed out the window. She saw the guys sitting on the porch steps. Her eyes grew large, the way they did when she was happy. She wobbled toward her record collection and flung records wildly. *Goddammit, where the fuck is it? You kids take everything from me, everything.* And then just as suddenly, she laughed crazily, throwing her head back and waving *The Sound of Music* furiously in the air. She ripped it out of its cover, throwing the jacket on the floor, and clumsily put the record on the phonograph. The needle fell onto it before she turned on the stereo, making a small, squealing sound. Before I could stop her, she was standing in front of the opened window, her robe flung off. High pitched and off tune, she sang along as the record played the song, *The Sound of Music.*

I shut the window and tried to pull her away, only to have her slap me across the face and open the window again. Stunned, all I could do was stand there and watch her dance and sing naked in front of the opened window.

She had asked me not to tell Dad. *We can't make Dad jealous, please don't anger him, there's my girl.*

I never did tell Dad. I had known Mom wasn't okay, but I had kept telling her she was. Just like I had tried to reassure David that I could help him, but he saw through my lies, my imposter self. I deserved his rage. That's what negativity like mine did. Attracted death. I had probably made Mom that way. Surely, Damien had dropped me now, like a hot coffee pot.

I was shattered, all due to my own undoing. I felt grainy and filthy. I picked at my nails, feeling the grit under them. I closed my eyes and opened them again. There was no difference, black was all around me.

～

THE FOLLOWING three days stretched out like the sky, endless and wide. I ate little, and did what I could with prayer. On the third night, I knelt on the hard-wood floor, kicking the round scatter-rug away. "Dear God," I said, my hands clasped together, "if there is help for me, if I really have a True Self then please show that to me." I stayed kneeling, until my knees ached. I missed Damien so much. I thought of him in those foster homes, where there hadn't been any love at all. If he could make it through years of homelessness, I could make it through three days of being all alone. I lifted my head and started to get up. But he'd never killed anyone, he was never that negative. I fell to my knees again.

I pictured Wendy and me, years ago. She'd been so young, maybe four? Mom had been playing the piano, and Wendy was crying. I went to pick her up, but she'd screamed as if I were murdering her. Mom stopped playing, and wobbled toward me, yelling, *Stop playing mother, Wendy isn't a doll.* She'd grabbed her from my arms, and Wendy yelled even louder. I was on my tippy toes, trying to grab her back. And then, Dad walked in. Mom held on tight to my sister and wiped her tears. She cooed, *Clara's at it again, making Wendy scream like this.*

Wendy had held out her arms to him, and he took her gently from Mom. I stood there crying, and Mom said so only I could hear, *You are nothing but trouble, I should have left you in the garbage when you were born.*

Mom had been right. I thought, as I climbed into bed. She should have left me in the garbage.

～

THE FOURTH MORNING, I didn't want to face anyone. I pulled the blankets over my head, wondering if I could simply let June know I was leaving. I'd sneak out and hitch a ride to the airport, even though I had no idea how far or close it was, or of the probable dangers involved in such a plan.

But there was a sudden knock on my door and I heard Damien say, "Good morning, hon, your three days are up."

I slowly pulled the blankets off and looked at the door, as if I were hallucinating.

"Are you in there?"

That was June.

I opened the door, and Melissa, to my great surprise, threw her arms around me.

"I'm back," she cooed. "Helen needed me these last few days to help you."

June and Damien spilled in behind her. They all clambered into the small cabin. We stood in a circle looking at each other.

"God, you look awful." June rummaged through her bottomless bag and pulled out a tissue, which I didn't take.

"Listen, hon." Damien was standing across from me. His gorgeous eyes shone into mine. "Helen's weeping like she's never wept before. On the heels of David's death, Becky leaves. She's losing sleep and can't imagine what's become of you."

"However, even in her grief, she never stops thinking about you." Melissa said, taking the tissue from June and wiping her eyes.

I looked at June, but she averted Melissa's gaze. I noticed the dirty floor. Even though I had swept each day, I should have asked the person who had brought me food and wood for some soap and a scrub brush.

No one cared. Damien said, "Helen has bought a restaurant property in Boston. Melissa and I are flying out tomorrow morning to scout the area, find housing for the two of you, and something nearby for myself..."

"I'm staying here," June croaked, sounding like a frog. "But I'll be moving as well, shortly."

Wait. What? I shook my head trying to make sense of all of this. "What do you mean...?"

"Oh hon, where's your smile? Your True Self, huh? Helen wants you, Damien and me to start up ASI Boston! Mary told her you needed a brand new environment!"

"Well... I do. This is so sudden." It was as though there were cobwebs in my ears. Was I hearing right? I'd be moving to Boston, with Damien and Melissa? I wasn't being thrown out for being a murderer?

Damien said, "What is going on with your fingers? You're bleeding..."

I had bitten two nails down to the skin. They were raw red and dripping blood. I put them both in my mouth. He moved closer to me, taking more tissue from June. He gently wiped my fingers and pressed the soft Kleenex into them.

"I told you a long time ago, this school is full of surprises." He was standing so close, I could smell the whiskey sweating off his skin.

"Come on," June said laughing. "I'm getting hungry, it's time for breakfast and I know Helen's excited to see you."

She pulled me by the arm, but I put mine through Damien's. He escorted me to the main cabin. Melissa was hanging onto his other arm. But I couldn't deal with that just now.

FORTY-SEVEN
WENDY

I was like fucking furious. My fucking anger was fucking bigger than the fucking universe. Huge waves of frustration were keeping me up all fucking night.

Jake and I were in the Mission, eating at La Ciudad De Mexico. I was like on my second burrito. He just shook his head.

"Just stop stuffing your fucking mouth for a minute. It's like you're not even tasting ."

I hated that he was fucking right. I put down the burrito, sucking my greasy fingers. And then I bit into it again. Fuck him.

"Fucking Patti Jenkins knows fucking nothing... and fucking Kleep knows fucking nothing."

Jake shook his head. "Fucking, fucked up."

He was so calm about it. "I mean is that like all you can say? Don't you like have any suggestions?"

"Like what?"

"I don't know. I don't fucking know." I like hit my fist on the table. "It's time to call that debriefer Beatrice person. I found her card two days ago in my fucking pocket. It was like a sign. I need to call her."

"What the fuck is she going to do?

"I don't know. Maybe she'll have some suggestions..."

"Fucking call her."

I fucking loved Jake.

~

I PUT on my Jax outfit to meet Dr. Beatrice Goldman. I like rode the bus downtown and walked into 450 Sutter Street. It was a huge fucking building with a gold-gilded lobby that had marble looking floors. I felt like I needed a fucking mink stole. I rode the elevator to the 22nd floor. The long corridor had a blue-grey rug. If there were like ever spies wandering around this building, you'd never fucking know. Everything was so like quiet.

There was gold lettering on her front door. *Beatrice Goldman, Ph.D. Clinical Psychologist and Debriefer.* I stood up straight... I can't swear, and I must act educated, calm and serious. I would tell her that I was studying family therapy and psychology. I had to be like fucking legitimate. Trying not to wobble in my high heels, I opened the door.

There was a secretary behind a long desk. The desk was filled with piles of paper, a typewriter and a yellow phone. The secretary had her like blonde hair pulled back in a ballerina bun. She wore a red suit and a white blouse that didn't have like a single spot on it. A blue pearl necklace.

"May I help you?" Her voice was soft, welcoming.

I sat on one of the red leather chairs, like large enough to seat both Jake and me. I wanted to kick off my shoes — they were fucking killing me — and curl up on the seat with one of the magazines. Dr. Goldman came out of her office.

She shook my hand, her small blue eyes like looking straight into mine. "Come, we'll talk in my office." I loved her fucking red hair. Not one strand out of place. I touched my own, falling down my face.

We walked into her large, like super fucking plush office. I couldn't fucking believe it. Everything was red. The two leather chairs, just like in her waiting room, and the fucking leather couch. All fucking red.

A desk sat in the corner, near the windows, neatly piled with papers and note- books. A wooden bookshelf lined the side wall next to me; had she really like read all of those fucking books? Fuck.

"How may I help you?"

I sat at the edge of the huge chair, trying to keep my fucking back straight. Just pretend you're a fucking professor. Just don't like fucking swear, whatever you do.

"I... ah... met you in one of my family therapy classes. You were like lecturing on mind control..." My heart was beating really fast. She nodded, like she remembered doing that.

"And I know someone who's missing..."

Her eyes were intent on mine. She had millions of freckles, but I could see like care and intelligence in her face. She wasn't a joke. She was like serious about her work.

"I... ah like I need this to be fucking confidential..." Shit. My neck was fucking burning redder than her fucking chair. I squirmed. She was fucking staring at me. "I mean, please like don't report what I'm going to tell you to the fucking police or the news reporters." Fuck. Stop the fuck swearing.

"Unless you report illegal activity, everything you say here is confidential."

I looked up into her fucking caring eyes and took in a long deep breath.

"My sister, Clara, has been fucking missing for a long time... I'm sorry I keep swearing..."

Dr. Goldman smiled, and dimples appeared around her freckles.

"No need to apologize, dear. For how long?"

I crossed and uncrossed my legs. She was really nice, and beautiful. She was writing things down in her notebook. I mean like how amazing was that?

"What are you writing about?'

"The things you're telling me, that way I won't forget. How long has she been gone?"

She looked at me again and smiled. Someone like her could forget stuff? I totally relaxed. I unwound my legs and sat more forward. "I don't know exactly how long. But, at least two... or three years. My dad and I are so worried."

Dr. Beatrice raised her eyebrows. "Oh, I'm so fucking worried..." I kept repeating like an idiot. And then I started bawling.

"Well, of course you are. And you have already told me you don't want the police to know she's missing?"

Still crying, I shook my head. "No, I wanted to know more about mind control, how a person can be brainwashed, when they're so fu... I mean smart, like Clara. She's the smartest person I know..." Please, please, please, can I please stop swearing?

"Well..." Dr. Goldman sighed. Her eyes looked tired. "...it can happen to the most intelligent of us. We meet someone, or a group of people we think understands us... we confide in that person or group, and before we know it, we have become vulnerable and dependent on their direction and guidance."

"That sounds like it could've fucking happened to *me*, ... but not Clara." It was hopeless, swears just kept falling out of my mouth.

Dr. Goldman was looking at me like fucking intently. It was like she was getting into my head.

"Did you and your sister experience a traumatic event when you were growing up?"

She was a fucking genius. If ever anyone was ever going to find fucking Clara it was going to be her.

I told her about Mom dying

"So, both your sister and you were already vulnerable, looking for a mother figure. It's very possible that your sister has joined a group of people run by a woman, someone she could identify as such a person."

Fuck. Dr. Goldman had Clara fucking pinned in like *under thirty* minutes. I made another fucking appointment with her. I'd get Dad to pay for my sessions. I'd like to get him to come in too.

FORTY-EIGHT
CLARA

Fall

It was my last day in San Francisco. I took a lingering walk toward Baker Beach. It was hard to believe that I would be on a plane the next morning. The familiar blocks behind and ahead of me hadn't changed. Yet everything had.

I reached the beach. The clear sky was filled with gulls. They swooped down onto the sand and swelled up again, winging through the wind. Even these god-awful creatures could be happy.

Boston. Helen saving me. Another privilege handed to me. I picked up a handful of dry sand and watched the grains fall through my fingers. Looking at my opened palm, I brushed the rest of the sand off until there was just one grain. I looked down the stretch of beach. All it was, was millions of tiny grains. Missing one wouldn't make a difference.

But missing one person did. David, Mom. Miriam came to mind. I asked her, *did you ever feel this way?* Her eyes were serious, and her mouth was turned down. She opened it as if to scream. I shuddered. *What would you do, if you were me?*

I moved toward the ocean. They'd found Mom on the rocks, and David in the smashed truck. *They said he was drunk. He drowned in alcohol, like Mom. But I, Miriam, I killed them both.* The ocean was roaring up to my feet. I took off my shoes and socks and waded in. I splashed water over my face, the salt stinging my fingers where I'd bit them. What if I kept walking in? And let the ocean swallow me. After all, I was nothing more than a grain of sand. Even more meaningless than that. I wiped my face. Stupid idiot for crying. For whom? For what? The tide was pulling at my ankles. I kept walking in. My jeans, waterlogged, weighed me down. Better the sea take me before I killed someone else. The waves were crashing and churning from every direction; I lost footing, and the strong undertow pulled me out and under, rocks and sand tumbling over and all around me. I was somersaulting along the sandy bottom, water raging through my nose and mouth. Every attempt to stand or crawl, or to writhe like a snake and move toward shore, sent me back and under, my back hitting the bottom hard, often.

I stopped fighting, stopped turning in what I thought was the direction of shore. I couldn't breathe. Just take me... I was whipped to the bottom and choking in what felt to be the whole ocean. I pushed with all my might and managed to get my head above the surface. Sputtering and coughing, gasping desperately for air, gulping it in and out, I kept pushing against the tide, struggling to find a place shallow enough to stand... which I managed to do. Standing, I braced my legs as the tide went out and let the tow pull me closer. Slowly I waded back, too cold to feel the cuts on my battered back. I looked up at the sky filling with fog, gulping breath in through my mouth as I kept breathing in the water inside my nose.

Finally up on shore, too exhausted to sit, I stood, looking at the Golden Gate looming above; I saw June and me, struggling to light her cigarette. That was eons ago and difficult to hold on to. I felt as heavy as the sea, water dripping everywhere, and sand stuck to my clothes and skin. Even so, weirdly, I felt tied to it, to this sand and rock and angry gripping tide; it had felt normal, or like I deserved to almost die. I saw my shoes, dry as you please, sitting a few hundred feet away. My socks were tucked inside, the sneakers neatly tied together. They seemed surreal, pristine. They were the only dry things I carried as I walked like a turtle up the dunes, feeling my breath return, even as the weight of my jeans and my hair, soaked with salt and sweat, slowed me further.

Sitting at the top, the wind blew the water out of my skin, chills on chills. I couldn't get warm, but I didn't mind. The bridge was still and quiet, unmoved on its

solid red-golden legs. How much had it seen? Could it see me now...? The undertow, though known, is the Ocean's invisible, breath-ripping, death-steep toll.

Mom couldn't fight that, and I could only barely do so. I'd escaped with small cuts on my red hands, imprints of pebbles and rough sand; the same was probably stuck to the cuts on my throbbing back. But the sea had eaten Mom, perhaps swallowed her in one gulp.

I looked out across the beach, down to the pathway I knew so well, the one so close to home. And though I was near, I could never go back there; never be alone with Dad, ever again. I pictured his face at those awful dinners. His chin long, his eyes unbearably sad. And now I was leaving for his and Mom's hometown, and Grandma was still there. But that didn't matter. Dad had probably gone through my things and given them away. He probably had found that necklace and earring set, and given them back to her. *She's so ungrateful.* They had most likely agreed.

Looking at the ocean, at its terrifying, deceptive beauty. Would Boston be like that? Beautiful, terrifying and deceptive? Damien would be there but so would Melissa. I sifted piles of sand into my shoes and pounded it down. The sun was sinking, and I knew I had to leave. I picked up my shoes, impacted with bits of the dune, and carried them down, the weight of water in my clothes stopping me from tumbling.

FORTY-NINE
WENDY

"Just be yourself. You don't have to wear a suit, but don't wear jeans either."

Freddy had actually fucking invited *me* to do my internship at the Monterey Center where I had received help fucking two years ago.

"Stop pacing. You're going to do great, or I wouldn't have asked you to run these groups."

How could he fucking know this about me? But, fuck, after meeting Dr. Beatrice, I wanted to be just like her, looking so professional and fucking confident. I'd wear a plain dress and put my hair up. Shit.

THERE WERE FUCKING fifteen people sitting around. And Freddy, thank God, was with me. I swear I fucking wobbled to my seat, as if I'd had a fucking whole bottle of whiskey.

"This is our new counselor? She can't fucking walk, shit."

"Yeah like she's fucking wasted. Bringing a fucking wasted..."

"That's enough Natalie." Freddy hadn't even sat down yet, and my face was so fucking red I couldn't turn around.

"This is Wendy Greenwood. She's gone through the program just like you. She'll be running your groups from now on."

I finally sat down and smiled stupidly. Each one of these addicts could like see right through me.

"Laura," Freddy spoke to another girl, probably sixteen, chewing bubble gum and blowing huge, pink wisps, snapping it down, only to blow it out again.

"What the fuck, Freddy. What's up your ass today?"

"You've got something up yours, to talk to him that way." I had no idea I was going to say that. I stared her down.

"Leave Laura alone, bitch."

"Terry, that's enough. Laura, what's up with you today? Tell us how you are." Freddy's voice was so fucking calm. But I wouldn't be called bitch. I walked over to Terry. She was a tiny kid, probably weighed 100 pounds. Her head wouldn't even have reached my waist, and I wasn't tall. Shit.

"Who do I fucking remind you of? Your mother? Your sister?" Oh fucking God, my head was spinning.

"Come sit down..." Freddy's voice was far away.

"Get out of my face, bitch."

"Listen, you're talking to the worst of 'em. What happened to you? Did you lose a mother, too? Is your fucking sister..."

"Wendy!" Freddy was pulling me away.

Terry had her fists up. Laura was right beside her.

"Fight, Fight, Fight..."

The fucking place had erupted.

"Fuck you."

"Shit get the fuck off of me..."

"Fucking bitch..."

The room echoed with yelling and swears, tears...

Freddy stood in the middle of it all. Somehow he'd managed to call for help, and a couple of policemen showed up, or Ward Guards, as they were called. They swung batons, but I stood in front of them.

"It was all my fucking fault. Don't bash them. We need order. Fuck. Please..."

The girls were spent. They sat down without being told. The two guards stayed by the door.

Freddy said, "We've had enough for one day. The meeting is over..."

"NO!" screamed Terry. She had her head down, hands over her face. Snorting, crying. "I want to talk. Shit. This is the only place I've ever felt safe. My fucking father beat my mother... but she fucking drank all the fucking time. And he left me to look for her. Sometimes he brought someone else home, sometimes she did..."

"That's so fucked up," Laura was near her, stroking her hair.

She should've sat down, but neither fucking Freddy nor I stopped her. Laura was still talking.

"Like, we're all just fucking swaying in some kind of fucking field, and everyone keeps stomping on us..."

Shit. So greatly put. I had felt that way often. Stomped on by Clara, following me to the fucking beach every night. Getting in my face. Yelling at my boyfriends, *You're too old for her. She's twelve*! And that's what made them not give me pot, which got me smoking in seventh grade. But shit, now... I had God in my heart. He was helping. He kept lifting my spirits. I'm not that girl anymore. Nothing was anyone's fault. Ever. And I remembered a different field. And I said,

359

"I wandered lonely as a cloud
That floats on high o'er vales and hills,
When all at once I saw a crowd,
A host, of golden daffodils;
Beside the lake, beneath the trees,
Fluttering and dancing in the breeze."

Terry's head shot up. "Huh, fuck?"

But I continued, 'cause it was fucking God talking through me. My voice had never sounded so strong, so clear.

"Continuous as the stars that shine
And twinkle on the milky way,
They stretched in never-ending line
Along the margin of a bay:
Ten thousand saw I at a glance,
Tossing their heads in sprightly dance."

"All of you, fuck, are in a field right? Maybe you can think about this differently. Stand up. Be in the field you're in now, being stomped on. Feel how fucked up that is. Then look up. Pretend you can see those stars. Pretend you can see the dancing daffodils in the field next to the one you're in. See the stars lighting up the path to it.

"The waves beside them danced; but they
Out-did the sparkling waves in glee:
A poet could not but be gay,
In such a jocund company:
I gazed — and gazed — but little thought
What wealth the show to me had brought:

For oft, when on my couch I lie
In vacant or in pensive mood,
They flash upon that inward eye
Which is the bliss of solitude;
And then my heart with pleasure fills,

And dances with the daffodils."

"Come on you fucks, move like you can really see this. God gave us these daffodils, this new field. See it. Be it. You can, *'cause it's really there."*

We needed music. So I hummed Mozart's Concerto in C major, in order to create a really different, calming atmosphere.

As they moved about, I looked at Freddy. His mouth was open, his eyes wide. He even joined them, spreading his long, thin arms out as if to make the field boundary. The newly recovering addicts moved in a wave toward him and stayed within the bounds of his arms, really and truly looking like dancing, fucking daffodils. If only Dad were here. And Clara. This was something she did all the time in her dance classes. Maybe if we did this long enough, I'd find her. As I stood humming, I could see Mom at the piano, her body swaying as her hands ran up and down the keys, me beside her, watching. And it was as though the music just beamed through me. *This* was what it meant to have God inside your heart; only God could have done this, could have thought of this whole fucking daffodil thing.

PART 3

ONE

CLARA

Fall

When I first stepped into the hallway of the two-bedroom apartment Melissa had rented, my heart sank. The entrance was dark and musty, and it stank like old socks. *It's a dump,* I wanted to tell her.

Sensing my discomfort, Melissa pulled me by the hand, shaking her head. "Wait till you see it, hon."

The hallway emptied into the living area... a circular room complete with shiny wooden floors and windows halfway around. A comfy brown couch with matching recliner chairs filled the space. It was even large enough to hold meetings. It was too nice. Beautiful, in fact. I wasn't good enough for this.

Solemnly, Melissa took my hand and led me into the enormous kitchen. There were more counters than the restaurant; a round wooden table, large enough to seat eight, sat in the middle of the stone floor; a microwave was built into the wall above the stove, and to the left of the sink, a working dishwasher.

My bedroom had hardwood floors, and the walls were painted lemon yellow. Charming cream valances drooped over the large windows. I gazed down at the weedy garden, the one cherry tree already turning orange.

I could see into the neighbors' well-kept yards, bursting with maples and oaks, their leaves beginning to turn yellow and red. The sky was endlessly blue, and the sun was flooding the room, leaving pools of light near the king-sized bed and the tall oak armoire. There was even a smaller, matching cabinet that I could use for toiletries.

We walked back into the kitchen and sat at the huge table. Melissa sitting across from me was nearly six feet away.

It was all so strange and too rich for me. Boston, I had always felt, housed really smart people; they were the graduates of Harvard, MIT and Tufts. They published important works and found scientific and medical cures for all kinds of illnesses. It was the hub of the best hospitals. And I was here, starting a restaurant and beginning ASI, Boston. Our new recruits would be these heroes. I saw Miriam floating in my mind, pointing to so many memories...Grandma Shirley giving me that necklace so long ago. *You look elegant*, she had said, her smile as wide as the sea. Patti and I dancing to Joni Mitchell: Patti had said, *You take to dance the way the waves do to the ocean*...and her beautiful blonde hair flowed past her waist. And lastly, the Golden Gate Bridge standing tall, surrounded in mist, foghorns warning and bringing wobbling ships from far out at sea to safety. I broke down, crying.

MELISSA AND DAMIEN were on me for everything. *Time to get up hon...* 5:30 a.m. I was on the trolley riding into Boston. It was a crowded and messy experience, people sleeping, full cups of coffee spilling. Hundreds of others standing and swaying so close, someone inevitably fell on me. The stench of stale beer, Coke, B.O.

The phone rang the minute I got to the restaurant. Damien: *Did you buy the furniture yet? How about the paint? I'll be there in a few. Helen understands your reluctance, and she isn't happy...*

The restaurant was located just a few blocks from the Boston Ballet, on a small, side street, just a hop away from the Boston Public Garden.

On my third trip into town, my head pounding from all the demands and being pushed off the train by so many hurried and frazzled people, I broke into a run. I entered the Garden just as the sun was rising.

I stopped suddenly, the cold wind biting through my light jacket. The Garden looked like a nature museum. The layout was exquisite. Cherry, willow and magnolia trees lined the paths, along with maples and oaks. Grass covered the area and wove in and between the flowerbeds. Ducks floated on the pond; the orange sky tinted the dark water, and I breathed in freshly mowed grass. Orange, red and yellow leaves floated like dancers onto the grass, landing gently, randomly, freely.

I drank in the utter beauty, so different from San Francisco... no fog, no Golden Gate Bridge. I remembered seeing the Charles River yesterday. I had never seen a city with a major river running through it, or with a garden like this.

Damien had told me that public hangings had occurred right here until the early 1800s. I tried to imagine the criminals hanging, from a maple or an oak. I could almost hear the snap of that rope and shuddered. I felt the pull of the ocean swallowing me into the roaring darkness; felt that same helplessness.

I put my own hands to my neck. I saw Mom's face, then David's; her huge green eyes and his small grey-blue ones. Drowned, crashed, drunk, dead. Was it really suicide? On both their parts? There was a squabble in the pond, two ducks were at each other. The wind picked up, and I stuck my hands deep into my pockets, as if to bury the thoughts.

I walked even more slowly, and followed the pond. This wasn't Baker Beach, but it could be a place to turn to. I stood watching the fighting ducks, the filthy water smashing up against the sides.

What would Dad think? Mom? Here I was back in their hometown where they grew up. As children, did they stand in this very spot, looking at the ducks? Did Grandma give them stale bread, the way she did Wendy and me when she had taken us to Golden Gate Park? I pictured Dad at age thirteen, maybe sharing a bag of that bread with Mom. Perhaps they stood close to the bank, taking turns throwing the food toward the floating birds, laughing at their squabbles. I imagined Grandma calling to them for their picnic lunch, spreading out a blanket in front of the signs I was staring at now, that read: *Don't feed the ducks*.

I also remembered a weird conversation I'd overheard years ago. Dad had been talking to Grandma... *You didn't see what I saw, Shirley. Fingers, toes...* And Dad had kissed all ten of my fingers one by one, then he did the same with Wendy's. After, he'd say, *Good, all ten fingers are healthy. Be grateful.* He'd smile, his sad eyes on each of us, warm like the sun.

Miriam was nodding, crying. A milk mustache on her upper lip.

But after that day, there wasn't any time to stop at the Gardens. Melissa was on me constantly. *You didn't go to the restaurant as you were told to do the other day, I called you many times. You're not understanding how close you are to becoming psychotic.*

And then Helen called, her voice was low and seething. "Mary is coming through... You must work off the negativity that killed David and do every single thing you are told to do with absolute perfection. If you don't, your body and mind will become so twisted it will show up in everything you do. You'll end up in a state mental institution for the rest of your life as will probably happen to June and Tim."

June?

Mary continued, "She's been kicked out and has left in a very negative state..."

We never did have a chance to talk this past summer on the farm.

Mary was droning on, "Not one chair can have a scratch on it; not one radish stem can be left on a kitchen counter; not one customer can complain..."

Every limb in my body felt like it weighed one hundred pounds. I moved like an old lady as I worked. The kitchen was freezing except when the stove and its burners were lit. Apparently, it was one of the coldest Octobers on record. My fingers and toes were red and raw, and I wore a stupid itchy, green wool hat all the time.

DESPITE EVERYTHING, the restaurant was hopping from the day we opened. Customers were saying there was no other café like it. We were the only ones using foods from local farmers, both vegetables and meats.

Dancers, musicians, students, scientists, store owners and business managers frequented the place; there was a small line outside the door as I opened each morning.

Damien ran the kitchen, being the main cook for the time being, while I was hostess, waitress and bus-girl. Melissa took care of orders and deliveries, and she was often away, visiting nearby farms.

The days were so dark and cold. The lights in the kitchen blinked off and on, and it was impossible to see at 5 a.m. I did everything by rote, mixed the batter for the muffins, chopped the vegetables, scrambled the eggs. And Damien was always there, *Even though we're off to a good start, hon, your negativity is seeping into everything.*

I often faked a smile, like I did then. If I pretended to be positive, maybe I would be. *If I'm not feeling joy all the time, I'm being false.*

Damien hugged me. *I know you'll come through, hon. I can feel it.*

And then we started sleeping together again. I noticed him drinking more; I figured it was the stress of the job. Or maybe it was me. Maybe my negativity was getting under his skin. I vowed I'd try harder.

369

≈

By early November, the café was filled with dancers; their soft, enormous bags hanging over the chairs, their feet turned out as they sat, hair oiled tightly into buns. They pecked at muffins and had thirds and fourths on coffee, talking with each other, long fingers gesturing. There were many who came in regularly and greeted me by name.

"Clara, do you have those apple muffins again today? We'll take a half dozen for the table."

This morning, I lingered at their table, asked them about the shows they were auditioning for, performing in. Then one said, her blue eyes glowing, "It's exciting, Patti Jenkins will be our guest choreographer..."

I spilled coffee on the table. My bleak energy was spilling out everywhere, just like years ago when I had knocked over the box of Captain Crunch cereal, spilling it all over the floor. Wendy had been screaming, *No yucky Mommy!* while Mom had yelled at me, *You can't do anything right!* and her opened bottle of pills dropped on the floor. I created chaos everywhere. It didn't matter that Patti was here, she'd probably run from me. When Patti had asked me, *What do you want to do with your life?* I had always said, *Own my own dance studio...* I had been so naïve. I knew now that it would never happen. To make matters worse, when I walked into the kitchen Damien wasn't happy.

"Waitresses don't do that."

"Don't do what?" The empty coffee pot shook in my hands. I carefully placed it under the brewer and turned it on. When I turned around, he was pouring the last dregs from a large whiskey bottle into his coffee.

"Don't gossip with the patrons."

I stared at him. I didn't remember him ever drinking while serving in the kitchen.

"What are you looking at? I said, don't gossip with the patrons."

He moved closer to me but something was burning. French toast. On the stove.

The pan hissed and steamed as I tossed it into the sink. I grabbed the fresh pot of coffee, a plate of muffins and stumbled out of the kitchen. He was right. No matter what I did or said, I brought everyone down.

I placed the muffins on the dancers' table and carefully poured the coffee. They looked up at me, laughing, but I only smiled and whisked myself away. They would have never guessed that I had been Patti's number-one teacher, that we had been on a first-name basis. I had asked Patti, *And you? What is your deepest dream*? She had said, *To become a famous choreographer*. Due to her purity, that dream had come true.

When I returned to the kitchen with a tray of dirty dishes, I almost dropped it. Damien was slumped on the floor near the stove, the bottle of whiskey broken, thick glass pieces around him; coffee staining his white apron and blue jeans.

I stood there, stiff. The restaurant was completely full. There was a line of people waiting. Jesus, I had no time to clean him up *and* cook *and* wait the tables *and* wash the dishes.

I knelt beside him, careful not to sit on the glass. I stretched my arm and gently rubbed his soft, wrinkly cheek. Should I slap him, just hard enough to wake him? I called his name and pinched his cheek. I closed my eyes. How many times had I done this for Wendy? For Mom? And how many more would I now for Damien? When I'd found Mom slumped on the love seat, I'd picked up the empty vodka bottle. But Dad had come home just then. His eyes were so sad, *What are you doing with that*? His voice was angry. *You have no business here. I'll take care of your mother*. But he couldn't. She'd died a few years later.

Damien finally came to. I helped him up and grabbed a towel to wipe down his wet clothes.

"I'm prone to fainting spells, okay, babe?"

"You're a fucking drunk" The words just fell out of me. I threw the towel in the sink, and it missed and fell to the floor. Was that what Mom had been? A drunk? When I bent down to pick it up, there was a huge cockroach scurrying under the stove.

"Look, babe...." He turned me around to face him. His eyes were ugly, bloodshot. "Drinking has nothing to do with this. Liquor helps, so don't go worrying Helen with this shit, okay?"

"I won't tell Helen. There's no need." I was good at lying, used to it. Mom had said to me so long ago, *That's a good girl, fill this little bottle for me, you mustn't tell your father. It will be our special secret.* This would be Damien's and my special secret. And anyway, he had a fainting problem. The guy was sick. Mom had been sick too. Had Wendy?

I softened my tone. I took a wet, clean cloth and gently washed his face and then gave him a fresh apron.

"We'll be okay, hon, right?"

〜

I HAD FINALLY FOUND decent winter clothes at Filene's Basement. Dressed in my new down jacket with a furry hood, strong leather gloves, heavy-duty snow boots, I clambered onto the bus in the darkness, no moon, no stars. 4 a.m. I wanted to walk through the Public Garden before work. Give myself some space to think. At that hour, there was hardly anyone riding, the lull was comforting.

I felt rested as I entered the Garden. The lamps lit up the trees in an eerie way. They looked like negatives of themselves. The water in the pond lapped gently, more heavily, due to the cold. Ice covered the fallen leaves. I crunched my way through the darkness.

Damien's fainting spells were getting to me. I couldn't stand his stinky breath, nor the smell of whisky oozing out of his skin. I lifted my feet higher and walked faster; the wind was picking up. The ice crunched and cracked, and long thick lines ran along the fallen leaves. Helen should know about Damien, but with me being so negative, she wouldn't believe me, the way Dad hadn't. I tried to run but I felt so damn heavy. The coat must have weighed a hundred pounds, and the shoes felt like they were made of bricks. I must have been awful to deal with when I'd found Mom slumped on the love-seat that day. Some drool had spilled down her chin. She was still in her blue bathrobe at 2:30 in the afternoon. Her face had been so pasty and ugly, I took a step back.

Days of Our Lives was on the TV. The foghorns blared so loudly it was as though they were right there in the room.

I stared at her and shivered. The windows were open, letting in all the mist. *Mom?* I whispered.

You betrayed me again.

I took a step into the room.

Mom?

I took a few more steps. Her pills had spilled all over her lap.

How could you have done this to me?

I'd called Dad. By the time he'd come home, I was just about to fill her empty vodka bottle. But Dad had said, *What are you doing with that bottle?* He'd had Mom hospitalized.

I slowly walked back to the restaurant, still thinking about her, memories flooding me. A stray white dog limped up to me. He might have been blind in one eye, as I could only see into one of them. His coat was matted, and he looked cold. I wanted to pick him up, but as I reached out to him, he growled, baring his teeth. Startled, I left him hurriedly. He could have given me rabies. I was just so stupid, the way I gravitated toward hurtful, sick energy. The way I had been in that car ride with Mom. She had been hospitalized so many times. And one time, she didn't want to go back. She'd been having a fit on the couch when I'd gotten home from school. She banged her small fists against the cushions, got up, grabbed her small pocketbook sitting on the floor and pulled out her flask.

Here, fill it and hurry up. We need to go. I had run to the liquor cabinet above the fridge and, on my toes, pulled down the vodka.

Hurry up, she'd yelled from the living room, *What the hell is taking you so long?*

I'd had trouble opening the new bottle. Wind blew in through the opened windows and chilled the back of my neck. My hand was cold, and it was impossible to twist the top off. I picked up a napkin and twisted as hard as I could, feeling my cheeks redden and pain rise in my mouth from my clamped teeth. I brought the filled flask back to her.

She took a long drink, looked at me smiling. *Come, my good girl,* and she grabbed me by the arm, her nails digging into my wrist.

You must come, do you hear? And then she'd laughed again, her throat sounding as though it had cracks in it.

At first she'd driven super slowly, and cars had been honking like crazy behind us. She was whispering something about LBJ while drinking.

I do wondrous things all day that no one knows about. I wasn't supposed to tell you about my connection with the President. But for a while I've been a member of an elite US governmental committee. And that committee chose me, do you understand? She turned her head to look at me, her eyes bloodshot. *Chose me to deliver certain messages to the President.*

What the hell was she talking about? She'd spoken so rapidly I could barely understand her. But she'd put her foot to the gas pedal then, not stopping at a single intersection, as we sped up and down dangerously steep hills, headed for Ghirardelli Square.

Stop, Mom! My voice had sirened over cars screeching to halts. There'd been a trolley coming right at us, and Mom had sped up even more. The driver had leaned on his horn, and I covered my ears, screaming. We trundled over the tracks, just missing the trolley.

I'm going to miss my plane, Mom had yelled. *There is such an important message I must give to LBJ.* She opened her window. A tirade of *"fuck yous"* and *"what the hell are you doin' lady"* had hollered in, but Mom had screamed back.

Because of all of you I'm going to miss my plane! You have no idea of the importance.

Mom, just shut the goddamned window and stop the car! We'd been going in the opposite direction of the airport.

She'd pressed the gas pedal to the floor, and her entire body leaned in toward the windshield. We were going so fast, and the bay was right in front of us, I knew we were both going to die. *God! Mom! Stop!*

At the end of Beach Street, she'd come to a screeching halt, sending me bouncing off my seat, my head pointed toward the windshield. Somehow, I had missed it and fell back, my butt hitting the vinyl seat with a huge thud. She put her cheek against the steering wheel and sobbed. It was as though an inflation inside her body had, suddenly, collapsed. Her hands were on her lap. She looked tiny. I put mine on top of hers. *Mom, Mom...*

Just stop, you don't understand me, no one does. And you mustn't tell your father, do you hear? She'd raised her voice again and her hands were shaking. *You mustn't tell your father.*

She was crying hard. I'd stroked her matted hair, stiff with too much hairspray. I looked out at the Bay. What good would it have done to tell Dad? I'd only get her into trouble. We sat quietly for a while. Cars honked and drove around us.

It's okay, Mom. I won't tell Dad. You're beautiful, and... and special... and..

She cried harder and leaned her head against my shoulder. I put my arm around her and continued to pat her hair down. I whispered, as if singing a lullaby, *It's really okay. You're fine, and of course you need to get the President his message. And you need to sit up and drive safely to do this.*

Then I got an idea. I sat up straight and turned toward her.

Mrs. Greenwood, I said in a deep voice. *I am secretary to the secretary of Lyndon B. Johnson. I understand you have a very important message to deliver. You must drive your daughter back to her home safely, and then I will speak to you about getting that message to LBJ.* Mom had shot her head right back up. She wiped her nose and patted the tears away from her cheeks. She moved away from me, looked straight ahead and began to drive again, this time more carefully.

Yes, you see, I will get you home safely, and then I will deliver the message to LBJ. It's a secret message. That's why you can't tell Joe. Once I get the message to him, the whole country will be safer.

There was a line outside the restaurant. For a second I didn't understand, or realize where I was. Oh my God, was it already time to start serving?

Hastily, I let everyone in and told them there had been a problem with the stove. I ran into the kitchen and threw some cold muffins into the microwave. Thank God I was the only one here.

I took orders, apologizing again about the stove. Breakfast would be a bit late; did they want to come back? Wait?

As I ran back to the kitchen, I couldn't get Mom out of my mind and stood, staring at nothing. The scrambled eggs could wait. The cold morning sun slanted across my face and down across the stove, making it shine.

The sizzling eggs made me look at them. I didn't remember turning on the stove. My heart skipped a beat; I had better focus, but something was unscrambling inside of me. Could there've been a time when Mom wasn't so crazy? Dad's colleague had been over for a dinner one evening when Mom had been in the hospital. *The Valium is highly addictive,* Dr. Weinstein had said. *Yes, but I didn't know,* Dad had said, frowning, his eyebrows crunched. None *of us did,* Dr. Weinstein had said.

Mom had needed help, as did Damien now. I had to tell Helen. I felt all that negative energy unwind. Telling would be right for me. I didn't have to keep secrets anymore. And, I had to dance again. I'd raise money and put on my own dance show and surprise everyone. By doing so, I'd become a teacher.

It was a relief to be alone now in the mornings. Due to Damien's periodic fainting spells, he was only coming in the afternoon and evenings.

It was a joy to work by myself, pouring muffin batter into tins, chopping vegetables for omelets.

I brought out the piping hot food, apologizing profusely to my waiting customers. And suddenly, I had an idea. It tumbled out of me, unexpectedly. I said, "We're having a fall special today, baked apple muffins, omelet with extra cheese; fresh-squeezed orange juice and coffee. Three dollars a plate."

Could they hear my heart pounding? Three dollars a plate! Twice the expense!

And yet, just about every customer wanted one!

I whipped from table to kitchen, feeling my mind clear, hope running through my veins.

I wrote out the same checks twice, one for the customers and one for the register. The customer checks were written on the white notepaper from the kitchen pads, with the price I had quoted. The checks for the cash register were written on the normal waitstaff paper that showed the breakfasts charged at the normal price. By the time breakfast was over, and Damien had walked in, I had pocketed $30 -- a fortune.

The breakfast shift was easy to do on my own. Neither of us said a word to Helen about Damien only coming in to do lunch and dinners. It was all going quite well. I imagined saving $500. My energy was changing, and surely Melissa and Damien would notice and tell Helen. And when I next spoke with her, she would hear the litheness in my tone, *feel* my new energy over the airwaves! And then I'd tell her that I had a grand surprise for her, a dance show I'd be planning, maybe even with Patti Jenkins! And, it would bring in a ton more students! I was so excited, I mentioned the idea to Damien, who said that Helen hated surprises, and it wouldn't work. *Leave the surprises alone, hon, and just focus on becoming your True Self.*

~

A FEW DAYS LATER, we were all in Melissa's room, watching her pack her bags. Damien was sitting on her bed, laughing.

"What's going on?" I asked.

"Oh, what a surprise we have for you! Helen is so happy that you are better! Damien and I have seen such an improvement!" Melissa sang.

I stood staring at her. She flipped her blonde curls away from her face, as she pulled another dress from her closet.

Damien was grinning widely, "Hon, I wanted to please you, so I've told Helen that I would love to put on a dance show either in San Francisco or in Portland, Oregon, as a means to bring in more students, and I thought that Melissa would be the perfect manager for that. You've been negative for so long that none of us had wanted to give you such a huge job. But since you've changed, we'll bring you onstage..."

"And Damien, hon," Melissa chimed in, "you forgot to say that you'll be moving in, as I'll be gone for a while."

I'd no idea how I looked to either of them. My entire body was inflamed. My throat was on fire, but I was too shocked to speak. And thank God, for I had no idea what I would have said or done, what I was capable of doing in that moment.

I stomped out of the room, into the kitchen, Damien following me.

"Why are you so sour, all of the time? This is your dream, isn't it? I'm worried, hon, your moods change so suddenly..."

"Shut the fuck up."

He was in my face." You're too negative for this school...You've betrayed this incredible teaching long enough. You may already be psychotic, the way you destroy the good everyone else is trying to create."

His words stung. Did he know about the "specials"? I pushed him back and ran to get out of the kitchen, but as I reached the doorway, I tripped over Damien's foot. I went flying and landed on my right ankle. I was squirming. And when I stood up, a sharp, unbearable pain went up and down my whole leg. I fell.

Damien poured himself another drink. "Cut the shit. This is exactly what I mean. You exaggerate everything for attention. You are such a fucking no good, fake bitching liar."

I was crawling back to the table, but the pain was so bad, I stopped and curled into a ball. Darkness.

Wendy had been three. I was six. She was crawling all over the table and had pushed Mom's grapefruit plate to the floor. *Get a rag and wash this up now!* Her hands were shaking as she popped a bunch of pills into her mouth.

But I couldn't leave Wendy... she was now reaching for Mom's coffee cup, and I swiped her hand, but that made the Captain Crunch crash to the floor.

For God's sake, Clara, get your fucking sister off the table.

I pulled her by the legs, she let out a piercing scream.

Give Wendy your glass of milk.

What, Mommy?

Wendy, kicking and biting, fell and was eating the spilled Captain Crunch from the floor.

I bent down and tried to pick her up; it was impossible while she was kicking, and crying.

Then I'll give her yours. Mom came over to us with a glass of milk in her hands. She put the glass on the table, picked Wendy up and sat her right down on the table, too. She held her down, flat on her back. *Grab the milk, I said...Jesus, why are you so difficult? Grab the milk.*

I grabbed the glass of milk.

Take the pills on my plate and drop them into the milk.

She was still holding Wendy down who was squirming and spitting.

I picked up the blue and pink pills, a handful of them, and did as Mom told me.

Sit Wendy up now.

I bent over her and tried to pull her up by her tiny waist.

She spit at me and tried to bite.

As soon as her mouth was open, Mom spooned milk down her throat.

Wendy choked and coughed, but even then, Mom kept spooning the milk down her.

No, mommy, no, yucky. She spit and screamed, and Mom held her mouth open and spilled the rest of the liquid down her throat.

The pills calm me, they'll calm you.

A few days later, Wendy was almost dead.

Dad had come home furious.

Mom was at the piano, and I had been dancing.

Why the hell did you give your own daughter pills? Anna, what the hell were you doing? He was at the piano, in her face, his fists clenched, his face white.

Daddy, it was me. I gave them to her. I did it, I did it. I ran to him, raised my arms up to him. His face turned red, pure raw, red, red, red. He was roaring.

*Those pills are dangerous. You almost killed your sister. **Killed** her, do you understand? How could you do such a thing?*

I told you she was no good. I told you, Joe.

Goddammit why can't you keep an eye on your own children? You knew those pills were dangerous, you knew this.

Daddy it was me, it was me, it was me. No, Mommy, please don't be mad. Mommy, Mommy, play the piano for me. Mommy... I was crying, begging. Dad's fist was raised, his mouth closed. He brought it down on the piano, and one of Mom's paintings of the Golden Gate banged to the floor. He brought his fist down again and again.

I didn't know. It was Clara. It was her. She's no good.

Dad grabbed Mom's shoulders and shook her and then suddenly stopped. He put his hands down. His head sank to his chest. *Jesus... Anna... Anna.* He held her. He stroked her hair. And then he looked out the window and put his hands to his side. He turned around and whispered to the air, *their fingers, their toes ...* He walked over to me and picked up my hand. He counted my fingers and kissed each one of them. He left the room and thumped up the stairs to his bedroom.

Mom at the piano bench was as still as the crashed painting, her head bent. She raised it and saw me. I was standing there, my own head down, looking at my bare feet. My baby toes were crunched inward.

Clara, you must fill this for me.

I looked at her. She was holding a small, funny bottle in her hands.

Fill this for me, from the large, tall, thin bottle with the white writing across it. It's on the kitchen table. Don't tell your father. It will be our secret, and I won't be mad at you. If you do this, I'll be happy.

I ran to the kitchen table, relieved to have something to do. I lifted the tall bottle. It was awkward, heavy. Don't spill a drop, just don't. I walked carefully back to the living room. Trying to smile, I handed it to Mom.

There's a doll, she said, grabbing it from me. She drank deeply and played the piano again.

"Clara? Clara?" Melissa was stroking my hair and calling my name. I looked up at her.

"Oh my God, you scared me. It looked like you'd fainted."

Had I? "I don't know..." I tried to sit up, but had to lie back down again.

"You know, she's always faking something..."

"Stop. She's crying." She placed her warm hand on my leg. "Where does it hurt? Here?"

I winced. "Everywhere."

She was concerned. "You need to see a doctor, *now*. I'm not sure this can wait, and I'm afraid you need an ambulance." She went for the phone.

I closed my eyes and saw me giving Mom her flask for the first time; always telling lies for her. Always.

~

"DON'T WORRY," the doctors told me. "It's a clean break." They put me in a cast up to my thigh. "You'll have a walking cast in three weeks and be back to normal in six." They sent me home with pain medication and medical orders not to work for four weeks.

The next night, Damien was pissed.

"Because you can't work for a month, and because Helen wants someone looking after you, we now need another student living here with us to take care of you."

He smiled the way he did when he was angry. I smiled back. I never knew what kind of mood he'd be in. I thought about my saved money. That, at least, brought me some comfort.

"And who would that be?"

"Judy. Remember her?"

"Wasn't she kicked out a few years ago?" I asked, surprised.

"Yes. That's her. She's back now. She'll be moving in with us tomorrow."

~

A FEW DAYS later when the phone startled me awake, I couldn't grab my crutches fast enough to get to it. By the time Judy ran into my bedroom, breathless, I was ready to bash her in the head with one of them. I hated being this helpless.

"It's Helen!" she said, her brown beady eyes as wide as she could get them. I imagined the crutch falling on her head, the blood spurting. Instead, I slowly swung myself toward the living room, the floors creaking.

If I slipped and fell on a sock or paper towel, I'd have to go to the hospital. Maybe if I stayed there for a few days, I could figure out a plan to leave. I'd bring my cash and ask one of the nurses to buy me a plane ticket.

I was watched all of the time, but I didn't know why. *Did* Damien know about the specials? There was nowhere I could go, not even the bathroom, without Judy saying, "Leave the door open, hon, I want to make sure you don't fall."

When I reached the living room, I hurled myself onto the brown sagging couch, its feathers flying out of the cushions. The rickety wooden table was covered with a red plaid cloth that Judy had thrown over it the minute she moved in. She was, like my mother, meticulous about things like that. She handed me the phone. It was 4 a.m.

"What's going on in Boston, dear?" Helen's too-soft voice came over the waves.

I kept silent and waited, knowing not to say anything.

"Everything going well with Damien and yourself? I hear there are a couple of new students?"

Helen didn't sound excited. Her tone was dead nice.

"I know the restaurant has already taken off," she continued. Her voice became lower, even softer, "Damien found $250 in cash in your dresser."

How the hell did he find it?

Judy hadn't tightened the faucet on the kitchen sink well enough, and I could hear one drop of water after another pinging onto the tin surface. I played with the phone cord and put it around my neck, my fingers pulling it tighter, anything not to answer Helen.

"You know Damien," Helen continued. "He loves to surprise, and he thought he'd do some fall cleaning for you since you'd broken your leg."

The pinging water wouldn't stop. I pulled hard on the cord. It was tight now, around my throat. How was it that I hadn't noticed that it was gone?

"He wondered if you were going to give me the cash as a Christmas surprise and if so, he's sorry. The good news is that he has already put it toward our restaurant expenses. But we'd like to know where it came from?"

I choked. I watched my fingers pull the cord away from my throat just far enough so I could breathe.

I formed several pictures in my mind, the way I used to do when I painted as a child. I filled in these pictures with words, coloring them in unexpected ways. I knew how to lie. As I spoke, I loosened the cord a little more and began scratching the freed area.

"Helen," I finally said, reading the words I had drawn in my mind. My voice sounded hoarse, choked. "Damien, as you say, has been great in the restaurant and has pulled in many new students, so it's hard to tell you what I'm about to say. But I do need to let you in on some things I've noticed about him. I think he's losing it. I mean, how in the world would I ever have $250?

"You take care of all my expenses. In addition, you entrusted me to run this incredible restaurant, and you have no idea how much love, work and presence of mind I've put into it.

"But Damien, now, he can't hold his liquor. Has he told you about the times he's come in dead drunk in the middle of dinner on Friday and Saturday nights? He staggers in, his shirt half-unbuttoned and wet with spilled whiskey or whatever he's been drinking. Black hairs bristle out of his chest, and he shouts out my name, demanding me to do things I can't possibly do. Patrons hurriedly pay their checks and walk out, leaving their meals untouched." I was really enjoying painting the picture for her.

"And when it happened again a week ago, I had to tell him not to come in drunk anymore. Damien lashed out at me, calling me all sorts of horrible names, loud enough for everyone to hear. I had to escort him out.

"How do you know that the $250 Damien claimed to find is mine? Maybe he drank away all that ASI money you trusted him with and became frantic to get it back. Maybe he didn't know how he was going to explain putting the cash back into the account, and so he told you an impossible story about finding it in my room. I think he needs time to sober up. Flying him back to San Francisco wouldn't be a bad thing. As you see he's really falling apart, and I'm worried."

I paused, taking in a deep breath. Helen was silent for a while.

"Well, one of you is lying. And in time, I'll find out who."

TWO

JOE

Fall

T he last thing he wanted was an interview with a major television station. He'd put it off for as long as he could. All he wanted was stability, people to be reasonable, unchanging in their decency, The news glorified pain, made shams of others, showed them to be whom they weren't. He liked poetry because the words never changed no matter how often he read them. Science. Cells and bones and blood. Everything connected. Beating the way it should. And when something was broken or irregular, there was a way to fix it. Death would be more welcome than this interview. There were so many imperfections on the ward. Ed was incompetent, and they still needed a decent psychiatrist. He agreed to help Aaron with this ward because he wanted to help. That was all. It was nonsense, this television interview, making it all about him. The ward was for the struggling, young adult drug addicts. They didn't need any more glorification. God damn it. He'd refuse the interview again, that's all. The less others knew about him the better.

Sandy appeared out of nowhere. She was running like a frightened antelope down the hallway. She bounced up to him, eyes red, cheeks streaked with tears. Her hair tangled.

"Fuck, do you know why we have to live only to die? Do we have a fucking purpose...?"

"You're upset. Slow down..."

She'd run past him, wildly, and he followed slowly. What had she taken?

He saw her dash into her room, and he stood in her doorway. "You shouldn't be alone."

He sat with her. She'd denied taking anything, and yet the speed in which she asked questions defied her statement.

"I just fucking want to know what the fucking purpose of life is, anyone's purpose, I mean do you know yours? Do you ever wonder who the hell you really are and why the fuck you're *alive*...?"

She was suicidal. Her medication needed to be changed. He thought of Wendy. He smiled in spite of himself. She, Wendy, would actually be good for Sandy. She was a professional counselor now, and when she stopped swearing, perhaps she'd be willing to help here on the ward.

"Doc, are you laughing at me? Stop it. I know I'm fucking weird but you don't..." Sandy was jumping up and down, pulling her hair out."

"Sandy, shhhhhh... you're upset. Come, walk with me to the nurse's station."

The idea startled him. *His* Wendy helping on *this* ward? As he calmed Sandy and walked slowly with her down the hall, he understood that his purpose was to bring sanity to the world. To help others understand their own powers of reasoning.

At the nurse's station, he asked Nurse Linda to take care of her. He ordered blood tests for her and thanked the nurse. "You'll be fine, Sandy. Just fine."

Yes. All he wanted was to help others find their own common sense. That was why he'd wanted Clara to quit Modern Dance and why he liked Poe. Poe understood suffering. Poe understood the hovering dark clouds experience brought. Wordsworth and Yeats had worked when he was younger. They were both naive, unaware of suffering. *I Wandered Lonely as a Cloud* was good for the children; his suffering, all suffering, wasn't just a "pensive mood" to be cheered by a field of daffodils. *The Song of Wandering Aengus* was good for Anna, but neither poem held any meaning for him any longer, at least not for many years. Poe's poetry helped him through these sleepless nights, wondering always where Clara was.

Whitman was the opposite of Poe. But self-centered. Joe would have nothing to do with him. As he walked into his office a poem came to him. He removed his black journal from his shirt pocket, sat at his desk and hurriedly wrote:

> *Daffodils, Golden Apples, every atom...*
> *but when you're in a storm*
> *and the wind carries the stench of blood,*
> *and the rain is the sound of guns,*
> *and so many loved ones die*
> *and your daughter disappears...*
> *apples and daffodils are a sweetness*
> *belonging in fairy tales.*

He put the journal back into his shirt pocket, stood up straighter. Maybe now that he knew what his purpose was he could do the interview. Maybe.

THREE

CLARA

I t was the third Friday in November, 3 a.m. Damien came home yelling my name at the top of his lungs. Judy obediently came out of her bedroom to inquire. I don't know what transpired between them, but my door swung open, banging against the wall.

"Hi hon, I have a surprise for you." Damien sat down on my bed, beside me.

He began stroking my hair, and I turned away, trying to push him off. He stank of whiskey. His god-awful breath made me gag. My heart was racing. There had to be a way out of bed. But before I could think of what to do, his tongue was in my ear. "Feel my surprise, okay sweetie?" He grabbed my hand and wrapped it around a gun he was now pointing into my palm. "Isn't this beautiful? " He forced my hand up and down it, and then held it still on the barrel. "Nice and hard, just as you like it, right hon?"

I went numb.

He began kissing my cheeks and running the weapon slowly up and down my back, caressing each vertebra, pointing the barrel of the gun downward. He leaned into my ear again. "Don't you ever lie to Helen again, okay hon? Slandering your teacher is never a good idea, is it sweetheart?"

I slowly turned over, making out the shapes of my crutches where they leaned against the night table. The gun was now at my throat, and Damien was kissing my breasts.

I pulled him toward me and put my tongue in his mouth as I caressed the gun, running my hands up and down, feeling his stubby fingers clasped around it.

"Don't think I won't pull the trigger, even if we do fuck tonight, which we will."

I entwined my tongue around his with all my might, and then pushed his head down onto my breasts. I raised my hips and whispered, "I can't wait to feel you against my broken bones." His clothes were still on; his shirt unbuttoned and his jeans unzipped.

As I licked the inside of his ear, I managed to free my hands. He was moving more on top of me now, eyes closed. Although he was heavy in his sweaty clothes, I pushed us closer to the side of the bed and hung out one arm to see if I could grab a crutch.

He took that arm and placed my hand on his penis, sliding it up and down. Then he took his gun and rubbed it on my vagina.

It was impossible to grab the crutch. I bent forward, whispering that I wanted to feel his new toy with my hands. He forced it inside me; the gun was cold and huge, and I was as dry as drought. The pain hit nerve after nerve. I screamed. Where the hell was Judy?

He removed it immediately and forced the weapon into my mouth to stop my yelling. The thing was down my throat, choking me.

He laughed, "You look so sexy with a gun inside you like this. What if I pulled the trigger now?"

I knew then he wasn't going to stop fucking with me; that he was actually going to kill me. Everything inside my body dropped into a deathly quiet.

I raised my hands and reached out again, for a crutch. I managed to grab one. He knocked it out of my hand. This got the gun out of my mouth, and I started screaming again, pushing him off of me with all my might. He was still holding the weapon.

We both fell to the floor, the gun fell, right between us. I reached the fallen crutch, still screaming for Judy. I swung the thing every which way, sliding it along the wooden planks. My leg was screaming with pain. Before Damien could stand up, I hit him good and hard in the groin. I heard him cry out and roll away from me.

Judy finally came in, saw us both on the floor, and Damien, with his jeans still down to his ankles, was doubled over, the gun still there, between us. She didn't ask a single question but rushed to Damien's rescue. Ignored and shaking, I pulled myself up, slipped on the smelly, long shirt I'd worn three days in a row, slipped on my shoes, grabbed my heavy coat and swung myself out of the apartment. I'd grab some pants at the restaurant. There were pairs hanging up in the back closet.

FOUR

JOE

J oe had fallen asleep in his study. Aaron had insisted he do the interview, which was to be this morning. *Just be there for the kids. It will bring in more donors. Besides, Mrs. Lincoln has agreed to join us. She loves us for saving her son Kevin..."* Joe had finally agreed. Kevin had actually shown up on the ward six weeks ago. Skinnier and weaker than a long piece of thread, he was passed out on the ward's doorstep that cold foggy morning. Joe had him rushed to the hospital and called Mrs. Lincoln immediately. He stayed on the phone while she cried. He'd wondered what it would be like for him to find Clara... Imagining the impossible never worked for him. He hung up with Mrs. Lincoln more abruptly than he'd intended. Berating himself for doing so, he'd told himself he'd be more patient with her the next time they spoke. Agreeing to the interview was like making it up to her.

On the morning of the interview, he'd woken up suddenly at 6 a.m., found himself at his desk and quickly changed, relieved he wouldn't be late. He had just enough time for a cup of coffee and to glance over the headlines of the morning paper. Sitting at the huge kitchen table, he read:

November 18, 1978

Massive Suicide. Over 900 follow Reverend Jones in Georgetown, Guyana.

Included in the 900 were 200 children who were considered murdered...

Immediately, he imagined Clara among the dead. Had she gotten caught up with Reverend Jones? It was so unlikely, yet he'd no idea. Miss Jenkins had had no word from her. His heart was clamping shut. He stood up and keeled over.

FIVE
CLARA

As soon as I got out of the apartment, I got on the trolley and headed straight for the café. I'd stashed some more money there, inside a small wooden chest I had bought at a second-hand shop. There was a large cabinet underneath the sink that held huge Ajax bottles. I'd placed the chest in the back, beneath the cobwebs.

I put my head against the window pane, the lolling bus reminded me of other bus rides up to Oregon. David. Dead. His image rolled across my mind. All he wanted to do was make me happy, make love to me and share the rest of his life with me. That walk... just a couple of days before he met me in the almond tree orchard... Right after class, around 5 a.m. we left the lodge by the back door. The sun was just rising. The rays spilled onto the grass and the vegetable garden we were passing through. "Look at that!" I cried. The lodge was bathed in fire: red-orange hues. I leaned into David and felt, for once, how good it was to have his arm around me.

He pulled me toward him and said, *I can only imagine how lively and beautiful our children will be as long as they have your genes.* I ever so gently ran my fingers down his cheeks and around his mouth. He held me tight. I could tell by his shallow breathing how tight his chest was.

His tone told me he was choking back tears. I hadn't known what to do. I couldn't ever help Dad when he was sad like that. It's this inability, this insensitivity that I have, that hurts others so much. And because I don't ever do anything about it, my negativity becomes lethal. Somehow, someway, I was responsible for his death.

My head pounded with every sudden stop and start the bus made. Its screeching noises made the ache endless. More memories jolted into my mind.

Dad... all alone at that big kitchen table.

Wendy on drugs. That time I tried to pull her away from those guys on the beach. *I'm my own woman now. Leave me alone.* Wendy had said. And the guy with long blonde dreads laughed. *You're like the Road Runner*, he said. Wendy laughed. Her eyes dilated, her voice cracking. *Always running after shit.*

You need to bring Wendy to the clinic. Dad had said.

No Mommy yucky. Wendy had cried.

She did it, Joe. She's always been wicked. Mom yelled.

I put my aching head in my palms and shook it until I was dizzy. When I stopped, I saw the morning's newspaper on the seat next to me.

The headlines read:

November 18, 1978

Massive Suicide. Over 900 follow Reverend Jones in Georgetown, Guyana.

I began reading the article next to it. The FBI was now investigating every cult in the country. ASI was among them. I read the same lines a hundred times, and nothing registered. My thoughts were knotted, tight, and repetitive. I could smell Damien's whiskey-sweat, and felt the cold, piercing pain of that gun in my vagina.

ASI was being investigated. Wouldn't *I* be the one investigated? Hadn't Mary through Helen tried to help me, not just once, but many times?

There can be no tears in your auric field, Mary had warned. But I probably had thousands of enormous holes. They would be impossible to repair. And hadn't Melissa and Damien both tried to warn me? They kept pointing out my irritability, my ineptness and I did nothing about it. Nothing. It was never my intention to hurt anyone, but I had been harming others my whole life... The hidden nature of this is what's so toxic. I spew hatred from my very breathing. That's why Damien almost killed me. I brought this on myself.

And, the very place I've called home for the past three years and the very people I've called family are being investigated. And because ASI was now being blamed for God-knows-what, Damien would be after me.

The bus aisle creaked as I lunged toward the front door. I hobbled down the two stairs carefully and managed to get to the café.

I grabbed my cash, pulled on a pair of wide, bell-bottom stretch pants that were too big for me and hobbled out as fast as I could. I'd go to Grandma's. I'd no idea how she'd treat me, but it didn't matter. I had no other place to go. If she threw me out, I'd understand. I'd deserve that.

My cash in the bag, I hurriedly hailed a cab. Damien and Judy would get hell for my disappearance, so I could be sure that the search for me would be thorough and strong. They'd probably already told the FBI everything about me. Could it be possible that both Damien *and* the FBI might be following this cab? I shuddered.

I closed my eyes. I saw in my mind a message lying on my bed. I'd seen this note a day after I'd returned from the doctor's after I broke my leg and had completely forgotten about it. The note was in Judy's handwriting. It said, *June just called, call her back.* Her phone number was clearly written.

What had she wanted to tell me? Could she have known something about ASI's recent investigation? Oh, I was crazy. How could June know anything? She was in bad shape. Melissa had her kids. Or maybe she didn't anymore. Maybe June had called me for help? Could she have been in some kind of difficulty? My heart dropped, my head ached.

900 people massacred in Georgetown. They'd followed the mind of one crazy guy, like Damien, who had almost killed me. I was in love with a murderer, in love with the farm, with Helen. It started snowing suddenly. From inside the cab, I could hear the howling wind but couldn't see out the window. The cab had to pull over.

Damien was pushing the gun inside my mouth, my crotch. Nerve upon nerve screaming inside every cell. The heat was up, the doors locked and the windows tightly closed. How was I going to escape? Someone was yelling something about, "Are you OK?" No. No. No. I saw the cabby's face looking like Dad's, all grim and worried. "Are you OK Miss?" The cabby had turned around to look at me. Apparently I was banging on the window, crying.

The storm stopped, and the cab rolled slowly down the snow-filled street, until we reached Grandma's. The cabby opened the door for me.

"It's very cold, Miss, can I help you out?"

I must've sat there for a while, unable to move.

"Do you want to go somewhere else?"

I was so nervous, I could hardly step out, and the ice was everywhere.

The cabby helped me, holding my crutches, as I held onto him and he led me to Grandma's brownstone. I asked him to ring the buzzer for me.

And there was Grandma's voice, soaring over the intercom, clear and kind as ever. "Who is it?"

SIX
WENDY

When I read about fucking Jonestown, I called Dad immediately. I knew how *I* felt: was Clara fucking a part of this shit? The People's Temple wasn't run by some fucking mother figure, and Beatrice Goldman would probably say she wasn't involved, but who could fucking really know? I had no idea how Dad would take this news. Praying that he hadn't seen the paper yet, it was fucking early enough, I dialed... but he didn't pick up. I called the hospital and had him paged, but to no fucking avail.

Jake and I rushed over to the house. Dad didn't answer the door, and that was fucking weird.

We ran around the back and into the yard, hoping he'd answer the back door. And through the glass doors that led to the garden we saw him slumped on the fucking kitchen floor. But I didn't have a fucking key with me. Shit. I had left it at home, somewhere on my fucking table. So we like ran to the nearest store and called 911 on a fucking pay phone.

Dad was raced to the ER at Mt. Sinai. He needed heart surgery like immediately.

~

Six hours later, the doctor said he'd be fine.

I hugged Jake. "Fuck ablation surgery. Whatever the fuck that is. Jesus."

When I saw Dad lying there in that small bed, with a white sheet and thin blanket covering him, he looked fucking dead. His face was whiter than the sheet. And he was mumbling something. I bent my ear to his mouth to hear better. What the fuck was he saying, mumbling in an unknown language, like he was fucking talking in tongues.

I ran out of the room. "Fuck, Jake, find a priest. Dad is possessed."

"Of course he's not..."

A priest showed up soon enough. I think a nurse saw my freaked out face and summoned one.

Dad was still mumbling when he walked in. The priest said, "That's Hebrew."

"What?"

"Your father is speaking a Hebrew prayer. I'll get Rabbi Daniel."

I looked at Dad, still mumbling, color coming back into his face. Just then Rabbi Daniel walked in. He was short and balding, wearing one of those black, silk caps on top of his head. He shook my hand firmly.

"That's the Kaddish." And then the rabbi chanted with him. Only, he turned to me and said, "He's translating it too, and speaking to others, Miriam and Anna."

I felt faint. What the fuck? "This doesn't make any fucking sense..."

And then Dad's eyes opened and he was still saying the prayer. I took his hand, and he squeezed mine. "Wendy-Bendy... it's good to see you."

What the fuck? I couldn't think. I couldn't talk. "You were fucking speaking Hebrew. This is Rabbi Daniel, he says you were saying the prayer for the dead... that you were fucking talking to Mom and Aunt Miriam, and they're fucking dead..." I swallowed my tears. I was pulling my hair. I wanted to punch something I was so fucking confused and scared.

Dad nodded to the rabbi, who squeezed his hand and left.

"You're Jewish," Dad said, reaching out his hand for mine. "I escaped Nazi Poland in 1939..."

I was still. My hand froze in Dad's. Whispering, he started to tell me what had happened to him. But I put my fucking hand to his mouth to stop him. He looked so tired and his face was like pale again. "Get better," I whispered. "Tell it all to me later, in bits. Not so much right now." When he was quiet again, eyes closed and breathing steadily, as best he could, I started to tiptoe out, when his room phone rang like a fucking fire drill.

"It's Grandma, dear. I must speak with your father."

Her voice sounded muffled, urgent.

Dad's eyes were open again; I gave him the phone.

"We'll be there tomorrow, first thing," he said.

My eyes bulged out of my head and I couldn't breathe. Jesus. Fuck. He's not going fucking anywhere. But, as he clearly said, "She's found Clara," he was also pulling out his plugs and tubes, and mumbling, "...damned doctors. I know what I'm doing. I'll be fine."

SEVEN
JOE

As Wendy and Joe entered Shirley's apartment, Wendy bounded in, shouting for Clara, her arms wide open. She suddenly screamed and as Joe followed, his legs weakened, his heart beat a little too rapidly. After all it was normal to be excited...

He stopped in his tracks.

Clara and Shirley were gagged, had their hands tied behind their backs and were being held up by an unshaven man with a gun. An older woman, with thick black hair had grabbed Wendy, who was struggling and punching her way out of the hold. The guy holding the gun, breath smelling of whiskey, turned toward Joe.

"I'm taking Clara back with me, and I'm going to have to kill the rest of you. You get to choose who goes first. Your beautiful blonde daughter here..."

"What the fuck, let me fucking go, you fucking bitch..."

Shirley's cheeks were wet, and she too was struggling with the ties tightly wound around her wrists.

Joe lunged at the man, knocking the gun out of his hand; a shot rang out. "My leg." Joe gasped. Falling to the floor, holding onto his calf, he saw the woman wrestling with Wendy. Wendy slapped her hard across the face, it seemed many times, screaming, "You fucking bitch, you fucking shit of a fucking bitch," then his daughter shoved her against the wall. Wendy ran to Shirley and ungagged her.

Damien had Clara in a choke hold and was pointing the gun toward Wendy. Wendy grabbed Clara's crutch, leaning against the chair close to her. She swung it at Damien hard, hitting him in the face. He let go of Clara and dropped the gun, shouting in pain. Wendy bent to pick it up, and Shirley screamed, "Watch out!" Wendy just managed to dodge the crutch that Damien held. "You fucking shit of a drunken shit fuck." Wendy tried to grab the crutch from him, but the woman got to it first. She swung it at Wendy, who dropped the gun.

Damien picked it up.

Shirley was looking urgently at Joe and saying something crazy, "... Jewish Joe. I just need you to know that before I die. So was Anna." But she screamed, as her head was pulled back by the man, who Joe now saw was pointing the gun at Wendy's back. Struggling, Joe stood up, and with an inward, raging fire burning up from his groin, steaming through his blood, he lunged toward the unshaven man. But Clara was already hitting him with a crutch. She was saying, "I'm a god-damned murderer, Damien, and now it's your turn." The gun fell to the floor. Joe grabbed it and aimed it at the man, but Shirley was yelling, "No Joe, don't do it again... Oh God, I should have told you, we're Jewish, your father, Anna, me..."

Shirley, his stepfather and Anna were Jewish? What did she mean, *don't do it again?* Clara was swinging the crutch every which way, hitting the man and the woman who was trying to hide behind him. The woman's face was bleeding, her nose was out of shape, as she grabbed the man. Joe dropped the gun and lunged at both of them, spewing, "God damn Nazis," and threw his body on top of both. They all fell. Wendy had the gun now... the blood pouring out of Joe's leg didn't make any sense to him. His heart had almost stopped.

The bodies he was on top of... were his Mama's, Papa's, Miriam's. From his gut, he howled, "NO." He rolled over and off them. Clara was at his side. "Oh God, Daddy, no, no, no." His fingers. She was kissing them, counting them. "They're all there, Daddy, remember how...?" As she spoke, there were the sounds of sirens, and then complete quiet.

EPILOGUE
CLARA

Summer

Dr. Beatrice Goldman worked diligently with Grandma, Dad, Wendy and me to help us all understand what had happened to me. It took a year and a half. As the process of debriefing unfolded, she showed me slide after slide of ASI; all of the ex-students reporting the abuse of the institution, June among them. Beatrice showed me medical evidence from the numerous mental hospitals where Helen had been hospitalized. She, Helen, had been diagnosed with a psychotic delusional disorder. Damien who had a history of crime, was diagnosed as a psychopath.

In many individual sessions, I had learned that nothing had ever been my fault. I was still digesting the fact that I wasn't born hateful, that my very energy was not inherently harmful to anyone.

During this same time, Patti had also worked patiently with me, and now, eighteen months later, I was dancing again.

∼

Waiting for the curtains to go up, I looked at Patti, who smiled that dimpled, wonderful smile of hers.

I started in a bowed position, and as I raised my head, I saw Dad, Grandma and Wendy in the front row. The music from the *Nutcracker,* Christmas Tree Grows, lifted me, as I sculpted the air, my body conforming to the notes like magic. I saw Dad and me, going to our doctors' appointments together, his stories flying through my mind... *The Nazis shot Papa in the head, then Mama. Miriam had turned to me, she had a milk stain on her face...Mama had had no time to wipe it off. They toppled on top of me, all of them. I had pushed their fingers and toes off of me...* Dad wiped his forehead, and his eyes. I saw him, again, putting Wendy and me to bed years ago, kissing each of our fingers, *good you have all ten, be grateful.*

My torso felt heavy as I reached for the growing tree, trying to stretch to its heights, to shake what I'd gone through out of my mind. Helen's face loomed over me... She'd had a psychotic history miles long, and nothing she'd said was real. And yet, I'd believed every word, thinking she was my mother, my family.

And there was Dad again, showing Wendy and me a note that Father John had written him. *Father John helped me escape and find the Greenwoods,* Dad had said, fingering the note the way he'd held our hands, with great care and gentleness. And as I floated closer to the tree, reaching higher with my arms, my legs, I heard Grandma saying that there'd been so much anti-Semitism in the '30's that she'd converted, denying her Judaism, and adopted a Jewish boy to assuage her guilt. As the music came to a crescendo, I saw Miriam reach out her arms, and she lifted me, lifted the tears lumping in my throat. *It'll take such a long time to understand all this Jewish stuff,* I said to her. *Grandma, Mom, Dad, Wendy, me, Jewish. Jew-ish.* She was saying, as she helped me pirouette slowly, and face Dad. *You've always known, remember how you'd wanted a menorah?* I couldn't see Dad's expression, but there he was, sitting in the front row, as I danced.

He'd *loved* to watch me as a ballerina. *My Mama took Miriam and me to watch the ballet in Krakow twice a year.* My dancing had reminded him of his sweet memories, and when I quit ballet, how else could he keep his Mama and sister alive, with the horror he had gone through? Miriam shook her head and said, *Neither of you had known what the other held in their heart.* My chest softened; the music was about to change. I carefully, slowly, moved into modern dance. I moved my head about and undulated my torso to Leonard Cohen's, *Bird on the Wire.*

I joined ASI to be free, not realizing that I was moving into a greater and more toxifying cage. Images of Damien stomped through my mind. *Never will you find a community of support like ASI...* his eyes so intently on me, feeling his soft kisses on my belly... I could smell his whiskey breath, feel him pinning me to the bed, moving the gun inside me, my vagina screaming, him pointing that gun at Grandma, all tied up, crying, struggling.

I was the beast that brought them all to Grandma's apartment; Dad lunging toward Damien, and Damien, colder than winter, shooting him. I had allowed Damien to put his claws into me, turning me into the same clawing monster. It was so hard to believe that this wasn't my fault.

But, here we all were. As Wendy had said, *It's a fucking miracle. And Dad fucking came away with just a limp.* And Damien was in prison, the last I'd heard.

But I looked out to the audience and glimpsed a figure, standing in the back. He was in the shadows and had Damien's build. I froze, but forced myself to stomp in circles, pounding out the image, facing the audience and pouring out my arms, pleading with my eyes as the song continued. I promise, Dad, I'll make this up you. I promise.

Miriam pointed at Wendy, and I could just make out her face, hearing her voice, *Oh, my fucking God, Dad and I went crazy searching for you. I thought you had disappeared because of me. I had to find you.* They had been searching for *me*, who had almost killed them both... and Wendy, so alive, not dead at all. She'd burst out, *We are back together again, like, we're all family. And God, is like that spirit that makes us a family... but what the fuck? I mean God is inside that love, and that love is like inside God, and all of that is inside each of **us**...* I let my head drop and whispered, *Dad, Wendy couldn't have said it better and this song is for you.*

As I slowly paced across the stage I didn't see the shadowy guy again. Miriam nodded, smiling. *You've always loved your family, and they you. They're the most important people in the world.* I knelt toward the audience and lifted my arms, as the tears ran down my cheeks, *This song is for you, Dad,* I whispered again.

I stood slowly, as the music changed again and brought me into the Beatles song, *In My Life.* My legs lifted of their own accord, and my arms felt surprisingly light, like feathers, and Mom twirled through me. I saw her, Wendy and myself on Baker Beach, so long ago. Barefoot, we had made dancing footprints in the sand. I saw them sparkle and disappear. *Just like fairy dust!* Mom had said. I felt that lump in my throat again as I remembered the sand castles we built... *that reached the clouds.* Rings of shiny sunlight had crowned her blonde hair like a queen's. Her green eyes were wide and sparkly like the ocean.

The song continued, and I kept thinking of her. *Oh, Mom, no one can compare to you. You, like me, tried so hard to be yourself. And we both clung to false Gods. You to alcohol and Valium, and I to the cult. We were so similar.* And my chest softened and opened as I saw how music saved us both. And I could hear in my mind, Grandma saying, *When you dance, my heart smiles. You are as beautiful as these sunsets.*

I came to a still point, the lyrics sending this love for mom into every cell in my being. My chest was beating like a hummingbird's, so quick and sweet, as I flew into the last piece, Mozart's Concerto in C Major.

How she'd loved to play the piano for *us;* especially the songbooks of A.A. Milne's poems put to music. She'd changed the words from Christopher Robin to our names; singing, *And Clara and Wendy, go hippitty hippitty hippitty hop.* And the higher Wendy and I had jumped, the more Mom laughed, adding to the wonderful music; and that was what had inspired me to create my own steps. She was the one who had said to Dad, *Oh Joe, she would love ballet lessons, don't you think?*

Miriam held out her hand again. As we twirled together, she said, *Your Mom has always loved you. Always.* Her milk mustache was gone; she was smiling as she pointed upward. I saw Mom floating above me, her curls looking like an angel's, sitting at a piano. A golden menorah was on top, its light surrounding her, as she played Mozart with the orchestra.

As the performance finished, with a standing ovation, I bowed. To Dad, to Wendy, to Grandma. And finally, to her.

Miriam, I said, *there's been a break in the fog, we're a family again.*

And as I stood up from the bow, there was Dad, in the front row, smiling wider than the sea, holding a bouquet of daffodils.

ACKNOWLEDGMENTS

To my Editors:

Mary Reynolds Thompson who showed me the importance of voice and suggested the title.

Sophie Wadsworth who taught me how to develop characters.

Julia McNeal for her brilliant insights, sensitivity to the nature of the characters, and ability to read the manuscript many times over.

From Grub Street, Boston MA: Steven Beber for his invaluable suggestions.

To my Brother-in-Law Dan Rosenheim for his generosity, time, heroic edits, and invaluable understanding and wisdom regarding copyright laws.

To **Jamey and Peter Faust**, authors of *The Constellation Approach; Finding Peace Through Your Family Lineage,* whose trainings in the Constellation Approach taught me how to deepen my connection to family.

To my Photographer Karen Borchers for her huge generosity and amazing photos.

To my Daughter Sarah Weidman, who, by example taught me focus and discipline, and that laughing often makes everything better.

To my Sisters:

Hillary Kambour for her enthusiasm and particular insights that would have gone unnoticed otherwise.

Cindy Salans Rosenheim for her brilliant, stunning, and amazing cover illustration and particular insights that would have gone unnoticed otherwise.

To my Nephews:

Zach Kambour for his wise advice on all things suspenseful and horror.

Nick Rosenheim for his marketing and book cover help.

To my Friends:

Muggsie Rocco who read the manuscript many times and offered astute suggestions.

Michael Rosenblum for his brilliant interpretation and translations of the Kaddish.

Debra Rosenblum for her undying support, patience as I took time to write, and wisdom to keep me grounded.

Nancy Capaccio for her undying enthusiasm, faith in me, and friendship.

Bill Winn for his marketing expertise and being such a good friend.

Virginia Slep for taking the time to read my manuscript twice, offering invaluable suggestions.

Sarah Fletcher for her ongoing support and sense of humor.

Omi Preheim for her faith in me and spiritual guidance.

To my Writing Group:

To Lyssa, Elizabeth, Ellen, Katharyn, and Catherine, whose friendship and encouragement I couldn't have done without.

To the Seven Bridges Writers Collaborative:

Paula Castner and Ann Frantz, thank you so much for your guidance.

Ursula Wong for her classes and individual help with the self-publishing process.

To the Book Designer, Copywriter, Website Developer, and Host:

Melinda Phillips for her book cover design.

Dale T. Phillips: for his keyword search, formatting, invaluable writing tips and advice, and most importantly for his patience.

Kayleigh Nutter for her support with copy.

Geralyn Miller for her interest, enthusiasm, and careful creation of the beautiful website.

Keith Dawson, website host extraordinaire, including tech support I could not do without, and profound positive comments.

To all of those in my Meditation and Healing Groups:

Omi, Arraya, Lorrinda, Cindy, Laura, Deb, Lee, Shayndel, Kathy, Kathy, Suetta, Joan, Marylou, DeLores, Joanie, Marylin, Walia, Barb, and Beth.

To my Research Sources:

The Groton Public Library, Groton, MA.

The Map Store, Cambridge, MA.

Without all of you, his book would not be. A huge, and mighty, heartfelt thanks.

OTHER BOOKS BY MOLLY SALANS

Storytelling With Children in Crisis

A Break in the Fog

ABOUT THE AUTHOR

Photo: Karen T. Borchers

Her love of literature and deep spirituality eventually brought Molly to earn her M.Ed. from Cambridge College in 1988. She then went on to obtain her license in Marriage and Family Therapy from the Kantor Family Institute in 1991 and a license in Social Work from Boston University School of Social Work in 1995. Her first book, *Storytelling with Children in Crisis,* is based on her social work experience in home-based crisis intervention.

Prior to pursuing her education in counseling and social work, Molly was a member of a prominent cult for seven years. Though she left in 1982, her experiences as part of the group haunted her, leading her to write her newest book, a psychological fiction novel titled *A Break in the Fog*.

Though not autobiographical, her insider understanding of the way cults operate informed this integral part of the dysfunctional family narrative. Feeling this was a story she had to get out, her wish is for readers to find hope in the family's quest for redemption.

f facebook.com/abreakinthefog

instagram.com/abreakinthefog

15229164R00233